KEPSTADUR KEEP

ISBN: 979-8-9995060-0-9

For Linda and Mary

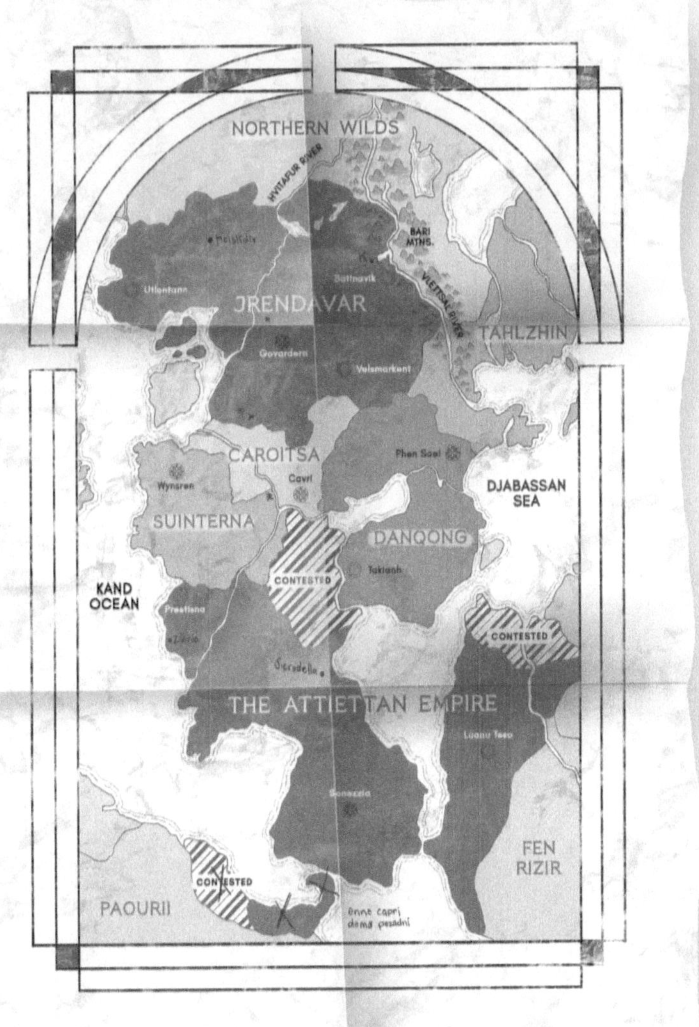

NORTHERN WILDS
HVITASFUR RIVER
BARI MTNS.
VLETTSAL RIVER
JRENDAVAR
Battnavik
Utlentann
TAHLZHIN
Govardern
Velsmarkent
CAROITSA
Phen Soel
Cavri
DJABASSAN SEA
Wynsren
SUINTERNA
DANQONG
Takianh
CONTESTED
KAND OCEAN
Prestisha
Livio
CONTESTED
Sicradella
THE ATTIETTAN EMPIRE
Luanu Teeo
Sonazzia
FEN RIZIR
CONTESTED
PAOURII
enne capri dema pesadni

01

MAGE'S PRICE

Eastern sunrises weren't unlike those in the west, maybe even more beautiful as the layered colors stretched above the mountains — but Sonja couldn't excuse the smell. Maybe it was the tinny soil or the hint of sour ocean breeze. The farther she traveled, the more she missed the aroma of stubborn grapes blooming around her homestead. Standing in the morning-blue shadows between buildings, Sonja mostly smelled liquor. The immediate area was clean, as far as alleys go, all thanks to an unadvertised business settled three bays away from the inn's service entry.

A rock the size of her skull held the oak door ajar, teasing glimpses of brass lanterns inside. Near the handle, a wooden placard boasted a carving of three interlocked circles. Despite delicate scrollwork along the edge, the pegs holding the sign to the wall didn't seem permanent. Most cities Sonja passed through accepted, even encouraged, the slow rise in magic-users, though very few knew that meant supporting businesses like this one. Without the law to fall back on, all dealers were wild cards. She steeled herself. The town was sales-forward, so she would be as well. No smiles today. Sonja pushed inside, rattling a small bell that summoned a merchant from his front sales room. If she'd counted right the day before, his street-facing business sold textiles. An unusual mix compared to the large, unmarked kegs, but she tried not to consider whether blood and draperies complemented each other.

"Welcome!" His smile stretched too wide for such a narrow face. He stepped down a row of stairs to lean on a polished stone counter, quickly scanning her. Straight, dark, Jrendavarian hair, rounded features, a fraying summer cloak, and a faded rucksack. She suspected he labeled her "Westerner" before she even opened her mouth. "Yours is an unfamiliar face, friend. Moving to town, or are we simply a stop on a longer journey?"

She offered a shallow smile. "Time will tell." From a belt beneath her cloak, Sonja unhooked a bloshul and laid the empty leather hide limply in front of him. She let her hand linger so that three rings glimmered in the candlelight. Black gloves wrapped part of her palms and her smallest two fingers, the backs stitched with the same interlocking circles displayed by the entry. In the borderlands, many merchants wouldn't sell to non-mages, so she'd learned to get that out of the way early. "How much to fill it?"

"Right to business." The merchant straightened with a prodding grin. "I respect that. Just a single litre?" He was careful not to look too pointedly at the empty loops along her bag.

"For now. How much will it cost?"

The merchant made a face. "For one, I'd need six and fifty."

Sonja scoffed. "I'm not interested in games. No one is charging four across the whole nation."

"Times are hard, ma'am. I do sympathize, but it's the best you'll find in town. I assure you it's morning-fresh and high quality. The price drops for larger quantities, but one simply isn't economical." His false empathy was thick enough to taint the air.

"You won't get more than three and fifty." She leaned forward, examining the casks behind him.

"For three litres, the price drops to twelve even. How does that sound? A real steal."

"Still four each? Not a chance."

The merchant paused at her quick response, examining her again with greater interest. "Okay," he mused, "three for ten, then."

She faked a glower, adjusting her pack as it grew heavier. "I'll have two for your original six and fifty."

He tapped fingers pointedly on the countertop, searching the space above her head. Counting, perhaps.

"That's three and twenty-five a litre," Sonja said. "Still overpriced, but fair enough. Take it, or I walk."

With some consideration, the merchant nodded, his grin taking on a distant quality. "This is agreeable."

Sonja laid a second empty bladder next to the first, then doled out six ronad and five smaller veyilir, keeping them stacked closer to her side of the counter. She waited for him to start filling the first bloshul before perching on a nearby stool. It was at least clean on this side of the shop. Many alley-facing dispensaries operated directly out of storage rooms or nearby sheds. While not as bright as the day-lit front-of-house, polished lamps cast shadows across wooden walls and a few small paintings of a bright, four-winged canary. Behind the counter, impressive floor-to-ceiling cabinets loomed over the row of casks, not shaped right for rugs or tapestries. Sonja cleared her throat and clinked the coins against each other. "You're from here originally?" she asked.

"Born and raised," he said, half turned over one shoulder. "Second generation to run this shop."

"So you know a good deal about the area?"

"Of course, of course. I've got trade routes memorized, know the best ports, and, for the right price, I can even find people who cross the Bari Mountains."

"I'm looking for a city." Sonja dropped five more veyilir slowly into the pile. "Been walking for weeks, and no one can ever point right to it."

"Which one?"

"Kepstadur."

The merchant's eyes flashed something bright. He forced an easy laugh, shaking off a bit of blood he'd splashed on one hand. "I hope you didn't walk too far for that old rock heap. You don't sound like you grew up here in the foothills, if you don't mind me saying."

Sonja shrugged. "It's been a long road, but I'm close. People have been saying it's 'to the east' for a while now. There's only so much 'east' left in Jrendavar."

The man sealed her first bloshul and started on the second, not rushing to fill the silence. "I know what you think Kepstadur is, but it's not just some forgotten corpse."

"I'm aware." She retrieved the bladder, dribbling some onto the counter to check consistency and color. Not immediately watery. A good sign. "Which is why I'm here, interviewing the locals."

"And you know what you're doing with this stuff?" His salesman's tone slipped again, revealing more of an accent. "Really's none of my business, but..."

She rested her second half-gloved hand on the counter, tapping three more rings against the surface, each representing a year of mage's training, with a seventh hanging on a metal necklace. That one was rarely worth bringing out. Most people only cared about full sets of three. Her little brother had been young enough to complete all nine years before aging out at twenty, but... She pushed the thought away.

"You don't have to worry about me."

The shopkeep grunted without turning.

With a breath, Sonja cast a small identification spell, fading the surrounding colors. Two energies flared to life. First was the merchant, while the second floated on the far side of the wall, maybe shopping or tending the front of house. Each glowed with a soft light, radiating from a series of threads bundled loosely inside their chests. These energies looked a little different for everyone, assembled in distinct patterns or hues, sometimes appearing longer or shorter. The shopkeep's were dim, with thin threads pulled taut. It was barely noticeable, but Sonja had become accustomed to sickly auras. He likely didn't know yet, not fully. But what would he gain from a stranger's unwarranted diagnosis? She hadn't traveled across the country to become some kind of mythical medical monitor.

Sonja dropped the identification and checked the small red puddle, glad to see how little had wicked away.

He met her eye, having turned to see her testing his product. For an instant, his self-satisfied smirk dared her to say his original price was unfair. It was, but maybe not as outrageous as she'd first believed. The merchant recovered his passivity and sealed her second bloshul, setting it alongside its twin. He crossed his arms and looked meaningfully at the remaining puddle, as if to invite Sonja to finish her little experiment.

So be it. In a ripple the man wouldn't perceive, Sonja sent out a much larger identification. Her surroundings faded grey and black, contrasting sharply with any nearby life. Energies glowed through walls and streets away in all directions in her mind. She counted out the heartbeats and was again pleased. Nearly ten for a small amount of blood. The salesman might've been honest about harvesting it this morning. When the spell ran out, she swiped a hand over the perfectly dry surface. Not even a hint of water or residue remained.

"I'll admit," Sonja acquiesced, fishing in emptying pockets for spare coins, "that's good stuff. You'll forgive my wariness. I've been the ignorant wandering mage a few too many times in my years."

Some of his bravado faded as he leaned against the nearby doorframe. "There's a caravan to Tharvik that leaves the north gate. It's usually some time midweek, but I don't keep track. That's the closest you'll get."

"Tharvik," Sonja repeated. "Understood. Thank you." She pushed the pile of coins across the table, adding two more ronad for quality and his information. A painful amount to pay for blood and directions, but she was running out of both. The closer to the ruins, the less people would say. With a nod, she checked her seals and hooked the bladders on either hip.

Sonja was nearly at the door when the merchant spoke again. "Mage." She turned, and he stepped into the textile shop, gesturing for her to wait. Long moments filled the emptiness, an unsettling amount of time that stood her hair on end. Was he reporting her? For what, she could only assume. Was it unwise to ask about the castle? This man surely would remember the day it happened. Would've been the first to hear, maybe went to see the site for himself.

As she considered making an escape, he returned alone, handing her a fabric bundle tied with twine. "Rice cakes. For the spirits," he muttered, swiping a thumb superstitiously up the bridge of his nose. Funny to see a backstreets blood salesman acting so rattled, but people didn't like what they didn't understand. Kepstadur Keep was clearly something that few people, even here, understood.

She offered him a small smile, then left on quick steps.

Despite the early hour, nearly every business in the city's heart bubbled with activity, bartering strange wares over the sounds of hooves on smooth cobbles. Stacked stone arches welcomed merchants into the streets of Batinavik in six different languages, though all the shops on the major thoroughfare spoke exclusively in the local Jrendavarian tongue.

Sonja weaved north through the crowd. She left the bustling commercial center unobstructed, finding humble but well-maintained neighborhoods where the paths were worn yet the shops were empty. The northern gate was quieter than others, despite the row of fountains marching along the spacious road. Sonja approached three chatting gate guards with a smile. "Is this the road to Tharvik?"

A square-faced woman grunted. "Yes'm, but it's a long way. About a three-day, unprotected walk."

"Excellent, thank you." Sonja moved to step around, but the woman shuffled in front of her. "I understand," Sonja said. "If you knew how far I've already walked, you'd see that a few more days isn't much to write home over."

"It's less the time, miss," the woman said. "We don't encourage lonely travelers down this path. Best to travel with the caravan."

Sonja nodded. "And when does the next caravan leave?"

The guards exchanged nervous glances. A man with a hooked nose spoke up. "Well, there's only one that makes this route, and they left this morning."

"Probably be back in, what?" The woman looked between her colleagues for confirmation. "Say a week or so? And then it'll make the trip again."

"Unfortunate," Sonja said, "but I can't wait a week. I'll just catch them on the road."

"Helmi travels with a good number of donkey," said the third, an older man with a soft voice. "They've got hours on you. You won't find 'em by sunset."

"So be it." Sonja squinted at the midmorning sun. There was plenty of time to catch up with a handful of donkey carts.

"Ma'am, it's really not the safest path." Hooknose looked younger and smaller by the second. "There are dangerous animals out there. We can't in good conscience let you go."

Sonja stepped away from his outstretched hand. "The longer we chat, the later I'll find the caravan." Sonja regretted the tired edge in her voice. These people were doing their job. Three years ago, she would have been more compassionate. Three years ago, she'd have never argued, leaving her sister to handle the literal roadblock head-on. But Thonra wasn't here. "I apologize for my insistence," Sonja continued with a softer tone, "but you would have to arrest me to prevent this." Tense silence stretched between the four.

When Sonja, again, walked around the watchmen, Square-face held up a hand to the others. "I mean it," the woman called. "You watch for beasts. There's a reason ole Helmi is the only one to take this haul. If you die out there, we'll never know to mourn."

Sonja walked on. It often wasn't worth explaining her advantages. So many common people knew magic as a chaotic force, taking lives without warning. Unstructured. Unpredictable. That was far from the truth. Ninety-nine years of scholars had built a chorus of experiments and understanding, voices still joining every day. Magic wanted to be paid. It was that simple. The untrained didn't know to tell the magic what to take. If left to its own devices, it chose its price instead. That was hard to track, unfortunately. The public claimed that any sudden death was a magical mishap.

Sonja opened a tiny drip on one bloshul, offering payment to lighten the weight of her pack. It was a warm day, but summer was generally the only pleasant season in Jrendavar. A breeze rustled hardy wildflowers and grasses. Short trees littered the hills, growing dense with evergreens closer to the mountains. She picked up her pace, jogging through midday's meal, hoping to make up lost time. Despite the bold sunlight, an unexpected chill rolled off the lake from the borderlands.

Even with a petal-light pack, Sonja's legs and lungs burned as the sunset cast purple shadows across the clouds. Best shape of her life, yet she dragged through the hills. Just as doubt nestled into her mind, she heard the first signs of the caravan.

Those sounds, unfortunately, included screaming.

Carefully but quickly, she closed on the yells and crashes, heart alternating between exhaustion and adrenaline. At last, Sonja crested the hill blocking them from sight. Wagons lay on their sides, donkeys bucked, and a spattering of armed caravan guards circled and danced back from a brutish creature. Bears were large near Sonja's home in the west, but here by the mountains, they were massive. With a haunting groan, a matted brown bear swiped at the guards, who scattered, luring the beast away from the desperate caravanners. Another slash, and the slowest man's spear clattered to the ground an instant before his body.

Sonja faded into the tree line and scurried downhill, discarding her pack along the way. She poured a thicker line of blood behind her. Animals often had fewer energy threads, but they worked much the same as a person's would. With enough payment and careful targeting, a talented energy mage, an alternator, could briefly disrupt a being's aura, as if strumming a lyre. This would leave the target dazed, disoriented, even nauseous — in this case, allowing the guards a safe strike. Closing in, Sonja masked the sound of her footfalls with an illusion spell and broke out from the trees. She sprinted at the beast's back, letting gravity do most of the work, reaching for its threads.

Her fingers contacted the energy in its chest. A silent instant of dread stalled in her mind. The bear bellowed and jerked away. Then, in that stillness, the pain registered, shooting up her arm, a shuddering tuning fork made of bone. Momentum carried her forward, despite the way her knees buckled. She tumbled to the ground and skidded through the dirt as waves of pain resonated along her arm. Up and down, up and down.

The creature rampaged on, stumbling, but it didn't fall. Maybe even angrier. That was not supposed to happen. That had never happened to her before.

In the creature's confusion, another guard connected with a halberd, gouging under its ribs. Undeterred, the bear batted the guard away. The weapon clattered to the road, bloodless. Sonja's stomach churned and rolled as the world pitched under her elbows.

A bloodless wound meant magic.

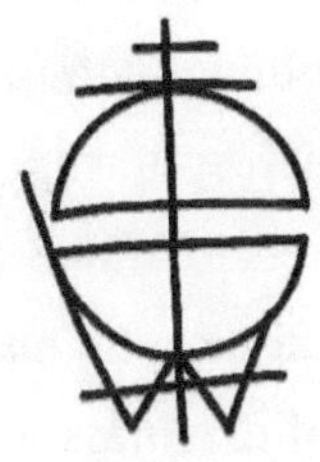

02

SOMEWHAT DEAD

The bear was magical. Sonja's mind whirred through memories of lectures greyed from decades. Bloodless wound. What were the options? The bear would bleed if it was innately magical — some kind of half-breed atrocity. Possibly an energetic parasite? Up close, this was clearly not the beast's first encounter with humans. Its fur grew patchy over deep scars all over its body. Scars that would kill. Few scholars successfully studied magic-infected animals due to the unpredictability, but, blessedly, they reported how to fight back: fire. Sonja clutched her shaking arm to her chest and searched for the strength to sit. The closest guard dragged her upright and farther away from the rampaging monster.

"Find a torch," she told him. "Light all the torches."

The man, sharp, with hazel eyes narrowed in concentration, was slow to react at first. She slumped against the nearest trunk, vision still spinning. Never had touching an energy hurt. Gods, why did it hurt?

She blinked to focus, searching for the guard again. With a sickening thud, another body crumpled. Not the same one. He'd been light-haired, right? Deep olive skin and an Attiettan jawline. He was there. Near the supplies. Fumbling with flints. Sonja raised a hand for another spell, an expensive perception spell, manifesting heat around the head of the torch. It flared loud and bright, first burning a pale lavender before fading to orange. The man stumbled backward, but only for an instant. A wave of dizziness washed over Sonja, meaning the blood line she'd laid was spent. That spell, hastily cast, had taken from the blood in her own body.

The fire caught the bear's attention. It hesitated, dropping to all fours, chuffing and growling. It shuffled in place and batted timidly at the closing humans. More guards dashed for torches until the flames burned through the dusk, and the monster ran. Pouring out a small payment, Sonja identified the unusual bear, finding two strange things. The first was its bright cluster of energy, tangled together and knotted in the throat, more like a rope than any individual threads. The second was even harder to parse. A cloud of mist radiated out in all directions. It followed the bear's escape like a swarm of locusts. The knotted energy likely caused her first spell to fail — too dense to dislodge — though she didn't know what parasite might cause that. Dowerjays, a common bird in the vineyard, fed their young off the energy in anthills until the babies could digest solid food. Could this be the reverse? Fleas or mites that both protected the bear and consumed its energy? She didn't know.

Her magic faded along with the rampaging footsteps, leaving behind only a deafening silence. Those with torches were wise enough to set a perimeter. Of the three guards struck, only one survived. Caravanners stacked scattered supplies and righted overturned wagons.

The original fire guard approached again, but she didn't accept his proffered hand. "I need a moment. Thank you, though. If you don't mind, actually, I left a travel sack in the tree line up the hill. Could I bother you to find it?" Little more than a nod, and he was gone. She gingerly kneaded her hand, confirming the pain had been completely energetic. There were no broken bones or even bruises. Neither stretching the joints nor applying pressure caused additional pain. There was only the memory. A hammer striking an anvil.

After observing for a short time, Sonja easily determined the person in charge. Amid scared merchants and flustered guards, a stocky older woman stood straight, giving directions as calmly as one might explain a recipe. Helmi, the gate watchmen had called her. Once Sonja's lightheadedness passed, she pushed to her feet. Helmi noted her approach with mild interest, giving a nod of acknowledgement. "Don't know what you did, but it's appreciated. That bastard shows up sporadically. He's got to die one day." Helmi crossed thick, suntanned arms. "How'd you know that about the fire?"

"Magic and fire have a lot in common," Sonja said. "They're tied together but don't always like that. I gave an educated guess."

"And you just happened to be passing through, then?" Helmi's tone wasn't accusatory as much as wary through her thicker accent.

"I was actually chasing you. You're the caravan to Tharvik?"

The older woman raised her eyebrows. "Walked all this way to join late? I hate to say it, seeing as you scared off our old reliable abomination, but I still charge transport fees to ride. Can't get around it by avoiding us in the city. Been doing this far too long to be burned like that."

"I'm willing to pay."

Helmi grunted her approval. "Ten ronad now, six on arrival. I'll knock some off for your educated guessing." The caravanner accepted payment, then raised her voice to everyone in the area. "This is camp for tonight."

Somewhere in the organized chaos, Sonja's pack found its way back to her. She built and tended the group fire while the others cleaned and repaired. One efficient hour later, nearly thirty people clustered around the flames. The caravanner in charge of dinner offered her an apple in addition to the provided travel ration, and Sonja invited herself into the group circle, listening to subdued stories as shovels broke ground a short distance away. It was sad but matter-of-fact, and as the camp settled in to sleep, very few ventured away for a moment graveside.

With restless weeks compiled behind her, Sonja unrolled her mat near the fierce woman with the halberd and prepared for another night staring at the stars, only to be nudged awake the next morning in the same position she'd laid down in. A dreamless black sleep, but it was far better than nothing.

Helmi led a small service in the pale dawn. A prayer of rest and peace, but only one of the fallen had been a long-term companion. There was something hollow in the memorial, a callousness that Sonja had learned to expect during her travels. Eastern Jrendavar didn't honor graves with stone or sprinkle salt across the top. People died, and the living moved on with heartless efficiency.

She bitterly hated their indifference.

Once settled into her niche on the penultimate wagon, Sonja spoke precious little for the first few hours, as if the party would notice her quiet displeasure — or care. Check-ins happened less frequently as time passed, and the following day, she may as well have been produce herself. Caravanners worked back toward speaking openly, even well within her earshot. They gossiped about competitors and complained that the wasted torches would take from their pay. Once her bad mood simmered, Sonja considered joining the chatting but always decided against it. She didn't want to overstep and lock the workers into a conversation out of obligation. But it was boring, sitting and watching the rolling hills.

If only the road was smoother. A night or two of decent sleep couldn't undo her months of built-up lethargy. She could use the nap.

On the third day of travel, hesitant rain fell just before noon. Helmi stopped the procession early for lunch at a crossroads, failing to hide from the rainfall under the branches of a grey willow.

"Getting colder," Sonja said, having fished out her heavier cloak and covered her channeling gloves with fur-lined mittens. "Winter is really nipping along the knees."

"Stay long enough, you'll get used to it," Helmi said around a mouthful of jerky. "Always cold in Tharvik. Seasons don't matter a damn out here."

Sonja frowned, peering out from the soft branches. An odd thing to say, yet it seemed true; farther down the paved path, rain flurried like snow. "Where does each go?" She pointed to the empty signpost.

"Both to Tharvik," the caravanner said. "That's quicker, safer." She gestured left to a narrower dirt path, barely wide enough for a wagon to sail through tall, starving grasses.

"More wildlife along the other?" Sonja asked.

Helmi let out a bitter laugh. "Not usually."

The lake weaved into view, the sweeping Bari Mountains as sentinels behind it. Thin clouds melted around the caps and taunted the party with beams of bright summer sky. Along the right path, there was something more. Possibly just another rolling knoll, but no, it speared up, a jagged stone with the lake expanding behind. A dark mountain in its own right, boasting rooftops and turrets and spires. "How much longer is the right path? I'd pay for the effort to—"

"We won't be traveling right," Helmi said. "Waste of time and energy. Nothing good happens on that side of the road."

Sonja nodded, finished the last of her bread, and took another pull from her canteen. "Understood." She rummaged through her pack, pulling out a handful of ronad. "What do I owe you for the ride?"

Nearby conversations slowed as roadies turned to stare Sonja down. Helmi's face gave no reaction. "You pay the rest upon safe arrival to the village, miss."

"It's best I pay now since, unfortunately, our paths diverge."

"Ain't nothing to loot there, mage," rasped another merchant, a palpable hatred in his scowl. "Keep of a Thousand Souls always makes room for another."

Finally. This was it.

Smothering a triumphant grin, Sonja shouldered her supplies and proffered the remaining coins. The older woman refused, then waved her off. "The largest gate leads to Tharvik," Helmi grunted. "Don't you forget that. See town if you must, but only a fool would stay out past dark. That place needs more than little fire tricks."

Sonja only hesitated briefly. With a subtle hand to each partially filled bloshul, she felt enough for several minor spells. "Thank you, ma'am." Sonja ignored baffled eyes as she lifted her hood and stepped into the drizzle.

The path leading toward Kepstadur had clearly been the intended route, using the same wide paving stones and colorful brick lining. Unmaintained, yes, but the fact it existed was important. Everything Sonja saw supported her understanding of events. Kepstadur was a port city crowning an inlet lake along a common trade route. In its prime, it had been the only stop between the secluded north and the Djabassan Sea. Most interesting were the claims of the regent's immortality. Not one little rumor, but dozens of firsthand accounts and documented interactions. The Kepstan name was widespread, even region to region, as numerous cities claimed encounters with this incredible woman and her ancestors. If the Kepstan's wanted something, they'd send a single negotiator. A negotiator blessed with immortality. Until suddenly, maybe fifteen years ago, the stronghold was found empty. No disease or sign of attack. No bodies left behind. A candle's flame pinched out.

Contrary to logic, this sudden extermination only added credence to the story. Many scholars, Sonja among them, considered it likely that whatever protected the Kepstans had backfired — a relic or natural phenomenon — and the cost had been the city itself. Its people were absorbed by an unimaginable power, never to be seen again. If the events *had* been magical, it likely left behind proof.

Sonja had spent years cramming claims of immortality and resurrection from across the nation into her notebook of rumors. While most sites took up a page or two, she devoted the last half of the book to Kepstadur. Accounts varied wildly — most outrageous in the far west near the homestead — but after a few months, she could point to some consistencies. She refused to believe anything not directly related to the family's resilience. The regent likely didn't float. She couldn't read minds or speak telepathically. She didn't sweat gold. Her voice wasn't abnormally loud, and if she could see through walls, it was only in the way any alternator could.

These stories were uncommon, which made them less likely. Sonja focused on immortality because of the facts. Not for her own hopes. Not for her desperation. There would be signs of magic here. There had to be.

With the foggy form so close, she started looking for familiar signs. She'd seen relics that made plants grow off-color, and some that made stone pliant like sap. The steady change in weather was also worth noting. Sonja flagged it as a good question to ask in Tharvik. As the sounds of the caravan faded, so did her fancy avenue. Sunken treads and reaching weeds, a tree downed across the road, and the faintest smell of rot. Sharp like an animal corpse, dead in the nearby ferns.

But that didn't matter. This was Kepstadur. Gods, it was here. It was…skinnier than she'd expected. The whole settlement was tall and narrow, reflecting double-height in the subtle waves. Perimeter walls stepped in tandem with the craggy cliffside and plunged into the water. Strange, flared roofs lined the battlements, many collapsed under what had likely been harsh snow seasons. In stark contrast, the castle proper seemed more traditional, wide and ostentatious, peering out from behind the defenses with a cluster of craning rooflines.

The lake crept inland, reaching farther into the rocky land until she came to a lattice of battered wooden piers supporting the road. Before she could overthink it, Sonja bounded across the parts that seemed stable, each step creaking louder. This was bad weather for a swim. Her gaze drifted beyond the castle, where spindly docks stretched out like skeletal fingers over far colder water.

Breath plumed out of her cloak, and rain froze to her shoulders faster than she could brush it away. While a midsummer snow was not unheard of, this felt different. Batinavik had been almost hot when she'd arrived, yet the plants growing lakeside looked small, bowed, and long dormant. She twisted one ring mindlessly around her finger, searching her memory for explanations. The bear and the weather were both promising signs of magic. It was just a matter of uncovering what was at play. Excitement welled in her chest, radiant against the cold and gloom, as the memory of Thonra's rare but passionate optimism rang like morning bells. *"The Kepstans didn't have to know the specifics to be right. Whatever they had, it's better documented than any other fjarfest we know of. When we get there, you'll see."*

Sonja could almost hear Ulrik's laugh. Thonra would meet her here. They stretched ever closer to going home. To bringing him back to life. This would be the one.

After an hour or more, she stood in the shadow of the tallest gate. The shining sun did little to combat the temperature. She took note of signage to Tharvik but turned away, walking over a small moat and into the keep proper. Sonja hadn't known what to expect, but it wasn't this. The walls held a solid perimeter. The streets were time-damaged but bloodless, and she smelled no decay. Morbidly, she was almost impressed. Squat stone homes stood firm, lining precise arterial paths that sloped in long Z shapes, down toward the waterside castle. The stables were in great condition but held only the memory of horses.

Sonja first heard news of the Kepstadur Fall as an adult, though she couldn't pinpoint how old. Maybe nine years ago? Ulrik hadn't still been training, had he? Regardless, the details that made it to the west never agreed. The city'd been burned or drowned or cursed; the gods themselves had swept it all away. She ran her fingers across a dusty window, all in reasonable condition. Standing here in the streets, the rumors felt overstated. It was empty, yes, but nothing told of the "greatest Jrendavarian tragedy" of Sonja's lifetime.

Her last site had been heartbreaking. A sizable village in the mid-south, blinked into obscurity during a harrowing winter storm. They had been so isolated or unnoteworthy to die without leaving even a name. When rediscovered, it was lauded as a haunted location where the spirits were strong enough to reenter their bodies. The so-called leading specialist had named the discovery after himself: Einar Village. A minor noble with nothing better to do, he'd preserved the placement of the bones and commissioned in-depth, first-person dramatizations of every villager's last days. For the most notable corpses, Einar wrote their stories himself. He'd been difficult to work with, and his fables were shit. Had the revived townspeople proven true, Sonja would have struggled to remove any fjarfest or artifact without attracting the attention of his crude band of Attiettan mercenaries. She shook away memories of their blunt faces and hateful stares.

In the empty streets of Kepstadur, Sonja found very little of value. Unlike in Einar Village, barely a remnant of humanity remained. The outer ring of homes and shops had been looted dry, though no doors were broken down. Most hung open, and those that were closed proved to be unlocked. She collected the occasional goblet or empty jewelry box, winding closer to the castle at the center. The deeper she traveled, the steeper the slope, until the road flattened into the first of three broad plazas. She toed at the lifeless dirt, imagining grass stretching between the mirrored buildings. The architecture was stately, with pointed windows and decorative trim. To the left, doors gaped off their hinges, framing a dim, disheveled library. Its twin was a temple, as told by a row of small covered altars. They were shorter in the east, barely to Sonja's hip, each marked on the side with a common prayer word and a corresponding glyph carved on the top.

Wisdom. Generosity. Protection. Harvest. Satisfaction. Wellness.

She rustled to find the merchant's bundle of rice cakes and stepped forward to study the glyphs. Some were standard: *HEAR* mapped to wisdom, *GIVE* marked generosity, and *SAFE* for protection. The standard *GROW* for harvest had been replaced with what Sonja read as *TRADE*. Interesting. The fifth glyph had faded past the point of legibility, but the sixth stopped her with a jolt. In a flurry, Sonja turned on one heel, slapped the bundle onto protection, and trudged from the courtyard. Kepstadur must have been backwards before the mystery, or maybe the carver hadn't known how to read glyphs. It was a crass mistake, but she tried to see it as such. A mistake. The altar for "wellness" held a glyph for *LUCK*.

Backwards, heathen bastards, all of them. As if Ulrik was just unlucky. As if there was nothing that could be done. She imagined some northern mystic bringing this idea down the river, planting it like poison.

Sonja re-centered with a hand on the smooth stone railing, taking the first clear look at Kepstadur Castle. Two more tiered plazas wrapped like an amphitheater, centered on the unreasonably large front door. The chamber beyond marched up to a level of massive rooms and glittering windows. Defensive towers framed the entry. Ostentatious, but she wouldn't deny the beauty.

She continued to the next level and stayed right toward the port, noting the placid water flooding the city's lowest tier. A series of metal grates stood locked but lopsided, corroding in the saltwater. The ships moored inside showed signs of rot, most sitting low in the shallow bay. Castle windows reflected evening sunlight as Sonja climbed onto the railing to get a look inside. The stained glass masterwork, with intricate wavelike designs, was unlike any other part of the structure. The delicate pieces danced with vibrant colors and reflected the line between lake and land. She frowned at a puncture wound through the design. Several panels had been shattered, gaping with a stark darkness against the color.

A voice broke through the silence of the empty city, speaking quickly and slurred. Sonja stepped away from the ledge, searching the open doors behind her, one hand resting on the fullest bloshul. A second voice joined, but the words were wrong. The language resembled Jrendavarian, but as the third voice cascaded in, she recognized what was happening. She couldn't pinpoint a direction because the voices weren't in the street. Perception magic. There was a mage nearby.

She ran. Louder and louder, more voices tumbled over each other. Speaking turned to shouting, crying, screams. Sonja jostled into walls and knocked over hollow barrels in her haste. At the top tier of the city, the voices were gone, but that didn't mean it was safe. Keeping track of the large gate toward Tharvik, she slinked through the alleys and hollow shacks until she found a niche to sit in and watch the exit.

The two bloshuls she'd bought in Batinavik were still mostly full. She wore two more across her chest; one was dry, while the other had been the drip for her bag's weight. Not much to work with. She pressed her palms together to stop the shaking, watching as the sun slipped away. There was no telling how far she needed to walk to get to the village, and stalling would only make it worse.

Sonja stopped the drip, settling the pack heavily onto her shoulders. From a fuller pouch, she started a new stream, faster than the first.

It pooled at her feet. One, two, three…she paid it to the magic and disappeared. Not a complicated illusion, but Sonja was less talented in that branch of magic. She excelled with energy spells — identifications, manipulations, sympathy. But Thonra was their usual cloak. An alternator and an illusionist. They'd been a good team.

Invisibility in place and the constant flow of payment, Sonja padded into the center of the road and scanned the area. Kepstadur was as it had been. Silent. Empty. Still. But Sonja didn't stay for more than a breath. She snuck across the bridge and trudged farther from the eyes of the city before dropping her illusion. Not half an hour of walking, yet the nearly full bloshul was all but dry. She sighed. An expensive escape, but the knowledge gained had been worth the cost. Kepstadur was real. The cause of its abandonment was not immediately clear. There were no apparent precautions to keep the curious traveler away.

And most notably, there was a mage hiding inside.

03

THARVIK VILLAGE

The evening's chill spurred Sonja onward. By the time Tharvik crested into view, the spiteful cold and fading adrenaline slowed each step. Compounding the effects, she'd reasoned that it was best to save her remaining bloshuls for emergencies, meaning she shouldered the full weight of the pack longer than she was used to. Thonra would have chastised her reliance on magical manipulation, and she would be right. Sonja hadn't checked in with her sister since leaving Batinavik. That would be a priority tonight.

Stone-based torches marched in long lines down the main thoroughfare, attracting clusters of townspeople to stand and warm their hands. Runes wrapped the stems, hard to discern in the flickering light. As the sky melted black and blue, Sonja asked for directions to a series of inns, reluctantly trusting that the Gaadi Inn was her best bet, per a bit of gossip from last night's dinner. Like many other nearby buildings, the details were hard to parse by moonlight.

The first hostel she passed was ominously subdued, while the second had boards nailed over dusty windows. Gaadi's twin hearths blazed away the cold, supported by the light of dozens of candles and lanterns. The stench of ale and sweat battled against bundles of cinnamon and clove hung around doors and placed decoratively at tables. At least they were trying.

In the center of the mess hall, a worn rug stretched from the entry to the bar top, where a spindly, grey-haired woman nodded a greeting. "All can I provide, ma'am? We've another hour for warm dinner, and four for warm drink." The barkeep gestured to Sonja's pack. "If you're after a stay, we've room in the main wing."

"Do you offer private quarters?" Sonja asked.

The barkeep stooped and thumbed through a small ledger.

"Carita," whined a drunk nearby. "When's your opening for *my* private quarters?"

"Shut it. Did your ole mother not teach your damn mouth to lock when two respectable people's having a talk?" The barkeep, supposedly Carita, looked at Sonja and softened her voice. "I swear, some nights, it's a shattered bowl cupping water around these parts. Anders there is harmless, but he's not worth the space in your ear if you can help it."

The drunk cackled and lashed something back that Sonja didn't understand. Many dialects here felt incomprehensible, growing thicker the farther north she traveled. It was all but a new language in some smaller towns. In Batinavik, merchants had slowed their pace to match Sonja's own western accent, sometimes insultingly so, but at least she'd known where one word ended and the next began.

Carita ignored whatever Anders had said, leaning closer to focus. "I've got four singles left available this evening. Lowest at forty-nine and highest at—"

"Lowest is fine," Sonja cut in, trying to imitate the quick clip.

"I don't need much space. Just a touch of privacy. I wouldn't mind starting with something warm before I go up."

"A stew and two drinks can round to sixty."

"If you stock anything from Snow's Grove, I'd take one instead of two house ales."

Carita nodded, swiping Sonja's money smoothly from the marred counter. "Whatever seat you'd like, ma'am." She poured and passed a goblet of wine. "Food'll 'rive shortly."

The dining area was neither full nor empty, with small groups scattered in every corner. Sonja settled at the most secluded table available. Far too large for one person, but a healthy distance from Anders, humming loudly to himself. Off her feet for the first time since lunch, Sonja resisted the urge to rest her head. The wine passed her lips and burned sour on her tongue. She choked it down and masked her disgust. This was in no way her family's wine. The more popular the name grew, the more often she ran across low quality copycats. Was it worth mentioning to Carita that the Gaadi Inn was being scammed?

With her bag safely between her knees, Sonja rolled her aching neck and stretched the stiffness from her shoulders. The hearth fire spread soft fingers across Sonja's back, melting tension from her brow. She could almost fall asleep here in all the noise…if she…just…

"Anyone is seated here?" The smooth, deeep voice held a thick foreign accent.

Sonja cracked one eye to find a trio of burly mercenary-types standing across the table. She took a breath to sit straighter, using the adjustment to rest one hand on a bloshul still hidden by her traveling cloak. "Not at all. Please, take them with you."

The speaker hesitated, a sharp, Attiettan-looking man, with a sparkle in his eye. "Is it accepted to join instead?"

Sonja studied the three faces. The Attiettan, a redheaded woman with a long braid and flat nose, and a wide man with piercings. It was the last who registered first. He'd been the very tail of the caravan's traveling party, one with a hammer the size of his head. Flicking her eyes back over, Sonja recognized the others as well. Red was the menace with a halberd, and the Attiettan was the guard who'd first run for the torches. Sonja gestured to the table. Red and Torch took seats, but Pierce stayed standing. "Glad the caravan made it into town."

"We could say the same about you," Red said. "Miss Helmi was in knots when you left."

"Worried?" Sonja asked.

The woman laughed. "Frustrated. Way she saw it, her stock was safer with you than any number of us."

Sonja openly examined their heavier armor and weather-hardened faces. "Unlikely, but I appreciate her confidence."

"You walked to the keep?" asked Torch. "Some expect to see you return, running as the first."

"No," Red said, "they never expected to see you again. Not much to visit at the end, far as I've heard."

Carita delivered Sonja's food without waiting for the conversation to stall, one eyebrow raised. That look implied the older woman would gladly remove these surprise dinner companions. Sonja gave a smile and a subtle shrug. The guards were fine for now. They'd been cordial on the trip when checking in with her. "It wasn't terrible," she said as the barkeep left. "An interesting piece of history."

"Is that what you went for?" asked Pierce in a shockingly neutral, Central Jrendavarian accent. "History?"

Sonja sipped at her soup. "What other reason would there be?" It was best to mask behind vagueness in these situations.

"And what did you find?" Torch asked.

Sonja took time to cool her stew and shovel a few bites — thankfully far tastier than the drink. There were three hundred different ways to answer. "The city was beautiful, but something is there," she admitted.

"I don't know what, but I see why it's called dangerous."

"How is this dangerous?"

She shrugged. "It's hard to say. I didn't stay long enough to really understand."

"And you go back?"

"What would I gain from that?" Sonja dodged, letting her voice grow colder.

Torch nodded, undeterred. "And to return for dinner, the path here was easy?"

"It was fine," she said. "No half-dead bears jumping out from the trees to maul me."

Red snarled like she might spit but thought better of it. "That bastard's a menace."

"And it's been here for a while?"

"Long before I started running these roads near six years ago. Still haven't figured out how to kill it."

"If you knew the journey was unsafe, why start?"

"I'll track these roads raw till the thing's dead and damned and ripped to shreds."

Sonja flinched, trying to cover with another sip of bitter wine. The commitment in the woman's eye was familiar. It was Thonra's rage. Sour spite churned in Sonja's chest. She knocked back the terrible concoction with another full gulp to truncate her suffering.

Nearby conversations seemed to swell in a brief pause before Torch spoke again. "The creature is killed before, yes? Simply does not stay dead. As is anchored in the soil."

"Won't die 'cause it's a demon," Red hissed. "Can't stab it. Can't drown it. Can't cut off its head. And it's a gamble if or when we see it. The times we've been well-manned, it's smart enough to stay away."

"Beast'll dig up those graves," Pierce mused. "Miss Helmi watches the sky, but the rest of us know."

"Well, with that pleasant image," Sonja lifted her pack, "I'll be off to bed. Thank you for the company." These three were working up to something. Best to leave now before she had to turn them down. She was tired and, frankly, out of charity to give.

"I'll pay your night's sleep if you tell us how to end it."

Sonja turned back to meet Red's eye. This guard couldn't be all that old, early twenties, yet she simmered in a bitter hatred that put bags under her eyes. "If I knew how to help, believe me, I'd tell you everything. Fire will scare it off, but I don't know how to…unmoor an anchor, as you call it."

Thankfully, they didn't insist further.

Carita called over a young boy to carry Sonja's bag and show her to her room. He favored the barkeep enough. Maybe not a son, but a grandson or nephew. Red stormed out, knocking over her chair and muttering vitriol. Carita hollered at the guards, but Sonja gently urged the boy to lead. He scurried up two flights of stairs, unlocked a small room, lit a few lanterns, and handed her the key. The boy spoke only when she thanked him, responding too quietly to understand. Then she stood alone again.

This cupboard with a window was horribly overpriced. There was a cot and a narrow desk, but barely room to fit her bag in between the two. The vaulted roof helped the space feel less claustrophobic. Not ideal, but it would do.

She locked the door and settled in, taking off the bulkiest pieces of travel ware and pretending she was comfortable, leaning elbows against the desk from her seat on the cot. After drawing the single curtain, Sonja pulled out a hollow rod the length of her forearm. It was a Tahlzhian export, supposedly some kind of tree or weed or something. It was watertight, and that's what mattered. She worked out the cork stopper and carefully removed a rolled map to relax onto the table. This page had been two pages adhered together. The top was empty and thin enough to show hints of a map underneath. It was hard to discern details through the top sheet, but over the months, she'd traced key landmarks to make it more functional. The most important marker was a circle drawn near the mountains. Sonja ran a finger over a small series of holes in the page, then dug through her pack for more supplies: a bag of salt, three smooth stones, and a wide, shallow bowl. To her loose bemusement, the bowl hung halfway off the table. A bad item to balance, she set it on the floor with a dull plink.

First, the salt. Sonja untied the top and sprinkled a circle close to the center of the table. After cleaning the edges, she laid three of the incense burners in a triangle, sure that the points intersected correctly. It wasn't her prettiest vel, but it would do. Many tools were nothing to look at; that didn't make them less powerful. Vela were simple devices to help with the heavy lifting, making difficult spells easier and less expensive. The best vela were often mundane items used with intention. They were the opposite of fjarfest — any relic that itself held magic. She placed the map on top, then balanced each stone at the intersections. Next, she poured a careful amount of blood into the bowl at her feet. The nearest candle burned overhead at arm's length, so she brought it to sit on the table.

Sonja pulled a small knife from her boot and held the tip in the center of the flame. Then she unfocused her eyes, her finger pinching lightly on a loose corner. After a few breaths, tendrils of energy branched from the thin top sheet in all directions. Most were faint and scattered. Leaves, seeds, or any other byproduct from the tree that had made it. One thread, however, shone bright and strong. The process of making sympathetic paper was unique, yes, but just another vel. It wasn't magical in its own right. It spent months curing after production, energetically adapting to the idea of being a singular object. The longer it sat as a conjoined page, the stronger the connective thread would be. Sonja latched on to the link with her mind.

Sympathetic magic was the costliest of the energy magics, with the price growing exponentially depending on any number of factors. Distance, relation, task — it compounded. Setting up a few vela could help disperse that cost, but only so much. Grasping the thread tightly, Sonja opened her eyes and found the approximate location of Tharvik. Before the blade could cool, she placed a single diagonal line. The energy left the room in a gust of wind that rustled the hair on her arm. She heated the blade again, then used the flat as an arrow toward the circle. Toward Kepstadur.

Satisfied with the directions, Sonja let the link slip away. She slouched on the narrow bed, frowning up at the joint between wall and ceiling. This was their agreement. They'd split up to explore twice the number of rumors. Riskier to travel alone, but efficient. If the leads ran dry with no success, Sonja and Thonra would regroup at the base of the Bari Mountains.

Sonja carefully extracted the map to look for new updates. Just before Batinavik, Thonra had transferred a second thin slash near her first, upgrading a report from "promising" to "very promising." It was the first hit they'd had in a few months. Crossed diagonals marched around the country, documenting all the "promising" leads that became "dead ends." Sonja's marks left a grey or black char from the burn, while Thonra's transferred only precise holes. It would be the opposite on the twin page. That difference in color made it immediately clear that Thonra had chased far more rumors between the two of them. Gods, did she ever rest?

Too tired to pack her supplies, Sonja lay down. She hoped to find the same rest from the nights before. Her groggy mind raced with memories of home. This little room reminded her somewhat of the old barn. Up in the rafters where she and Thonra and Ulrik would build hideaways with other children from the vineyard. Those were the early days, still at the first farm, when their parents had strictly forbidden the children from using magic. They'd saved every spare veyilir, hoping to afford any amount of formal training for all three. Times were hard. Worker families came and went. But the siblings remained. They fought, yes — Thonra and Sonja more than anyone else — but they took care of each other.

Sonja had long since realized how dangerous their secret alcoves had been, but those were some of her favorite memories. Back then, their few luxuries had been enough payment to practice magic. Chocolate from birthdays or stolen glasses full of unprocessed wine. Ulrik had once nearly killed the barn cat trying to practice. He'd been young and didn't understand what he was doing, so Thonra's subsequent lectures had been too harsh. The guilt haunted him for months. At seven years old, he starved himself in recompense.

They were adults when Ulrik gave more context to the story. As a boy, he stumbled into a method of energetically stabilizing that old cat, using his mashed dinners as payment. Thonra, again, had been furious. Her husband gaped in disbelief. Sonja had cried, vividly remembering the trembling husk of a child in her brother's bed, resurfacing the memory of tense dinners as their parents paid for doctors they couldn't afford. But Ulrik only got better after that damned cat fully recovered. Had she known, Sonja could have helped with the healing, but sweet Ulrik had believed it only worked as well because of his shame. That was, supposedly, part of the cost.

He'd saved that wretched animal. Twenty years later, Sonja had failed to save him in return.

31

04

SHAMAN

In a dark sanctuary, near a loud city, on a hot day, Thonra waited. The woven cushion beneath her knees had been almost comfortable at first, but after kneeling for half an hour, each damp fiber dug into her shins like a gravel beach. She had never cared for incense, and this short room held enough burners to smoke out the sun. The oil was similar to lavender but with sharp undertones. Which did the shaman want? To relax or to stay alert? The whole temple had been a mix of antithetical practices.

Thonra turned her ear toward gentle footsteps as other supplicants arrived and left around her. Her eyes remained closed to display a solemnity she didn't feel. The only thing keeping her in place was a simple task she'd given herself: count the water drops as they fell to metal drums. Her patience would wane before another ping brought her back to her task, mentally shouting the numbers. Had "the Pilgrim" designed this waiting area to be so intentionally frustrating? Many recollections of the mysterious tul-Habao considered her opaque; some of the more critical called her a trickster. Whatever she had been, she knew more about creating fjarfest than anyone else known to history.

A gentle hand fell on Thonra's shoulder, and she regretted how dramatically she twitched away. She hadn't heard these steps drawing closer and surely hadn't expected to be touched. "The shaman beckons," said a soft voice.

Thonra stood with as much grace as she could, her cramped legs rippling. Were she taller like her siblings, she would have ducked through the low-ceilinged space as the guide did. She didn't know what to expect from this meeting. This place was clearly not a temple to the gods. Not any gods she knew, at least. The wide colonnades contracted to narrow passes of natural rock formations. There were no great art pieces or altars. And she'd be damned before she ever sat and waited like that again. Damned cushions on the damned floor. She hadn't expected to miss the creaky old benches and long fasting tables from the temple of Tsultsve or the dances held for Uskieru's harvest. She felt too old to be crawling around on the ground.

Her guide weaved through dripping formations, resting a hand on one in particular, one that looked notably phallic to Thonra, though she kept her expression under control. Bragi would find it funny. They would hardly have to glance at each other. The thought of shared smiles, as with most memories of her husband, only rekindled a quiet anger. She tugged on her carved wedding earring out of habit, wondering if the old fables were true. If they were, did Bragi feel her frustration with him each time she brushed against it?

The acolyte continued in silence, leading deeper into this gods-forsaken hole in the ground. Turn after turn until the faintest sounds of running water began echoing along the halls. Not simply the drips on stone or chimes against metals, but melodic tones like rain on a lake. Despite the effort of the walk, the depths held a cold that summer couldn't banish. After ducking through another low passage, the guide bowed and gestured Thonra past.

Around one final corner, she faced a room taller than the new house. Maybe the new house stacked on the old house. Her stomach churned as she realized how far down they must be. The slope hadn't seemed too steep, yet…

Thonra forced her focus. At the far end of the chamber, a thin figure in yellow knelt beside a sweeping pool of cloudy water. No sitting pad in sight. Thonra banished her own deepening frown, clasped her hands in front of her chest, and strode forward, stopping a few paces behind the shaman. Locals called him ba-Olafur.

"I apologize for your long wait," ba-Olafur said, a long, golden braid waving against his back. "It's good to commune with our structure."

"Of course," Thonra said, as if the phrase meant anything to her. "I understand you're a busy man."

"A meaningless distinction, busy. We are only as available as we allow ourselves, traveler."

Thonra disagreed with that assessment but didn't argue. She stepped through a narrow path of three hundred candles scattered on the floor. Gods, it was unnecessary. However, she couldn't help but bask in the gentle, all-consuming warmth. The air was its own blanket against the unnatural chill.

"From where do you travel?" He still did not turn to face her.

"The west, teacher."

"Clearly, as the sun originates from the east. May I ask you to be more specific?"

Thonra considered. This was a widely known and respected holy man. One who kept his practices fully separate from worship to the gods. That held a certain gravity. He might trick the simple, yes, but she humored the idea that ba-Olafur was at least competent.

"Helslidir," she said.

"Beautiful pastures. Did you watch after any animals?"

"My family lives on a farm," she replied vaguely, though he seemed thoroughly preoccupied with his *communing*. Did her reply matter?

"And what started your pilgrimage to us?"

"I simply seek to learn. There is a broad world of knowledge beyond the fields."

"Ah, your first time away from home, then?"

"No, teacher. We boarded with tutors as children."

At this, ba-Olafur turned, the multiplicity of candles casting a pulsing glow from below. His features were wide and attentive, hinting at some Tahlzhin heritage despite naturalistic Jrendavarian speech. He held her gaze for several breaths before studying the rest of her appearance. Thonra adjusted her stance, feeling exposed in the simple worship tunic.

"Is there something wrong with that answer?" she asked sharply.

"Not at all, traveler. It was simply the tone with which you said it."

Memories of an abandoned abbey returned unbidden. Her first time from home had been a disaster. The tutors forbade the children to discuss private lessons, claiming that each had their own journey.

"Comparison leads to distraction. Distractions kill mages."

But Thonra remembered her sister's tired eyes during lunch period. She remembered her brother's sudden, hostile turn. Such a sweet boy, acting completely unlike himself. She remembered the shame of her ignorance. It had taken her far too long to tell their parents. To beg for a different tutor. "I meant no tone at all."

The shaman's concerned expression did not change; he only turned to face her fully, legs crossed. "Ah, you must forgive my presumptuous nature. Searching for answers between the words often leads me to find those unintended. It seems you have specific hopes for this conversation. Perhaps it's best that you tell me your story."

"There's little story to tell," Thonra said. "We aren't taught about tul-Habao in the west. We studied runic theories in great detail but never attributed to her. Suddenly, I'm confronted with hundreds of accounts of an incredible fjarfest-crafter, supposedly taught by magic itself. I've seen the relics they credit to her. I need to know if the legends hold any truth."

"The Pilgrim was very much real. My father met her when he was a child. It was her third venture to these caverns, the very last time anyone saw her here."

"What was so special?"

The shaman blinked before a broad, stifled grin pressed along his lips. ba-Olafur gestured to their surroundings. "She spent much of her time beneath the surface with the rivulets and pools. Many believe she valued springs and waterways after a life near foreign deserts."

"That's nice," Thonra interjected before he could start reciting the First Pilgrim's biography. She'd read that already. "So these caves were like her home? Or a resting spot along a common route?"

"The caves themselves? No, not at all. Other villages rejected her, but my people knew. She stayed with a different family every night and answered questions in the square."

"And her magic? She taught, yes?"

"Oh, no, tul-Habao was no mage."

"You're so sure?"

"We have no record of the Pilgrim's magic."

Thonra bit back an impulsive response. Implying tul-Habao had no magic was like implying lightning never struck the dirt. There was plenty of evidence left behind, even if it was rare to personally witness. Neither spoke for a while, leaving only the steady water dripping into pools and echoing along the stone.

"Is this all you were curious about?" ba-Olafur asked lightly. "Whether the Pilgrim carried magic—"

"I've studied a good deal about tul-Habao," Thonra said, squatting to be level with the shaman. She selected each word cautiously, making sure they were even. This was not someone to threaten lightly. She had to — *needed* to — convince him that her intentions were innocent. "I've read several accounts of her skill as an alternator, and even a few implying she could perform perception magic. To say she was anything short of extraordinary…it's an insult to all scholarship in her name."

"And this is what you seek, mage? Scholarship?" His tone never wavered. "It is wise to remember that many people have been extraordinary, even those without such gifts."

He had no reason to believe Thonra was a mage — she'd left her mastery rings behind for this encounter. She decided not to acknowledge it. "All I request," Thonra softened her voice like Sonni would, "is travel information. Everywhere I look, her records are in shambles. Woven maps burned through the middle. Storytellers using imaginary cities. Sections blotted from scrolls."

The words echoed between them and against a hundred jagged edges. All the kindness faded from the shaman's face. Not dissipating completely, but retracting. "I fear you know why. As a scholar, I expect you understand that some information becomes lost." His jaw flexed. "As a mage, I expect you understand that some information is dangerous. Too tempting to keep accessible."

Shit. She contorted her brow into a look of confusion, but it didn't appear to be enough. The rigidity in ba-Olafur's gaze was firm. He knew that she knew of the Second Pilgrim. The Pilgrim of Sorrow. This conversation had ended. As she moved to stand, something caught her eye. The pool behind the shaman spanned to the wall, nearly as far away as Bragi was tall. The wall itself was relatively flat for a cave but carved in patterns and lines that ferried streams of water from the dark crevice above. At the very bottom, the rock stepped back, creating the reversed ledge where the drops collected. From this angle, around the shaman's head, Thonra caught a glimpse of a necklace — a wide, flat stone bound with several woven cords. It hung under that ledge, collecting streams, half-submerged. Thonra noted the deep grooves of a carved glyph. Unrecognizable. Not outdated or a foreign style. No. A glyph worn away unevenly through the years. Streams from above eroded the top, and the water below faded anything beneath the surface. A fjarfest, a relic, destroyed.

Thonra met ba-Olafur's eye once again, feeling his fear acutely. Was it her face? She tried to neutralize the disappointment but had no method for gauging success.

"You are not the first to copy her footsteps," he whispered. "But I beg you will be the last."

Thonra's body groaned as she straightened. "I don't know what you're talking about," she lied. "But if this legacy dies, it is your guilt to swallow. Yours and everyone like you. Magic will never make advances if we hide and destroy everything of value." She said it with as much conviction as she could muster. These words were unlikely to change the shaman's mind, but Thonra couldn't help it. She would say anything in hopes of breaking through to these types of people.

The fear melted from ba-Olafur's expression, along with his welcoming posture. "The last person who searched for tul-Habao's legacy burned half of our city to the sod. He terrorized us with our own dead. Invisible assailants and bouts of madness. Hundreds of citizens, all dead. I looked into his eyes as he killed my predecessor. He was smiling. The Mage of Voices didn't have to reveal himself, but, if not me, who would tell his story? Yet, even with all his power, he disappeared into obscurity."

The Mage of Voices. The Hand of the Dead. The Second Pilgrim. Valtyr of the North. Names Thonra had become too familiar with. And this fool all but accused her of admiring his callous cruelty.

This day was a waste of her time. But she wouldn't leave empty-handed. She spoke again, forcing forward gentleness. "A last question, if you will."

He watched her with snake's eyes, cold and narrowed, body coiled. Would a shaman be armed? That was a sick fascination, but she didn't fear him, regardless of weapon.

Thonra retrieved the paper from her simple rope belt and held it for him to see: an advertisement for a pair of mages offering services as experienced tutors.

A sneer flashed across the shaman's face before neutralizing. Good, he knew these people. "You are far too old for training now, are you not?" ba-Olafur said cooly.

She refused to rise. "Are they still here?" It was a battered, faded page, but new enough to read.

"He spends his summers in the port."

"Which port?"

"Out of the eastern gate; take the first fork south. It's only a few days by foot to Seglaborg."

"Thank you." She spun promptly to leave. The force flickered nearby candles, blinking a few out completely.

"You cannot live forever," said ba-Olafur.

Thonra didn't turn back. "I don't want to."

05

WILD HOGS

No matter her efforts, sleep taunted Sonja. It stood out of arm's length and laughed. After a few hours of restless thrashing, she sat up to clean her runes, returning all the salt to its pouch and spending a pinch of blood to search for anyone awake nearby. She tried documenting the bear encounter in a small journal, which made her sleepy, but the feeling disappeared when she closed the book and lay down.

As the sun returned, Sonja was there waiting. She locked her belongings away and met the new dawn in the streets. The city wasn't what she'd expected. To start, Tharvik felt empty, even as citizens started their morning routines. Sonja couldn't help but feel this was a town failing to fill out its shell. There were obvious signs of former glory: ornate doors, oversized windows, public statues, and more shops than Sonja cared to count. Yet so much looked long-since abandoned. Kepstadur's fall had consequences that echoed through time. A haunted trading hub appeared to be bad for business.

The community left behind was resilient, but there were signs of cracks. They grew cagey without warning. Sonja tried twice to pawn off the trinkets from Kepstadur, but the shopkeepers would rather sell than buy. A large announcement board in the town center boasted minimal posts — mostly decrees from a nearby lord whose name Sonja didn't recognize. Scattered among tax information, wanted posters, and seemingly-uninforced decrees, unofficial documents relied less on actual words. It didn't seem that the locals had lost literacy yet, but she saw it as a slippery slope.

After a few hours of wandering and another failed nap, Sonja shuffled through booths, restocking her supplies and chatting with anyone who seemed receptive. No one around town dealt in blood, but harvesting their knowledge was the most important task for the day. She avoided mentioning Kepstadur outright, guiding conversations subtly when possible. Of all people, the young adults were the chattiest. Those who could remember, if only vaguely, a time before the sun struggled to warm the soil. Many had been aware of the Kepstan family's rule but had no opinions of their leadership. They were possibly the most affected by the decline of population and commerce and education.

But Sonja was careful. She didn't want people finding a pattern, so after a quiet dinner, she paid for a night in the cheaper hostel wing, moved her things to a lock-bin, then left town before sundown. It was too costly for a second night in the tiny private room, and she didn't need to message her sister again. She frowned to herself, clutching the edges of her cloak protectively. Inside, she carried all of her bloshul and a length of rope.

One of the civilian signs from the announcement board had simply read *REWARD*, with a crude drawing of a boar's head and dark, hollow eyes. Below that, ten hexagons and a barn. The message was simple enough. The farmer would pay ten ronad for hunting pests. It felt like he could've offered more, but she didn't hold it against him.

Hogs in eastern Jrendavar were easiest to find right at nightfall; she suspected the same here. Sonja hiked into the woods, searching for traces of activity and a good place to hide. She manipulated her cloak to radiate small waves of heat. Summer really had no power here.

A stream traced the hills toward the lake, lined with wilting berries and dense grey fungus. She found a hollow to wait in and considered what she'd learned. Several patterns emerged during her conversations in Tharvik. First and most apparent, no one ever mentioned what had happened. Not even in passing.

"After our allies left us…" or *"The damn trade routes couldn't have held up one more season…"*

Further, several accounts related the uncanny weather with the events at Kepstadur.

"The farmer shammed prices like his's the only ass is cold."

Next were the raids. When former trading allies learned the city had fallen, there were years' worth of campaigns to claim those lucrative ports — and, by extent, Tharvik.

"Ship shows up one day, torments the shops the next, then they're fed to the earth. Never seen again."

It had been a few years since the last raid, but the older population didn't seem convinced it was over. These years of sporadic fear had left scars.

"This new lord won't honor the settlement. Won't hear a word. All that fighting for nothing."

Nearby, the smaller wildlife returned. Mice and squirrels, then even a few fluffy red birds. None of them would account for much blood, so it'd be a waste of life for not even one full bloshul. Maybe if a larger bird of prey dropped in, but those were hard to catch. She cut off the drip fueling her self-warming cloak, sparing her meager supply until she knew what this haul would provide.

Sonja's last intellectual harvest from Tharvik, and the one most popular with young children, were the fairytales. Those were harder to learn from. Sometimes the stories told of fiery green ships that ferried the dead. Sometimes there was a witch that drowned children or ate the minister. There were ghosts that screamed your name and magical artifacts that would turn you into an owl. Maybe there was truth in there somewhere, but Sonja put very little stock in it. Nothing more than interesting speculation outlining the terror these townspeople had lived in for years.

Nearby grunts brought her back into the present. She sent out a low-cost identification, finding a cluster of energies just out of view. With bigger prey so close, it was worth the cost of a silencing illusion to get to her feet and creep alongside the stream. Even before she'd crested the hill, however, the pigs caught her scent.

Moving on instinct, Sonja pulled the stopper on her only full bloshul and disappeared from sight. She created three basic, human-shaped illusions on the far side of the hogs, moving despite still arms and legs. Sonja willed the phantoms closer to her, noting the faces they wore. Familiar workers and farmhands she hadn't seen in years. The hogs squealed and rampaged away from the illusions, barreling directly toward an invisible Sonja. Maybe a dozen of them.

She reached out from beneath her cloak, strumming at the energy on the largest of the pack. The threads in its chest flexed and bounced, grounding the creature in a dazed heap. Unable to see her, the horde didn't know where to dodge. Sonja dove away, but one tangled in her cloak. The illusion dropped, and she fell amidst the swarm, slashing wildly and curling underfoot. A heartbeat later, Sonja lay near three stunned creatures. The way it should have worked with the bear. The first hog recovered, squealing, and stumbled away. She lunged for it, but another sprawled across her cloak, holding her in place. The big one escaped, but she had enough sense to disorient the others a second time. The remaining two weren't small, but neither would fill her bloshuls alone. She hissed out a string of curses, yanking her cloak free and fishing out her boot knife. With two swift punctures, the hogs stilled in the leaves.

Now for the messy part. She'd start with the bigger one. Sonja hoisted the beast carefully over the sturdiest nearby branch, using techniques Ulrik's in-laws had shared. She placed the drainage point, her first bloshul already uncorked and in hand. As was the glorious nature of the mage: crawling around after wild animals for blood. It was an uncommon bonus to get paid for something she'd have to do anyway. Money had been flowing one-way for a while now. Twenty more would continue to limp her along.

The first hog almost filled six bloshuls — gods, animals were so damn big in the east. She only needed about half of the second to top off the last bladders. Her tutors had preached the importance of watching her threes. If they'd known anything, they knew that magic loved threes. Carrying nine bloshuls was Sonja's way of adding to that lesson, because what could be more magical than three sets of three?

She let the second body down gently, paying its still-warm blood to manipulate both carcasses' weight. One over her shoulder and the bleeding one dragging behind, Sonja started walking. It was nearly dark, and if she was honest, she didn't know how to get back. She searched for any sign of the Kepstadur rooflines through the trees, hoping to find the road before it was fully night.

The land was quiet here. With so few birds, they were tragically easy to scare away. Sonja whistled to fill that void but struggled to keep the sound consistent. Lighted or not, it was still a difficult walk. If nothing else, she hadn't expected the carcasses to be so unwieldy. Smelly, yes. But a dead hog shouldn't fight this hard to rot in the forest. The sound of her boots on gravel startled her, soon replaced with relief. The stars had woken up, but the overcast sky reflected firelight. Tharvik's torches.

With a satisfied grunt, Sonja readjusted her grip and trudged uphill.

What happened next, she could barely comprehend quickly enough. A massive form slammed into her from the opposite tree line, and they skidded together across the rocks. Her mind flashed with images of the unkillable bear, and despite her last encounter, Sonja reached to tear at its threads. The bear raised a sword, then spoke — something she didn't register. But bears don't speak. Not a bear pinning her, but a man. He met her eye, confused, and lowered his weapon. She did not still her own hand. His energy threads flicked past her fingers, and he seized. Sonja shoved him down the hill, abandoning the hogs to clamber for his sword, but, even stunned, his grip held. She skittered upright, drawing her boot dagger, coiled and ready.

The man coughed and sputtered out something in another language. Sonja recognized the voice as he switched to Jrendavarian. "I thought you a monster." He proffered his hands, sword still held but only loosely. "I give apologies. Did not know, did not know…but what in the seven depths you are doing?" He was Torch, that Attiettan fire guard. The one who had found her at dinner the night before.

Sonja glowered and took a step back, still pointing her tiny knife at his chest. "You tackle me out of the woods and have the audacity to ask what *I'm* doing?"

"You are right. I give apologies." He sheathed his sword and stayed on the ground, only straightening the smallest amount. "Is a misunderstanding. I hear a broken song get closer, like forest demon. I hide. You walk by, I see a big…" He struggled for the words, gesturing at the carcasses. "You are as some hairy creature pig from the center of Tobequim. Hunched back, big ass tail. I don't know what I think. Just reacted."

"Why were you out here in the first place?" Sonja snarled.

"To visit the castle."

"And you stayed until after dark?"

"Is more of an accident. I stayed in one room with no windows, so time is difficult to trace. Then outside, is all shadows and sunset."

Sonja's knife dropped slightly. "What room? A room in the castle?"

The man nodded.

"You went inside the castle?"

He blinked slowly, mouth hanging open. "Yes? Like you."

"No, I only saw the city."

Of all reactions, he laughed. "I see how you return in such time. I believed you explored the castle too."

She stared for another confused moment before her mind whirred in a different direction. He'd gone inside. Why? What had he found? "Did you see or hear anything bizarre?"

"You ask many questions. May I now ask one?"

Her dagger wavered. "Okay?"

"Why pigs?" he asked. "And where from?"

The questions were so genuine, she almost smiled. "They're hogs from the forest."

"Is hog the same as pig? Actually," he waved his hands, "this does not matter. Why do you have this? And how?"

Magic was common, but mages were not. It was difficult and sometimes dangerous to tell a layperson about the sacks of blood she carried. There was a nuance to the matter they couldn't understand. "I stunned them and killed them."

"Stunned? Is the same that happened here?" He pressed a hand to his chest as if catching his breath. "Is uncomfortable feeling."

She blushed. "You're lucky. It's usually a bit more than uncomfortable." Probably iron in his breastplate — she didn't know how foreigners made their armor.

After another hesitant silence, he moved on without noting her vague answer. "And now, you carry pig-hog back to the village. For what reason?"

"The farmer offered a bounty on them. A couple of coins."

The man considered, still wrangling his heavy breathing. "I help carry pigs, yes?" He gestured to the bigger animal. "As apology for the, eh, confusion?"

Sonja nodded slowly, deciding he would have a hard time drawing such a large weapon with a hunk of meat over one shoulder. She, however, did not sheathe her dagger.

"I am Niccolo," he said as he stood.

"Sonja," she responded.

Niccolo bowed with a small grin, sandy waves falling around his face, before lugging the full weight of the carcass, un-lightened, over his shoulder. "With grace." After a moment, Sonja recognized the odd phrase as a literal translation. Her Attiettan was far from perfect, but the leap was logical enough.

A new tension settled over the moonless night as they walked together. The extra set of arms would have been more useful in the depths of the woods, but she was grateful for any help — less so since that help slammed her into the dirt. She checked each of her bloshuls again, not feeling any seeping liquid, but needing to be sure. If he'd ruptured one in the fall, she was not excited to replace it.

"So, you bring into the city?" Niccolo asked as they drew closer to the gate. "Bring to the farmer?"

"That's the goal, but, by now, he's probably asleep. Might not pay if I wake him."

"We are two strangers with dead animals in the middle of the night. That may be of worry."

She hummed her agreement. After minimal discussion, they picked out a tree a few lengths into the underbrush. Sonja clambered onto a branch to tie both creatures in place. She traded the last of the seeping blood to lighten their load. Her knots were sloppy, and the stiffening bodies sagged somewhat, but the job was done. The rest of the way to town, Sonja manipulated her cloak to radiate heat, purging any blood from the fibers. She would find a place to clean up tonight.

"Well," she pulled open the door to the inn, "thanks for your help." A twinge of fear struck as she realized he might be staying in the same shared chamber. Sonja regretted giving up her private room.

Maybe Niccolo could sense her discomfort because he smoothly fell out of step. "Good night." He strode to the bar and struck up a conversation with Carita, not glancing back as Sonja ducked into the dark corridor. If he left her alone for a few hours, she would disappear for Kepstadur in the morning. She wouldn't return until the magic was in hand, and by then, the Attiettan would be long gone with Helmi's caravan. Sonja slipped her dagger under the pillow and tried to get comfortable as a nearby family sang their infant to sleep. Memories of her nephew flooded her mind. Vann. He'd be so much bigger now. He deserved to have his father back. She couldn't wait to see him again.

06

MARKET OPTIMIST

"You've a delivery, miss."

Sonja stopped in an early morning sunbeam and turned to the bar. Carita nodded her over as she finished bussing a table's worth of breakfasts — Sonja wondered if the wisp of a woman ever stopped working. She met the barkeep at the counter, receiving a small pouch with a metallic clink. "Did the delivery boy note the sender?"

Carita shook her head. "Was one of them mercenaries with the supplier. Told me you'd find him in the market, should you be looking. Oh, and this as well." The barkeep produced a coil of rope, clean but damp to the touch.

Suspicion churned Sonja's gut as Carita disappeared into the kitchen. Which caravan guard if not the Attiettan? Returning her rope, cleaned and rolled neatly, alongside a pouch of coins only confirmed it. Tucked away from other patrons, Sonja sorted through the sack. Twenty-seven ronad. The farmer had only advertised ten per boar.

She shoved it all into an inner pocket with a huff. Fine. If the idiot foreigner wanted to hand out money, who was she to question it? The day was long ahead of her, and it'd be a waste of energy to chase him through the stalls.

She made it as far as the door before her frown deepened. He'd left twenty-seven coins. Three nines. Was Niccolo using mage's numerology to manipulate her? He didn't seem to know much about magic, but if that was a deception… Her sister wouldn't trust it. Thonra wouldn't care to know. But Thonra wasn't here.

Sonja turned toward the hollow shell of a market. Niccolo waited near the front, chatting with a younger merchant under an illegibly faded sign. She took him in fully for the first time. Tall for his people, standing around her same height, but bulky. Working-strong, but with an easygoing posture. Odd symbols lined his breastplate in faded blue paint. His coastal skin and light, wavy hair stood out in cloudy Jrendavar. He let out a hearty laugh that contrasted with such exacting features. A sculpture that sang and swayed. His sunlit amber eyes met hers, and the Attiettan grinned, crooked as the waning moon.

"You receive my letter?" Niccolo stepped away from the counter, and they walked among the limited wares.

"If there was a note, I didn't…"

He made a face. "No, no. I apologize. Is like a joke. May not sound well in your language."

Sonja raised an eyebrow but didn't argue. "So, do you want to explain your gift?"

"Is from the boars. I delivered them early."

"Sure, I understand. But you know you left more than the payment, correct?" Maybe it was unwise to point out, but Sonja's mind buzzed with curiosity.

"Yes, I know is more. Is a funny story, actually. The farmer. He does not pay the full price — probably think I do not count in your language. But when I go back, he says because two is a bundle price. We, eh, how say, ebb and flow for a time, but it is not worth effort. He closed the door again, and I am with two pigs. He does not want them on his land. So, I go to the only place I can think of."

After a pause, Sonja recognized his anticipatory expression. "And?" she asked.

"And so, I take them to the butcher. We barter, but he is kind and agrees to pay for the meat."

"At which point you brought it to me." Sonja narrowed her eyes. "Instead of taking the money and leaving. Some of which I didn't know existed."

"I keep some. But is important to be truthful. I mean this as an act of goodwill."

"And if that proves to be an effort wasted?" She jostled the pack she carried. "I'm not going with the caravan or hunting that bear."

"We go to the same place." He kept his eyes forward, guiding their steps closer to empty bays. "Is my opinion that purposefully traveling together is better than being at the same location by accident. Unless I am very misunderstanding, we will see each other again."

Sonja considered his words, kicking a loose rock farther ahead. "And what do you hope to gain?"

Niccolo lowered his voice. "Bringing a mage to a magical place? I believe is obvious."

"Not from a partnership." She matched his tone. "From the castle. Why are you going?"

"Sense of adventure. The, eh…adrenaline to see all that is secret in the world."

Sonja snorted. "So money. You want to steal anything left behind."

Niccolo smiled into the cloudless sunlight. "Money is nice."

Sonja turned toward the vendors, and he followed. There was merit to bringing such a strong build to help her explore. He could save a lot of blood, moving heavy objects manually. The idea of a useful travel companion was tempting, but she didn't know this man. Carita's title spun through her mind: mercenary. The Attiettans were a violent people. They'd been at war her entire life, most recently border disputes with Danqong. Never against Jrendavar, but their soldiers were supposedly excellent. Between mercenary or soldier, she'd prefer the former. Messy hair hung just below his jawline, with a knot holding the top half out of his face. Not exactly the image of a refined army man. Possibly a simple, greedy traveler, not unlike herself. He would be arrogant to go into the castle alone, but so would she. "What about the rest of your friends?"

A quick emotion burned away his easy smile, too fast for Sonja to fully interpret before it returned, smaller this time. "If you speak of guards from the caravan, I do not know them well. They have many stories, many sad stories with drink, but I know these only several days beyond you."

She nodded but was not naive enough to dismiss them. One mage against one fighter, she would have the upper hand. Add two more into the mix, and her odds went down. "I plan to stay until I've learned what I need," Sonja pressed on. "No traveling back and forth to civilization if we forget something. You need to be used to the idea of rotted out cots and haunted chamber pots."

"Haunted chamber pots?" Some of the life returned to Niccolo's expression, his steps slowing to a stop. "I'm sure there are worse things to find. So, this is an agreement? We are a team?"

Sonja looked between his proffered hand and his eyes. In the best scenario, Niccolo could be useful, filling a role Sonja lacked. Worst case, they would be isolated if she had to kill him. The idea was unpleasant. She had only come close once, but under the right circumstances, she had to be willing to take lives.

They grasped wrists. "As is ensured," he said in the old

Jrendavarian tradition. Well, almost. The word was "assured," but she acknowledged the effort. "Now, we share bread." Niccolo clapped her on the shoulder, moving back into the heart of the market. "Is correct in my home for bread and cheese and wine, but there is not that here. Bread and cheese will do."

"We have wine," Sonja said, but remembering the drink provided by the tavern, she amended her statement. "It's just rare. Not yet on this side of the country."

He scoffed playfully, with a quick exchange to a nearby vendor. "You have not had wine if you do not leave from your own soil."

She rolled her eyes as Niccolo offered a small bundle. The bread he purchased was more of a cracker, but the cheese was light and warm. "I'd like to go soon," Sonja said. "Do you have everything?"

Niccolo agreed, stopping only briefly by the inn to collect the rest of his belongings and square tabs with Carita. They left at an even pace, back onto the thin forest path. Sonja's eyes drifted toward the old tree where she'd last seen the hogs, then up the path toward Kepstadur. She waited to put some distance between them and the city before speaking. "You actually went inside?"

"The castle? Yes. Is very impressive. Different in Attietto. We use less stairs."

"But you heard nothing?"

"Heard?"

"Like with your ears. Any noises?"

He rolled his eyes in an exaggerated fashion. "I know what this means. No, I did not hear. There were footsteps, but they were my own. No one speaks but to myself."

Sonja flattened her lips. "In my defense, you'd never heard the word 'hog' before yesterday."

"And in my defense, why have two words for the same thing? 'Hog' has a silly sound."

She smirked as he hissed out the syllable. The man had a dangerous charm that she distrusted, though she was quietly glad for even brief company. The walk felt longer now that Sonja wasn't sprinting through the night, but Niccolo passed the time reasonably well. He could talk about anything. The castles across the sea, unexpected Jrendavarian food, the way the ronad was lighter than Attiettan coins, silly facts he'd learned about plant husbandry…

Mostly, she was content to listen, occasionally taking his bait to respond, but she focused on the surrounding woods. At several points, she felt silly — if he'd wanted to rob her, why stop and apologize the evening prior? Her stunning spell had barely affected him. What would she have done with her tiny dagger against a big ass sword? Maybe he was simply waiting until she had all her supplies. She tried to suppress the thought.

Niccolo, unfortunately, seemed very interested in the topic of magic. A topic she'd rather avoid. "In my home is one very nice man and his daughter," he said. "They practiced with nets and made for very good fishers. The method is a secret, but many people know it is the magic. Even in poor seasons, they bring in many. Keep the docks fed when others cannot."

"That was kind of them," Sonja said passively. She fidgeted with her rings. Without the right training, magic was unpredictable. It was dangerous to share vaguely how it worked, as that only led people to become more reckless. Better for the populace to know less. It preserved more of their reverence, both for magic and the mages who wielded it. This was the second rule her tutors taught.

"Is dangerous."

"Magic often is." Kepstadur gaped with the broken-jawed bridge. She noticed on this approach how one half was fully slack, implying a failure somewhere in the mechanism. "Speaking of danger…"

But he didn't laugh. She wasn't offended as much as surprised.

Along their walk, Niccolo had taken any opportunity to keep her talking. Yet, he was silent as they passed into the walls. No gregarious comments, not even a smile. He scanned the streets in even intervals, seeming to take in the details. The careful part of her mind wondered if his changing countenance was part of a greater goal. He stalled in the first courtyard, treading carefully around the stonework design inlaid underfoot. "Is so empty."

"I suppose that's why they call it a ghost town."

"Is not enough time to decay bodies," Niccolo whispered. "And little sign of animal."

"The animals would stop coming around when the food stores were empty. It's been something like twelve years. That's plenty of time for Tharvik to bury the dead. Last rites are important to some Jrendavarians." Her eyes shifted to the altars, where the collection of rice cakes had disappeared. "The siege was a long time ago. Any number of things could have happened since."

Niccolo shrugged. "Does not look like a siege."

"It could have looked like one right after the event." She wouldn't mention the possibility of magical interference until he did.

"Is not fighting here. Not even ten years. This city is built against the large army. Is important for defense." He gestured at a series of holes in the walls. "These throw water into the streets, knocking soldiers to the ground to slide into the grass." His gaze shifted to the second story of the library. "Arrows fall like rain. You have saying, yes? To kill snakes in a barrel? And all is if the walls allow entry. No raiders. This fight started and ended inside." When she didn't respond, he trickled down the tiered platforms, shuffling past empty buildings and untended gardens.

"You know a lot about fighting," she said. They were likely similar in age, somewhere around thirty, if she had to guess. "That comes with experience, right?"

Niccolo didn't react, as if he hadn't heard. Fine. She refocused on Kepstadur. Sonja could almost see the function of each distinct tier. Nearest the gate, shops faced out toward the city wall, with private residences on the other side. The middle, the largest tier, felt fully residential. With no easy way to move carts through a central axis, a spiderweb of homes sprouted around each other. At the bottom, buildings were wide and low, with signs that they had once been ornate. Buildings of state, maybe. These were in the worst condition of any, standing out starkly among what must've been amenities. Parks and fountains peeking between the forgotten grandeur.

Niccolo made no comment on any of it, leaning over the last outlook before the flooded bottom. "The water stands to my knees but can be passed on foot if you are careful with steps."

Sonja wrinkled her nose. "It's got to be freezing. This would be in shadow until midday."

"Oh, it was very cold." His voice flickered with an instant of his former humor. "I will admit to slow time to adapt."

"There has to be another way to get across. If it's not that deep, we could carry boxes or barrels for stepping stones."

"The boxes that are broken and rotting? You may pass across the top, but I know they collapse under me. If I have to go in the water, it will be on my own terms." He ran a hand through his hair. "I can help you bring some down."

"I won't have you move boxes if you don't gain a benefit." Sonja took another look around the lowest courtyard. To the far left, the most impressive of the gardens stepped up toward the keep's back. The tiers were tall, but they could maybe scramble up. Sonja strode past him, crunching onto the gravel and mulch of the public gardens. Her hopes of scaling the marble walls grew dimmer with each step. Another row run of steps elevated the lowest tier so it wasn't close to her reach, even, hypothetically, on his shoulders.

Niccolo shuffled past her, examining the ledge without taking his hand off the railing. "This can move us closer."

A narrow balcony ringed the perimeter, submerged but stretching to the front door with only the banister reaching from the water. "You're going to walk on a rounded handrail all the way over there?"

He dipped a boot into the water. "Is not deep."

Upon further inspection, Sonja found a lipped edge barely under the surface, thin but wide enough to walk on. Niccolo stepped out first, leaning on the railing for balance. They skirted the edge of the courtyard, taking on no more water than a puddle. Far drier than wading across smooth cobbles, though it did require a firm grip. Shallow columns guarded the door, but with room at the base to swap handholds. It took effort, but both passed onto the steps of the castle easily. No voices yet. Maybe they hadn't been spotted.

Sonja tapped one finger on the dark, intricately carved door, squinting up at its immense height. Taller than at least three of her, and it sounded solid. "How did you get in?" She leaned against it to confirm the weight. "These doors are meant to be manipulated."

"I pulled." Niccolo shrugged. "Only as open as I can slide through."

"And you closed it after leaving?"

"No. There were no places to slide my feet." He seemed to understand her implication.

Sonja offered a bit of her own body's blood, then gestured him toward the handle. He wrenched the door open, staring at her in mild bewilderment. "It only takes one mage," she said.

Light beamed inside over their shoulders, bouncing off marble and reflecting up a sweeping staircase — maybe the tallest Sonja had ever seen. Dust spun up with each step to glitter in the sun. Stone pedestals framed either side of the gaping entry like the terraces leading through the city, culminating in two more sets of doors at the very top. She could barely see parts of a gilded ceiling beyond.

"There was art," Niccolo whispered, his eyes following the arches spanning overhead. A few steps up the torn carpet, he pointed to the lowest ledge. Sonja forced the door closed, joined him, and followed his gaze. The terraces, even dustier than the stairs, showed remnants of footsteps among circular imprints and even a few dragged lines.

"Statues?" Sonja asked.

"Is what I believe. Dragged off soon after abandoned, maybe."

"It'd be a shame to show up too late. Is the entire place empty?" She ran a finger along the smooth stone.

"Is only the entry. Maybe one or two items taken from the welcoming room, but then it seems preserved."

Discordant voices faded into Sonja's mind. They were quieter this time and dissipated quickly, almost as if indirectly targeting her. "What's at the top?"

Niccolo smiled, turning to walk upstairs. "I could not describe. Is better for you to see."

She followed him past a row of windows that kept the empty displays glowing. Slowly, the next room glided into view. Cavernous, with a vaulted ceiling, speckled with skylights and pocked with crumbling reliefs. Ornate columns cradled the dome in smooth arches. The tile floor mimicked stained glass with vibrant colors and thin, gold-leafed dividers. To the left, a grand ballroom. To the right, a heavy dining room table. Twin staircases wrapped along either side to a low-ceilinged second story, strangely dark despite the sunlight. Between the stairs, a pair of thrones gleamed on a low plinth. Golden sunlight streamed in from one side.

"This place is incredible," she whispered.

"Had many defenses as well." He gestured to a row of dark lines.

She squinted up at them, slow to comprehend. "Arrow slits?"

"In the entry too, and with, eh, how do you say…they are more defenses…eh, anyway, a difficult castle to fight."

She stepped closer to a giant faded painting and traced the runes carved into the wood. *SAFE. GUARD. STRONG.* A whole line of what Sonja called warding glyphs. "Yet someone did."

Niccolo frowned. "It is difficult to think…"

His reply faded behind the returning cacophony. The voices were louder now, loud enough that she flinched back.

"Is alright?" Niccolo was at her side, a hand hovering barely a breath from her shoulder.

She stepped away, subtly dropping a small puddle of boar's blood. Toward the inner halls, her vision lit with blinding yellow, so bright, she couldn't discern what she was seeing. She broke her spell quickly. "Something is here."

"Trying to scare me away, no?"

Sonja shook her head. "Just be careful. It's very wrong." She turned toward the ballroom, but he remained. He traced one finger across the bottom of the painting, the same track Sonja had drawn through the dust. She held her breath, watching his posture for any change.

Niccolo met her eye. "Yes?"

"Did it…" Sonja fumbled for the right words. "Did you hear…"

He frowned. "I hear nothing."

Sonja examined the arrow slits, too dark to see inside. Stepping from the foyer didn't alleviate her discomfort. More dark lines marched over the doorway, as if to watch the lost revelry. Fewer footprints traced across the floor here, but she noted some were barefoot and pointed them out to Niccolo.

"Not uncommon. I see many. Perhaps those who remove their shoes to walk the waters?"

"Maybe. It's odd regardless, especially in a room cold enough to watch your breath."

He nodded, running a hand through the cobwebs draped over a lowered candelabra.

Windows along the left led to a balcony view of the castle town, while those to the right showed the ruins of the old garden. With direct access to large, fragile openings, Sonja understood how foolish it was to think those gardens would be easy to access.

As she met Niccolo in the foyer, the voices returned, clearer this time. "She will be thrilled to know! Write that down, write it down."

Sonja looked up to ask if he really couldn't…but the startled look on his face said he heard something. It spoke again, a single voice, then cackled. The sharp sound bounced off every hard surface.

Anything laughing in a haunted castle was, frankly, bad news.

07

ENTER OBLIVION

Adrenaline spiked through Sonja's veins. Was this the ambush she'd anticipated? The man with the piercings, the woman with the halberd — there was no telling how many lurked in the dank halls. What would mercenaries earn for a mage? Was there a market for that? But Niccolo had flinched beside her. Brows drawn, he scoured the balcony with shifty eyes and measured breaths. One hand clutched his sword, the other corralled her back. Would he continue to pretend as his own people closed in? Could he gain from a few extra seconds of companionship? He met her gaze, eyes narrowed. An expression that held a question: *What do we do?*

In a flash of instinct, Sonja latched on to his arm and dragged him under the stairs. He ran toward the throne room, but Thonra's voice screamed. Only a fool would let him rush her anywhere. Sonja veered right, moving toward a heavy door at the end of a shallow hallway. Niccolo didn't resist, even surged in front, postured like he expected the door to be locked. It pushed open effortlessly, hinges groaning, but they slipped in on silent steps. Sonja eased the door closed, pulling it up to stop the squeak. Niccolo's hand shot from behind to hold a narrow line of sight toward the foyer. His breaths brushed her cheek as he craned for an angle over her shoulder. And they waited. The voice remained, chattering nonsensically, echoing off every wall. But it wasn't coming closer.

She couldn't say how long they stayed crammed in that corner.

But hiding from what? Was it the illusionist? Worse, was this a trick to hurry them out of the foyer? What hid nearby? "I'll check behind us." Sonja slinked away, ducking under his arm. He shifted into the space she abandoned, barely acknowledging the interaction. The damned Attiettans were too used to being packed together.

Her cheeks burned as she stepped further into the hall. It was a dull space with plain stone walls and floors. Not stripped of art, but a place that never knew grandeur to begin with. A service corridor, maybe? Light bounced around corners, but it was distant, almost strangled. Pairs of shelves held simple candelabras, all coated in a decade of cobwebs and grime. The wood-slat ceilings were low and suffocating. She could only imagine it bustling with workers. Few footprints remained, all fossilized in deep dust.

With one last glance at Niccolo, still affixed to the door, Sonja dodged around a corner to find diverging paths.

To the right, a descending staircase, with half-doors at each landing. Straight ahead, Sonja saw only a blind turn. She chose the stair, peering into each room. The hinges relented to the steady march of time, sagging the gates to lean together in the middle. The first opening framed a large kitchen. Aside from abandonment, it was remarkably clean. Plates stacked neatly on shelves, pots and ladles hanging in place. Even the dishrags lay folded and flat on what must've once been pristine wood-capped countertops.

Down a level, Sonja followed a gentle clicking sound to the pantries. The memory of rot hung in the air. Small hums of glowing orange scuttled across the ground, most visible in the darkest shadows. She pushed cautiously through to get a closer look. Reminiscent of beetles but slow-moving, these creatures were nearly the size of her palm, with shells that glinted blue in the distant sun. She carefully pinched one up, the sharp, squirming legs unable to find her, and flipped it over to examine that light. The underside glimmered like a matchstick's flame, and she swore she could feel heat radiating out. It slipped from her grip and flitted away on reddish wings to rejoin its infestation. They rested on shelves and clung to the ceiling, with a noteworthy population collected on a stone strip jutting from one wall. Only one of her tutors had focused on biological studies, and he had never taught about bugs. Sonja was embarrassed to admit that if a creature wasn't familiar to the vineyard, she knew shockingly little about it.

The next flight turned into the brightest corridor. The smell of salt and stagnation grew as she stepped down. Whatever was in the sealed door at the last landing was likely in poor condition. Around the corner, floodwaters penetrated a green iron door, reflecting the small windows arrayed up the wall. Sonja tried to imagine where she stood in relation to the city. This area, a large delivery room, likely led to the ports. She picked out the shadow of what seemed to be a submerged desk in front of some built-in shelving. A few cubbies still held packages or papers, long faded and disintegrated by the saltwater. Across the flooded entryway was a nearly identical staircase leading up and around, turning toward Niccolo.

She was probably farther than was safe. Sonja passed the kitchens again, taking stairs in twos, but keeping her footfalls quiet. The Attiettan waited at the top, staring back toward the foyer. "Anything worth taking?" he whispered.

Sonja shook her head. "Rotten food, mostly. What was the voice?"

"I did not see. Stayed far, maybe upstairs." Niccolo's eyes drifted away, along the other path. "Is more?" When Sonja didn't answer, he led the way. Three doors waited around the last corner, along with the descending stairwell she'd seen from deliveries. The first two doors nearly aligned on either side of the hall. Niccolo approached the more ornate, finding it, again, unlocked.

Light from a thin window outlined a bunk room, cluttered with beds and layers of disarray. Deep in her mind, the wave of voices returned. They cried to her in unknown languages before fading to murmurs. She shuffled around discarded blankets, abandoned boots, and overturned chests until, with a thwip, the space erupted in a shock of sunlight.

Niccolo stood on the cot closest to the window, a rotten, utilitarian curtain in one hand, scanning the room, his expression empty. He almost looked sick. "Is strange to have none of the dead."

"Is it?" Sonja nudged through a pile of discarded objects spilling from an overturned trunk.

He stepped slowly down, bracing against the frame before shuffling to check the first unopened door. "There are no left behinds. There was... It is much..." Niccolo paused. "I cannot think of the words. This is first sign of conflict in the city."

"Maybe not. It could be messy servant's quarters."

He muttered something unrecognizable. "This room has a word that I do not know in your language. But these are not for servants. These are for soldiers."

"Barracks? This close to the kitchens? I don't know. The servant's quarters have to be somewhere."

He closed the first door firmly and scoffed. "Your country gives strong boots to servants, yes?" Niccolo shuffled to the next, careful to step around the mess. "For all the many walkings done between the stairs and the stoves."

Sonja frowned and knelt to open a trunk. Among civilian clothes and a few religious bracelets, she admitted he might be right. She picked through sheathed daggers and dented steel. On the closest bed, a battle horn nested in the sheets; it was old, with a thinning strap and fading carvings. She pulled it out to examine the outdated rune for strength. Her first runic tutor had taught that…that old runes… provided…

The voices in her mind crescendoed. A chorus of wailing fear. Pain reverberated between her ears, pressing out of her eyes and nose. Unyielding. Sound scraped her skin and rippled through muscle. Light lanced across her vision, resolving into a deep, red darkness.

It was night. Guards stumbled out of bed and scrambled into armor. Another squadron rushed out of the storeroom. The captain gave her a crossbow, his eyes steady and knowing. He spoke, and she replied, but she couldn't hear anything over the terrible horn. One of the new recruits, Captain's nephew, trembled across from her, ratcheting on his bracers as silent tears dripped down his face. Sonja reached out with a brutishly calloused hand and grabbed the boy by the arm. She pulled him toward the staircase. He'd have to learn. Protecting the regent was the most important part of the job.

The sights and sounds of the vision world faded, leaving Sonja with only a dull, broad headache. She blinked, then found herself on the stone, leaning hard against cold metal. Another heartbeat passed before she recognized the hand clamped firmly over her mouth and the arm pinning her back. A wave of dizziness saturated her mind as she tried to buck away.

Niccolo's soft voice broke through as the droning horn faded. "You are safe. It hunts each of us. You are okay…"

Sonja forced a few breaths, then tapped at his forearm. Slowly, he loosened his grip.

"Is passing you?" he asked.

She pulled fully away, settling heavier on her knees, feeling the cold seep up through the stone. Sonja tried to speak once, startled by the hoarse pain in her throat. Instead, she dismissed his concern with a flippant gesture.

Gods. What had happened?

Scholars knew a good deal about magic, but even the most well-read mage would admit that their understanding was limited. So she started with what she knew. Yes, illusion magic caused hallucinations. Yes, talented alternators could store energy spells in objects. But whatever that was, it didn't feel like an illusion. Sonja had *become* someone else. Never had she encountered perception magic strong enough to strip away her identity and replace it. She'd known things that she had never learned. Recognized people she hadn't met. Chills raked along Sonja's spine until her whole body trembled with the thought. She needed to write this down.

But Niccolo was there, wide-eyed and watching.

"Come on, then." She pushed to her feet, hating his pity.

"We can rest a moment."

"We can't. Let's just—" Sonja stumbled over her words, mindful of the false pretenses that started this alliance. "Let's find the expensive shit and get out of here."

His eyes focused on the war horn she'd found, seeming to decide something. Niccolo rocked to his feet. "This door is for weapons." He pointed to the far end. "All common and in poor upkeep. This is stairs down, and this is private quarters. Shared captain's room, very empty. I think we see what is at the stairs. In other castles, I see many coffins underground for safety."

"Coffers," she said, stepping around scattered personal items. "Coffers hold valuables. Coffins hold the dead."

He pushed the door open, squinting into a darkness that night couldn't rival. With a few quick strikes of flint, Niccolo ignited his torch. "Smells of home." He pressed it into a cage-like wall sconce until firelight bloomed in the circular room.

"Lamp oil?" she asked.

"The ocean," he said with a shallow laugh. The stone ceiling was low and sloped, mirroring the spiraling staircase. A limp wooden rail stood as the only barrier between them and a terrible pit in the center. A very thin barrier. Anxiety brushed up her arms just looking at the crumbling banister — held up by far too few planks, all thin, gnarled, and riddled with creeping blue moss and rot. Niccolo worked a loose stone out from the wall and dropped it into the abyss. "Is not quite the ocean here, but there is a word in my language. When it smells of salt and sweat." The stone splashed far below.

She stepped onto the landing and breathed in the stagnant air. "Long way down."

Niccolo shrugged, closer to the edge than felt responsible. "Are your coffers to be sealed from water?"

Sonja frowned. "I don't know much about that kind of thing." What protections *would* the Kepstans put around a valuable relic? Probably not water — not intentionally. Metal and wood shouldn't be left submerged. Something based in stone wouldn't rot or rust, but glyphs would fade. Maybe a textile? But who would want to wear a sopping wet glove or sock or cloak? "If it's here, it'll be protected." Internally, she carried a war. On one side, her curiosity begged to soak up any bit of knowledge left behind by souls who'd built their tower too high. However, logic reminded her that, as the expert on magic, she would face sudden dangers alone, at least until she could explain what was happening.

Niccolo bounded down the stairs, lighting each sconce as they passed. He was a decent companion so far, reacting reasonably to sudden changes, and she valued the extra supplies. Maybe she was overthinking things, but…no. No, hallucinations — perception magic in general — complicated their search. Her brother and sister, both more talented illusionists, had taught her a few things to look for, but adrenaline often overshadowed good sense. If she couldn't trust her own eyes and ears, what was safe?

With each new light, the shadows only retreated, pooling beyond the ledge despite the flames above. After a full circle of stairs, Niccolo reached the first landing. Again, the stone protruded out only a few feet, with a hollow core. Other than the continuing staircase, this level offered one other choice: a tunnel stretching deep underneath the castle. A dense, green gate blocked the corridor, and, for the first time, they found themselves locked out. "Cheery," Niccolo said, leaning the firelight into the hungry darkness.

Sonja reached for the padlock but stopped as the whispers edged back into her perception. She quietly dripped a small puddle of blood and conjured a ball of light, starkly blue compared to the fire. He didn't even flinch before she moved him out of her way. Regular openings marched down either side, implying more halls but nothing visible from their shallow angle.

"Could be a maze," Sonja said, pushing harder in search of the end. But it simply kept going.

Niccolo examined the hinges, only glancing toward the light in the moments before it blinked out. "Do we break it? Use magic?"

"Magic is weird about iron. Let's look for a key first."

A series of expressions flashed across Niccolo's face. He straightened, then gave a quick nod. "Your magic was bright. Does better than these."

She glanced between him and the line of torches sweeping their path, breath whispering out in the frigid air. "I assure you, fire is the cheaper option."

"Cheap as money?" he asked. "I do not know that to be true. These are, eh, much less in Attietto."

She shrugged and continued down. "It's just tiring. I'm not as good with illusions."

Niccolo followed behind, banishing more darkness every few steps. Another loop halfway around the circle, Sonja glimpsed the water for the first time. Like in the courtyard, the surface was still and glassy, filmed at the edges with lichen and grime. She waited for Niccolo to catch up. Several sconces hadn't caught or sputtered out after only an initial flare, including the last one in reach. Neither commented on the row of eight prison cells marching along the perimeter. All too shallow for most adults to sit inside. He knelt, holding the torch out toward the water before tossing another stone into the middle. There was no tap of rock-on-rock. "It goes deep."

Dripping more blood, Sonja projected her little blue light beneath the surface of the water. He was right. Farther and farther behind… Behind… She brought the light closer through wisps of dark seaweed, gently weightless. Another mass bobbed nearby, and another, slowly making sense in her mind. Not plants. Hair. Human hair. Attached to human heads. Attached to human bodies. Rows and rows of bodies lined up like little soldiers. A grey cast tinting their skin. "Gods incarnate…" Sonja whispered as the cool light faded.

Somewhere far above, the heavy thud of a wooden door registered amid her racing thoughts.

"This is part of your magic, yes?" Niccolo's smooth voice barely concealed its taut edge. "You open and close doors, yes? Is what you call a trick for parties?"

"I didn't…" she cut off as his posture flared. The torches above ticked out, one by one by one. Sonja searched for a place to hide. Not in a cell. Maybe an illusion in the shadows, but it could cost an entire bloshul. It might be worth it…

"Name yourself," Niccolo called, a deep resonance echoing up the hollow core. So much for any plans involving hiding.

Sonja swiped up her nose. They might need the luck.

No reply as more torches died.

Niccolo stepped back, forcing Sonja into the frigid water. It bit into the skin over her ankles. He flinched at its touch, but continued onto the landing, wary of the edge they couldn't see in the waves. They shuffled along the perimeter until Sonja bumped into one of the few remaining sconces, pulling his torch hand to light it as the last flame above faded. The oil caught, illuminating a human form off to the side. Not the one coming from above, but something ascending the drowned stairs, trudging out of the depths of the water, with slopping steps magically silent.

08

WATERS BENEATH

The creature lumbered from the wake with unnaturally straight posture, its thin hair clinging to plump skin and a twitchy neck. It wore a dress stretched over wide shoulders, seemingly old and papery. It appeared eyeless until firelight glinted off its inky black scleras. Another followed close behind. "Niccolo…" Sonja whispered as she poured out a healthy amount of boar's blood. With attackers on both fronts, she needed to know how many. She cast a quick spell and searched for energies. Illusions wouldn't have signatures, but these terrible things, these corpses, glowed with a hazy dust held in each limb, thin lines in the chest. Muted, muddled energies that pulsed sickeningly as they moved out of the water.

She looked up, searching for whatever was dousing their lanterns. Nothing. Sonja paid more and strained her mind's eye against the inverted darkness. Niccolo flared blue-green nearby. Far above, that blinding cloud of energetic mist clung to arches that she couldn't see.

But no living being approached.

Niccolo reoriented toward the revenants as a third and fourth emerged. *"Ast maegenia?"* he asked.

"Yes, magic, but I don't know how. These are alive, I think…I don't know…but whatever is coming down the stairs is an illusion. Strong illusions can still hurt you."

"Do not understand," he said calmly, eyes darting between the stairs leading up and those leading down. He passed her the torch and reached over one shoulder, gliding loose a shimmering black handle wrapped in sackcloth. The blade curved, a deep grin wrapping back in a wicked, crystalline sickle. It was beautiful — transfixing — in a dangerous way. Somewhat pearlescent, with delicate carvings along the handle. Sonja pulled her eyes away and moved to the next sconce, then the next. The bodies wandered evenly toward Niccolo. So many more than before, and all covered in silence.

Sonja searched through an inner cloak pocket, one she kept full of pebbles. She reared back and hurled the cluster through the air, casting an energy spell at the last moment to manipulate the weight. The smooth stones shot from her hand in a wide spray into the line of corpses. Many projectiles hit the walls and stairs with a crack. A few struck true, lodging into soft flesh, but others flew through corpses with no substance. Illusions. Mixed into the lot.

She took a breath to warn him, only to choke out a scream. A frigid hand sprung from the water, latched on to her ankle, and clawed up her cloak. Sonja used the lit torch to bat it away, cracking into the side of its head. The wail that followed was nearly human in the unholy silence, nearly heartbreaking, slipping back under the water with a gurgling croak. Thin, black ichor seeped from its temple.

"Sonja?" Niccolo called.

"More here." Sonja turned away, her stomach knotted, only to lock eyes with a dimly lit figure standing above the stairs, blocking the exit. Tall but slender, maybe a masculine build wearing heavy winter clothing, one hand outstretched. She couldn't discern features or expression in the darkness, but their eyes bored through her.

The torch sputtered and died as more revenants dragged from the water. Sonja kicked at the first, stumbling as her boot cleaved through empty air. Her pack caught on the wall, giving her time to rebalance and jam the torch into the flaming oil. Glancing over one shoulder, Niccolo was surrounded. The horde dove and slashed; she could barely find him in the mayhem. Sonja pulled the torch, blazing once again, more careful with her warding swings. She huddled close to the wall sconce, watching those black eyes fight the instinct to run. There were just so many. One lurched, and Sonja spun away, realizing too late that the fingers slid through her cloak. She reached for the sconce's rim, but real hands already had her.

Frigid water enveloped Sonja. Shoulder first. Every muscle clenching. Crumbling inward. Shattering. She could swim, but not well. Had to get the hands off. She balled her legs up and pressed hard into the chest in front. The creature barely reacted as she clawed at its face and ripped at its arms. Sonja reached behind, pulling hair and digging blindly at its eyes and nose. It readjusted its grip, forcing air from her lungs. The salt burned deep.

She forced her eyes open, flicked the cap off her most accessible bloshul, and painted the water crimson. Sonja clawed through the body's energy field, finding more resistance in the water than in the threads. She kicked again and propelled one corpse into the foggy distance. Ears popping, Sonja and the last revenant bumped against stone. Good. There was a bottom. She reached behind, raking through a loose field, too weak to even feel the strum. The revenant released her, arms drifting to either side.

Sonja thrashed, desperately trying to reorient to the surface. Her pack dragged down, pinning her shoulders, destroying momentum.

A final breath leaked out as she fought against her belongings. Every curated supply and careful decision was a stone. Sonja tried her lightness trick, but the bag would not move. With another heave, she choked on more burning water.

Leave it all or die.

Those were the options. The goal was in sight. She was going to find the relic. This was no way to die. Not yet.

Sonja slipped her arms from the straps and pulled a sash from around her waist. She kicked off hard, abandoning her supplies. Long heartbeats passed as she thrashed against the water, bumping into the legion of frozen corpses, dragging toward the orange light. Sonja broke the surface, still choking but alive. Her eyes burned, and all the shapes coalesced in a medley of grey. She stretched in any direction for the lip, but it was obscured under the rippling water. Still sputtering out brine. Nothing made sense.

A hand clamped on her collar, briefly dunking her before tugging up and out of the freezing torrent. It found purchase under either arm and yanked her like laundry from the wash, smacking with a metallic thud against the wall. Words spilled over her ears as she retched, shuddering at the exertion.

Niccolo prattled behind her, a tittering flute. Quick and lilting. But the words were less than music. Sonja squinted at the stairs, but nothing waited for them there. Where there had once been dozens of bodies swarming Niccolo, five remained, collapsed and unmoving in the shallow water. Three lonely lanterns provided the only light.

"You are gone. You here, yes? The you on the stairs…" The hells was he saying? "We need to go."

"Lost your…your torch," she wheezed.

He responded with something snippy and offered a hand. The room pitched around her as she hauled herself up. Niccolo levered one arm over his back, all but carrying her up the stairs. In the dizzying darkness of the next landing, Sonja pulled away, barely able to discern Niccolo's outline. "We should…be careful." Her words fluttered out between breaths, raspy and uneven. "It could be waiting. See if we're dead. Might be invisible. We'll do the same." She prodded the three bloshuls on her body, one of which was half-filled with water. Useless. Two reliable bladders remained. That wasn't enough blood.

"And you can hide the water path?" Niccolo pinched at her sopping clothes. "We do not need a trail where we run."

She nodded, fumbling to strip off her cloak, now infinitely heavier than normal. His hands were there, providing stability, un-catching ends, and together, they fumbled to twist it tight. After several compressions, Niccolo tugged the unwieldy fabric from her hands, giving Sonja the space to wring out her hair, the edges of her shirt, and her loose trouser legs. "Sit a moment, yes?" he requested.

Each heartbeat threatened to freeze her alive, but she couldn't warm herself frivolously. Two bloshuls. Not enough. She complied and squeezed uselessly at her boots, but she needed the magic. There was a solution, she just had to pay for it. If not from bloshuls, then from herself. Sonja focused on an amount — a ceramic cup she'd loved as a child. She imagined it brimming with red and called Niccolo over. "Stand with your ankles touching. Are your shoes leather?" The shadows fully masked his expression, but he confirmed and complied after a moment's hesitation. "Do me a favor," Sonja added.

"Yes?"

"Don't let me fall down the stairs."

He didn't reply as she pressed one hand flat across his shins. Keeping the firm memory of the cup, Sonja touched her own shoes with the other. This trick would do nothing for the insides, but it might save them from leaving an obvious trail. A shadowy outline hovered near the side of her face, close enough that she could almost feel it. With a surge of magic, water wicked out, dripping along the sides. To her surprise, she didn't feel faint. The tradeoff was a sharp headache, but she could work with that. Sonja took back her cloak and, somewhat recklessly, offered anything remaining in the mental cup to direct a pulse of heat through the fibers. The cloth hissed with steam that plumed between her fingers. Starlight burst across her vision, but only for a moment. "You don't want to heat clothes. Not while you're wearing them." She pushed weakly to her feet. "Even a second can burn. I would know."

Niccolo cupped her elbow. "Is this when you fall?"

"No, no. I'm fine." The cloak was still damp, but she stepped away and wrapped it on regardless. "But we need to go, fast."

At the very top, Sonja placed a shivering hand on the door. Her chest ached, but this was no time to rest.

Niccolo leaned close, barely breathing. "Will invisible help if the door still opens?"

"I'll take care of it," she muttered. "I can disguise us and the room together." Thonra was better at this kind of thing. The thought soured in her mind, dripping discontent. Sonja visualized the barracks. Each door, all the cluttered mess. Sometimes, in moments like this, she could feel the magic coalescing around the request, filling all the details she didn't have until, with a breath, Sonja twisted the drip on one of her full bloshuls and pressed through. A few drops collected on her arm before dissipating. As the illusion grew, the deep red tears blinked away faster than they could fall. The room appeared empty, waiting in the same disheveled state they'd left it. It might be overly cautious, really, but Thonra's voice repeated in her mind.

"Careful is the opposite of dead."

Sonja followed quickly behind Niccolo, searching the corners for any sign of change. They stepped into the low halls of the service corridor, but before she could even close the door, Niccolo shoved her back, taking up a wide, ready stance.

"What?" She righted herself and peered over his shoulder, tracing his eyes toward the closed door across the hall.

"He can hear us?"

That question stood the hairs along Sonja's neck on end. "Nothing can hear us. What do you see?"

"In the room." Niccolo tilted his head. "The man. He is there."

There was nothing but a closed door across the hall. Was Niccolo hallucinating? Only if the illusionist could see him, which no one but Sonja could. But this was magic. Whatever he saw meant something. If they could find a safe space to record this vision…except she'd lost her notebooks. Regret ached through Sonja's body. "We should go," she said, pulling him the first few steps.

They ran. Leaving was the safest option. Without her bloshuls, Sonja couldn't keep up with the costs. Niccolo stalled outside the service corridor. Was it following him? Sonja stepped toward the exit, only to hear the laughter from earlier, echoing somewhere in the foyer.

"It can see us?" Niccolo hissed.

At the shake of her head, he darted in the opposite direction. To the throne room. Shit, he was fast. Why was he so fast? The illusion faded with distance, and this idiot didn't seem to know that. Sonja sprinted after him, unsure if she kept him fully masked with his heavy armor and clattering supplies. She glimpsed enough of the throne room to know it was decadent. A smear of gold and marble and satin. Niccolo veered right. He clawed open a pair of oak doors and all but threw her inside. Sunlight evaporated when the doors thudded shut, replaced with a vibrant green radiance. Before Sonja could argue, the Attiettan dropped a drawbar into place, locking them, together, inside.

09

WARMING UP

Despite the aching cold, Sonja stood to her full height, unwilling to turn her back on the mercenary. She spared a fleeting identification spell, finding only Niccolo's dim energy in her immediate surroundings. A sparking green mist radiated around him, maybe an effect of his breastplate. He discarded his pack and sword and slid to the floor, heaving. Her adrenaline faded to a cautious mistrust and a gaping exhaustion. It was so cold, and the cloak was not helping. She stripped it away and pulled out a middling seat at the table, subtly retrieving the boot knife and sheathing it in her belt.

"Oye." Niccolo's suddenness startled her. "I must chase my breath, but this room is more than a room."

Sonja furrowed her brow, unsure what that meant, and shifted the seat out further.

He made a bizarre chittering noise, somehow reproachful in tone, before rolling to his feet, one hand clenched at his side. "Just wait."

Niccolo shuffled to a large stone inlay on the far wall. "I fix this."

"Fix what?" she asked.

"Trust me. Is a good surprise." His voice lilted with the same easy levity it always had.

She glanced at the lock again. On the inside of the door. This was not keeping her in but locking the illusionist out. Slowly, Sonja let her eyes wander the room as he fiddled with an array of metal rods. Rows of ornate shelves lined three of the four walls, each overflowing with books and scrolls, trinkets and plaques. A dozen or more mirrored lanterns held glowing stones responsible for the vibrant green ambiance, amplified by a smooth white ceiling. The centerpiece table, bright white to match, was built thicker along the edges, inset with an outdated territory map of Jrendavar. Small wooden blocks had been arrayed in various colors around strongholds and stacked near major ports or epicenters. This was a war room. She shuffled over, perching on the table's edge to watch him work.

"Is my turn to make magic," he said. "Is worth waiting."

Sonja raised an eyebrow, caught between mistrust, concern, and a bit of bemusement. Niccolo had shown no magical aptitude yet, nor had he seemed reckless enough to bother things that ought not be bothered. "Of course. The magic of sticks in the wall. I'm well-versed in this ancient art." She brought a leg to her chest, hugging it tight. This did little to warm her, but at least she could rest.

Her eyes closed for barely a heartbeat before Niccolo startled her with another irritated sound, not quite a whistle or a click. "Worth waiting," he repeated.

"You sound like a big, stupid bird," she said.

Another moment of fiddling, then a terrible grinding sound. With a flourish, Niccolo stepped to the side, gesturing her forward. Something in his giddy excitement softened her exhaustion. "Is safe to be close, if you want," he said.

It took only a single step before she felt it: beautiful heat, pulsing to a radiant rhythm. Heat with no fire. No burning coals or steamed rocks. Just a hole in the face of this broad stone… It was a chimney.

The thought of warmth made her shiver. Sonja leaned into the stonework, curling around the mouth, holding her trembling hands deep in the gentle waves. "How did you know this was here?"

"Is my magic." She could hear the grin spread in his words. "I do this magically."

"It's a vent, right?" she said, ignoring him. "Do you know the source? It doesn't smell like a hot spring, but coal and wood both require tending."

"Is impressive for a big, stupid bird, yes?" Niccolo rummaged through his pack, unfolding a long, woven mountain tarp. Beautiful quality, likely very expensive.

"Really. How did you find this?"

He dragged over one of the thick-limbed chairs and climbed up. "This is the room I found on my, er, I know the word. Investigate? This vent is opened when I find it. I come in from the cold to warm myself. Spent many hours here, but without windows, is difficult to know the time."

"Doing what?" Sonja flipped open a book resting on the mantel. "Reading?"

"Your language is less hard to read, more hard to speak, and more hard to listen."

"This isn't Jrendavarian." She skimmed the pages. "If I had to guess, it's Caroia or something similar."

"I give thanks that you believe I read every book in some hours." His smile only broadened. "In truth, I find one book and made efforts to read one page." He used his arm guards like a mallet to pin the corner of the tarp to the bookshelf.

Niccolo swapped sides, draping the wool temporarily over her head and again standing on a chair, quietly nailing the tarp into the soft wood. Once in place, he pulled the loose side to the table, using his two standing-chairs as the final points, collecting the heat around her. "Did that one page teach you about pitching tents?" Sonja asked with a smirk.

"One page teaches me that I am not as good at reading as I pretend." He moved to the far side of the canopy, rummaging again. "I learn the tent for myself. Heat is like money here. If you cannot control, you do not live the winter."

"Or the summer, in our case."

He laughed but hesitated to reply. "The supply you carry is no longer here, yes?"

Sonja frowned into the warmth. "It was too heavy to swim with. I left it at the bottom of the dungeon."

"It is what I thought you might say. But this is not teal-breaker." Without entering the makeshift tent, Niccolo tossed a bundle to the floor. "You will not be warm until you are dry."

She eyed the heap suspiciously. A clothing bundle. His bundle. Shame spread across her cheeks. "Niccolo, I can't…"

He chirped again. "This dumb bird will not argue. Even you winter stormcats cannot live in wet fur. Change, so this can dry. You use magic again, yes?"

"No, actually."

"Oh. Well, this is sad. But we can make this do."

She set her three remaining bloshuls nearby, not sure what to say about her supplies. The thought closed her throat. She was useless without that blood. He'd learn soon. Sonja unfurled the bundle. Simple, but sturdy. A familiar Jrendavarian weave pattern.

"What happened?" he asked quietly.

"In the water?"

"In all. These are the demons? The damned?"

Sonja frowned. There were enough factors that her mind couldn't decide where to begin. "I've never seen anything like it," she said honestly. "Maybe you're right, but I can confidently say they looked like corpses. My brother used to tell campfire stories about things like this. He'd call them revenants. I'm most concerned about whatever was dousing lights on the way down. They didn't have a signature; I checked. If I had to guess, it was a manifestation, but that creates more concerns. Wherever the real body is, maybe invisible nearby or hiding across the castle, that person is a powerful illusionist to both show some kind of dominion over the corpses and to create all those illusions. All of that *through* a manifestation? If it wasn't so terrifying, I'd be impressed." She examined her leathers for signs of damage, but they were too wet to tell. Sonja hung those closest to the warmth, aware that it wouldn't be enough. To fully dry the set, she either needed three days or a good bit of blood to spare.

After a long pause, Niccolo sighed. "How do you explain to a small child? A child with bad word remembering skills."

"Oh." Sonja blushed. "I'm sorry, I didn't think to—"

"Is better than to make every sentence slower. I like this more than people who only gesture." More rustling implied he was waving his arms. "But for this time, I welcome some gesture."

"I can start simple. You know what an illusionist is? Someone who uses perception magic."

"You know how Attietto learns about magic?"

The immediate reversal caught her off guard. "I don't."

"To learn magic, Attiettan children go to special training."

"It's the same here."

"Is not. Attiettan children go to training to learn your language. *Then* it is the same because they come here. That is how to learn magic. If you do not come here, you do not know. In my home, you learn to fish or sail or sell or fight. These are best options. No magic."

Sonja chewed on that thought for a while. "No local tutors? Not even now?"

"There are, but these die very easy. People do not trust the Attiettan teacher. Is best to trust here and trust Danqong before the war."

She nodded to herself, slowly hanging her clothes to drip-dry, bloshul belt slung over one shoulder. Sure, tutors were hard to find, but was Attietto really that far behind? Jrendavar's magical population was growing daily; would it not be the same across the other nations? Sonja stepped around the tent to find Niccolo cross-legged on the table, pawing at a wound at his side. His metal breastplate and thick underlayer laid on the table nearby, and his dense wool undershirt bunched into a knot by the elbow.

"What happened?"

Niccolo shrugged. "A knife, maybe. I don't know which hit me and could not find it anywhere. It is big to cut so deep." His eyes lingered on his armor and the gash trenched into the metal. "Sharp, as well."

"The knife might not have been real," Sonja said, choosing her next words carefully. "Some mages are good at pretending. They can put pretend images in people's minds, or they can make pretend images look real for everyone. Hallucinations versus illusions."

"Is what you do to leave the barracks, yes? Illusion for everyone?"

"It is. But some people are much better. Like in the bottom room when some corpses were only fake. That's an illusion too. Some mages are so good at pretending that they can manifest their pretend — they make it real," she added quickly.

Niccolo's brow furrowed, and he looked up. "Pretend to make pretend real? Do I not understand what 'pretend' is?"

"No, you get it. But that's the magic part."

His frown deepened. "You say that someone uses magic to throw pretended-real knives?"

Sonja nodded.

"Why…not make more knives?"

She couldn't fully suppress a small laugh. "That would make sense, yes. If one knife scratched your armor, imagine thirty-six knives."

He turned back to his injury. "I do not see how this is funny."

"I'm not laughing at you. No, it's a great question. It was just funny to imagine you yelling at a hostile mage that they were doing the magic wrong."

"Someone should tell him," Niccolo mumbled, but the defensive posture melted. "So, he mañie-vest one knife instead of more because of something I do not know."

"Manifestation is expensive." Sonja shrugged. "Could he have made thirty-six knives? Maybe. But it could have killed him."

"You say it again. Is expensive. It cost. Why? It cost what?"

Sonja flattened her lips. "That's complicated. Cost can be a lot of things."

"Like money?"

"Well, no. Not usually, or at least I've never paid coins to use magic."

He flinched and muttered something in Attiettan, perhaps having twisted too far. "Okay, so this is like the fire. You pay in warmth?"

Why was he so full of questions? "Do you need help?" she asked as he felt blindly at his back, a small jar of salve balanced on one knee. When he didn't object, Sonja sat to better examine it. The cut was about the length of her hand and still bled, but it was shallow. He was lucky. The plate had saved his spine. "Heat would be an interesting payment. For heat to be valuable, you'd need to be freezing. I couldn't pay with water while drowning, but it would be a powerful currency in a drought."

Niccolo fixated on the bookshelf in front of him as she applied the ointment, lingering in the quiet for longer than was comfortable. "What do you pay today?"

"Do you need help wrapping this?" Sonja resealed the container and glanced through a sack of similar salves. All labels in Attiettan, of course. She pushed back from the table, her eyes tracing trophies lining each shelf, any of which could be an artifact.

"My people say Death takes your years for magic. Is a demon of lifeblood. A gamble that your body may not have ability to give."

She considered him, leaving the table to pull down a helmet. It was an odd, square shape. Sonja flipped it over in the surprisingly thorough light. The metal was scuffed and dented, but there were no glyphs anywhere she could find. "It's not a bad rumor. Somewhat misleading, but best to be cautious. Magic will hurt if you don't *truly* know what you're doing."

"We have a saying: You spin circles and turn left so I cannot follow." He grimaced. "Sounds silly of your messy language. But if you will not tell what you pay, will you tell why?"

"I don't want to give you ideas."

"There is no magic in me to use."

Sonja doubted that, looking over a few more trinkets before selecting a gauntlet covered in foreign glyphs. Scholars disagreed on the topic of magical access. It was hard to track percentages while also teaching safety in fear. Personally, she agreed with the generalists, those who thought that most people could use magic; it was a matter of training. "Well, it's still morbid."

"So, this *is* lifeblood."

"I don't know what that means," Sonja said. Why did he care? Why did it matter? She cast a quick identification spell, which rang sharp against the pain in her head. The gauntlet wasn't magical, nor was the helmet, but there was magic here. A detached sword hilt, a pair of silken shoes, some kind of rock, a book lying open on the table behind her. Sonja dismissed the spell, collecting several of the items off the shelves and moving a chair to sit by the vent. She sighed. "I've never heard of lifeblood, but yes, blood is a more stable magical currency. That's what makes it dangerous. If you don't know how to clearly offer payment, it will take something high-value by default, and that's how people die."

"You use human blood?" His voice was quieter.

"I do not." That was a bad question. That was a question that encouraged the uneducated to jump to conclusions. Many felt a primal fear, terrified that, because they were full of blood, any mage could use them as a walking magic source. It wasn't that simple, but scared people didn't listen. Scared people killed the threat, perceived or otherwise. This is why the smartest mages didn't talk about magic. It was easier, safer, to keep the secret. "You should understand that payments are not inherently negotiable, but the most advantageous repositories are frequently those that are unyielding and versatile." If she was lucky, he wouldn't understand half of those words.

The slurry had barely left her lips when realization burned across his face. "The pig-hog. You did not drain to be less heavy. You drain the blood to use."

She started to deflect with the reliable lie that animal blood was disgusting…but his grin was so genuine. Not quite smug, but self-satisfied as he examined her belt of bloshuls. "Protect our secret, okay? Think of all the idiot people with no self-control."

He nodded and asked to warm in the tent, respectful of her drying clothes. "I have another question."

Sonja picked up the shoes, finding more glyphs she didn't recognize. Without her supplies, it was dangerous to use sympathetic magic, connecting to the energy of another being or fjarfest, so she'd have to test the usage the hard way. "Yes?"

"You can explain illusions again?"

"Things that aren't real, but they look real." She pulled at the laces and scratched the fabric. It didn't seem too protective. The soles were hard though. "Illusions are for lots of people to see, but you can't touch them. Hallucinations are just for one person. You can't touch those either."

"Is possible that the more corpses were hallucinations? Magic only for you?"

Sonja stilled her hands. "Meaning you didn't see them?" It wouldn't make sense to swarm Niccolo with bodies only Sonja could see, would it?

He didn't meet her gaze. "I did not, I do not think. I see five. Five then fall."

Odd. But she could test that. "What do you see here?" Sonja held out her hand, casting a cheap hallucination of a cluster of grapes.

He looked to her eyes and back a few times. "This is a joke?"

Interesting. To be sure, Sonja sent an illusion of a rock flying at his face. It passed directly through the bridge of his nose, yet Niccolo didn't flinch.

"Are you null?" Sonja asked, ignoring the numbness growing along her fingers.

He blinked at her several times. "Ah. Not a joke. This is insult."

"Not an insult. It's a kind of person. Someone who isn't tricked by illusions. No duplication, no cloaking, no alteration." This could not be more perfect. "I've never met a null. It means you're not affected by magic. Or not as much. It's like having a higher tolerance."

His expression was unreadable.

She slowed her excited words. "Think about alcohol. You and I have a drink. The first night, we both drink beer. It might take three beers before I get a buzz, but you might need six." He nodded, so she continued. "Say the next night, we drink liquor. Something strong out of Suinterna. After two shots, we'd both be tipsy. Hallucinations and illusions are like the beer. They're cheaper, so it takes more for you to see them." Sonja could feel her heart thudding in her chest. He didn't know how rare he was, nor did he see how that could be useful against an illusionist. "Do you understand?"

"I do," he said solemnly. "But one problem with your comparing."

"Which is?"

"Your people are very clear to tell me. I am, as is called, a lightweight. You will out-drink my liquor every time."

Sonja's expression flattened. "Dumb bird."

Niccolo chuckled, settling onto the floor with a book in his hand. "As is my curse." Of all books, he held the one from the table. The one with a magical signature. It wasn't terribly old, all things considered, leather-bound, with the imprint of a fluid, snakelike creature on the front. Null or not, perhaps he knew more than he let on. She simply had to get him talking. Maybe something specific to Attietto.

Sonja rested her head. "I have a question for you now."

"Be easy with me."

"What are your thoughts on the Waters of Life?"

Niccolo perked up. "This is not common here. Your people do not believe in this, no?"

"I don't know what people believe." She shrugged. "But I read a few books on Attiettan religion."

"What do you wish to know?"

"It's more general," she said. It had been a long time since she'd last encountered information on the myth. The details blurred in her mind, as it felt inconsequential at the time. "The revenants downstairs. They're in water. Could it be healing them? Healing them enough to revive them, maybe with the right spell or relic?"

The book slid closed in his lap, with a single finger holding his place. Niccolo's brow drew together, his eyes fixed on the middle distance. She could almost see the possibilities unfolding for him. "Eh, this may work, but below is not the Healing Waters."

"Could it be blessed? Made into healing waters?" Perhaps the right glyphs could make any water holy. That would make it easier to transport across the country.

"These are found, not made," he said. "And more, the damned living again, they are not healed."

She made a noncommittal noise and let the topic drop, returning to the relics in her lap. Gods, it was difficult to discern the function without sympathy…

"I have worries of the illusionist," Niccolo said unprompted.

"He complicates things, yes, but we'll be careful."

"I worry of a room of Sonjas and not knowing the real from the unreal. Choose wrong and die."

"You'd be a challenge to trick."

"But I am not safe from all magics." He hesitated, concern still deep in his tone. "I saw you on the stair. Down when we fight. You run up from the water and call me to run too. But I still see bubbles."

Sonja took in this information, piecing the words together slowly. This illusionist, whoever they were, had not only tried to drown her, but then used her own image to lead Niccolo away. She didn't want to think about that dungeon or the water or what nearly happened.

"You say a null is tolerable. A magic at the strength of liquor, and I will see, yes?"

She forced levity into her voice. "I never said you were tolerable."

Niccolo met her eye, apprehensive, then pressed on. "I have a friend who values secret knocks and hand signs and passwords."

"Sounds like something that only works once."

He sighed, rubbing his face. "We agree of similar conclusions. But something can help. Something not usual."

"Ah, what a shame. Because we're known for only saying usual things."

A smile crept along his features. "Yes. This is why I vote for 'haunted chamberpot' as code."

"Where'd you pick that up?"

"You. Is one of your very usual words that you say."

"Of all things to remember…" A genuine laugh escaped her lips; it was a quiet, strangled thing, but it took some of the weight with it.

"Is because I do not listen otherwise." Niccolo smiled. "I am sure you can find a silly thing in return. It is only fair."

"Like 'teal-breaker,' you mean?"

"What is of this?"

"Teal is a color. *Deal*-breaker is the saying. Something that cancels an agreement."

He snorted. "Is truly? In Attiettan, *teel* means this." He scrunched his fingers sharply at her. "Meaning it is not working because the bone is breaking. I use this wrong for many years now."

"Yours is brutal," she said. "But that's a reasonable mix-up."

"Is still funny. A very good passcode because it means nothing."

"Well, if we want it to be reusable, we should make a pattern," Sonja said with a yawn. "You use words that start with the letters H, C, and P. I'll include a color."

"Aye, yes. I am sure this will be simple for a man who barely speaks the language."

"Barely speaks the language, my ass. If you want to see 'barely speaks the language,' I'll show off all thirteen Attiettan words I can think of right now. But fine. We'll swap; you use colors, and I make up a phrase."

He smiled. "No, no. I only joke. Is a good idea. I will *have clever possibles*, yes?"

"Unless you're *yellow*."

He smiled, relaxing against the table.

In the silence that followed, Niccolo's breathing settled into a steady rhythm. They'd have to get moving again soon, but not with her few supplies still intermittently dripping. She was practically useless with so little blood left. But she couldn't quit now. Something within these walls could raise the dead. It was real. The smartest route from here involved hunting the illusionist. Eliminate the threat. But would that be a waste? What could she learn from this person?

She imagined a world where the Kepstans had simply revived themselves after fatal events. That would be the perfect relic. And, maybe under the right circumstances, she could convince the illusionist to teach them how to use its power. But with so little blood?

Sonja sighed, elbow on the counter and head against her palm, whole body still aching from the swim. She'd find the damn relic, with or without the illusionist, once she was in her own clothes again. Slipping something magical out past a null was the most ideal situation. For now, it didn't hurt to rest her eyes.

10

THRONE ROOM

Sonja stirred awake, her shoulder prickling with the unnatural posture. "Thonra? Ulrik?" she said through a dry throat. Stone flared out in all directions. The monastery? The tutors could always be watching. She searched the corners.

But this wasn't the monastery. A green glow. A makeshift tent. The war room. The keep. Kepstadur Keep. Their last hope for Ulrik. And with that, sorrow crashed over her fading dread. She was safe but alone. She was close to the solution. It would be over, and they could go home. She'd find it. She and the mercenary…

Where was the mercenary? Shit. Shit! Niccolo was gone.

Sonja scrambled to her feet, any sleepiness dripping away like heavy mud. He was gone. How long had she been asleep? Her clothwvvwere still dripping, but the armor would have to be fine. She rushed to suit up, wrestling the excessive fabric to fit tight under her armor and jamming her feet into damp boots. This was a disaster. She should have never come with this bastard. Thonra's memory didn't even have anything to say. What did the Attiettans know but gold? Bastards. All of them. Greedy, slimy…

She kicked something hard, skittering it across the ground. A sword and sheath. Niccolo's sword. That was a foolish thing to leave. His breastplate lay nearby, rend still clear in the lantern light. His pack slumped in a chair. The sickly, bitter rage melted into panic. If he hadn't left on purpose, had he been taken?

She checked her supply, knowing how much blood she would find. Her breaths came short and shallow, fanning little sections of drying hair. Where would he be? An image of the dungeon flashed in her mind. Surely not. Not floating alongside all the bodies that tried to kill them. Another in the collection.

Sonja lashed the sword to her hip, placing a confirming hand on the dagger in one boot. She looked at the armor. The gleaming metal would hold up far better than her old, damp leathers. She rocked it with a single finger. To call it heavy was an insult. Without a manipulation spell, it would only slow her down. Despite whirring fears, she remembered to check the door before bursting out of the war room.

Empty.

Without a dry cloak, the frigid air rippled across her skin. She searched for any signs of blood or struggle marked across the throne room tile but found nothing. Nothing but beams of sunlight and the glimmer of forgotten gold. The foyer next. Sonja stepped toward a fallen tapestry she hadn't noticed before, rotted and stiff at the foot of a door set into the shadows. She checked the handle, then slammed her shoulder at the opening, rattling the top while the bottom held solid. Unlocked, but wedged in place.

Sonja angled away from the service corridor, determined not to find him there. Dragged through decades of dust and thrown from the spiral stair… How would it feel to fall? No. She banished that image.

Focus.

Gods, the thoughts spiraled on without her. She couldn't differentiate her fears from the waves of voices. No sign of him in the ballroom, none in the dining hall. Her heart recoiled as she peered toward the entry. He'd opened that door before and could've done it again.

But he wouldn't. He left valuable supplies. He was here. She had to believe that.

Sonja flitted toward the throne room, eyes searching the top of the twin stair sweeping into the unknown. Two steps up the carpeted path, and Sonja's stomach churned. Blackness bled at the edges of her vision. The screaming started, low and distant, as her hand hovered over the banister. Now was a bad time for another episode. She backed away and ran into the dining room. Her grip tightened on the hilt, already sick at the idea of a kind man dragged across the castle and added to the rows of revenants.

Why take only Niccolo? The question sparked through her scattered thoughts as she found the doors into the kitchen. No one inside. Only the roving lights of the same beetles from the pantry.

Why drown the foreigner when Sonja was a much easier target? Gods, he was in that water. She knew it. Sonja bolted from the kitchen. How had the mage found them? Had she left a trail even after—

Sonja thudded into a body moving in the opposite direction, sprawling to the ground. She landed with the sword under her hip and scrambled for the blade in her boot. Her other hand gripped the last full bloshul.

Niccolo stared back, mouth agape. He was dripping wet and shivering, wavy hair dark and plastered over his face. Under his heavy winter cloak, Niccolo wore nothing more than his trousers. That bizarre sickle clutched in his lap, boots held in his off hand. Behind him, a wet slop of a sack. Sonja's drenched belongings lay intact, here on dry land. "I *have carried presents*," he said.

Sonja gawked for another few seconds. He was here. Gods, he was going to die like this. The bastard. Tears welled in her eyes. He could come back, but Thonra…Ulrik… Her whole damn family might as well be on the ocean floor. What was he doing out here?

Niccolo's careful words registered in her mind. His expression was intense, though he barely gave her tiny knife a second look. That phrase was important. Sonja snapped into her body and stammered for a response. "You're all but *blue*. Winter's witch wants her kiss."

He visibly relaxed. "Have not hear that before."

"It's just a saying. You're going to die of frostbite." She unbuckled the waist sheath, slid his sword across the floor, then pointed to her pack. "I'll take that."

"I am hopeful is all inside." His voice quivered around the words.

"That's not important now." Sonja stood and offered him a hand, then pulled him past her. "Come on, then. Hypothermia is not fun." Idiot. What had he been thinking? He could've died from the shock alone. All this for a bag he couldn't understand the value of.

They loped from the servant's corridor, and she swore it was even colder here. Maybe from the windows in the ballroom or the skylights in the too-tall foyer…

"And she will be highly displeased when I tell her." A thin, emphatic voice echoed through the hall in the moments after Niccolo dashed into the throne room.

"This is exhausting. Constantly, day and night. You'll put your differences aside, or I will force my hand. I swear… I will not be your friend anymore."

Sonja, slower and several paces behind, easily skidded to a stop out of sight. She peered around the corner to find Niccolo crouched tight to the far wall, backing away. The shallow antechamber offered nowhere to hide, and the width was too far for Sonja's magic. In a flash, he ducked into the first place deep enough to hide him, pressed tight against the jammed door.

"No! I expect you to get along," the same voice snapped. "Now, go deal with it somewhere else, I'm busy."

Finally, Niccolo met her eye, seeming as panicked and confused as she felt. Where could they go? Back to the service corridor? Niccolo would freeze. It would be the same for the dining and ballrooms, but with the added concern of finding a place to hide. Surely there was somewhere upstairs, if it weren't for those voices…

But Niccolo had made his choice. He pressed against the door until the rusty hinges creaked and groaned. Sonja gestured wildly to call him off. Even after noticing, he only studied her, wide-eyed. It didn't seem to translate, as he set his heels and applied pressure. She flinched at a wooden pop, peering around the corner to check on the stranger in the throne room. Yet, there was nothing. Niccolo pressed harder, shoving his sword into the jamb, legs sprawling farther into the hall. Shit. This wouldn't end well. If the door opened, it'd be loud. If it didn't…well, someone was going to find a half-naked Attiettan stabbing castle-grade hardwood.

Without a second thought, Sonja opened a drip, setting a tight sphere of invisibility and silence. She ran, arms slamming on either side of Niccolo, bag squishing into the wall beside him. The top of the door bent before snapping loudly back. "Go," she said at full volume. "Open it. Fast."

He took in her hunched posture and the disappearing drip of blood and seemed to understand. Wordlessly, he pressed harder on his levered sword. With a grunt, Niccolo slammed an arm back, scraping the door a few inches across the stone. Sonja took the hilt from him, shifting the angle and leaning in to drive it through the settled frame. She took a moment, morbidly curious, to check over her shoulder. The stranger stood deep in the throne room but perfectly in sight. Gods, he was dreadfully thin. He wore a lavish red cape, fur-trimmed along the edges, but too short for his long legs. His chestnut hair was scraggly and loosely tied back, with jagged lines cut to frame his face. He had to be nearly a head taller than Sonja, watching his own footsteps, arms outstretched like a circling hawk.

Niccolo slammed his shoulder into the wood, and the door gave way, crashing against the wall behind. They tumbled inside in a heap of limbs and murmured apologies. Once she dragged herself off of him, Niccolo snatched his sickle, his shoes, and her travel pack, pulled everything inside, and kicked the door closed behind them.

"You okay?" she asked over her shoulder. "The sword, did it…"

"I'm fine."

Sonja curled her hands into a plush carpet, surprised at the softness. The air was the warmest it had been since leaving Batinavik, and she nearly said so, but after one look at Niccolo, the words died on her lips. He seemed so small. His body pressed heavily against the door, his eyes cast down. Cloak twisted haphazardly at his legs. Soft daylight behind her highlighted chills across his bare chest and arms. She waited for several heartbeats, jaw clenched shut. There was a bolt lock above him that, with a bit of effort, slid into place. She capped the bloshul and let the illusion tick away.

Sonja pushed up and stepped deeper inside. The air grew warmer along the hall. Through a second doorway, a small room shone with daylight from above where short, dirty transom windows ran the length of two walls. A wide desk faced the entry, cluttered with notes and scrolls. She ran her hand along the surface, scattering pens and pages and a few beetles. The chair behind was tall and firm like those in the war room but padded with reddish fabric that matched several lounge seats by a familiar stone chimney. She sifted through the contents of an open drawer until her fingers brushed metal. A ring. A signet ring. The regent's study. A great place to hide a relic. A place that had seemed locked. If it wasn't with the illusionist, the fjarfest had to be here.

She looked back down the hall and paused, slipping the ring into her pocket before helping Niccolo into the warmth. His playful eyes were tired as they met hers, and his skin was clammy. He collapsed onto the couch closest to the vent as she ripped down a few tapestries and shook the dust out of them. The thickest, she draped over his shoulder. Sonja wanted to say something, but every thought held bitterness. So instead, she rummaged through her pack, taking silent stock of each item. Her sympathetic map looked safe, though many alchemical supplies were ruined. Salt, southern clove, ground sage root — none were safe from prolonged submersion. Clothing and blankets and her summer cloak would dry fine if laid out. She was careful about the food. If she found water inside the storage hide…but it was all dry. Ulrik's in-laws knew their way around waterproofing. From the very bottom, she pulled a jar of traveler's stew, broke the seal, and strode over to set it on the vent to heat.

Her frustration only built. "How was the water?" Sonja whispered. "Everything that you were hoping for?"

He curled farther into the makeshift blanket and gave a quiet, mirthless chuckle. "I am from a small fishing village forgotten by my country. This is clean to compare." He tousled his hair with one corner of the tapestry. "My cousins have name for me…eh, translates 'dive first, regret second,' but more crude."

"But I doubt the fish try to drown you."

"The dead did not move. Not once," he said lightly. "Is more easy than I think."

"But you didn't know that would happen."

Niccolo looked up at her, hesitating before giving a slow response. "No. I did not know. But these are important, yes?"

"More important than watching each other's back? They're not." She snatched a rubbish bin and picked a seat far away from him. Dust puffed out as she wrung out the first of her items. "What was your plan if something went wrong? You ran off with nothing but a sickle and an overconfident attitude, so sure things will work out. And if not? What does it matter? I'd realize you were dead, eventually." Sonja threw the shirt on the bench beside her. "Am I grateful for this? Yes. But you scared the life out of me."

He watched her work. "I give apologies," Niccolo said. "It was what I believed was best. I believe this is task I have skill for and will be helpful."

"Yet you waited until I fell asleep to leave," she hissed over the sound of water. "You knew I wouldn't agree. It was stupid and reckless, and then where would we be?"

A soft smile pulled at his features. "Who am I to stand against your magic or logic or whatever you mages use? I have apologies that this scared you, but I do not regret fully. Is only a gamble if you lose."

Sonja pushed to her feet with her fistful of wet fabrics in one hand. "It's done now. Just don't do it again. Gods incarnate." With a huff, she padded to the corridor. "I'm going to watch the kid, see if I can learn anything. Once it's clear, we'll go get our shit back. Eat the stew when it warms up. It'll help." Before Niccolo could reply, she retreated to the cool darkness, half closing the study door behind her.

Now that she had her bloshuls, she could spare some resources to steam her clothes dry. Sonja laid them flat and sat against the door, straining for the boy's voice. She was almost hopeful he'd left, until a clear proclamation shattered that.

"There's simply very little within my power that I may do to help. Your query is long noted as we seek further solutions, but your persistence wears upon the court's countenance."

Sonja dripped a tiny payment, blinking away the world's colors. The wall of light still hung somewhere beyond, upstairs over the service corridors, but that wasn't important. A single bundle of threads meandered in the throne room, stalked by a wave of mist. So this was not an illusion trying to lure them out. But it *was* familiar. Sonja thought back to the unkillable bear and the energetic mites that had swarmed its body. The dead in the basement had that too. Even Niccolo's energy. Was it endemic? Maybe it was in the water, ingested over time. But that wouldn't help Ulrik.

There was something depressing, yet fascinating, in the one-sided conversation. The self-important tone, the big words used incorrectly, the repeated responses. Over and over. Some kind of mad king, stubbornly guarding the only war room door.

Sonja stripped off her leathers and compressed fully out of Niccolo's line of sight, changing into her own spare outfit. It felt good to wear clothes that fit again. Her breezy summer cloak was better than no cloak at all.

She rejoined Niccolo in the warmth, tossing his spares beside him on the bench. "You won't be warm until you are dry," she said, trying and failing to mimic his silly chirping noise. "I will not argue with a big dumb bird." Sonja sat on the desk edge with all six bloshuls in her lap, turning fully away from him. He took a while to change, but eventually, the rustling started. "The kid out there thinks he's a king," she said, examining the first blood sack. "He's holding court, I think."

"Yes?" Niccolo asked.

She poured a tiny bit of blood into one hand, then tossed a charcoal. It floated, featherlight, all the way to the ground. "Talking about resolving the famine and getting their wells investigated. Farmlands and taxes. A lot of rambling." Her palm was dry. No water contamination.

"And the one he speaks to?"

Sonja puffed out a breath. "He's alone." The next desk trinket floated down the same as the first, but the third bag left brackish water in her palm. A contaminated bloshul. She frowned, moving it to the side. Paying from the bad bladder, she scanned behind herself, back to the boy again. An energy caught her immediate attention, far closer than the throne room. Niccolo's dull thread floated behind her and to the left, but the fog she'd seen before was different. She stiffened. He wasn't wearing the chestplate, meaning the mist couldn't be a side effect of iron. The greenish glow was fully detached from his body, lying off to one side. It sat still — or at least not breathing. While all objects had sympathetic connections, ordinary objects were far more expensive to identify. Two things carried such prominent life energies: living beings and magical investiture.

This mist was too still to be alive, even as the edges pulled and flexed. Niccolo carried a relic, and she had a strong inclination it was his strange grinning sickle.

What a great combination: a foreign mercenary and a magic blade.

11

NEW SUPPLICANTS

Well, shit. The null knew far more than he let on. Reading relic books, carrying relic weapons… What else was he hiding? Sonja pinched the bridge of her nose, dropping the identification spell. This was a problem, but not an immediate one. It was best to remain calm. If she could frame her knowledge casually, it'd give her one hell of an edge. She forced her mind back to checking the bloshuls.

"If he is alone," Niccolo's voice grounded her again, "we can go see, yes?"

"See?" she asked, nearly turning before remembering his undress.

"See, yes. As with the eyes," he said. "The boy."

The fourth bloshul wasn't contaminated, though the fifth was so diluted, an inkwell cap hit hard against the stone floor. "Why?"

"You say as he is unwell. What if we help?"

"I'm sure that joke works better in Attiettan," Sonja replied, searching for the leaks on the two bad bloshuls. They would need to be replaced, but she really hated making them from scratch. Neither Tharvik nor Batinavik had sold…

Niccolo stepped in front of her, suddenly fully dressed. "I am not doing a joke." His eyes seemed black in the fading light, coals ready to burn. "We can hide and soon it will find us, or we can go to him to see what he does. He is pretending as king? Let us be peasants."

"This is another of your gambles," she said, sliding off the desk away from him. "It could be a setup. Something attacked us, and we have no reason to believe this isn't it. What would we gain from talking to him over, say, following him?"

"You tell it costs to be invisible. Are there enough pigs to pay?" He let the words simmer before adding, "This boy is covered in filth. How long is he here? He can know things."

"Oh, so we just make friends, and he'll show us to the treasury." Sonja snorted in disbelief. "If he knew anything, he'd have left by now. It seems smarter to search the hidden room than to gallivant after this child." Every drawer and shelf overflowed with supplies. She busied her hands, rummaging through trinkets and taxes. More importantly, Sonja felt for hidden storage. "With our luck, the kid would lead us to another room of the dead."

"You are so sure the boy is related to the other, but I saw the man who waits. Is not the same here." Niccolo crossed his arms. "He who waits does not blink. His hair is of crows and skin never sees sun. He looked of death alive."

"Keep practicing your ghost stories." Sonja waved for him to search a row of drawers lining the far wall. "The thing about illusionists is they can look like anything."

"Any informals is more than we have now."

She ignored him. "I've found both jewelry and coins here. Watch for older mints, back before the Northern Famine. Collectors love that." After raiding the desk, she moved to a wooden wardrobe. Inside, lavish cloaks hung in ruin, eaten away by time — maybe those little fiery beetles had a taste for silks. Under the ratty garments, however, Sonja glimpsed something unusual. Careful not to make a noise, she stooped to retrieve an iron key tangled in the mess. The worn handle was simple and utilitarian, contrasting the intricate pattern of the blade. Whatever this unlocked would be thick. Her mind flashed to the gate in the dungeon, but she pushed the thought down. That was the last place she wanted to return, and only after checking everywhere else. She quickly pocketed it before continuing her search.

"You're really stuck on this kid, aren't you?" Sonja aimed for nonchalance, maybe weariness. If Niccolo believed he was close to winning an argument, she could "relent" in exchange for information on his fjarfest. And if that didn't work, maybe the mad king had some ideas for her new key.

Niccolo hesitated. "I think the goods are worth the bads. And if he needs help…"

"That's not my problem."

"You are so heartless?" Steps shuffled like he turned toward her. "You do not care at all?"

"For the life of a crazy child in an abandoned city? No. I don't. You say he's not the illusionist, so I care even less." The key was so old and heavy, it had to be to a significant door. "If he's not bothered by the haunted castle, then he's *part* of the haunted castle. Meaning, I don't trust him."

"I am not bother by the haunted."

Was that pain in his tone? Sonja met Niccolo's eye, his expression flat and guarded. "You know I don't mean you," she scoffed, shoveling through another cubby and pocketing anything interesting. "You're weird in a way that makes sense. Nulls are something I understand, at least conceptually. I don't want to understand rambling ghost boys."

"You do not find him of any import? Just ignore this as a nuisance?"

he asked sharply. "You can turn blind so willingly?"

She set her jaw, dumping a thin powder into one hand. "If I put it off long enough, I'm sure you'll disappear again." Regret washed in as soon as the words tumbled out. So much for moving past it. Long moments of silence suffocated them. But she wasn't here to make friends. Not with mercenaries, and not with crazy kings. She'd find the Kepstan relic, maybe make it out with some extra pocket money, wait for Thonra, then go home. That's what mattered.

"I am sorry." The gentleness of his tone stung; fingers of guilt wrapped around her throat. "I did not mean for you to feel unsafe because of my action. I try to be helpful, but I see the correct behind your anger."

She turned to face him, fumbling over her words. "No, that was bitter and unhelpful…"

"Is worth being bitter." He started to say something, then laughed dryly to himself. "In Attietto, this sorry means little. Is often used when the guilt is not on only one. But there are no words to translate a better apology for your language. We ask to trade. I give my large breath; you — er — clean? Is not the same."

"Tor instienan," Sonja said quietly.

Niccolo bolted straight, wide hazel eyes fixated on her. *"Repetita?"*

"You say *'retsirun e'lativio.'* And I reply with *'tor instienan.'* It's one of the first things they teach in Attiettan — apologizing." She shrugged defensively. "But that's all I know. I can ask where the grocer is, tell you the name of my favorite book, and identify a handful of animals, but they taught us mostly phrases to be used out of context."

"It is like my start," he said, picking up a few glass orbs, all rolling against each other. "My companions point to objects and repeat the word. I learn road and stone and tree before even learn to say hello or goodbye. I learn the best curses after."

She had little to say to that, but when another few minutes of halfhearted search passed, she circled back. "Let's talk to him. If he's been here as long as it looks, you're right, he could easily know something we don't."

"Yes? You are sure? I can talk if you stay to hide. Is smart to not show all our number until we know how he is. You wait with magic for when something is wrong."

Sonja hummed an absent response, her hand resting on her pocket, picking careful words for a trade. Information for information. "I can watch your back, yes, but do me a favor." She showed him the key. "Find out if he knows anything about an old door or chest. Do it subtly, if possible."

His eyes narrowed, taking it in without reaching for it. Slowly, he nodded. "I can do this."

Sonja offered a shallow smile. They needed each other here, no matter how briefly. It was best to give the appearance of working together. "My sister taught me a trick to keep our hideaway a secret." She didn't mention her struggles with this magic — a duplication illusion that would hide them among dozens of fleeing copies. Ulrik, the talented bastard, had believed that the best way to master a skill was in an emergency. Of her siblings, Sonja had been the only one who didn't live up to that spontaneity. She retrieved the worst of her broken bloshuls and settled on the ground near her drying supplies. "It might be best to conceal that magic weapon of yours. Not wise to let it out of your sight." She tilted her head meaningfully toward the couch, where the fjarfest hid under a cushion.

Niccolo gave her a searching look, sharply alert, with all emotions locked away. Good. Best if he was a little scared of her. After a long pause, he retrieved the sickle. "Is a shame I do not bring the case. I did not know to need it."

"Plans are fickle that way." In a pulse of energy, Sonja purged the water from her bag and a few of the fabric items. When the bloshul was empty, she used her boot dagger to dissect the bladder. She met his suspicious gaze, holding a hand out toward him. Another heartbeat passed before his expression went fully blank. He stepped forward and handed it down. As it touched her skin, Sonja's mind rushed with voices and cries, similar to the ones haunting her through the halls. But these were so quiet, almost far away. He took a seat nearby, lounging stiffly with his eyes turned away.

The sickle had a good balance to it. Lighter than it looked, but still substantial. Again, it struck her with its elegance. Crystalline ridges that curved like fish scales. The edge was thin as a whisper. She started cutting and wrapping, taking the time to examine the carved details along the blade. As with many powerful fjarfest, she found more than Jrendavarian glyphs — several Tahlzhin bases, others she didn't recognize. Closest to the handle was the rune for *STAND*, often used for endurance. Above that was unreadable, but the next looked very similar to an old symbol for *BIND*... Maybe family? Connection? An unusual rune, but she'd withhold judgement until she found a point of comparison. *SKIN, EDGE, DAM...* What she wouldn't give to study this against their runic compendiums back home. But not now. She needed information. "I've made quite a few sickle sheaths in my day," Sonja said. "My family runs a vineyard out west. We still make almost all our tools by hand. No time to repair poorly maintained equipment."

"This is not a common tool for farmers to replace?"

"They are, but it used to be this way for everything. Most traders stay in the east. Merchants have better rights here. I wasn't great at political studies, but it's something the crown finds useful."

"Political studies for mage?"

Sonja nodded. "It's irresponsible to raise mages who don't understand anything about the rest of the world. Power and context are best when balanced." She flipped the sickle over, pleased with her handiwork, when another carving caught her eye. Not a rune, but text etched along the handle, under the thick layers of wrapping, so she could only see the first few letters.

"The word is in my language," he said. "The name is carved. *Mietitore*. It means reaper. I do not know all that it does. But is easy to kill when I hold it."

"What does that mean?"

His frown deepened, voice colder than she was used to. "Have you ever hurt someone with your small sword?"

Sonja didn't respond, now very aware of the weight of her dagger.

"Is difficult to kill with one swing," Niccolo continued, slipping a belt to rest across his chest. He settled the sword to sit low between his shoulder blades. "A death strike is not always fast. But this…" he aligned the strap to pin Mietitore between sword and shirt. "This blade always kills first. Is not how a blade should work." His voice was unexpectedly raw. When his words didn't dance, they marched like mortuary poetry. Still beautiful, but firm with purpose. He cleared his throat, cheeks somewhat flushed under the cloudy afternoon sky. "This is done, yes? We agree on plans? I go to learn, I ask him of door, you save me before I die." The smile was hollow as the two stepped away from the inner study. Peering through the door's unsettled edge, the foyer seemed darker and more ominous. He tightened the cloak around his shoulders, almost like the armor he didn't have. Then, with a nod, Niccolo slipped into the foyer, sneaking along the wall toward the throne room.

Hidden in the niche, Sonja took time to wedge a small length of rope in the jamb. If the rope wasn't in place when they returned, someone had found their hideaway. To keep this a secret, she chose not to stay; with her own blood, she stole a moment of invisibility to sneak around the stairs. Sonja tucked beside a decorative column to wait, checking each of the four bloshul she'd worn. The chilly air wrapped in tight as she slid to perch on the stone base.

Far out of her sight, Sonja knew the moment the mad king spotted Niccolo. His words faltered, and his response broke away. "See him in," the boyish voice called. "Rare to find a new face seeking my favor, least of all a foreigner. Do you have a name?"

"Yes, Highness," Niccolo's tone held gravitas and power. "Niccolo son Adelma. I am of Ziania of Attietto, and look for the grace and wisdom of your people."

"Enter, but understand my position. I hold this land until my mother returns. I am no lord, but the crown prince. My word is law, and I offer my ear. Speak, Niccolo son Adelma."

"I travel here with news from war in my homeland. It is not as—"

"War?" the mad king — rather, mad prince — hissed. "In Attietto?"

"Yes, is as that," Niccolo said after a brief hesitation.

"For how long?"

"Many years, Highness. Many fights against Danqong. A war we believed is for good."

"Why has no one told me anything about a war?" The prince sounded flustered. Not quite angry, but pouty. Several seconds passed before he spoke again. "Well, that necessitates a change. I'm going to need to speak with him this afternoon. Mother will not be pleased to come back to a poorly informed information ring. It defeats the purpose right in the name."

The room surrounding Sonja grew brighter, like dawn over the horizon or a forest fire catching in the brush. She squinted against it, checking that she wasn't touching even the bottom step. But when her eyes adjusted, she cowered in a very different room. The skylights above showed an inky night, contrasting a golden chandelier. Everything sparkled. From the filigree decorating the columns and trim, to the vibrant frames with paintings several times larger than Sonja herself. The grime and wear that had obscured the art, gone. A regal portrait of a man and woman shone next to a landscape with a boy and a bear wearing matching formal smocks. A sprawling tree filled with colorful birds of all sizes. It was the same foyer, but alive.

A party spilled around Sonja, flitting across the polished marble floors. Men and women dressed in rich silks that would stand no chance against the cold. Sonja herself still felt it, the chilled stone wall pressing into her back. Her breath still rolled from her lips. The party was quiet. Clicking footsteps sounded as if from down a long tunnel, and conversations were unintelligible regardless of proximity. If she focused hard enough, she could still find Niccolo's voice.

"…a story of betraying that still follows as a shadow. I was once captain of a unit. Good soldiers who want to save, eh, shield the home."

A regal woman and a scar-faced man exited the dining hall, their prying eyes locked on her. The partygoers bowed but received no acknowledgement. This was the same pair from the portrait, presumably Regent Kepstan and her warlord.

Illusion magic. Sonja was sure of it. Her pulse thundered in her ears. She was exposed. Someone could see her. Gods, they'd played right into the illusionist's hand. She was not safe.

Niccolo's voice danced through the distance as the royalty advanced on her. "My allies agreed. We leave our post before the generals asking to do more pain to those we protect. But this is too late. The march became a fight. The fight became a fire. Large fire that spread in the docks and burned in the city. Proud Attiettan soldiers with torches. The homes and businesses too close to stop."

The words struck Sonja. She knew about the burning of Ziania. She knew of the storehouses and markets. She had known the situation very…intimately. Affianced to a wealthy merchant, who left to tend his stock. Who'd never come back. Who sent a brief letter to cancel the arrangement. Attiettans sympathizers had burned Ziania, not the soldiers. Everyone knew that. It was turncoats. A betrayal. Why would the army attack their own port? Could they be so ruthless?

She couldn't give more thought to the matter, not as the royals continued to approach.

Even the strongest mage had limits. For illusions, the limit was often distance. For hallucinations, it was often keeping the target in line of sight. Either way, Sonja needed to move. She stepped carefully around the column, backing into the ballroom, rewarded with a flicker of weakness. The vibrance leeched away at the edges, seeping inwards. Until, suddenly, the lights returned, and the colors were more garish than ever. Through the windows, Sonja was startled by the clean night sky, freckled with stars over the castle city. The gardens grew lush, all the way to the tiers with the government buildings, budding with exotic plants formed into geometric designs. The golden decor gleamed by candlelight, casting odd shadows across small groups and couples chatting in corners. Ominous partygoers turned and stared, moving slowly toward her, silent as the moon. Regent Kepstan's face grew more concerned. The warlord waved for Sonja to follow, unsheathing a decorative sword and guiding the regent away.

Sonja had to stay calm. Magic like this would be expensive. It would run out eventually. She swept warding hands through the forms as they closed in. This wasn't real. It was too big to be manifested. Just figments. Falsehoods. Keep breathing, and get to Niccolo. She'd gone too far. Where was his voice?

With as much confidence as she could, Sonja stepped through the finery, back toward the foyer. The Kepstans waited for her, hands outstretched, pale frowns marring their faces. A thankful breath escaped her lips as she caught glimpses of the castle ruins smeared underneath the decadence.

She heard Niccolo again, if only distantly. "Not enough of us. Too few of all. And we trusted one untrustworthy. I asked that we wait for one I know many years. A great friend. He arrived but with forces. He gave chase, and we few escaped…"

But the spell was not over. The scene flashed and flooded with intangible hands clawing for purchase against her clothes and skin. It was startling, yes, but it was fine. It would be over soon. She would get out. Everything was…

Something behind Sonja caught her by the hair, jerking back and down, untucking the braid from its long-suffering bun. Sonja spun with a wide arc, clawing at the forms as black hair unraveled across her shoulders. Her fist ripped through open air and smiling faces. Something tangible had touched her. This was no longer a safe illusion to ignore. She retrieved her boot dagger, flailing again.

Nothing.

At any point, a knife could manifest straight through her throat. She'd pay every bit of her blood to the floor. Niccolo was too far away. If something went wrong, he'd never know. Not until she was already cold. Spirit whisked away to the Sapphire Orchards.

Why hadn't it killed her yet? What was it telling her?

In a flash, a sword cut through the line of pursuers. With a fluid dance, half of the partygoers crumpled to the ground. "Go!" shouted the warlord. "Run while you can!" He defended as she stumbled toward the regent, the woman's words too far to understand.

No. This was wrong.

Sonja changed direction, tripping in her haste, dagger bouncing away. She dove after it as the illusions swarmed her again.

"Niccolo?" she choked out his name.

His words dropped off, and she called again, more steadily. Sonja's tone wasn't without fear, but she hoped he would react calmly. The crowd backed away, leaving a pair of familiar boots standing close, and a man with one arm outstretched. Her eyes slowly traced up his trousers and breastplate, meeting the fear in his hazel eyes.

The prince's pathetic voice peaked. "You cannot leave without finishing the story!"

Niccolo blinked down, mouth slightly ajar. With a shuddering breath, Sonja closed her eyes and slashed across his chest. Her blade sunk in like he was made of sand. The metal didn't make a sound since, of course, that armor was still locked in the war room. Then he was ash, falling on her arms and collecting at her feet, spinning up in reaction to her fear and panic. A manifestation. Just a strong illusion.

The court closed in again. Sonja fought against patterns or forms, terrified to catch another physical being. Terrified it would strike her first. While they were easy to dissipate, manifestations were not harmless. Deep in her mind, a last horror repeated: how was she still trapped here? How could anyone have this much to pay?

She yelped as a hand caught her wrist, prying the knife away.

"I am very sorry, Highness." Niccolo's voice called from right next to her. "We still have many injuries from the events. My partner overcomes much. In three months, her entire back was *red* with scars, but is getting better now." He pressed the dagger into her hand, his eyes searing. Intense eyes. Compassionate eyes. "The pain is much sometimes. But is no longer colored *blue* on cold nights."

Colors. He was giving more colors. This was Niccolo. "*Hallucinating crowds of people*," she said.

"You are safe," he whispered. "No more visions." He helped her slip the knife away before they stepped around the staircase. The filthy castle had returned in full, leaving only weak raincloud light from the many windows.

"She is a local guide for us. Speaks much better than I can." Niccolo turned to the prince. "In the city when the attack. She is of your country, but as in danger as the rest of us." With one arm held over Niccolo's shoulder, every time she stepped, he rocked her with a false limp. After a moment, she adopted it without his help.

"And the traitor?" The boy stood in the center of the room, perfectly poised at the intersection of a large design in the floor tile, his bony arms crossed tight. Sonja couldn't quite place his nationality. Maybe some Jrendavarian heritage based on his height, but it was hard to tell with so little of him left. How far would someone walk to make it here? Had this skinny vagabond stumbled in on accident? "What became of him?"

"My country believe that he is no traitor, but a hero. It is my name they call traitor. We come here in search of your aid. A power that can undo this fate. For allies and for salvation. We wish for your blessing."

The boy didn't seem to like this answer. His bright green eyes flitted past them a few times.

"You are now a part of this story, Prince Leif," Niccolo added. That seemed to improve the prince's mood.

Leif, apparently, considered. "Yes, yes. You shall wait a moment as I consult with my advisor." He strode toward the throne plinth, speaking emphatically to the emptiness beside him.

"Your thoughts?" Sonja whispered.

"He is important," Niccolo breathed back. "Is here for a long time."

Before she could press further, the prince's eyes locked on to her over one shoulder. "Yes, she's pale, I agree. Would Nurse keep medicines for that? Go ask her to prepare." He nodded vigorously, then stepped toward them. "Madam, your name?"

"Sonja Vinzler, Highness."

He nodded again. "And you were hurt?"

"Yes, Highness."

"That makes sense, of course." With two small claps, Leif paraded past them. "Come now. Arvid is alerting Nurse. I will take you to her myself. She will help."

Sonja recoiled. "Oh, I…"

Beside her, Niccolo pulled on her arm. They locked eyes, his expression encouraging. "We will go together, if is acceptable," he answered the prince.

"Yes, yes. Come now. Nurse hates to wait." Leif bounded from the antechamber and through the foyer, disappearing around the banister.

Sonja slowed their pace. "There's something wrong with the stairs." She barely moved her lips. "It might cause another…another vision."

"Do we refuse?"

"I don't know. Maybe not. That much magic is almost always hiding something. We'll likely need to investigate, eventually."

He frowned. "Is worth it? I can go alone?"

"No. We're a team. I've got tricks to help. Just be there if they don't." Sonja opened a small drip on one bloshul, letting it fall for several steps before reaching for the magic. First, an identification. Starting their ascent, she peered up with inverted vision at the immense energy floating to the right. Her feet dragged, but Niccolo added support. It was exhausting to filter the dominating light, but it came with a reward. Columns of energy staggered across the steps, some kind of net or barricade. With a confirming tap, she slipped from his grip, weaving carefully between the lights. She twisted her rings to stay grounded, hearing the voices without being overtaken.

Leif bounced impatiently at the top, speaking to the nothingness nearby. "No, Elvy, it's fine. Nurse will fix it quickly. I'll tell her to do so, and we'll go." He scampered toward the energy, disappearing to her vision altogether.

Sonja blinked away the spell, so close to the source that it burned. Niccolo pressed a gentle hand into her back and gave her a questioning look. She nodded to inspire confidence but only felt more tired. If only she had something to connect to sympathetically, a vel to reduce the weight of the presence leaning against her. Shouting. Crying. Pleading. She set a focus, touching the first three fingers of each hand together. It helped direct the magic, somewhat simplifying what her mind's eye saw. Since many of her bloshul had come from the same animal, they were typically easy to link sympathetically. But their lines wavered with the distance. Early in her travels, she'd learned to use these links like a magical scaffolding. At the time, it had protected her from a fjarfest capable of repeating human speech — a relic she'd underestimated. She focused on those lessons learned through the years. Sonja was stronger than she'd ever been. Focus.

Along the hallway, clusters of doors snaked around each other, guarded by beautiful statues and velveteen curtains, yet the hall itself was windowless and shrouded in sharp darkness. Niccolo pointed to a worn line in the carpet going in the opposite direction. No sooner had Sonja turned to look did the voices magnify. Quick, like an arrow that pierced her ears. There was no time for a scream. She fell wordlessly into sudden night.

12

RIVERSIDE

Seglaborg was a speck on the darkening horizon when Thonra spotted a familiar cart, tall and fully enclosed with colorful wooden boards and carved detailing. The shack on wheels was even rattier than when she'd last seen it. Little had changed, from the hateful mule glaring across the pasture, to the words *Spells of Scholars* scrawled in chipping paint.

The caravaneer recoiled when Thonra informed him she'd be dismounting here, his eyes flicking to the scholastic shack and back. "Miss, I wouldn't…"

"It's fine. I can walk the rest of the way."

He exchanged glances with a few nearby guards, but they put up little argument as she thumbed out the rest of her payment. The pack seemed to trundle on even slower after she disembarked, possibly expecting her to change her mind and wave them down.

Thonra stared at anything to keep from making eye contact with straggling merchants. The sky glowed a violent orange, and the landscape was serene despite the river's torrent raging off a shallow cliff. The area had a particularly rainy spring, according to her ride, who grew nervous when the path veered too close. Their conversations had hinted at a recent drowning but nothing more specific.

She waited until the cargo had faded into the mist before strolling over to slam the butt of her dagger into the rickety door. A woman screamed over the sound of a man's dazed grumbles of, "Gods flay my bones! Who the hells's there? The hells do you want?"

"Bendik, open up," she called between rounds of metallic knocking. Even the ever-nervous Sonni refused to call the Myhrs by their surname anymore. They'd lost that right.

At her words, something in the internal chaos changed, like the two were considering their next move. They might act rashly, and that simply wouldn't do. Paying the tiniest bit of blood, Thonra cast a powerful light illusion that beamed out through the tight cladding. Another slurry of cursing preceded a rocking as his gravelly voice called out again, "Back off, will you? I'm working on it." The wagon continued to jerk around as its occupants jostled inside. Thonra made eye contact with the evil old mule as it bucked against its stake. The wheels ground against large stopper rocks. She pushed on the closer of the two, but the stone seemed sturdy. A bulky man unlatched the entry and barged out wearing nothing more than faded old trousers and the stench of liquor. Gods, he looked old now. Would he be sixty yet? Bendik slammed the door shut, clutching his shoulder. His disheveled hair was thick but grey and fell in a greasy sheet. Wary eyes skittered over her features, one light brown, the other dull blue, deeply set in sleepless wrinkles. He looked like the knocking had fully startled him awake, despite evening just starting. "What do you want?" The tone was guarded as he squinted at her face.

"I'm here for my lesson, teach."

His frown deepened, though it seemed to take even a few more moments before recognition overtook his expression. "So, the Vinzlers live on." He spat near her feet. "I'll pray harder next time."

"I need a book," Thonra replied.

"Ah, of course." He bowed sardonically. "No one told Miss Mulled-Majesty, but my humble library has been significantly depleted over the years. Travel's an expensive task when you don't have Mummy's money to get you what you want."

"You have none of my sympathy. The way I remember it, you didn't struggle getting what you wanted back in the day."

"Don't tell me you chased me here to dredge up your own lies and slander. Guilty conscience? I won't be accepting apologies."

Thonra snarled, "You're a wretch. Play the victim, but you know what you did to them, and you'll live with that till the day you die. I hope it burns you from the inside and chokes you with the guilt." She stalked forward, reaching toward the cart, but his hand shot out to block her. The moment his fingers grazed her skin, she smiled, opening a small drip on one bloshul.

Bendik's clammy palm latched on to Thonra's wrist, but she only closed her eyes and cast out another shocking light. A tight silence wrapped around them, absorbing his yelp of pain and surprise. She swung her fist up, still clutching the dagger, making a far firmer connection and shattering his nose. With two quick steps, Thonra dropped into a ready position, watching for his next move.

But no. Bendik dropped to his knees and curled in the wild grasses, mouth ratcheted in a scream consumed by her magic. He tucked his head in defensively and shuddered, but he didn't strike against her. She waited several moments longer, sure of a feint. He continued to writhe, squirming away as if she would kick him where he lay.

It was pathetic. Over before it started. Bendik hadn't taught her for long, but memories of his martial lessons left bruises on her soul.

He and his wife had been formidable. Or had he only been strong when compared to children? The last image of this man as a force of nature crumbled in Thonra's mind. The monster who had caused her siblings so much pain yet had never shown that side to her. They rarely spoke of those days, waking to the Myhrs watching them sleep. Even as adults, it was a sore topic. Sonni had stayed in Thonra's room well into adulthood — until the day Bragi proposed. Ulrik's night terrors could wake the whole house.

She dropped the silence spell so that the old man's groans scraped across the evening breeze. Inside the cart, Thonra found an unfamiliar woman in silk dressing robes, huddled in the corner, long red hair cascading over piles of feathery blankets — not at all the face Thonra had anticipated. She looked terrified. She looked young.

Thonra's ebbing rage reignited, bottlenecking at the base of her skull. A pressure she couldn't release here. She rocked onto the creaking vessel, pulling open the cabinets that had once housed hundreds of books. Bendik and his wife, Edel, had forced the students to pack and unpack the supplies at the beginning of each quarter. Trudging the tomes in and out the monastery walls would "build character."

But the cabinets were, in fact, empty. Of the original collection, six books remained. Fortunately, these were the best. The pile included a smooth leather sketchbook, spewing loose pages and frayed bindings. The Myhrs had curated this one personally, purchasing anything claiming to be a relic diagram, then using tree sap to stick it all together. She took a moment to examine the pages, careful to mind Bendik's continued wails outside.

Now that she was familiar with the name tul-Habao, Bendik's notes attributed many of the sketches to the Pilgrim. A spiraling dagger, a wristlet with gems and chains, a pair of round spectacles, a single fur-lined glove, several river stones marred with different glyph combinations. Yet she'd been overlooked in the lesson plan.

She skimmed handwritten notes, flipping quickly through the pages until she found the word she was looking for.

... Provide theories to the Kepstan family relic. Scholars conclude the glyphs recorded on the heirloom diadem are unlikely to support the proclaimed protection.

Below the original text, notes scrawled out a list in red:

Stitched undergarments? Jewelry? Diadem interior? AGT - 243.

The final number had been circled several times in a third type of ink. Thonra glanced at the woman again, finding her staring with wide, watery eyes. "Old Edel finally left, then, did she?" Thonra asked. "They used to fight like badgers."

The woman hesitated. "She died. It was last year. Coughing fits that ate her up."

Thonra nodded, flipping through the remaining pages. "And how do you fit into this?"

"He offered to teach me…"

Thonra jerked to study the woman's face. "How old are you?" The way the woman shifted her gaze confirmed that she was not a legal student. Still, she was far from the old man's age. Thonra softened her shoulders, motioning to the bed. "This is his payment, then? He'll teach over-age students if they'll sleep with him?"

Red curtains covered her face. "There were still payments."

In a sharp flurry, Thonra shoved the notebook into her satchel, followed by the few remaining books. The last caught her eye, *Advanced Glyph Theory*. She took a centering breath and cast a shaky identification inside the cart. It was fast and expensive, but energies flared in all directions. The woman's strong spirit nearly blotted out a glimmer of light hiding under her.

Thonra waved her out of the way and pulled up the mattress. Beneath the heavy blankets and lumpy bedding, she yanked open a secret compartment. Thonra shoved past full purses clinking with coins until she found a small redwood case. The lock at the lip was slender and broke under a few thuds of the dagger. Inside was an assortment of junk, but in another surge of power, each object glowed. She slid the box into her larger pack and pocketed several bundles of ronad.

"If you want out," she said to the woman, "I'm leaving for town now." Without waiting, she dropped from the cart to loom over her old teacher. Bendik had pushed to his knees, still cradling his ruined nose in blood-streaked hands. Thonra lowered her voice, just above the sounds of his whimpers. "Let me guess." She lifted his trembling chin with the toe of her boot. "She's mature for her age?"

His eyes flickered behind her on all sides. Thonra pushed away and followed his gaze, only to find dozens of children standing in the evening mist. Not just any children. Sonja and Ulrik, repeated again and again, from all those years ago. They were thin from missed meals, with hollow eyes and tight-pressed lips.

Thonra hadn't helped them. It had taken her so long. Guilt and hatred burned away at her soul.

Forcing confidence into her trembling hand, she closed off the bloshul still dripping at her side. One by one, the visages of young Sonja and Ulrik faded. She hadn't meant to cast the illusion, something that happened more and more with time.

She left him there in the dirt, pressing back furious tears. Soon after, soft footsteps pattered behind her, and the red-haired woman silently fell into step. Neither spoke for a long time while the stars blinked awake overhead. Sounds of the city drifted in, but Thonra felt distant from them. All her concentration funneled into taking the next step forward.

"He taught you all that?" The woman studied Thonra openly, a hopeful edge in her shaking voice. "The light and the images?"

Thonra considered how to respond. "Not much, no. The Myhrs were our first tutors, only for two mastery rings. They were...not a good match for my family."

"Did you earn the rest somewhere else?"

"Yes."

"You have all nine?"

"Five."

The woman's face fell. "You aged out."

Thonra pursed her lips. She had fought like crazy to stay in training for another year, but she'd received her final ring at twenty-one, and that was already a scandal in academia. "Yes. Only my brother was young enough to earn them all."

"And you still haven't found another teacher?"

"You don't always need a teacher." Thonra took another appraising moment. "What's your name?"

The redhead looked shocked for a moment. "Nalvina."

"And how many rings did you earn during childhood?"

"One — I was on track to earn them all, but the money ran dry. My uncle took me in at eleven. I tried to go back, but it never worked out."

The advice died on Thonra's lips.

Nalvina clearly read into the prolonged pause as a final damning confirmation. "There are tutors out there who know the age limit is pointless," she hissed, tears defining her tone. "Someone will teach me. I just have to find them. I'll find them." Nalvina's fervor echoed into the empty evening.

"I've been doing this for a long time. As arbitrary as it seems, the habits are easiest to instill early on. Are there people who may teach you more magic? Yes. But those people aren't looking out for you. It'll be more slimy old fools and selfish bastards who will take your money and disappear before completing their part." Thonra shook her head. "Take Bendik. How did he plan on getting you a new ring, much less eight? Who would he turn your paperwork in to?"

"He said resources!"

"His name is marked as 'discredited' in nearly every academic record across Western Jrendavar — he's holistically exiled from several regions." Thonra wished she found pleasure in listing the Myhrs' punishments. Instead, she felt nothing. "He's a predator, and his wife was no better. He took your money, he used your body, and he would have disappeared once you asked for what he owed."

Nalvina's voice dropped to a whisper. "You don't know that."

"I don't," Thonra confirmed, "but I have enough experience to believe I'm right." After a pause, she held out one bundle of ronad. "If I were you, I'd go home. It's hard to accept sometimes, but things don't always work out." Before the redhead could take it, Thonra added a second of the stolen bundles. It was likely Nalvina's money anyway. "You've got a lot to live for. Move on. Do what you can with what you have."

Thonra didn't wait for the woman after passing Seglaborg's gated checkpoint. Deep in the twists of the city alleyways, she paid for a private room and laid out the trinkets that the Myhrs had spent so long collecting. Thonra flipped through the sketchbook, tearing out and aligning any relics that seemed to match. First, a satin sack containing a large, dented amber. The associated diagram called it a troll's eye and described a darkness spell activated by blood. While Thonra would've considered it an illusory relic, the text implied this magic followed a theory called "energetic perception," a term Thonra had never seen before. Bendik had several questioning notes on that claim as well, but nothing particularly enlightening. Even with instructions, Thonra couldn't make it work.

Fine. It's not like she needed a trinket for darkness.

The next interesting piece was a thick vial of water, spinning and crashing in on itself, even when it lay on the floor. One diagram claimed the contents were a poison called "Will Waters" and would compel a drinker to work themselves to death, unable to sleep from energy or lie still from physical pain. The following pages claimed it was a healing springwater that flurried and grew stronger when separated from its source. The Myhrs had both included their thoughts on the tonic and the risks associated, but neither were helpful.

The little box held dozens of these trinkets, many associated with a string bookmark proving each to be more useless than the last. A young runner delivered warm dinner to her room as she was studying her sister's latest update on their sympathetic map. The landmarks weren't exact, but Sonni was closing in on Kepstadur Keep early. It had been over a week since Thonra had sent news, long before her encounter with the cave-dwellers. With a spoon in one hand, she fumbled through the steps to link to Sonja's twin page, then seared a mark through her approximate location, hoping it transferred correctly. Thonra had some access to energy magic but had been far stronger with perception. Having a limited time to learn, she'd focused on her strengths, only all these years later regretting the narrowed nature of her education. Sonni used sympathetic magic like she was breathing. Powerful, useful magic. Thonra struggled to even slash her location. And the cost? Outrageous, even from her oversized bloshul.

Somewhere around midnight, Thonra settled into the plush bed, flipped open *Advanced Glyph Theory*, and skimmed the opening pages. The text was in old Jrendavarian — not fully divorced from her own speech, but she had to concentrate on the meanings. Page after page, she realized that this was almost certainly the teaching guide the Myhrs had used nearly eighteen years ago. Inscriptions in the margins rang with the memory of Edel's shrill soprano and strict eye for penmanship.

"Glyphs are particular," she would say. *"Irresponsible markings will kill you dead."*

Thonra turned to the two-thirties. The last quarter of the book discussed relics created from living beings. She passed illustrations of thick hide armor stitched with gibberish runes. A sword crumpled uselessly nearby. Thonra imagined several ways to get past those defenses but ignored the urge to write the book off. The next pages implied that hairs from a particularly ugly dog would lend to strong wards. She skipped the following list of other organs that could be hardened or repurposed.

A dual-sheet, full-body illustration of a snakelike dreki stared up from two hundred and forty-one. Thonra ran her fingers across enlarged sketches of scales, wings, and eyes. Even before turning the page, she could see the feral scrawl of handwritten notes.

The Myhrs had found a lot to say about the Kepstan's fabled artifact. Much like the stories she'd collected through the years, the notes pointed in all different directions. But these theories converged: a method of carving glyphs into the crystalline structure of dreki bones or burning into the scales.

If one were to conceptualize a single lever, this is as a fjarfest of standard life. Beyond may hold that of the pure marrow of the midnight fawn, who steps up on air as stone may never be so solid. The wing of flame's louse calls forward the breath of life in winter's heartiest spite. These are as gears within the hope of every unknowable spell. But a wyrm that moves as silk through stars is the full assembly, lifting unseen boulders that the mage may naught but snap a request and be it done.

Thonra read the text over and over again. With the Myhrs' notes, she pieced together the relevance: if the Kepstans had a dreki-base relic, the family wouldn't need to be magical. The text suggested that dreki relics were inherently stronger than others — even other magically-inclined animals. The power would act without prompting once the defining glyphs were set. So little was known about the late Kepstan family, and expeditions, no matter how large, had resulted in little more than tragedy.

Without the notes, the archaic text could have taken all night to decipher. She almost felt bad for using magic to shift the rocks holding the Spells of Scholars wagon in place. In her defense, the stones could have remained firm. Bendik and his cart may be exactly where she left him. It was a meaningless claim, of course, as she didn't care if he lived or died. If the gods chose to roll him into that river, so be it. Thonra had simply given them the chance.

Of all the six books, one more stood out. The thinnest of all the remaining collection and one she had nearly left behind. She held it in her lap, leafing through the pages, but nervous to open it. The simple title glared at her in bloodred writing: *Voices from the North.* A biography. Several historians had written similar accounts, collating information and speculating on unclear events. Yet, somehow, no reputable book collector ever owned them. Libraries and repositories often reported them as missing. Valtyr of the North was the reason tul-Habao's story had been obscured. Thonra understood that her current mission looked suspicious. Her path seemed interwoven with Valtyr's eradicated legacy, and, if it were anyone else, people would be right to fear. She, however, accepted the consequences. She knew better than to seek immortality. This was about justice. About an unfair world. About her own failings. Thonra was a special case.

She opened the book. It was not the first she had found, but Thonra drank in the story every time. His early years as a raider, the illusions he would cast so each man fought his brother, a theory-riddled relic that could control the bodies of the dead. This book was unique in its "definitive stories" of his youth. A supposed plague that had swept his land, a supposed family that had died, a supposed breakdown over his own mortality. Thonra almost found it funny. As if anything could justify this life of destruction. She nearly skimmed over the most important element of the text. Not the print itself, but another nugget left in Edel's penmanship around the middle of the book.

Cannot hold the dead here, but directs before departure. Immortality or soul collection?

An arrow pointed to the word *wristlet* underlined in the center of the page, amid a list of possible fjarfest. Thonra rolled to hang off the side of the bed and pulled over a pile of sketches. She remembered the image of a wristlet somewhere in the mix, and, upon finding it, noticed a small note circled in the corner.

VFTN - 37

Laying her head on the hard pillow, Thonra decided it was imperative to beat Sonni to the walls of Kepstadur Keep. The more she learned about this man, the more she theorized his success was not completely skill-based. He had the perfect mix of relics and the knowledge to become the bane of the mountains. If the Myhrs could piece together all these theories, it was a matter of time before someone else discovered the breadcrumbs to Kepstadur. Potentially someone equally capable of directing the magic as Valtyr had been. Her sister was a skilled mage, but Thonra wouldn't take any chances. The magic to revive Ulrik would almost certainly be energetic. Sonni was vital to their goals. If she got herself killed, what good was Thonra? Simply the last Vinzler child standing, haunted by the ghosts of the siblings she had failed.

13

PRIVATE QUARTERS

The hallway tilted, melted, dripped, and submerged Sonja fully in an instance of darkness.

There was no hallway.

Only dawn in the kitchens. The Kepstans often slept in on stormy mornings like today. Her knees and wrists popped with the rain, as soft hands kneaded bread. She considered how best to tell her husband she was pregnant. He'd be thrilled, but she had a feeling it was another boy. They'd both wanted a second daughter. All the same, this was a gift from the gods, especially at her age.

A cold sensation like rising water wrapped up Sonja's legs, but the woman in the kitchen didn't register any fear. Under the waves, her vision faded. Sonja heard voices as she floated alongside the darkness.

In a blink, she stood in the forge. The fire burned bright, but she couldn't feel its heat. The same odd green as all the castle vents. Her hands were thin and rugged and covered in black grime, holding a hammer in one and a rag in the other. Was it rude to stop by the library a second time in the same day? Probably. Especially wearing such filthy clothes. It was a bad impression.

The forge washed away without warning.

Ulrik smiled back at her. The grin that told her he'd said something clever. Well, he thought it was clever.

Then it was midday. She stood on top of Kepstadur's wall overlooking a bay brimming with merchant ships. She was short, sure, but tall enough to see past the parapet. Still, her comrades on patrol rarely missed an opportunity to poke fun. She liked to believe it didn't bother her and told them as much when they asked. She only replied with meaner jabs. In a way, it really was fine. She knew it to be a sign of affection...but sometimes, she considered telling them that those jabs struck deeper than she let on.

In the void, Sonja rocked like so many of those boats. Drifting up and rolling back. A giant, erratic breath.

The voices returned, but when she rolled her head toward them, Sonja was bedside. Back home. In the garden house. Ma didn't know what was making Ulrik sick. He could be contagious. Thonra stood over him, face pulled taut — an anger that shadowed pain. Sonja tried to speak, but Thonra turned away. "I can't do this right now, Sonni. Just watch him."

Another blink.

She sat in a dark space, holding a deck of foreign-looking playing cards. These were bad cards. Bad, bad cards. But she couldn't go out on this round. There were at least four thugs behind her. She leaned back with a smile, forcing her thundering heart not to rattle her breaths. Convince one more person to fold, and she'd gain back a couple of coins. As long as she had enough to buy in again, she could win it back. Just lie a bit longer.

Sonja's vision only flashed a moment between locations. A distant thud registered in her mind, something akin to a slamming door. The voices were closer than they had been…and familiar. Sonja could almost reach out and touch the words on the wind.

But at the end of her hand was a line of light. She'd felt a fair few energies in her time, but none this thin and brittle. Ulrik had been asleep for three days. It was early in the morning when his threads started to flake through her fingers. She called for her sister, and they held tight enough to draw blood from their palms. Thonra's rage echoed across the vineyard, waking the rest of the family with the knowledge he was gone. Ulrik's wife was the first into the room. His widow. Her grief had been quiet and stuttering, holding their son, too young to understand. Ma and Dada clung to each other outside the door.

Stories tumbled in and around Sonja, growing dim with every new vision. Somewhere in the mix, she grew cognizant of her state. These were only hallucinations, though the texture felt wrong. The magic from the foyer had been a soft summer linen, a foreign silk tied over her senses. This was a burlap sack. Pinpricks of reality flashed by, but it was hard to keep track of any one.

She learned to observe from a distance, turn away from appearances of her family, and press forward any time Niccolo's voice broke through. The rocking boat soon neutralized to a hard cot under her shoulder and hip. The last image to fade was Thonra. She was the shortest of the siblings, with their mother's chestnut hair and their father's grey-ice eyes. Her obstinate glare, however, always made her seem larger. Sonja remembered her as she'd been on that last day. Tired and thin, with bright red cheeks from southern windburn or rage or barely contained tears. Sonja was unsure which.

The memory of Thonra stood with her, watching as she rested, even as Sonja's eyes focused on the room where Niccolo's accent twirled in the emptiness. Deep evening shadows stretched across the stone, combatted by the soft glow of a heat vent. Sonja shivered despite herself, drawing up and rustling the heavy blanket — no, a cloak. One far thicker than her own. It had a supple oak smell and a wool-lined interior. She focused first on the chimney, fully open and pouring warmth into the space, all the while fighting back a powerful draft of icy wind from somewhere behind her.

A soft laugh caught her attention next, where Niccolo sat bedside on the floor with her hand draped over his shoulder. She flinched, drawing into the cloak that must have belonged to him. He didn't react to her sudden movement. "No, is not as that," Niccolo said. "We watched for careful moments. It is good to know when the time is to attack with force — to uproot earth and sand to defend. When to be behind the enemy so that they do not know you hit them. We *hold caution precious.*"

Sneaky. The code phrase blended into its context. From the echo of his voice, Sonja guessed the room extended far beyond her. The thought was ominous, as her still-whirring mind offered images of folkloric monsters standing in corners or hanging from the rafters.

"What happened to them?" the mad prince Leif asked, sitting cross-legged with a straight back. The seriousness of court had dissipated, and Niccolo's words enraptured him. It made him look younger. His full-length trousers only reached to mid-calf and strained at the knees. His eyes, brimming with wonder, starkly contrasted the lines of exhaustion trenched across his face. He leaned forward intently, and Sonja couldn't tell if he was young enough to be her son or old enough to be her father.

Niccolo took a long pull from his canteen. "Adelma traveled with us. She and I see many cities together. Castillo is sneaky, if not smart. I am sure that he will come back one day."

"Which was your favorite?"

"Battle?"

"City."

Niccolo's shoulders relaxed. "Those nearby have many nice things. I see more of my people along the coast, but also trade routes sometimes. When we first come here, I did not know what your people think of Attietto."

Sonja studied the room, taking in the shelving stocked with medical wraps, old vials of ointments, and rusted implements.

"I'll travel the trade routes," the boy said. "I'll see all of them, and you should join me and tell the stories of my travels."

"I am very honored."

"You'll have to wait for my parents, though. I'm in charge." Leif raised his chin. "Everything must be running smoothly upon return."

"You do a great job, Prince Leif," Niccolo mused, catching Sonja's eye with a gentle smile. "Your people seem very happy."

"They would like you, I'm sure. My parents, that is." Leif crossed his scrawny arms and flexed his jaw. "It has been a very long time since they last wrote."

"What have they been doing?" Sonja asked, pleasantly surprised to find her voice unstrained. Maybe this fainting episode hadn't involved nearly as much screaming.

"Nurse!" Lief sprung to his feet and scurried off behind her.

"Travel with the army," Niccolo responded to her question. "*Heralds carrying peace*, as we are." His tone was genuine, but something in his expression reminded her of a parent continuing a make-believe story. "He says they will be back soon."

"Does he know anything about our *green* key?" Sonja whispered as she pushed upright, swinging her legs over the edge beside him and offering back his cloak.

"Your lips, they are still cold," he said, reaching to still her hand; his other arm rested dangerously close to her leg. "Hold for longer. Until you feel good."

Something swelled in her stomach at his gentle touch and casual closeness, but she tried to move on as effortlessly as he had. Damn Attiettans. "I'm sorry for fainting," Sonja muttered. "More weird visions. They weren't the same as… Well, don't worry about it."

"The boy faltered too." Niccolo spoke quietly, barely moving his jaw. "Did not fall, but hears something terribly loud. Holding his ears and stumbling and telling for someone to make it stop."

"And you heard nothing?"

"And I heard nothing," he confirmed. "Your bag bleeds, though. I found to make it stop, but I fear it stains your clothing." Niccolo held up her summer cloak, dyed red. "This gives him great concern."

"I'll take care of it." What a waste of resources.

"He speaks little of the castle," Niccolo whispered quickly as the boy's footsteps drew closer. "Little of its belongings. Rather listens to stories than tells them. He believes to be prince. Believes that his mother returns one day. Believes that staff remain. He only waits."

Prince Leif turned on a heel at the foot of the bed. "See? You can fix her now."

Sonja exchanged a glance with Niccolo from his spot on the floor. He gave an encouraging nod, and Sonja fought back a sigh before holding out one arm. A few silent seconds lapsed with nothing more than Leif's occasional interjections.

"Overnight?" The mad prince squinted into her face. "No, that's not it. I just hadn't thought it to be so serious. I'll approve the fresh tonics, yes." A moment passed, and he grew exasperated. "Hush, Elvy! This is important. It's an expense worth taking for our new friends. We'll find another blanket. And Niccolo, you'll clearly have a place to stay in our guest rooms. Yes, *these* guest rooms. Why are you so fussy?"

Sonja's back went rigid. As if she would stay here alone. Her throat closed at the thought of this dark room, with nothing but the child's manic ghosts. Of Niccolo disappearing into the hall and being lost to the wind. Leif turned back to Sonja with a smile, but she cut across him. "Highness, there is one other thing we need to tell you. It's regarding your mother."

The young man's face contorted. She hadn't expected that kind of pain when the idea flashed across her mind. Sonja started an apology, but Leif turned to the space beside him. "That's all for now, Nurse." He watched the air as a person only he could see left. "What do you know of my family?"

"More than you might think, Highness," Sonja said quickly, searching her mind for long-forgotten history lessons. Her heart thudded an uneven rhythm. What *did* she know? She'd heard many stories on this place, but those had mostly covered the fallout of its loss. Theories about the disaster. Not good to mention here.

"She's returning soon, then?"

"We are not so important to know details." Niccolo covered her hesitation. "But she sends us early with…" He looked for Sonja's approval and she nodded subtly. "She sends us with a key."

"Which one?"

Sonja produced the iron from the study and leaned in conspiratorially. "Your mother said you would know where the lock is."

The color faded from Leif's face. A feral spark glinted in his eye. "I know which, but I'm not supposed to…"

"Is okay," Niccolo said. "Is important we go. She gives permission."

After a moment of consideration, Leif strode to the hall, not waiting as they scrambled to follow.

Sonja returned Niccolo's cloak, spending the blood in her soaking summer wrap to stay warm. "I'm sorry if that was reckless," she said, "but I'll be damned before a ghost boy locks me in a medical ward."

The infirmary exited to a wide corridor's dead end. Leif backed toward the wall, eyes fixated on the blind turn and gentle sunset. Fear dragged along his features.

"Highness?" Sonja whispered and clutched at a bloshul. Niccolo dashed out, sword drawn defensively. But there was nothing. It was an unremarkable corridor by Kepstadur standards. Vaulted ceilings, marble columns, and stone — all covered in a decade of dirt and grime. The carpet was stained black as pitch in the strangled dusk. But the three were alone. Supposedly. Sonja offered a pinch of her blood from the stains to identify the hall, flinching away from the same blinding mist beyond the stone.

"Something is there?" Niccolo called, though it was unclear who he was asking.

She pursed her lips, wishing she could say "no," but this wasn't something he could fight.

Leif took a deep breath and blinked a few times before shaking his head. He stole a suspicious look at Sonja. "Nothing is wrong. We'll use this stair." Behind them, Leif pushed through a thick drape that wept dust over his arm and into his hair. The boy didn't seem to notice. He entered the gaping hole in the stone.

Sonja stalled, curiosity pulling her to understand his fear.

"Is where you fall," Niccolo cautioned. "There are doors on that wall — farther than where we see. This is where you both are unwell."

She frowned and relented. "Multiple doors? Were the they opened or closed? Could you see inside?"

"Two together." He aligned the edge of each hand. "I did not open, only follow Leif when he runs."

Sonja turned to the dead end and stepped into the shadows. It was unwise to go back so immediately. If walking past it had caused such an onslaught of visions, she couldn't imagine what might happen to whoever touched the damn thing. Unfortunately, with the bizarre magical signature, she expected to be the one who would find out.

A stair spiraled down in a tight circle, with walls enclosing both sides. The boy pushed through a door, leading to a colonnade lined with the backs of familiar curtains. They were in the dining hall, skirting along the outside where messy functions were hidden from guests. Leif wore a scrunched frown. "It's important I get back soon. Cook doesn't like it when I'm late for dinner." He nodded formally into a dark room, then flapped into the primary space. "You'll eat with me, yes? Cook always makes more than enough."

"Cook" didn't seem to make much of anything as they passed the silent kitchen. What *was* the boy eating? Sonja imagined him chasing those little fiery beetles, catching them up, and…she didn't like that thought. Niccolo took up the reply, keeping their charge distracted with questions about food and drink.

Upon exiting the dining room, Sonja's stomach dropped. Leif set his shoulders to point between the twin stairs, directed toward both of their safe havens. Two rooms littered with supplies as proof of their sneaking about. She prayed for a secret tunnel under the thrones, but that hope felt pointless. "Do we distract him?" she hissed to Niccolo. "Keep him away from our things?"

"No, no," Niccolo said, "this is important. He shows us this place of importance. We let him, yes."

The prince came to a stop beside the study, hesitating for a long moment before kicking the fallen tapestry out of his way. "It doesn't open, unless she gave you another key."

Sonja was ready with a response. "It's about knowing how." She swept a hand across the wood, casting a hallucination of three glowing runes. They were overly complicated, unlikely to spell anything, but the simple glyph for "open" wouldn't have appeared impressive.

Eyes wide and sharp, Leif's breaths stilled, waiting as if he didn't believe the magic would make a difference. Sonja verified that her little rope had stayed in place before forcing the door open. It dropped out of sight. Most of her travel items were still drying fireside. It would be too expensive to keep up even a low-grade hallucination.

But Leif didn't seem to care. He gawked at the walls, spinning in all directions with tears in his eyes. He touched every tapestry, ran his fingers across the smooth wood, leaned on the desk. It was a compelling reaction, but she forced away the instinctual empathy.

Sonja perched against a bookshelf and narrowed her eyes on the boy, mentally listing all that she knew. First, a mage wandered these halls, definitely an illusionist considering the multiplied corpses and the extravagant party hallucination. These events might not be related, though she believed they were. The hiding man flashed in her memory, the one only Niccolo had seen, waiting behind thin invisibility for them to escape the dungeon.

Second, the revenants had been dead. They'd sat in the water until silently summoned. That was at least in part a hopeful sign for Ulrik. While an army of bodies was notably not good, *something* brought them back. She still didn't understand what magic kept energies attached to those husks, nor why they attacked, but something had resurrected them. It was possible. The knowledge hid in these walls.

Unfortunately, that led back to Leif. He was not himself a manifestation, but that meant very little. Perhaps an illusionist would hide behind this frail image. She frowned at the boy pouring ink across his open hand. Could he seem more harmless? If this skinny squatter wanted them dead, he should have done it while she'd been unconscious in the infirmary. Choosing not to attack didn't tell Sonja anything about his intentions. Bringing him here might have been foolhardy. It exposed half of their supplies and gave away a safe location.

But this act was convincing.

Niccolo had fully melted into belief, even if Sonja hadn't. He watched with a painful compassion as the boy picked gingerly through drawers and studied seals. That said, Niccolo was his own issue. Some kind of mercenary or soldier, she still didn't know. And why was he here? He couldn't read the books. He hadn't gathered many trinkets. Was he really looking for a vault, or had he known they'd find this child? No. No, Leif was unexpected. Niccolo had seemed so surprised. Even now, as he stood and watched, his hand rested on the pommel of his sword. Maybe she'd misjudged. This wasn't a passive observation. Leif was unpredictable, and Sonja appreciated the wariness in Niccolo's eye.

Leif had abandoned his mutterings, neither talking to the real people nor to his imaginary staff. Something about his posture...the mad prince showed a deep reverence for these dusty artifacts.

She wanted to believe. What happened? When had he arrived? Where had he traveled from? Was he a Kepstan? Had they really left? She wouldn't put too much stock in it yet. If she were an illusionist trying to trick explorers, what better idea than to pretend to be some kind of remnant of the past? Something that leaned into the rumors of immortality. Something to give people like her hope. She couldn't trust anything here, and she knew it. But Sonja wanted to believe.

Especially as Leif knelt to the edge of the rug and started to pull.

14

SHIFTING TUNNELS

Without needing to confirm, Sonja and Niccolo stirred to action, shifting the sturdy wood furniture, then rolling the heavy wool rug to rest against the desk. A second covering lay beneath but jumbled easily out of their way.

And there it was. A trapdoor, the handle and padlock both inset to lie level with the surrounding floor. If ever there was a place to keep a vault, why not the secret door in the hidden room? She'd searched the entire time Niccolo had been recovering and never suspected a thing. Sonja's mind buzzed with possibilities of what they might find. She dropped to one knee, guiding the irons together. The key slid in effortlessly and clicked at the first full turn. She wrangled the padlock away, then moved for Niccolo to haul the door open. He heaved once, the hinges groaned, and a gust of warmth flushed the room. Chains on either side stopped it from crashing into the cabinetry behind.

Rather than a small cellar or vault, Sonja peered down a long row of dim steps. Heat lapped at her eyes, along with a smattering of bugs scattered across the tar-coated underside. Several flitted up and around the study — the same little fiery beetles that infested every corner of this place.

That rolling heat was familiar; realization and disappointment settled over Sonja. "It's tunnels for the vents. Goes to the hot spring or whatever runs the chimneys." No sensible person would keep vaults in so much heat. Most valuable metals melted easily. The ronad was especially sensitive. Beyond money, Kepstadur's relic would despise the heat. Or would it? What specifically did magic hate about fire? Sonja didn't know, but she had her doubts.

"We can go look." Niccolo seemed stiff as he rushed to remove his cloak and roll the sleeves of his tunic.

Leif hesitated. "Down is very bad."

"You cannot see your own castle, yet you wish to travel the world?" Niccolo's voice was sharper than she was used to. "There are many bad things. Is best to start to conquer here. Is important to see."

Sonja frowned. Why bring the boy? Was it part of the lie?

She didn't have time to reply before Niccolo guided Leif down the stairs. "Is your first great adventure, yes? Come now, it will be good." She tried but couldn't catch Niccolo's attention. "You know of these tunnels before, Highness?"

He did not wait. With a start, Sonja threw a few supplies into her bag, shoved a damp sock into the interior door jamb, and scrambled after them. She imagined flaming corpses, unbidden in her mind. The perfect antithesis to the waterlogged revenants in the dungeons. Dozens standing in their eerie lines and boiling the air. Would they be immune to fire? Resistant to anything, save that mysterious Reaper blade? She shuddered the thought away.

At the bottom of the stairs, the stone tunnel sloped at a noticeable rate. In place of torches, sconces held mirrored orbs that reflected a smooth light, barely bright enough to see by. Clusters of beetles formed their own little lanterns, adding to the air's ambient charge. Paths diverged in every direction, even one that turned back alongside the stairs. Niccolo was nowhere in sight, but Leif's words guided her around a few short corners. "Well, I'm making my own decisions now, Elvy," he said to no one, voice still shaky. "They could have told me if they were going to be gone so long. Do what you want, but I need to know what is here."

He loped after the mercenary's purposeful gait, arms outstretched to touch both walls flanking him. The blue-shelled bugs scuttled away from his fingertips. They were bigger here, upsettingly so. Along one corridor, a flash of orange the size of an alley cat skittered out of sight. Sonja hurried to catch up.

"You seem pretty sure about this," she muttered, a pit of anxiety growing in her stomach. This was not the first time that Niccolo had pressed for them to venture into the castle depths. Possibly a coincidence, yes, but there was something starkly impassive in his eyes. "And the kid?" The words barely floated over their heavy footsteps.

"This is good. Is a place to hide secrets." He still didn't glance her way, not fully, instead twitching around to study each intersection they passed. "We will find this."

Sonja considered her response, but Leif spoke first. "Not the next one?" The tone was trapped between a question and a statement. Before she could ask for clarity, Niccolo turned the corner and came up short. A large metal panel hung down along deep grooves in the stone, blocking off the hall, all but a few fingerspans at the floor line. It couldn't be solid iron, yet the texture was right. She'd never seen such a massive panel.

Leif huffed and crossed his arms. "Were you not listening? She told you this way was closed."

Niccolo hovered a hand next to the metal. "Who told?"

"Elvy." Leif bubbled with irritation. He gestured up to his imaginary companion.

"Ah, yes." Niccolo followed his eyes. "Elvy's accent, it is difficult to understand." He fixed Sonja with an uncertain expression, though she gave little more than a shrug in return. "If Elvy sees, please tell me so, Highness."

Leif nodded, but Niccolo had already thundered deeper into the maze. The air grew warmer, stale and arid. Continuing down, they passed several smaller burrows. Some bored into the ceiling, around the size of Sonja's fist, while others twisted into the walls and floors. Joints seemed especially hollow, as if the mortar was too soft. More frequently, they were deterred by metal, needing to backtrack along the shallow incline to a clear path. Deep trenches marred the walls, acting as tracks for these panels, stored overhead when open. "Elvy" gave more information of what would be ahead, despite the way Leif dragged behind. This seemed to only spur Niccolo on.

After half an hour, the heat was unbearable. Sonja was sure they'd been walking in circles, but Niccolo hadn't slowed his pace. He must expect one great coffer in the very middle. She kept her mind occupied with ideas of what they might find. A mineral hot spring with magical properties still sounded lovely. They could bring Ulrik up and pour a vial into his mouth. He'd glow, then rise off the ground and sputter awake, where he'd insult them before pulling his sisters and wife and son into a hug.

Better yet, it could be a strong fjarfest, invested with the hopes of an entire line of royals. Maybe a tall staff, a golden scepter with a glowing emerald crowning the top. Thonra would pierce the soft dirt, and all the alternators at the vineyard would come together. They'd pick the nine best to hold hands and will the magic forward. Ulrik would appear as he'd been. Healthy and weeping happy tears.

The last concern was the firebugs, as Sonja decided to call them. These tunnels resonated with their clicking, and some of the larger beasts had taken to following them. Sonja stalled to watch the rear, occasionally turning to clap away any that got too close. The smaller ones were just as annoying. She was constantly batting them off Leif's arms or dodging those that Niccolo shook away. But the deeper they went, the larger the firebugs grew. From what she could tell, they were the same creature across all sizes. Likely magically attuned, with abnormal growth variation, but something was truly upsetting about the texture and tones along the carapace. If a breed of jackalope were found to be significantly smaller than other nearby species, it was cute. But big beetles? Pointedly not cute. And the bigger ones were becoming more common.

The breath before she voiced her concerns, Leif said something Sonja didn't catch, but his panicked tone dissipated her words. "Hide where?" he continued, sweeping more firebugs off his arm. Another heartbeat passed before Leif vanished.

Illusionist. Leif was an illusionist.

But that was the least of her concerns.

Sonja turned at the sound of skittering claws, her hands reaching instinctively for her bloshuls. A giant, glinting shell barreled down the hall. A firebug larger than any of the others she'd seen. Shoulder-height as it reared back to expose a broiling underbelly, flickering orange, feather-like armor. Each leg was its own saw, with teeth marching along the backside and angry talons at the tip. Sonja dodged out of the way as it crashed down, flaring sharp legs like whips. As it raised up a second and third time, Sonja timed her strike. With boar's blood pouring out, she lunged forward and batted at its core to disrupt its energy. Heat seared her fingers, and pain clawed up her arm, but the monstrous thing flinched and shuddered. Niccolo shoved it to the side with the flat of his sword, keeping it from collapsing on her. The monster was nearly half as wide as the hall itself. Its back rocked against the wall and kept it from tipping.

A harsh burning smell overwhelmed Sonja, but her thoughts were dull and slow. She processed nothing more than the sensation of clutching her searing arm to her chest.

Bright red wings flared as forelegs clambered into place. Niccolo scrambled to keep his footing. The metal bounced uselessly from the hard shell. He spun away and grabbed a space in the air, latching around an invisible post. Lief yelped in alarm, flickering back into view, and they sprinted away. "Sonja, come on!" he called, jarring her into her body. The giant firebug was recovering. Bloshul still dripping, Sonja kicked the creature's closest leg and manipulated its weight. Down, down, down. The bug screeched and pivoted, now magically too heavy to move. Then she dashed to catch up.

Niccolo hurried her in front and kept pushing. "Is dead?"

Sonja struggled to run and speak and fight pain that rolled in like waves of sickness. "Use the other blade," she finally coughed.

Niccolo grunted, but didn't reach for his sickle. "Find the metal walls," he said. "Any of them. We hide in quiet, and they will pass."

"Go right," Leif called. Sonja followed out of instinct and ran a ways longer before he repeated the command, and she turned again. The hall grew warmer with every step. At the next crossroads, Niccolo pulled her back, tucking into a niche next to another gate. If she'd been sweating before, she now melted. Looking back, Niccolo guarded Leif from a wall of radiant metal, the younger man desperately wheezing. Amid the racing, incomprehensible thoughts and the pulsing under her skin, Sonja squared her shoulders in the corridor's mouth, waiting and listening. In the breaths of anticipation, she grounded herself and examined the hand. This was happening too often, facing consequences when disrupting the energies. First the bear with its stubborn threads, now these bugs with underbellies too hot to touch. That defense was second nature. This was punishment for her flippancy. The gloves had protected her outer fingers, but the tallest two and thumb stung. Red ribbons already wrapping the exposed flesh and pulsed with her heartbeat. She blinked away tears. Could be worse…

Claws clattered across stone, and all three held their breath. Sonja rested her off hand on the next bloshul, tense until the two firebugs buzzed by. A cluster of smaller creatures fluttered in their wake. Neither of the boar-sized bugs seemed to register them. Another few minutes passed, and the largest limped by in the opposite direction, again, not reacting to their huddle.

"Cannot see through the heat," Niccolo whispered after the scratching had faded.

Sonja gawked openly at this declaration. He knew about these things? She hadn't believed him to be stupid, but where the hells had he learned about giant, glowing, heat-vision beetles? "We should regroup," she whispered. "I don't have the resources to repeatedly deal with something that big."

He waved a hand, peering out at the smaller lantern beetles climbing the walls. "We avoid big. Do not worry. We are very close."

"Close to what?" Sonja snapped.

"To answers. Highness, you want answers, yes?"

Leif looked terrible. Exhausted and shaky as he picked at pests from his clothes. "Mother wants me to be ready when they come back." That didn't quite answer the question. He stepped on a firebug's shell, tiny compared to what they had just seen. It held firm, more akin to stepping on a rock.

Sonja ran through solutions. She could go back. There was nothing stopping her. Even as Niccolo marked the wall with arrows pointing toward the exit and escorted Leif around the next turn, she didn't have to stay. The soldier was slipping. She couldn't quite identify it, but he was different here.

Did she care? She could make it back to the study. It would be easier to avoid the firebugs alone. But would he tell her what he found? She thought back to the twenty-seven ronad that he'd given her, unprompted. Would he maintain the same generosity if something lifesaving waited in this vault?

Could she blame him if he didn't?

Thonra's voice raved in her mind, but the words jumbled together. Uncertain panic rippled under her skin as he left. Another moment of hesitation, and Sonja chased after them.

Niccolo waited at an intersection, waving them to stay back. Smaller beetles riddled his chest, upwards of a dozen. In the hall beyond, a few mid-sized creatures wandered by, antennae flared. Once they were out of sight, he shook his collar, spitting at them as they flailed. Several opened reddish wings, but most pattered like hail. The soldier continued doggedly on.

Leif panted behind him. Hair plastered down his face, knees trembling between steps, his expression that of someone about to vomit. Digging out her canteen, Sonja handed over the remainder of her water, then followed Niccolo's marks along the wall.

"Are these what your parents warned you about?" she asked softly. "These bugs could be big enough to hurt you."

He showed great restraint not to gulp down the canteen's contents. "They didn't tell me why. Just not to go."

Sonja collided into Niccolo's back as he suddenly drew up short. She peered around, finding locked grates seeping with motes of light. A steady breeze whipped loose hairs back from her eyes.

Niccolo staggered forward, barely stopping himself from clutching the metal bars. "Hello?" he bellowed. A flurry of wings erupted in the chamber — a constant noise that Sonja hadn't fully registered. Niccolo waved over his shoulder. "Leif, please. You have seen it, yes? You can call it?"

When the mad prince hesitated, Sonja stepped up. Inside were more firebugs than she cared to believe existed. Several landed on the bars, too large to get through, while smaller individuals settled along Niccolo's shirt. The room itself dropped off starkly, with jagged stones scattered to mimic a cave, though the shape seemed geometric. Along the high perimeter, more doors peered into the maw, guarding from familiar tunnels. The flooring had a metallic sheen, though damaged. It was bright, but unnaturally so. A green light somewhere beyond their view flickered like flames, outshining the hive's orange. Shadows cast inside were too sharp — long and dark lines radiating from a single point barely out of view.

Niccolo stepped back into the hall, kicking an approaching head-sized firebug with a dense thud. She flinched away. The outburst was sudden and understated, but the beetle lay stunned for several long moments.

Sonja skirted behind him as he traced close to the cavern perimeter. An iron panel blocked the next tunnel, leaving a few handspans at the bottom. He tried to lift with the top of his boot but jerked away instantly and prowled on. The third grate was once again accessible. Beside her, he craned to see the floor. Sonja gawked along with him, absorbing all the details. The difference in stone texture, scratches along metal walls, patterns in how the lantern beetles clumped together, the unnatural fire. If he was going to be so difficult to work with, she'd figure it out on—

"Hello?" Niccolo's second call, while weaker than the first, still startled her. "Hello…"

"Who are you yelling for?" Sonja hissed. "You're going to attract more beetles."

"I…" His eyes flicked between the cave and a silent Leif several times before settling on her. Reflecting green with the vibrant firelight, Niccolo's gaze felt empty, as if all that determination had sweat out of him, wicked off. "Is not here. Only bones of greatness."

She moved him away, finally glimpsing the light source. A massive flame burned in a collection of smooth, glittering rocks. Maybe burned into shape? "What is it?"

But Niccolo was already gone, walking back the way they'd been, with Leif magnetized at his side.

"No." The word slipped from her lips unbidden, only to be followed by more. "Absolutely not. What the hells is going on down here? You're going to answer me, dammit!" She chased after them, latching to Niccolo's arm. "What is that thing?"

"Just…" He sighed. "I will explain, but…"

Leif stooped, proffering a rock, though Niccolo didn't seem to notice. Sonja glanced over — not a rock. One of the firebugs, but its underbelly light had faded almost completely. Before Sonja could lash back at the Attiettan, a distinct tapping caught her attention. Heavy. Carapace on stone. "Run," she hissed, pushing them forward. "Get us out of here."

Turn after turn, they looked for a nook to hide in — any of the dozens of iron blockades obstructing their path. But they hadn't followed the arrows. They found nothing. Their footsteps only drew more attention. Firebugs took note from all sides. Smaller creatures scuttled away while larger ones hesitated, drawn tentatively closer, as if the trio seemed more vulnerable now.

With a sudden curse, Niccolo tumbled to the ground, tripping over a beetle as tall as his knees. In the chaos and the closeness, Leif and Sonja flailed alongside him. The firebug screeched, flailing on its back. Sonja detangled herself and kicked it away. More large beasts closed from several directions. Some seemed manageable, but a few were absurdly large.

Niccolo was slow to react, grabbing a smaller beetle and chucking it down the hall. Its wings flared open to right itself before crashing into a larger firebug, one hip-height and missing a leg. There were few clear halls left, but Niccolo wasn't getting up. He batted at another with his sword flat, a cymbal of metal and shell. Sonja found her pouch of pebbles — not pebbles. It was the ronad from the boars. With a curse, she loosened one bloshul and scattered a handful, amplifying their weight as they flew. In a way, paying money for magic. Who could've predicted it...

Leif stood over Niccolo, tugging at his shoulder as the mercenary slowly got to his feet. She launched a second handful of coins down a different hall, looking back in time to see a large beetle rear up. It crashed down, pinning Niccolo's leg. His shout bounded off every surface of the small space. Sonja swatted at the closest bug before rushing in. Leif threw her canteen, the little water remaining splashing over the beast's shell. She pushed Leif behind her, snatching the Reaper blade off Niccolo's back.

Lief pulled on her shirt and pointed. The beetle in front of them hissed and scuttled several steps away, bashing into the walls. "The water," he said timidly. Were these creatures actually made of fire? Sonja racked her mind for anything like this.

The broken-legged beetle closed in.

Maybe they could extinguish the heat underneath. But she had no more water. She had blood.

Talons flared overhead. Crawling along the ceiling.

With a manipulation to lighten its weight, she shoved one back to tumble, thrashing and disoriented, down the hallway. Sonja followed a step and slapped across another's back. She manipulated the shell to freeze. Colder and colder, calling all the spite of Winter's Witch and pouring it into the spell. Sonja surged with a yell, prying open another bloshul, but it was too dry for ice to form and melt.

If blood wouldn't work, a fjarfest would. She tore the leather wrapping free and brandished the Reaper, spinning in all directions.

A moment of stillness passed in the hall. That breath was eerily silent, with a tension that stood the hair up along her neck. In an avalanche, everything moved at once. Smaller firebugs spread gory red wings and flew like arrows toward her. Those nearby clawed upwards, hot coals along her clothes. The larger beasts scraped across the stone with a new frenzy yet unmatched.

Sonja had made a terrible mistake. Her grip loosened, not even sure which direction to look.

That's when the first drop fell, and the hissing began. The soft stone turned a stormy grey. Slow rain fell from the ceiling, water mixed with the grit of sand. Manifestation sand. She looked to Leif and found his face strained. Bloshul still dripping, Sonja joined him, spending a great deal to manifest water. She focused on the ash left by the magic, convincing it to become wet again and again as it tried to fade from their existence. It was a little cheaper that way.

Firebugs fled; any too slow or too close seared and smoked. There was a putrid smell to their death. Not the woody smoke of a healthy fire. It was sour bog fumes, excreted as so many embers faded.

Niccolo — miraculously released from his stupor — stood in front of her, his hands holding her at each elbow. Sonja looked back to Leif. "That was incredible. Such a powerful spell…" she whispered.

The boy wasn't there. Yes, his body stood behind her, but deadman's gaze had turned his eyes to glass. She dropped everything, stumbling to her knees to catch him.

—  —

15

LITTLE LEFT

Gods, he looked like Ulrik.

No, he didn't. Her brother had midnight hair and a thin beard that still hadn't fully grown in. Leif was nothing like Ulrik. Except he wasn't breathing. Her heart stuttered, and tears pricked her eyes. Part of her was aware of the blood pooling at her legs. She paid the price and reached for his life threads. The mad prince was still there. His soul was still bright.

Niccolo stepped in front of her, scooping up the boy. "I get us out. I get us out."

And he did.

In her dazed state, no more than a heartbeat passed before they were in the study, slamming the trapdoor behind them. Niccolo was talking to her — at her, rather, since she didn't care. The colorful study faded as Sonja paid for an identification spell. Ulrik had survived several nights where his energy would hover loosely in his chest. This was nothing of the sort. Leif's threads pulled taut along his spine. Eddies of mist rolled around him. Mist, like the rest of this godsforsaken place. She moved her cheeks over his mouth, where the softest breath brushed her tears. Releasing her grip on the spirit, Sonja watched it settle firm.

"He wasn't…" she whispered. "I know he wasn't breathing."

A metal plate ground shut somewhere in the vents, struggling after years left open. "And he now is?"

Sonja sat back on her heels. Niccolo's hand fell lightly on her shoulder, but she jerked away. Thonra would feel rage. Thonra would demand to know everything. Thonra would be right to tear into him. But Sonja was empty; the resurfacing ache of Ulrik's loss twisted in her throat. She rested her head on the arm of the bench and breathed, squeezing the burned hand to her chest. "I need you to explain yourself," she said. "I don't want apologies or half-truths. Explain. All of it."

The room was silent for a moment. Quiet as the dead, but she could feel his eyes boring into her back. After several long moments, Niccolo shuffled. Sonja turned to find him sitting cross-legged on the ground. The sickle lay bare in his lap. He examined it like an antique rather than an active and magical weapon. He waited. Leif's breathing steadily grew stronger. One of the small firebugs fluttered from the bookshelf, followed by two from the vent, all flocking to land on the sickle. Another, then another.

"I start with the easiest. These have a long name in Danqong, but I learn to call them matoa bugs." He ran a careful palm across the surface, sweeping most of the pests together. With the other, he retrieved the bucket of water Sonja had used to wring out her clothes. He dunked the bugs in, frowning at the carcasses as they sizzled and sunk. "That is new to me. If I know the water to kill them, I can be, eh, prepared." Niccolo pulled one out and examined its fuming shell.

"These work together with dreki; they eat a moss that grows in the scales. And when there is no moss, these eat old scales to make room for new. After a dreki dies, these eat what remains. Remains like teeth and claws."

Sonja observed the curvature of his sickle again, noting its awkward connection to the handle. "And this is a dreki weapon," she said.

He nodded. "Danqong does many tests to find what is most powerful. They send the best skilled soldiers with these and similar." She pursed her lips, waiting for him to continue. Eventually, he did. "Sailors of Attietto believe a dreki guard this city. Some believe the city falls because of this monster, and it eats them all at night, and no one is left. Armies come, and it eats again."

"You came to Kepstadur looking for a wyrm? A dragon?" Irritation seeped through in her tone. "Were there any firsthand accounts? Anyone who saw it circling the city?"

"Is a secret dreki that lives in the tunnels under."

"And you wanted to find it to, what? Kill it? Make more weapons?"

"No," he snapped, before forcibly settling his tone. "I speak to it."

Sonja's immediate response clogged behind her teeth. He wasn't serious. He was smarter than that. She studied his face in the ambient shadows, finding him unreadable. "Speak to it? Like talking?"

"Yes. Talking."

"Dreki don't speak."

"Danqong says these do. There are many stories of speaking."

Sonja frowned, tending to Leif as his breathing became wheezy. "Myths. Maybe some religious teachings. Dreki do not speak."

"And you have seen one to not talk to it?" He crossed his arms. "You know they cannot? Or is this that they do not speak to you?"

Sonja gave him a blank stare, too tired to even scowl. Dreki were real, if uncommon. Yes, their bodies made for fantastic relic bases, but that lore was so easy to exaggerate. They were animals. All of her tutors agreed — simply animals with access to energetic magic. She brushed hair from Leif's face, then glanced back to study Niccolo's firm expression. "What did you want to talk to it about?"

Niccolo hesitated. "When I leave Attietto, is with many people. A city is on fire, and very few arrive to your country. Not as fast or as quiet or as lucky. It takes four months to reach your border. If you do not know where is Ziania is—"

"I do," Sonja said. "I...knew someone who made that trip often. That would be slow travel."

"We could not find ships to accept Attiettans. Suinterna spoke alliances with my home, agreeing to help capture *disitorre*."

"You must know really great secrets to have two whole nations hunting you."

Niccolo huffed, his taut smile looking more like a sneer. "Is in place before we leave. We are not so important as to create panic in the army. Instead, my name is known for the misfortune of friendship. He and I are from the same place, recruited on the same day. I am considered traitor, yet he holds torches against those we swear to protect."

"We were told a much different story about Ziania," she said.

Niccolo pushed his hair back and shrugged. "Not surprising. Is a bad look for the soldiers."

"But wait...you're saying the friend you enrolled with, he just accepted burning his home to the sod?" He looked confused, so Sonja clarified. "You told Lief you were born in Ziania."

"Ah. Yes. This is a lie to make the story more..." He waved a hand dramatically. "Most is true, but details are, eh, not important. Is burned by Attiettan soldiers while some soldiers refuse and die. We are lucky and escape, even with Castillo's chase. And is the last time I stand on Attiettan soil. We cannot go home. So, we do not. We travel, and I am separated from the other survivors. I come here to talk to this dreki. If it sees my good intention, it will grant a wish for reunion."

There was no response that didn't dash his dreams against the stone. Dreki don't talk or grant wishes or protect castles or read hearts. These were children's tales at best. Legends from foreign mystics. But how could Sonja tell him that? She said nothing, instead holding her uninjured hand toward him. He passed her the Reaper sickle and laced his fingers. She examined the runes again, wondering how many innate abilities this blade had started out with, even before the intricate line of glyphs.

"So, you will tell me now?"

Sonja looked up. "Well, some runes are older. I can try, but…"

"Not these letters. What is your reason? Why are you here?"

"I'm here for the payout." She clicked her jaw shut.

Niccolo attempted a smile. "I identify mercenaries. I smell greed. You do not have the…er…the committed for money. Not to kill."

She summoned the will to disagree, but the spark never caught. Sonja simply remained quiet, accepting it was just as damning.

He scooted closer, only a few handspans between their knees. "You would like many of my friends. We are a strange group. Some soldiers, a priest, a botanist, a merchant. It is much like the beginning of a joke." Niccolo met her eye. "Is a very long time since I see them. We separated slowly: one, then the next. Life is many partings since my draft. Some too quickly to say goodbye. We protect who we can," his voice cracked, and he failed to laugh it off, "and remember who we cannot."

Sonja's eyes unfocused for a bit. She had no response for such a raw and honest admission.

He started to say something but seemed to change his mind at the last moment. "When fleeing my lands, I learn to study people. Sense deceiving before more betraying. When I read you…er, you are…" he stumbled over his words before taking a breath and starting again. "If you seek money, it is not for your own benefit. I do not believe otherwise. I am uncommon to be wrong." Quiet confidence bolstered his statement, resonating off the soft words.

She broke his gaze first. "This place has lots of rumors. Some about dreki in the basement. Some are about immortal royalty. This family who couldn't die...Until they did."

Niccolo gestured at Leif. "You look for him?"

"I don't know what to think about him," she muttered. "It's not impossible that he's something important, but I can't believe that immediately. In the current circumstances, Leif poses more questions than answers. He's a liability."

Niccolo grunted. "He is unwell, but he believes this to be his home. This place of painful memories. Is something for him. I have a good instinct. You seem to agree, crying for his loss."

Sonja pursed her lips.

"I can ask you something?"

She resisted the urge to respond harshly. "It depends."

"Is a silly question." Niccolo seemed to labor over his words. "Many people say... Eh, well, they may not mean... Is not that I do not believe them, or even that I do, but this is nice if it works out..." He muttered something in Attiettan, then took a breath. "The boy. Can he be answers for both?"

"I don't understand."

"He is your immortality, and he is my dreki. These are the same."

"You want to know if Leif...is a sky serpent?" Sonja couldn't keep the incredulity from her tone.

"Half sky serpent," he clarified. "All Danqong rulers are children of dreki. Why not is true here too?"

Sonja scanned his face. "You're not serious. This is a joke question?"

He didn't answer, his posture sagging. He secured the Reaper behind his back again and cleared his throat. "Your hand? You are hurt?" Niccolo said before she could apologize. "I have salves to help this, but is with my supplies." He seemed emptier than he'd been before, as if comprehending every non-answer she'd given him.

The remnants of her defensiveness puffed steadily away. "He doesn't remind me much of my brother," she whispered. "Only rarely. But looking at him like this, they are similar in size those final days."

"Final days," Niccolo repeated, prodding at a bleeding line scraped at her wrist.

"He was sick, and no one could stop it." She let out a mirthless laugh, slowly tearing at the carpet fibers. "I'm here to rob a corpse of immortality, and you want to ask a monster for a map."

His lips curled to a despondent smile. "I need more than a map. My friends are with your brother. I am the last of us. It is a large wish."

Sonja's shoulders took on a great weight. "All of them?"

"Two in a bar fight. One freezes to death. The last, Adelma, the army captured her. Executed as a deserter. Is my fault we were traveling so close to the border. To hang is my fate one day."

"You lost your mother?"

He furrowed his brow.

"Niccolo son Adelma. You have a parent named Adelma?"

Understanding flashed in his expression, even a breath of a laugh. "Is a lie. I do not tell true names to skinny boys who speak at ghosts. She teaches me better than this."

"Oh. Obviously." Sonja blushed.

He softened, seeming to notice her tone. "And we were also not cápitan. Both no more than foot soldiers."

Sonja didn't want his pity or excuses or anything. She turned to check on Lief again. Still stable, still recovering. A damn mystery. "Why change that detail?" she asked.

"If we are cápitan, we can stop it from happening." Niccolo's response was so immediate and striking. His voice rumbled around the words. For an instant, he was a version of the Niccolo from the tunnels. Fixated. Callous. But the regret bled through. As if he blamed his own station for what he witnessed. He shook long hair over his face, then pushed it back again. "If I go for my pack, I also have food. You have hunger, yes?"

His sudden shift in topic was jarring, especially as more questions formed in her mind. He couldn't return home or do magic to revive his friends. If there was no dreki, what would he do? Leave? The thought hurt in a way she hadn't expected. Maybe she didn't want an answer. "Should we relocate to the war room?" Sonja asked, reluctantly allowing the conversation to pass.

"The war room is only one door. That is good for some and bad for others. If it finds us, how long is defensible with no exit? How long can we be sieged by the dead?"

"Would we do better here?"

He considered for a moment. "Yes. Most think this door cannot open, so is less likely found. And there are two exits. We have a place to fall back." He pushed to his feet. "Let me retrieve it."

"I'll go with you."

"No, I can. You watch him."

Sonja stood regardless. "If this place is defensible because of its secrecy, you need my invisibility spells." It was late. She was tired and hollow, but she didn't need him getting killed in the night. "I'm no healer. I've done what I can for now."

Niccolo nodded mutely and stepped away, motioning for her to lead. After checking the sleeping prince one final time, she stepped into the secret hallway, pleased to find the rope still pinned in place. They slipped out and wedged it closed as her fifth bloshul bled away. Dodging moonbeams and shadows nearly too dark to see, they scurried through the halls under Sonja's silent invisibility.

Barely three steps into the war room, Niccolo snatched Sonja's wrist as she reached for the bloshul, backing her intently away from one corner of the room. "Did you hide the open door?" he whispered without letting go, eyes trained on the corner behind her.

"Yes." She searched his line of sight. Her gut tied into knots as he reached for his sickle. "Corpses or man?"

"Is the dead, I think," he said.

"Don't kill it. That might alert the illusionist."

"You are sure?"

"No, just a possibility."

He met her eye and lowered his weapon. "So we grab it and run?"

"If there's only one, that's probably what it's watching for. We should focus on the most valuable things from inside."

"Your cloak and the armor?"

"Too visible." She pushed him to the chair. "Grab everything you can. But make it look like you didn't touch a thing."

He loaded her arms first, rustling quickly through packages and bundles. The breastplate was tempting, but it sat centered on the table. After a brief argument, both agreed it was too risky. His mail and leathers, however, seemed fully obscured, making them much safer to retrieve. Sonja couldn't ignore the longing in his eyes as he left the plate behind.

In a flurry, they scavenged as much as they could reasonably take and bolted from the war room, careful of the door and their undead watcher. The bloshul dripped drier by the second, but when Niccolo guided her to the side in the foyer, she followed. He pulled her close to keep her out of the path. Another revenant.

Warmth radiated from her back, and she felt his drumming heartbeat. "Is only one," he breathed. She could see this one, walking from the foyer toward the throne room. It seemed to be a woman with hollowed cheeks and thin, frosty hair. The eyes were the same obsidian scleras from the basement. The dead woman loped closer, but not close enough to touch. Niccolo tensed, one hand still tight on

Sonja's hip. The revenant made the wide loop into the throne room within a few paces of where they stood.

Niccolo moved to leave as soon as the corpse had passed, but Sonja, arms full, pinned him back with a shoulder. "We need to know if it knows." He didn't respond, leaving her in that vibrant silence. To Sonja's relief, the corpse looped up and turned left toward the garden. "A patrol, maybe. It…" She turned her head, met his eye, and froze. He was almost himself again. A soft, open expression, far from the manic determination that had driven him through the tunnels.

And he was very, very close.

Sudden, giddy nervousness bloomed in Sonja's gut, burning red across her cheeks. She stumbled away and muttered an apology. His wide eyes faded to a tired smile, with a small laugh to relieve the tension. "We check for more?" Niccolo whispered.

Another quick minute distanced them from the encounter as they ran a cursory search through the main spaces. They spotted two more corpses patrolling the halls, and Niccolo pointed to invisible sentinels near the dining room, in the entryway, and along the stairs. Locked inside once more, Sonja closed the bloshul, and Niccolo took several precarious items from her hands. She stayed by the door, somewhat expecting the creatures to slam in and shatter their peace.

When nothing happened, Sonja was surprised to find Niccolo fighting back laughter. She nudged him deeper into the study, shutting the second door for more privacy. Every emotion competed for her attention, but laughter had not been near the forefront.

"What's so funny?" she asked, adrenaline still shaking her arms.

"Gods, we should have died." He placed each item carefully onto an empty couch and cupped his face. "Is not funny," he said despite the dull grin. "I feel as a child running through the streets after dark and hoping the adults do not catch."

"That's how you felt breaking curfew as a kid?" Sonja strode over to Leif — exactly where they'd left him and steadily improving — but she cracked. Niccolo's reaction was infectious. "What is wrong with you Attiettans?"

He shook his head, responding first in his native tongue before swapping back. "Is not the same exactly, but in part is like we got away with something. Like we should have trouble but were too smart. I cannot explain. Is just funny, but in a scary way. I do not know what to do but laugh."

"Well, to start, open the damn furnace. Leif is shivering now." She was thankful for the smile she couldn't fully force from her voice. The uncertainty of the last few hours had worn her raw. Laughing seemed far more appealing than crying.

Niccolo did so, then covered Leif with the tapestry he'd used earlier. "But shivering is alive?" Focus settled in as they checked his temperature and organized the haul, passing around dry rations and full canteens. "I am so hungry, this tastes as my maman's cooking." He laughed halfheartedly. "She would hear that and put me to feed the trees without a hymn to sing."

Sonja studied his face. "Are your parents still…?"

"Oh, yes." He waved a hand, shoving the rest of the bar into his mouth, as if stalling his reply. "Is probable, at least. They are still in well health at the draft. How is your burn?" Niccolo reached for her arm, his eyes evasive.

She ate more slowly with her off hand, studying him as he worked. How old were Attiettans when drafted? Was there an age? Ziania burned years ago, yet he spoke as if he'd been gone only a few weeks.

Niccolo pulled the first of her rings away but hesitated with the two on her middle finger. "These are not good. They, er, squeeze for burns. Can get stuck. I do not mean bad by this." He waited for her to remove them.

"It's no problem," she said, transferring the set to uninjured fingers.

"It works best to have them all in a particular place, but the magic doesn't stop because I'm not wearing them."

"These are for magic?"

Sonja nodded. "Somewhat for show — it's a schooling thing — but they have runes on them that help. We call them vela."

He blinked at her a few times, seeming to chew those words over. "Is well," he said finally. "And this?" He pinched softly at the two fingers of her glove. "Also for magic?"

"It is. Our last tutors emphasized hand focuses, especially for stronger spells. With the stitching on the back, they help some, I think." She pulled it over her smallest two fingers, exposing the entire hand, hanging the thick fabric off her wrist. Even Sonja was surprised at how immediately the burn line stopped. Not a sharp edge, but a quick gradient.

Niccolo's hands grazed across her palm, applying small amounts of pressure to the places already trying to blister. It stung, but only mildly. Heat built in her cheeks and pressed against her lungs. She tried not to look at him.

"This is not deep. If we hide infection from this, you recover quickly." He pulled a container of salve — something fresh-smelling, with sharp, coastal notes — then smoothed it across the angry skin. The balm was cool and glossy, leaving behind a slick residue. He secured a bandage loosely, face tightened with concentration. "This will swell, but maybe only a small amount. Try not to bend. If these break," he pointed to a few blisters, "medicine hurts more."

Niccolo looked up, his jaw slackened and lips parted softly. Electric hesitation caught her breath. He wore that same expression from the hall again, the one that melted the furrow between his brows.

Sonja felt nauseous. The hand still holding hers trembled slightly, or maybe she trembled against him. He rested the back of his palm on her thigh, frozen and waiting for her reaction. Gods, was he going to kiss her? It had been years since she'd kissed someone — well, that wasn't true. Those informants along the southern border who wouldn't take her money…but since she'd meant it? That had been a while. Gods, did she still know how? His eyes dropped, then lifted back to hers.

But she hesitated. The memory of panic raced along her spine. Waking alone on the floor. The man he'd become in the tunnels… Or maybe this was the act. Charming, kind, and funny.

What did she know about this foreign soldier with his dramatic lies? Would she become his next captive audience?

Would that be so bad?

Sonja had no time to decide. Niccolo sensed the change in her posture, straightening with a forced smirk. Maybe they hadn't been that close at all. It had been a trick of the light or an effect of breathing in all the little sparks in the tunnels. He placed her bandaged hand gently into her lap and got to his feet. "I can keep primary watch over Leif." His tone was starkly neutral and terribly quiet. "I am sorry, er, as I am the reason you are both hurt."

"I'm sorry," Sonja breathed, without fully calling for the words. She questioned if he'd heard her as he busied himself across the room, but the last step faltered. A different discomfort smothered them.

"You can explain what happened to him?" Niccolo asked, clearing his throat. "Why is he like this?"

"I can guess," she replied. "He manifested that water on the walls. That's the strongest form of perception magic. It would have cost a lot. He didn't have enough payment, so it apparently took from his body."

"But that is to kill him?"

"Not always. It took enough to make him faint, but he's stable."

A heartbeat passed as she peeled away her leather armor. "You mages…" Niccolo finally said. "Always fainting, then?" His tone tried for a levity that Sonja didn't feel. She failed to laugh convincingly or think of a clever defense. After a time, his tone dropped again. "And if he did die? If he is the immortal you look for?"

Sonja's brow tightened. "We'll have to keep him alive to find out." They accepted the uncomfortable silence, keeping hands and minds busy and separate while preparing for bed. "Do me a favor tonight," she said, smothering any bitterness away.

"Yes?"

"If you're planning to rove the halls, at least invite me."

"You have my complete promise."

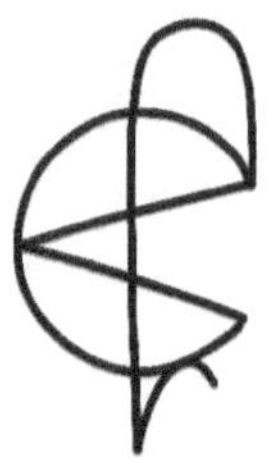

16

EYES UNCOVERED

Morning broke through high, slim windows. Sonja woke feeling almost rested, though she didn't trust it. Sleep had become a cycle. Fight for weeks, count every star, pluck every blade of grass, and stare at the insides of her eyelids, then, miraculously, she'd crash. Bask in a few days sleeping nearly through the night, then go right back to exhausted struggling.

It was the air. She was sure of it. So humid out east, in the lowlands and fields. The weeds smelled like rotten lilacs, and the sheep's damp musk permeated everything. Maybe that's why it was easy to sleep here. Kepstadur itself didn't smell like much, especially considering the dead in the halls. It should smell terrible. It simply didn't.

She rolled onto her back and gazed at the wooden shelves. The study was grandmotherly in the dawn light. Dust coated the books, yellowed and dulled. The fabrics were all crisp. Not foul, but distinct.

As she stretched, Sonja became more aware of the nearby snoring.

It was a miracle that she'd slept through it. Leif had shifted some in the night — a good sign — and this sound that rolled in his chest had a healthy rhythm to it. She ran through the facts again, focusing on one: Leif had been fully unconscious when they'd met those patrols. That was a good thing, yes? It was at least a fact in his favor. He could still be suspicious for a dozen reasons, but he wasn't the same illusionist who'd nearly drowned her.

Niccolo lay on his stomach, his fingers curled lightly over the hilt of his sword. His was the bench nearest the door. Coincidentally, that was also the farthest from her. She dragged her eyes away. On her gentlest steps, Sonja slid through the study door and crept down the hidden hall. As tall as she was, she had a decent view into the foyer. She counted to a couple hundred, but no patrols wandered past.

"There is something in the *white* light?" Niccolo whispered from the study.

"*Haven't caught a parade*. Not unless they're invisible," Sonja said, waving him over to look.

After a moment of searching, he shook his head. "I see nothing."

"Just a patrol at night, then? I'd like to check on our watcher from the war room."

"If I gave ronad to bet, this guard remains." Niccolo led back into the study and rooted around for breakfast. "It is the place we are expected to return."

She hummed an affirmative and placed another container of traveler's stew over the heat vent. They kept their distance, neither commenting on the night before. It was better this way. Gods, she'd kiss anyone these days. She needed to go home.

A choked sob caught Sonja's attention. She spun to find Leif sitting upright and clutching his tapestry blanket. His wide green eyes flitted from corner to corner until tears spilled into the fabric. Niccolo knelt in front of him, trying softly to draw his attention.

"How could you tear it down?" the mad prince whispered. "This is wrong, and it's your fault."

"I am sorry, my friend. We hoped to keep you warm. You have hunger, yes?"

Leif's eyes narrowed, focusing on a proffered travel ration. "Cook will have breakfast for me," Leif said stiffly, but he leaned forward. He waited a few moments before taking it in hesitant fingers.

"You feel better with food." Niccolo smiled and stood, raising subtle eyebrows at Sonja.

"You were amazing in the tunnels," she said, aiming for a soothing tone without being childish. The longer Sonja spent with Leif, the less confident she was about his age. For some time, she'd seen him as a lanky teen lurking in forbidden halls. That felt wrong when cautious fear deepened the lines around his face. It ticked like a pendulum clock. A child fumbling with his understanding, then an adult realizing an enormous oversight. She continued forward. "That was impressive magic. How did you do it?"

"Is this the blessing food?" Leif pressed fingers into the aged cheese, looking past her to Niccolo.

Niccolo hesitated, flashing Sonja an apologetic look. "Perhaps. I do not know this. Is a tradition?"

"Blessing food has extra magic to make me stronger."

Sonja furrowed her brow. "Is that how you manifested that water? With blessing food?"

"No, I can do that all the time," Leif sniffed. "But that felt bad. I need to tell Elvy to pick up my practice again. Have you talked to her this morning? I told her to wait here." His voice wavered, eyes scanning the room again.

Sonja braced and took a chance. "We actually struggle to hear Elvy. She's very quiet, so we need your help to hear her."

He processed, then grunted, nibbling on the cheese. Leif closed his eyes as he chewed. "You must share the secret. Cook doesn't know how to make it right." He gnawed off a much larger portion. His posture sagged, trembling less behind a clenched fist of tapestry.

"Could it be that Attiettan food is more blessed?" Sonja fished.

"Is possible." Niccolo's face told her the food wasn't from his homeland, but he understood the importance of keeping the boy talking. "From where do you get blessed food? There are traders?"

Leif shrugged, stuffing the rest of the cheese into his mouth. "It usually comes to the altars. Arvid brings it back to me so I don't have to leave the castle and hurt my friends. Cook has made copies before, and it's not the same."

"What of this stew?" said a shrill, unfamiliar voice. "When it is complete, we may bring more samples to Cook and request he make another attempt."

Sonja stumbled back against the desk, searching the small room for the source. Niccolo stared at her as if looking for direction, hand resting gently on his sword. He didn't seem to hear the voice.

"That's a great idea," Leif said. "And with our new friends, I'm sure Cook can figure it out this time."

The voice — Sonja locked on to its location near Lief — made a smaller harrumph of ascent. "It's time for our dear Cook to rise to the occasion." It sounded older, feminine, and authoritative. The tone was posh and the accent aristocratic, with hints of a rich, southern Jrendavarian dialect.

"I'm sure we could spare some supplies or knowledge," Sonja replied to the emptiness. "Should we set out a fourth portion?"

"No, kindly. I appreciate the offer, but I've already eaten this morning, vieran."

Sonja flinched at the old Jrendavarian honorific, not only for its outdated usage, but for the choice to use the title for a married woman. "Will you join us for lunch, then?" Sonja offered a bit of her own blood and checked for energy readings. Shimmering mist glowed in a crown above Leif, dim compared to the pale yellow of his woven threads. It spanned in a fluid circlet as wide as he was tall. She turned her head only slightly, glancing back toward what she believed was the throne room, comparing the distant brightness that churned somewhere beyond stone and mortar.

Sonja refocused as the voice spoke again. "This is far from proper, vieran, but I appreciate such consideration." Sonja narrowed her focus to a dense portion of fog. A thicker, silvery glow hovering chest-height beside the couch. "Best if the young sir returns to his schedule."

"I'm tired, Elvy," Leif whined.

"Highness," chided the voice, "shall we discuss after you eat?"

The shimmer faded as Sonja's spell was spent, but the voice remained. Niccolo met her eye, doling out the lukewarm broth. The expression hung somewhere between confusion and anticipation. He was completely in the dark.

"What is on the prince's schedule today, Elvy?" Sonja uncorked a bloshul on the desk, letting it slowly tick away. She touched Niccolo's arm with her thumb and first two fingers. A three-point connection. With a small push, she attuned to his energy, mentally reaching out and grasping it in a sympathetic link.

In the following silence, she worried something had disrupted the voice, but Leif nodded to the emptiness. Elvy replied slowly, suspiciously. "The young sir has more responsibilities than are simple to recount."

Niccolo's eyes snapped to the invisible source, lips parting.

"After breakfast in the Great Hall, he has lessons in the arts, then a morning stroll. The young master must tend to the letters from foreign dignitaries before the performers arrive at midday. Petitioners query him shortly after."

Leif slurped down the meager stew, ignoring irritated ghost noises, and walked purposefully toward the exit.

"And what will you be doing, vieran?" Elvy's voice floated behind the prince as he struggled with the exterior locks.

"Regent's business," Sonja said. "It's proprietary. She wishes to tell you about it herself."

Leif offered a reserved smile. "You'll join me for dinner, then?"

"Of course." Sonja followed him to help with the exit, Niccolo a few paces behind. "But promise you'll be careful, okay? We've seen some concerning…changes across the region. Monsters, the living dead, able to hurt people."

Leif scrutinized her in the ambient lighting. "Living dead? How can you tell?"

She ground the lock free and gestured out into the foyer. "The black eyes," she said.

There was something of a pause as Leif glanced toward the throne room, then Elvy responded. "For once, Counselor, I must agree. These are childish stories. I insist you refrain from filling the young sir's head with frivolities."

Agree? Who was Elvy agreeing with? Sonja decided not to ask.

Leif studied his shoes. "Don't worry about it, Elvy. It's best to heed all warnings."

Niccolo nodded to the importance of vigilance. In a moment of instinct, Sonja set an encouraging hand on Leif's shoulder. Already attuned to one, she felt his energy in waves. With a deep breath, she mentally latched on, the way she used to see her brother's imaginary friends.

Colors erupted across the foyer. Not the crisp golds and marble from the first vision. Rather, the floor glittered with blue and silver stone and inlays. The tall room warped with flowing filigree vines twisting around the caps, and purple murals of exotic animals. Paintings on every wall showed the same three people. The regent, her warlord, and Leif. Not a child, but at his age today. He was fuller in the paintings, still narrow but not so sickly. He stood on his own now, though hunched and staring across the room. At the end of his gaze, the over-saturated light dripped like paint near the bottom. The grey and grimy reality grinned through the playful scene: rotting, jagged teeth in stark contrast.

Beyond Leif loomed a stern, middle-aged woman with slim, foreign features under Jrendavarian hair. She stood head and shoulders above Leif, who was himself tall, but there was something absurd about her proportions. Her long skirt billowed a fingerspan over the ground but started so high that Sonja wondered if this woman had a ribcage or was just a pair of legs. When she moved, the skirt did not kick out with steps to match a soft clicking noise. She stood between Leif and the slow-mending rips in his fantasy, bringing his attention to her.

"We'll start with a visit to Cook," Elvy said from the tall woman's lips. "It's best not to waste time between tasks."

"Arvid, bring the letters, okay? I'd like to multitask." Amid all the changes to the space, Leif spoke to no one. He laughed after a moment. "Just like she would."

Elvy looked first at Niccolo before locking eyes with Sonja. Her face twitched around that pointed gaze. "You are well occupied, then?"

Sonja hesitated, still searching for this "Arvid" character. "We need to be about our business."

Elvy did not spare a courteous smile for them. "I will be around to check on you soon, vieran. It is best if you stay on task."

Sonja felt a rush of dizziness as Elvy escorted Leif toward the Great Hall. The bloshul ran out. Her trained instinct cut the spell, crashing back into reality's sad truth. Thonra would have lectured her for days if she knew. She was growing lax with her magic, not setting conditions every time.

"Is incredible," Niccolo said as he bolted them back in the study.

"At least you saw it too," she muttered.

"You are not happy with the magic?"

"Just frustrated. I did something stupid."

"Because you show me?"

"No." She met his expectant gaze and sighed. "There's a safe way to use magic. You tell the spell to stop if it runs out of a specified source. It's an extra step that I've been neglecting."

"Is why people get hurt?" he asked. "They do not tell the magic to not hurt them?"

"They don't know how, usually. It's not instinctive, communicating with magic. You have to know it's there and train intentionally." She busied herself, organizing and cataloging their remaining supplies. "Could you hear or see Arvid? The one Leif spoke to at the end?"

Niccolo looked up in confusion, squinting as if convinced he'd find a second meaning. "We establish I do not see much, no?"

"You saw the rest of it though?"

"I see Elvy." He gestured a line at his chest — a reference to her skirt. "Some silent servants by the stairs. I see the displays and art."

But nothing of Arvid. Sonja chewed on the thought. The Elvy hallucination seemed tied to an energy. Maybe Arvid needed a mist to be seen? No. The paintings didn't have energies, yet they changed.

"Something is wrong?" he asked.

"That trick has never hidden part of the vision."

He flashed a consoling smile but offered no suggestions. So they worked. Niccolo's food helped replenish the soiled packs from the corpse water. An idea that still turned her stomach.

"What is it?" Niccolo asked suddenly.

"Hm?"

"What is that you speak to? For the magic? Is a god?"

"Oh. No. Not really. Some believe that it's the purview of Neska, but most of my tutors disagreed."

"Neska," he repeated. "This is strange connection. She is warrior maiden, yes?"

Sonja frowned. "Well, not exactly. I mean, she is, but that's not what she's really for."

"She is Taziche, yes? Is for prayer in battle and generals."

"What?"

"Neska." He took the desk chair, eyes gleaming with eagerness. "Neska is the same as Taziche. Your gods, my gods. We have different names for the same. Taziche is god of battlefield plans. Generals pray to Taziche for, eh, inspiring."

"I mean, maybe. I don't know many soldiers, and I've never seen war. We pray to Neska for plans, I guess. Plans for harvest, plans for drought. I've never thought of her that way. She's like the instinct to react. She is experience and learning and gambling."

"Gambling?" Niccolo crossed his arms. "What does this mean?"

"Gambling is this hobby—"

"I know this word. It is not for Taziche."

"You never felt like generals gambled your life in a strategy?"

Niccolo took in a breath to respond, only to pause and let it out. "Had not considered, but I see. Tsalvi would ask the best questions." His heavy tone made her pause.

"Tsalvi was your priest friend?"

He nodded. "They teach many things I did not know. Very fascinated with connected gods."

"And your other friends?"

Niccolo's expression was hard to read. Almost pitying? "You are kind," he whispered, finishing his immediate task before relenting to fill the silence. "Lohn kept very large books of notes about plants. It was his job. Botany. But he wants to write for many languages. Ginevra is of here. Sold warm clothing to Attiettan travelers. Warm clothes and mushrooms." He made a spinning motion by his eyes.

"Very strong. Lohn took many notes on effects. Tsalvi is the most, er, happy of the sad group. Always looking for the best pastry of the world. And Adelma… She was as a sister."

Sonja thought back to his hopes for the dreki and felt guilt for her earlier callousness. She searched fruitlessly for something comforting to say but found nothing. "Well," she cleared her throat, "all the same. Some people think magic comes from her. Some think magic comes from the stars and you pay the night sky. In Danqong, the wind supposedly takes the payment."

"Many things are as monsters in Danqong. Wind is among them." Niccolo leaned onto his forearms. "Which do you believe?"

Sonja smoothed out her empty pack to check for wetness and counted her remaining bloshuls. "Magic feels newer than any of those things. My grandparents struggled with the rules in their day. I don't know what takes it. Maybe a new god."

The words hung in the air for an uncomfortable breath. She swapped packs and organized salves. He tapped slowly on the desk and studied a stack of the regent's papers. "I would be scared to pay for something to one I do not know. Litres of blood at a time. What god wants this?"

What an unsettling comment. She shrugged, feigning indifference. "I'm not sure. But it takes from far more people than me." She cleared her throat before the silence could settle. "We should explore upstairs. We've gone down in every available location and only found horrors."

"Last time we went up, you nearly die from walking."

"That's not true. And now that I know what to expect, I can work around that." He frowned, so she continued. "We'll start on the opposite side. But that much magic is hiding something. We can't ignore it forever."

He wasn't looking at her anymore. Sonja cinched the pack and dragged it upright, feeling guilty. She'd prodded painful memories. His friends, their deaths. What had he thought when she'd collapsed upstairs? He said Leif had been affected too. How would it feel to be the last person standing? Again and again.

"So now what?" she said. "Where else could your dreki be hiding?"

"We found it." His expression hardened somewhat, a crease splitting his brows. "Is below. Is dead. Only the heart blazes."

Sonja struggled with a response. "What does that mean?"

"What do I know? I only tell you what I am told. The heart of dreki burns after death. Burns for hundreds of years. You do not know this? All mages do not study dreki?"

"I've learned about them, yes, but never anything like that."

"What happens to the heart, then?"

"What happens to yours?" she countered. "It decays. Like everything else."

"Then how do you explain the fire below?"

Sonja didn't have an answer. "That fire could be any number of phenomena. Listen, we'll keep looking for your guardian dreki. And if we can't find it, well, I'll help bring them back."

His hands stilled, and he kept his eyes down. "You don't have to..."

"It's what I'm here for anyway," Sonja grumbled. "If the magic exists, I can help a few more good people."

No response. She turned back to her supplies. There were only three bloshuls remaining. It was jarring, the rate she was going through the blood. Niccolo donned the retrieved armor and sheathed both weapons. He offered to carry the pack, but she needed him mobile if they found something unexpected. It was light anyway. Not even worth manipulating the weight. Leaving the study, Sonja wedged her little rope in the doorframe again.

"What you did," Niccolo said, "it was incredible. The colors..."

"It was Leif's vision," she said. "I connected us all sympathetically and — well, don't worry about that. But I think he's hallucinating what the building looks like. As in, with magic."

"Is this magic from the illusionist?"

"It could be, but I don't think so." They shuffled across the foyer, checking more intently for signs of the dead. She had a small theory but no real way to test it. They'd seen Leif's power in the tunnels. What if he was using magic on himself? It felt too ridiculous to say outright, even to a null. "Leif can go anywhere in the castle. Most illusionists would struggle to keep him under such a big spell, as much as he moves around." There was nothing in the ballroom. Nothing in the foyer. Nothing upstairs.

"Is the voice watching him?"

"Elvy?"

"Yes."

That thought unsettled her. "Maybe, but I don't know how. I'm more concerned about Arvid, the one we couldn't see. More than that," Sonja hesitated before lowering her voice, "something is wrong with Leif's spirit. It doesn't seem to be all together. Like oil and water, there's a portion that—"

Niccolo grabbed Sonja's arm and dragged her into the dining hall. They ducked behind a wall as he covered his lips with one finger, his other hand pressing over her shoulder. "We were see-able?" he breathed, inches from her ear.

She nodded, throat dry. They were still visible now, but she didn't say that.

"Person enters from the city," he whispered.

How loud had they been speaking? Had their voices carried? She didn't have enough blood for this. Sonja pushed away, then led behind the kitchen curtain. She checked for an ambush, then rejoined Niccolo as he peered out into the foyer. "Looking at the painting," he said, pointing to an area of emptiness.

"I don't see anyone. Is it a corpse?"

"No."

"Could be our illusionist."

"We can capture?"

"Why would we do that?"

He shrugged. "Answers."

She watched Niccolo's eyes as he tracked across the foyer. He made a sudden motion that Sonja didn't understand. He repeated it, and she got the impression that the stranger was coming into the dining hall. Sonja nodded, and, to her surprise, Niccolo gave a quick smile and glided along the curtain. He waited only a second before padding out into the room. She hadn't even known to stop him.

Sonja angled along the divide, watching him sneak through dusty daylight. In a burst of speed, he ran, wrapping arms around a place of dense nothingness. She tore from behind the curtain and leapt onto the table. He yanked a travel pack away, scattering it out of the spell's radius before straddling the air, using both hands to pin invisible wrists.

An unseen force buffeted Niccolo as Sonja jumped down, bloshul ready. With the intruder held, Sonja could guess at the placement of energy strings and stun them long enough to gain decisive control of the situation.

Niccolo recoiled, turning back with spit on one cheek, but he kept any anger controlled. Sonja knelt beside him. As she tensed to unstop the bloshul, the first sound escaped the void beneath Niccolo. A familiar cloak materialized, trimmed in beautiful maroon stitching. The woman's eyes, like rain clouds, stared past a deep blue scarf. A gift from her husband, but battered and worn.

"Sonni?"

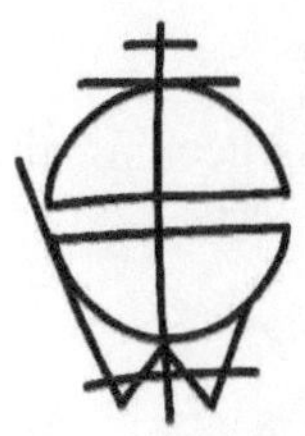

17

THE PILGRIM

Sonja's fingers went numb somewhere along her periphery, dropping without opening the bloshul. She stumbled to push Niccolo off, falling to her knees as Thonra sat up. Gods, she looked so tired. Traitorous tears pricked at Sonja's eyes as she embraced her older sister, rediscovering the faint smell of home on her clothes. It felt unreal. One more step, and they would all be home again. Together.

Niccolo quietly collected the pack and scattered items, set it beside them, and leaned against the table several paces away. Thonra pulled back to search her sister's face, then glanced over with a cold eye to study him. Her impassive expression melted into something crude. "I see you picked up a.... helper. Who's the strapping stallion?"

Sonja flushed, hoping the implication was lost to Niccolo's very specific vocabulary. "Drop it," she replied. "This is Niccolo. Niccolo, this is my sister, Thonra."

"With grace." He nodded a bow. "Is a surprise to see you, yes?"

Thonra made an indistinct noise before Sonja cut in. "This was always the plan, actually. We were always meeting here." She turned back to Thonra. "But I didn't realize you were so close. Did your last lead fall through?"

"I see you haven't been checking the map." Thonra stood and sharply dusted herself off.

Sonja frowned. "Been busy."

"Nonetheless, no. It's the same elk path. Same man mired in his own mythology, but all roads led me here." Thonra examined her sister again before strolling along the table. "What've you found?"

"Kitchen, pantry, and staff quarters behind this curtain. An armory and barracks beyond that. There's a dungeon too, but let's address that later." Sonja stood and pointed across the foyer. "Ballroom and gardens there." She thought better than to mention the study out loud. "In the middle is a throne room and a war room inside. We were about to explore upstairs."

"There will be hallways wrapping above. In the atrium," Niccolo added. "I will like to see them."

Sonja fought the urge to react. If he knew a word like "atrium," he could have easily understood her sister's earlier implication.

Thonra raised another eyebrow. "How do you know?"

"Holes for archery."

"Arrow slits," Sonja clarified. "This place was defensible."

"As much as I loved that sweeping architectural tour," Thonra said, "surely you found something more relevant."

"I'm sorry. Next time, I'll lead with the basement full of bodies," Sonja snapped. "I didn't realize you were on a timeline."

"Slack the press, Sonni. I'm only trying to catch up. What do you mean, bodies?" Thonra glanced out the window before stalking toward the drape that hid the kitchens.

"The dungeon I mentioned. There are dozens of preserved corpses."

"Recent?"

"Probably not."

"Well, let's go, then."

Sonja stopped with heavy bootfalls. "You don't want to do that. It's an army of revenants."

"Even more reason." Her response was piercing in a way it hadn't been before. Yes, Thonra had always been coarse, but this didn't feel the same.

"Not like this." Sonja's throat tightened around the words and burned to her core. "He can't come back like them. It won't be him."

Thonra paused, turning, not to her sister, but to Niccolo. "Stallion knows?" He gave no response, but Thonra didn't need one. "Don't hurt her. You look hard to kill." The tone felt too serious for her smirk.

"She's kidding," Sonja lied. Thonra hadn't killed the last one, but that was before Ulrik... She didn't fully know what her sister was capable of anymore. Sonja herself had changed so much.

"You don't have to worry of me," Niccolo said evenly.

"After that warm welcome, I'd disagree." Thonra rubbed at her side. "Is that how they greet people in Attietto? *With grace*?"

He returned a flat expression, subtly quirking an eyebrow at Sonja. "Your word is 'consistency,' yes?"

She smothered a treacherous smile, remembering Niccolo tackling her in the forest. Unfortunately for Thonra, the stone floor would have hurt far more than dirt.

Thonra moved past the curtain, seeming to check rooms from the sound of her steps.

Niccolo made a face, shifting closer. "Is really your sister?" he whispered.

"She's an acquired taste," Sonja replied, then clarified, "She's always been like this. It got worse after Ulrik."

"Ulrik is your brother?"

Sonja confirmed.

"When?"

She dropped her eyes to the slow-rotting tabletop. Her smallest finger traced the grain. "Almost three years."

"Two years. Five months. Six days." Thonra pushed out of the curtain and back to the foyer, leaving with her typical quick gait.

"She's going to be an ass to you." Sonja lowered her voice further as her sister entered the ballroom. "Her husband traveled with us at the start but went back for the harvest. According to her, this search shouldn't involve anyone else anymore. She'll go back to normal once this is all fixed. One look at Bragi, and they'll make up. They're perfect for each other."

"You are sure?"

"She's only mad because she cares. It's annoying, but it's consistent." Sonja huffed a small laugh. "Consistent is the word."

They followed. Niccolo checked every corner for invisible watchmen; Sonja counted the drips of red dissipating from her sister's back bloshul. She missed her thicker cloak as they stepped out into the gardens but tried to seem unbothered by the cold. Nearby, Niccolo nestled inside the warm fur of his collar. Attietto was far enough south, had he even seen snow before he'd fled? In his defense, the wind was the worst part of Jrendavarian weather. Thonra dropped to a knee and hunched over a portion of the planter, digging with her hands. "So, tell me about the bodies."

Right to business. Typical Thonra.

"There's a whole army of them in the dungeons," Sonja said. "I'd guess they don't breathe and probably don't feel pain. They seemed reliant on this one mage — an illusionist, we think. He tried overwhelming us with duplications. They looked for us last night, which was unsettling. I worry they have some way to report back, be it directly or indirectly. We don't think they know—"

"Only at night?" Thonra looked up, focusing longer on Niccolo. "Nothing during the day?"

He shrugged. "I see nothing but at night."

Thonra dug out a gnarled root ball, eyes narrowed as clumps of damp soil fell through her fingers. She broke off a few thorns along the stems, then kept digging. "What do you know about the mage?"

"Only that he exists," Sonja said. "Someone has been in the city since I first arrived, and Niccolo saw—"

"Did you tell anyone you were coming here?"

Sonja stumbled over her reply. "I'm sure some people might…but I don't think that's—"

"How many people know?" Thonra stilled her hands, jaw set.

So many faces flashed in Sonja's mind. The blood merchant, the gate guards, the entire caravan. "Everyone around here is too scared of this place," she snapped. "And anyone I told would have to sprint to get here first. I wasn't announcing my plans before taking a nap. I came straight here, and something was waiting."

Thonra went back to work, pulling long-dead plants to lay nearby. "An illusionist and a puppeteer." She discarded the original roots, knocking the dirt from her hands, then rummaged through her cloak pockets. "If the mage is still here, he hasn't found the Kepstan relic, and that's what matters the most. Did you happen to see him wearing this?" She proffered a folded page, then went back to digging.

Sonja held the sketch at an angle for Niccolo. It was a drawing of a bracelet with little chains and rings. Vague glyphs marched around each perimeter. The print wasn't Jrendavarian, but the handwritten notes were. They were somewhat familiar, though she couldn't fully place it. "This is the Kepstan relic?"

Thonra shook her head. "No, but I do think it's another powerful fjarfest in play here, possibly one of many. This mage I was following, Valtyr, some call him a pilgrim. I believe he was a collector. Decimating entire villages, stealing sacred treasures, and terrorizing the region. The living dead is a reoccurring element in his stories. He briefly had a cult following with a lot of iconography around hands and burial rituals, so several sources theorize he had something like that." She gestured vaguely. "From my research, he disappeared from record pretty close to Kepstadur's fall, though no one else is talking about this connection. This is the kind of place he would want to go, and the kind of item he would steal."

Sonja chewed on the words, clutching the diagram against the bustling wind. "Hoarding too many artifacts can come with unintended consequences," she murmured to Niccolo. "Implying this Valtyr character tried stealing the Kepstan's relic but set off a magical reaction." She turned to examine her sister. "That *is* what you're suggesting, yes?"

Thonra gave an innocent shrug. The kind she reserved for these breadcrumb situations. She wouldn't just say what she thought. This was a game, leading people to make her conclusions. It gave her a sense of superiority.

Sonja hated it.

"Whether he caused it or not," Thonra gave her sister a significant look, "if he died here, where would that leave his trove of artifacts?"

"Here in the city," Sonja whispered, eyes pulled toward the energies on the second floor. "Waiting for someone to find them."

"Which someone, apparently, has." Thonra stood, dusting any remaining dirt onto her pant legs. "But let's get inside before poor Stal starts growing icicles." She strode toward the throne room, casually examining tall windows spanning between arched columns.

Frustration brewed in Sonja's gut, hot enough that she considered chucking a clod of dirt at the back of Thonra's head. It was unnecessary. Meant to get a rise. Logically, she knew that, but, gods, her sister was a nightmare.

A gentle hand brushed her wrist, and Niccolo's steady smirk rested over her. "Is a shame, she is right," he whispered, "but icicle elbows are great weapon. The mage will never expect this."

"Ignore that kind of thing," Sonja grumbled. "She thinks she's funnier than she is, and she kicks anyone who tells her otherwise."

"I will keep this in mind," he said, bowing Sonja past him. "If I decide to say so, I stand far from her legs."

Sonja almost laughed, moving to catch up to her sister on the throne plinth. It was spattered with gold detailing that Sonja hadn't originally noticed through the grime. Thonra traced a hand along a cluster of delicately cast birds arranged around the throne backs.

"Does the name tul-Habao mean anything to you?" Thonra asked unprompted.

Sonja was disinterested in answering, but Niccolo lit up. "Is a Danqong prophet. Prophet of Sound."

"Prophet of Soul, but that's pretty close, Stallion. I'm impressed." Thonra didn't sound impressed. "I'd never heard of her before finding this through-line. Apparently, she was a real person. A Tahlzhien polymath with a soft spot for alchemy. A few texts call her the founder of runic studies. You know what makes her special, Stal?"

Niccolo's face flashed with confusion, then neutralized. "Eh, is very smart. She traveled many places. She lived many years."

Thonra grinned. "She lived a *very* long life. Hundreds of years. Supposedly already practicing magic at the dawn of discovery. This is one of the most widely educated mages ever to exist, and she spent decades in and around these mountains." Thonra twisted and wrenched a bird statue, snapping it from the throne. "Her symbol was this four-winged canary."

"Gods!" Sonja hissed, stepping to guard the rest of the sculpture. "Are you compelled to break everything, or is it a new hobby?"

Thonra showed no regret, slipping the bird into an outer pouch and turning to study the dreamlike painted ceiling. "For our purpose, tul-Habao had nine recorded trips through this port. I'd wager she left something very important behind. Mix that with the immortal Kepstan mythology… We'll be westbound in no time."

The pit in Sonja's stomach deepened as she followed Thonra's quick steps across the room. She imagined a world where Leif held this precious relic. It wasn't sitting on a corpse or hidden in a vault. It was on a living person. Possibly a royal. Alive because he could not die. Sonja flexed sweating palms and tried to neutralize her face. "And if it's all cheap propaganda?"

"What? Just because these people couldn't handle it?"

"Lower your voice."

Thonra did not. "Alternators were uncommon in the east. Still are now. Maybe someone with even my skill could make it work, but with you? With both of us? Child's play." She meandered toward the war room door.

"Don't open that."

To Sonja's surprise, her sister listened, turning suddenly to close the distance. "He'll be home," she whispered. "We'll bring him home."

Her grey eyes, Ulrik's same grey eyes, brimmed with thick hope. This was, finally, the end of the line. Those damn grapes had never been so close.

Niccolo's boots shuffled behind her. He was a part of this too.

"Before I show you the rest," Sonja said, "you should know I've made promises."

Thonra's glowing confidence dimmed to distrust. "Within reason, Sonni. I can entertain promises within reason."

Resentment was the syrup that Sonja couldn't choke down. "I wasn't asking for permission." She couldn't bring her sister to Leif. What would Thonra do? Honestly, Sonja didn't know. But what was he compared to her brother? Just a kid. Yet, if Thonra killed him over some theoretical relic, it'd be the same as Sonja holding the knife herself. It wasn't worth the chance. She couldn't expose Leif. Not yet. "Come on, but be on the watch," Sonja said. "There's one last place you need to see."

"Let the null lead." Sonja hadn't mentioned Niccolo's ability, but he *had* tackled her while invisible. Thonra fell into step with him. "How long have you been in Jrendavar, Stal?"

"Some years now," he said.

"What're we really talking? Three or four or five? Some could really mean anything." Her words flowed together. Sticky. Indistinct.

"Seven, eight. I do not know."

"I see. Dd you move here to work? For curiosity? For pleasure?"

"Thonra, leave him be."

"It's a harmless question."

"Is fine," Niccolo said, his singsong accent suddenly thicker, slower. "I come here leave army."

"How did you get out alive?"

"Much luck and care. An amount of cleverness. Sold one eye to Tobequim."

Sonja yanked on her sister's arm. "Leave him alone."

"These are normal mercenary questions." Thonra broke away from her grip, eyes dead and cold. "I need to know the sword behind me."

"He's not a mercenary."

Niccolo didn't defend himself.

"I can see that," Thonra said flatly. She mouthed another phrase before extracting her arm and following Niccolo out of the throne room. Even silent, Sonja understood: "I'm worried for you."

Sonja could have beaten her sister's skull in. She could have screamed. She could have fallen to the ground and cried or taken a nap or become stone itself. In their thirties, yet they still fought like unstable teenagers. When things had started to improve between the sisters, Ulrik had gotten sick. Stayed sick. Not a fever or a cold, just weak and weary, like he was saving their damned barn cat, and they were powerless all over again. Thonra had regressed. Not that Sonja handled it better. Gods, they knew how to irritate each other.

The day's frustration was exaggerated, and Sonja understood that. Thonra was hurting. Deeply. It was apparent, down to the way she breathed. Two years of solitude had made things worse. The search seemed so promising in the beginning: a few weeks of research, a few weeks of travel... As if necromancy could ever be so accessible. As if their education would show them three easy steps to fix the family.

Ulrik wasn't supposed to be dead. She shook the thought away.

At the base of the stairs, Sonja started a small drip. "Step where I step," she told her sister, then waved for Niccolo to lead. Sonja squinted up as the color faded away, finding the stair empty. No columns of light to weave around. Beyond, the strange torrent was smaller, maybe tighter. Less oppressive overall. It was unsettling. Had something changed? Sonja tried to remember the last time she'd heard the voices in her mind, but the castle had been silent for so long. Since the illusion of the party. Since meeting Leif.

A weak cry drifted in the silence, followed by the trembling words, "Please, help." Through the sobs, she recognized the prince's voice.

Niccolo bolted toward the darkness. Faster than she'd seen him go. He was water rushing to a cliff's edge. Toward the doors framing the darkness. Those same doors that held secrets and brought mages to their knees. Toward the remnants of the energetic wall.

Leif was inside, bleeding.

18

KEPSTADUR'S FALL

Sonja scrambled after Niccolo as he vanished into the cursed room. Each heartbeat seemed to pass as slow as three. The world's colors faded back to normal, and the door looked nearly benign. No taller than the others, but stepped back a body's length, giving a cave-like appearance. Sonja feared what hibernated inside. Swirling iron filigree reinforced the dark wood, and oversized handles dominated the edge. Was it all iron? Maybe some of it, but twisting vines mixed into the details. Shadows obscured everything more than a few steps within the chamber.

Sonja yelled Niccolo's name, but he wouldn't hear her. Not over the memory of a bar fight, a frozen night, and an execution. Not with someone waiting to die. He would get himself killed in that room.

Gods, he was fast.

The voices returned. Shouts and wails as she careened toward him, the room beyond fading in as if behind a mist. Another antechamber, filled with the remains of art and culture. Past a second set of open doors, a colonnade faded into darkness. Dull purple plants strangled every surface, bearing thorns the size of her fingers. The wicked tips flared in every color of paint. Deeper still, a massive bed stood framed by an even larger stained glass window. The sun's bright beams reached through but barely rattled the darkness.

Sonja called his name again, but she couldn't hear her own words. Was it the voices? Was it a cloak?

Then there he was. Barely visible through that thick shadow. Niccolo danced around piles of vines, the Reaper blade in one hand. He slashed his way to Leif. The boy heaved each breath, his eyes fluttering. Vines twisted at his neck and clawed his face to the side. He had a single arm free. The rest of him lay flat against the wall, coils holding him upright.

Sonja was careful to follow, until the mad prince met her eye, tears streaking dirt from his face. The voices buffeted her mind and screamed for her attention. Niccolo raised his sickle.

And then he was gone.

She patrolled a long, dark hallway on a peaceful night. A trio of windows overlooked the keep as it slumbered. A few gambling houses stayed open this late, but the bars were supposed to be closed by now. Something was happening in the streets, too far away to understand detail. She could only see torchlight. Maybe another raid looking for that thief's den, Big's Hoard. It was a good night for it. The star-speckled sky was the clearest in months. She liked full moons. It was so much easier to see, yet, tonight felt...hesitant. The air was waiting for something. Or was that her imagination?

She shook the feeling away and continued the route, looking out over the empty foyer and nodding to the guard posted deeper in the dining hall. They didn't acknowledge the gesture, but it could be hard to see the House Kepstan uniforms in the dark. She hadn't crossed her hall buddy yet. He was still new on nights, so his name escaped her. She passed the royal bedchambers, the guest rooms, and the infirmary, noting nothing of interest. Maybe her hall buddy had gone to peruse the kitchens. He seemed to love those little sweet loaves left by the staff. She pushed past the tapestry and into the dim passage. Halfway down the hidden stairwell, she tripped on something large and soft, barely catching herself on the narrow walls. Light reached from the bottom, just enough to make out the features of the second patrol, eerily still. Her heart rate spiked, and she stumbled to lift him, finding a deep tear in his neck. Living Spirits, he was dead. But there was no blood. Had he been attacked elsewhere and relocated?

The door behind her swung open, adding more grey light to the scene. Before she could turn, pain pierced her back. A sick scream echoed off every stone. Her breaths stalled, and her arms grew leaden. Tears eluded her. She collapsed onto her fellow guard. Shit, what was his name?

It was an odd sensation to know her body was dead. She'd always imagined death as something more...powerful. Was she a wisp? She felt no control over her movements. Was that normal? She feared this was it, damned to watch her own body decay. It wasn't fair. She didn't want to die. This wasn't fair.

Gravity changed. She fell up and sideways, through the corridor, through a wall and into the royal bedchambers, her body left behind. Other faces orbited the plush four-post bed, eyes glazed over. No, no, no, no. Below, the regent stirred upright, waking her warlord. They spoke in hushed tones, far too garbled to understand. He reached for his sword and pulled a thin cable. The bell in the captain's quarters. This was her legacy. She'd raised the alarm. Her final scream would save the regent. She died for that. This wasn't fair. So sudden. Understated. In a servant's stairwell without a scrap of dignity. Not even facing her killer. She didn't want to be a wisp. This wasn't fair.

A jolt of dull pain registered as Sonja's body impacted the stone. For a moment she found the will to push against the foreign consciousness, to search for reality. There was no rocking boat this time, only a rampaging storm to drag her back under. Sonja clawed over the images. Thonra's voice registered as if beyond the horizon. Niccolo tore through Leif's bonds, carefully extracting him from the wall. The prince coughed blood. He was so small.

A new vision crashed down.

She was in the barracks, crossbow clutched in white knuckles. A gaggle of soldiers stood in the captain's quarters, staring into a dark staircase topped with screams. The passage to Regent Kepstan's chambers. Another body tumbled down the spiral. The fourth one. She didn't check on the dead, using the lull to surge up. At the top, she loosed a standard bolt before registering her target. The sergeant collapsed, narrowly stopped from slashing through another line of support. He had been kind and soft-spoken. What would've driven him to kill his comrades? She couldn't think about that now.

The trapdoor opened to a marching colonnade casting harsh moonlight shadows. Green and black uniforms tumbled over each other in a gory mess. Only the Kepstadur Guard. Had someone stolen the laundry? No. She knew the faces of every soldier present. This was madness. They gutted each other without remorse. Not a drop of blood stained the hardwood. She took shelter in the shadows of the dressing area, noting a single stranger walking calmly through the mayhem: dark hair, with a billowing, embroidered cloak.

He ducked past her bunkmate, Niall, burying a knife in his neck. Hot fury swept over her skin as she leveled her weapon. The stranger weaved through the chaos, closing on the bedchamber. Her finger tensed, but something caught her attention. Niall, head held unnaturally high, creaked to an upright position. He leveled his sword at a new recruit, who was battling against the empty air nearby. She flinched away as the body crumpled, aiming to send a bolt through Niall's temple instead. He wouldn't want this.

But where had the stranger gone? She skirted around the room's edge, pulling one of her relic bolts and searching for that embroidered cloak. When she found him, it was too late. The stranger stood behind the warlord, a blade embedded in his soft organs. "Stay with me, sire," the man whispered, his accent round and northern. "You are my chosen to tell this story. Remember the name: Valtyr of Voices. Gather all your allies. Hire your best defenders. Put a bounty on my head. Make it one worthy of the man who kills your lover. Swear vengeance. But swear first that you will never forget this name." Valtyr cast the warlord aside, all in plain view of the regent and her immediate guards, yet no one seemed to notice.

The trigger compressed, slowly, treacherously in shaking hands. She was a decent shot — outstanding before joining the guard. One of only five trusted with these special arrows. The bow recoiled with a clang into her breastplate, moments before the bolt connected. Vines erupted from Valtyr's shoulder, and he bellowed in pain. Without walls to latch on to, hungry tendrils hooked around his limbs and burrowed into his skin, sprouting their thorns in an instant. The mage clawed desperately against their hungry wrapping, casting magical fires to singe the root. Gods, how was he still walking?

She dodged out of sight, fishing for a reload. It was a matter of time before the mage found her. But the room stilled. Soldiers defending against unseen forces hesitated. Those fighting each other gasped. Several figures with that unsettling upright posture froze entirely. Whispers and sobs roiled amid the columns. The cold fear in the air tasted sharp, almost metallic. But the moment was fleeting. Those terrible, stiff soldiers stuttered back into motion, with more martyrs rising from the ground as if held by a marionette's string. Swords clashed. Comrades fell. Panic returned.

She shot a standard bolt through the back of the nearest puppet's skull, then searched for Valtyr, reaching for another charge. The mage stumbled toward the regent, one hand pointing toward the madness and the other clutching a long dagger. Her fingers betrayed her, desperate to reload faster. A strange dust formed behind the hand guards, solidifying into knives. They fell only a moment later.

She settled the bolt into place but fumbled to draw, pulling back again only after it was too late.

The regent's blood spilled onto the bed, yet she did not fall.

"And they called you selfless," Valtyr cackled, readjusting his dagger and tearing at her clothes, drawing back with a crystalline pendant. The Kepstan Regent collapsed off of the bed and out of sight.

For no more than an instant, Sonja felt her curiosity split from the vision's anguish. Less than a breath between waves.

She squeezed the trigger, only to be buffeted into the wall, a sharp pain tearing across the back of her arm. Somewhere in the distance, glass shattered, barely discernible as her crossbow clattered away. Four of her friends — the corpses of her friends — closed around her, their eyes turned black all the way through. Her stomach roiled. Niall was among them, barely recognizable with that hole through his face. She drew her sword with the uninjured arm, swinging wildly while trying to escape the corner.

Sonja recognized the miracle and the tragedy. This body was null. She was the only one who could see her friends dying. But the null guard didn't know how to help. His one grace: Valtyr didn't seem to recognize what made this soldier different.

Sonja and her host battered the corpses back, defending valiantly until they could slip away. They sprinted for the bed, stooping to steal a crossbow from the body of one of their sharpshooter friends. Valtyr was gone, limping toward the door, still clawing at the slow-growing vines. With her shared awareness increasing, Sonja recognized that

Valtyr paid for magic with the blood of those dying around him. She and the host scampered across the bed, but the regent was dead. Where was the warlord? Had he not fallen nearby? There. Three corpses, with their terrible black eyes, carried the warlord away, feebly fighting their unforgiving grasps.

Sonja and her host reloaded the crossbow. This one was older than the last. Looser, and more worn down. They stabbed through Niall's pursuing body, leaving the sword in his chest and kicking him back, then took cover among the curtains of the bed.

Sonja and the host lined up the shot.

Valtyr examined the necklace and, in a flurry, turned back to the regent. "You half-breed bitch," he spat. "Where is the rest?"

But the regent wasn't on the bed. Sonja's host was. She accepted how this would end. This wasn't a hallucination, but a memory. She couldn't alter the events. Only one person had survived the disaster at Kepstadur, and it wasn't a null guard. Her host was a man, she realized. His name was Felix. His mother had said the name meant "lucky." It was important that she knew who had killed this monster.

Sonja let Felix pull the trigger. He had been a great shot. The relic bolt struck true. Valtyr stumbled back, and vines erupted around him. Thorns lashed backward, binding him to the wall. The revenants carrying the warlord stumbled, dropping his groaning body in a heap among them. Felix jammed another relic bolt in place as Sonja begged him to run. To take cover. Felix aimed.

Ice split his throat, and a hot spring emptied down his chest.

His finger tensed on the trigger. A simple reaction, but it was enough. Sonja stood beside Felix's spirit, willing the bolt to drop faster. Begging for a decisive kill. It shattered stone, a hand's width from Valtyr's neck.

Felix's last thought, lying in his disappearing blood, was that his mother had not named him quite right. Then his energy dulled and followed the magnetic flow toward the mage. A whirlpool of souls. And he'd be another.

Invisible currents pulled Sonja back toward her body, but she fought to stay, to watch Valtyr die. She needed to see it. The vines wrapped across his face and around his throat, but he clutched the regent's pale blue necklace and bellowed in rage.

A distant voice called her name, but Sonja resisted.

Valtyr thrashed against the bolts and bonds, drawing lines of blood. A body manifested beside him, but as it approached, it collapsed into dust. With effort, Valtyr selected one soul from his mix, sending it to the bed. To Sonja's horror, Felix's body righted itself, neck a gory mess, and stumbled toward the mage. His black eyes vacant, Felix took a longer route, retrieving a sword and piercing down through the warlord's chest, even as the spreading vines took hold of the royal's limbs. Felix's body turned toward Valtyr.

The instant the vines touched Felix, he collapsed, and the soul returned to the torrent. She was thankful to see them take hold. Hopeful that Felix rested here under his last powerful act. Grateful that he could never join the ranks of the dead. A sentinel guarding the place where Valtyr should have died.

Where Valtyr hadn't died.

Sonja jolted back into herself, woozy as she stumbled off the dormant relic plant. Niccolo sliced through the last vine. The manifestation of Leif faded to dust, and Valtyr, gaunt and skeletal, created a knife to force under Niccolo's soft armor. He battled the hand away and, in a fluid motion, cleaved through the mage's body.

The Reaper stopped with a *crack* a few fingerspans in, as if the mage had stones beneath his skin. Flesh parted around the crystalline blade. No blood poured out.

A bloodless wound meant magic.

Shit.

A multitude of Sonjas and Niccolos scattered around the room, bursting into existence with panicked breathing and illusory footsteps. Thonra's duplication spell. Some ran for the exit, deeper into the chamber, others for the broken window. Sonja couldn't tell the real from fake. If anyone could, it would be a null. She stood carefully, reaching and hoping Niccolo would understand, stepping slowly toward the foyer.

Had he fallen at the knife wound? Did he need her help?

A hand latched on to hers, rushing past like a storm. They bolted through copies of themselves and careened into the hall.

"Find Thonra," she told him.

"Try," he hissed back. "There!" Niccolo pulled her toward a closed door beside the stairs.

Sonja squeezed her eyes shut. Logically, the door was open, but her mind didn't believe that. They passed through the wood into a dim, blue-tinted corridor, leaving behind a pair of illusions struggling against the iron handle. Niccolo swung the door closed. The impact vibrated soundlessly through her soles. Sonja clutched for the locks, five of them at different heights, all a little stiffer than she expected.

Niccolo sank against the wall. His legs spanned the corridor's full width. An invisible foot lightly kicked Sonja's calf and broke her into the illusion. Thonra skulked away to watch her handiwork through the arrow slits. "Welcome to the den," she muttered, hands held out as a focus: the thumbs and first two fingers connected to each other in a sort of pyramid. A thin stream of blood flowed from a bloshul strapped to her chest, evaporating before reaching the ground. This was an enormous and complex illusion. But Thonra designed it all. From the unique escape routes to the cacophony of footfalls, and a last bit of attention tending this cloak of silence.

Niccolo furrowed his brow. "Den?"

"Like a fox," Thonra said. "More acutely, a thief's den."

"It's her name for the little game of hide-and-seek she plays while the rest of us do the dangerous work," Sonja grumbled.

"That's a bold comment about the only person who didn't rush headlong into the most obvious setup since Ulrik stopped hunting rabbits. Call it cowardice, yet you're alive because of it."

Sonja knelt beside Niccolo, ignoring the jab. "Are you *hurt, cut... poached*?" she asked quietly, reaching to the place he was bleeding. "It looked like he..."

Niccolo let out a dry laugh. "Mail. The *grey* guardian," he said, resting both hands over hers. "Is not my virgin fight. Is never been stabbed so lightly."

Thonra huffed behind them, something akin to a dry snicker. "Whoever told you that phrase might not be a friend."

"And the sickle?" Sonja pressed on.

He didn't reply immediately. "It has not ever failed to reap." Niccolo retrieved it from the stone floor, one hand clutching hers for a few extra seconds. "And worse, my eyes fail. I am to see through these things, yet... This is my fault."

"No, it's..."

Thonra cut in, her voice exact but not biting. "None of us could see through that, Stal. Some magic is too strong." The humor had evaporated. She wouldn't look at him, the corners of her mouth pulled flat. "What do you mean by 'reap'?"

"It's a fjarfest," Sonja said. "Probably dreki."

"What does it *do*? Poison? Mind fog? A non-coagulant? It looked like a clean hit. How long until the effects overpower him?"

"It just kills." He shrugged. "There is no more effect. Alive at once, then no more. Is instant. This failed, and I do not know why." He shook his head, then ran a thumb beside the chips in the obsidian blade. "Did not think it can break."

Sonja sat back on her knees, paying to check the energy. A thin line of green mist pooled at the cracks and rolled back toward the door. "You hit it pretty hard," she said. "He has the Kepstan relic. I have to assume that's why it didn't work. It's not broken, but it's leaking."

Niccolo's eyes widened. "Leak what?"

"Life, I think."

"Life. Oye. You say this as is so normal." He rubbed his cheeks.

She looked for the words to explain her visions when a force buffeted the locks. Sonja flinched, choking out a startled yelp. Long heartbeats passed before steps shuffled away. Sonja sat straighter, only to bump into Niccolo's arm, extended protectively behind her. His face tangled with emotions as he crossed his arms over his chest. He couldn't hold her eye, eventually leaning back against the stone.

"Maybe one day you'll be grateful," Thonra called over her shoulder. She sat facing the dark corridor, legs crossed and focus intact. Her bloshul dripped at a much slower pace, once every few seconds, as the only cloak they still needed was the sound negation. "First rule of hide-and-seek, you'd need to be quieter without me." Petty sarcasm rolled off Thonra's words. "I'll see if I can give you more space to whisper while I work. Let me know when you're good and ready to finish this. I'll try not to doze off in the meantime."

The day already lay heavy across Sonja's shoulders. She was more tired now than any sleepless morning. Tired to the core. Why was it always the end of the run that was the hardest to keep pace? "It's not as simple as walking up and taking it."

"I don't see why not. If that rotted body is who I think it was, he should be easy enough to push over. We need to go before he pays for reinforcements."

"He can't die," Sonja said, thinking back to Leif's fainting episode in the tunnels. Would a trained mage like this have ways around that kind of limit? "But he is only holding part of the magic."

"Part?"

She studied her hands, sorting the memories she'd witnessed.

"The condensed version, please," Thonra cut in. "I'm sure this is not the only spell worth paying for."

"Valtyr break in," Sonja used her most childish tone. "Try steal magic. Uh-oh. Relic broken. Regent has half. Where is the other piece? Got stuck! Can't look for it now."

"Sonja, I'm serious. Do you know where the other half is?"

It was unclear when all the pieces had clicked together in her mind, but Sonja had never been more sure. Leif was the son of the Kepstan Regent, and Valtyr's purge of the city had never found him. Or at least never taken him. The details were still vague, but she poured out a small pinch and searched through the walls for Leif's unique, braid-like signature. The castle buzzed with activity, mostly downstairs near the dungeons. Valtyr's torrent of souls was far beneath. Dredging up bodies from their watery waiting place. She needed to act fast. "A Kepstan survived," Sonja said quietly. Her panic rose the longer she searched. "Niccolo, where did he say he'd be?"

"Eh, many places. I do not know. Can you not…find him?" His eyes flashed to her bloshul as she pushed harder. Wordlessly, he extended a bloody hand toward her, luminescent blue in her distorted vision, his blurred expression solemn.

"Gods flay my bones," Thonra spat, sliding her sister an oversized bloshul. "Save your blood, Stal. That's not enough to help."

Red-faced, Sonja bit her lip and ran her own hide dry with surges of perception. "There's something over there." She waved vaguely across the atrium. "I don't know if it's him, or really where it is. This place is…"

But Thonra was already walking toward the exit.

"Ah," Niccolo said without moving from her path, "you know where he is, then?"

"We can't sit here. Sonni just has to find him."

"And if, instead, we do not go back into the open, but look at the secret hallway? See where it goes and if is defensible."

Sonja braced for a bashing reply. Pushing back only ever settled her sister harder into her opinion. Thonra stared down at him for a long moment before she extended a hand. "Easier to cloak in here." She pulled him from the floor and gestured along the archery corridor. "Lead on."

Had she heard that right? Not a single argument. Could this be an illusion? Not likely. Thonra spent so much time invisible, she didn't leave much to work with.

Sonja couldn't help the sneer that pulled at her cheeks. *Lead on.* Nothing snide or condescending. Thonra would disagree with a fallen bridge for daring to change her plans. Even reasonable requests could be dismantled for the sake of being the smartest person in the room. Niccolo offered Sonja a hand up after him, brow furrowed at her expression.

"Do we have any information at all?" she asked to shake off his silent question. Best to not waste Thonra's good mood.

"He tells to me that his door sings," Niccolo said. "This means something to you? Is magic?"

She took a moment to dust off her clothes. "If you're asking if it could be a hallucination, yes. I don't see why not. Visual, auditory, olfactory — I bet he smells every time his staff is supposedly cooking."

"That doesn't feel right," Thonra said. "The most powerful illusions form from honesty. Where would he get the idea of a singing door?"

Sonja exchanged glances with Niccolo, searching for the gentlest words to describe the boy. "It's hard to explain," she said. "Leif isn't fully with us… His mind, I mean. He's been through a lot…"

"All the more reason. That association likely started somewhere. What if the door looks like a mouth? Having it open could remind him of a singer."

"Is not unreasonable," Niccolo said, walking deeper into the archery corridor.

Flashes of the palace ticked by on either side. The dining hall to the left and foyer to the right, both silent and empty. At the corner, a door led to a claustrophobic ladder to the main floor. The hall widened along the front, maybe the size of Sonja's childhood bedroom, every wall covered in perfectly regular windows. Thonra continued, but Sonja and Niccolo stalled. The first few showed the lake, the city, and the softest white clouds rolling in over the sun. Several shorter openings peered into the entry stairwell. From above, the weighted door no longer dominated the space the same way. Square holes sloped down through the floor, fully open to the steps below. Sonja didn't want to think about what defenders might drop or pour on besieging armies. "What about statues?" she asked, observing the empty pedestals. "Could the room be near a statue of a singer? Maybe a painting?"

"If it's a painting, we'll never find it," Thonra said. "Not with all the grime and damage."

"Is good idea," Niccolo replied softly. "In Attietto, we have — eh, how to say — *yartiporta*. Is, eh, little men on the walls. Little statues to watch windows." He reached to the top corner of the nearest arrow slit and traced a space the size of his head. "Many singing or playing instrument to tell the home when intruder is near."

She nodded slowly. "A little bard carved on the wall would make sense. I can't say I've seen any around."

Niccolo's response was lost under an update at the far end. "The hall is a horseshoe shape," Thonra called. "There's another door. It leads to the far side of the balcony. Away from the regent's quarters."

Sonja tried another identification. Sparks like flint strikes danced over Thonra's shoulder, but Sonja couldn't parse that meaning. "I still don't see him from here. There is something weird, maybe something in these walls. Can we check the balcony?"

This wing of the castle was far shallower than its mirror, ending in the triple window Sonja had seen from the first guard's eyes. The city had been so peaceful that night. Four narrow doors marched along the far wall, their tone so similar to the stone, she hadn't noticed them in the memory. "Could singing refer to a stage?" Sonja offered. "Elvy mentioned performers, didn't she?"

"A stage like the throne plinth?" Thonra asked.

"Maybe a real stage. Even a small one. It could be behind these doors, with a view into the gardens?" Sonja turned for confirmation, finding Niccolo kneeling to examine the time-worn carpet.

"Is not a common place. Leif does not go to that side many times. He walks toward us." The path veered back toward the archery corridor. "Is for a reason, yes?"

"Maybe." Thonra stood with her arms folded, staring back toward the regent's darkened chamber. "Can you see him yet, Sonni? I don't want to know what happens if the Warlock Warlord gets both halves."

"Working on it," Sonja snapped, spending more blood now that she stood in the open. "I was hoping the archery hall was the problem, but still nothing. I've checked nine times now, but he's not here."

"Would he have left? Fled when Valtyr…"

Sonja didn't listen to the rest of the sentence, eyes tracing the bizarre, ember-like patterns dancing back toward the ballroom. They sparked and jolted out of alignment in unstable rainbows, but the color at the core of it all, that was right. Leif's energy was a soft yellow, bright enough to seem white. This was largely the same, only broken up and jittery. "What if the door doesn't have a mouth?" she mused. "What if it sings because it's metal? With enough iron, it could fully distort my magic."

Recognition settled in Thonra's expression, and she pulled out a familiar dagger to rap against the walls. It was good to see her using it. To know that both sisters carried a gift from Ulrik. Sonja stepped forward to help, pulling the twin knife from her boot. Metal on stone tinkered in the short, boxy wing. Niccolo disappeared into the archery hall for an instant before leaning out again, wide-eyed. Sonja followed him back to the blue shadows. With a coin between two fingers, Niccolo tapped on a part of the wall, dull and flat. No singing. Nothing. Before she could explain differently, he struck the stone right next to it. The hallway reverberated with metallic hums.

"Gods, Stal!" Thonra hissed as she joined them. "What was that? A dinner bell for the corpses? Be careful with that shit. I don't cloak everything."

"Others heard this? More than we three?"

"No, not this time, but next time—"

Sonja cut off the argument. "What happened to not wasting time? Help us get in." The dim lighting worked to mask discrepancies, but now that she knew what to look for, she could mostly identify the irregular outline. Niccolo traced the detailed metalwork, gripping at the edges. Without a place to pull, he leaned his shoulder until the assembly creaked.

"There's got to be a lock," Sonja said. "Leif isn't strong enough to force his way in."

All three scrambled to look for oddities around the invisible frame until Thonra called in triumph. A keystone slid smoothly through.

Sonja wiped sweaty palms down her hips. Gods, it felt like a mistake to expose this place. A mistake she couldn't undo.

19

CROWN PRINCE

Soft light poured into the archery corridor. Sonja instinctively drew her shoulders up. Was it bright enough to see from the foyer? "Thonra, before we go in, I need you to promise to be…gentle. He's been alone for a long time."

The elder didn't respond. She stepped after Niccolo, plugging her bloshul fully as the metal door swung shut. The trio stood in a shallow foyer on the remains of a vibrant rug. Something in the wall's animal murals spoke to a youth that twisted her heart. Sure, he'd seemed young, but this? To the right stood a deep closet of ratty shirts and trousers, but the shoes were the worst. Children's shoes. A young boy left behind. The next room only emphasized that. Light filtered in from thin windows overlooking the ballroom, casting shadows between broken toys. Too old for a toddler, but too young for a teen. Small recurve bows with broken strings. Tactics games set up for matches never played. Block towers in all states of disrepair.

Niccolo joined Sonja on the steps of a platform stage where she ran her fingers over a set of velveteen curtains. "I worry for this," he whispered, not looking at Thonra.

Sonja sighed. "I wish you could see the person she was. She was funny before she was bitter. She was thoughtful before it hurt. If she says one more rude thing to you, I'll beat the shit out of her."

The softness of his gaze returned. "I do not worry for myself, but I will not let her hurt him."

"I know."

Movement through the last doorway caught their attention. Matted hair obscured heavy-lidded eyes as Leif stepped from the shadows. "It's neat, isn't it?"

"The room?" Niccolo asked. "It is. The hiding door is very nice."

"Few people visit me here. Usually just Elvy."

Niccolo shook his head. "We need to find you."

The prince raised an eyebrow, glancing to the back of the room.

"Highness," Sonja drew his attention, "this is my sister, Thonra. She was part of our traveling party before we split. But bad things are in the keep. We're worried about your safety."

Lief's expression closed off, heralding in a hesitant breath.

Niccolo spoke. "You can travel as you want. We can help you travel until it is safe to return."

"You want me to leave my post? My people?" Leif's voice cracked. His eyes flickered around the room before closing tight. "Did Mother really send you?"

"You're in danger," Sonja said. "There are bad people here that want to hurt you."

"Prove it," he snapped. "Prove that you aren't bad."

Sonja knew only one path. Barreling in. The way Thonra would. "Your mother. She wears a crystal blue necklace, yes? It has some funny pictures on it? Glyphs you might have learned. Is that right?"

Leif fixed her with a vitriolic glare. His face gained that age again, that nebulous quality that took his features from being a large child to a ragged adult. How old had he been at the time of the attack? Six or seven? No. He was more mature than that, even in his youngest moments. Nine? Twelve?

"When did you last see her, Leif?"

He backed farther into the darkness of the bedroom. "It's been a long time."

"Your mother gave you a crystal like hers, didn't she?"

"No." His voice was clipped, laden with tears. "Get out. You're here to steal."

This felt terrible. Sonja sat on the stage, lacing fingers and softening her voice. "Someone stole her crystal, Leif. Did you know that?"

The prince didn't reply.

"The thief knows there's a second piece, and he's here looking for it. Looking for you."

"You leave for some time so that the thief does not get both," Niccolo said. "See the travel you want. Come back when is safe."

Leif shook his head furiously. "I can't."

"Why no?"

"Who will lead?"

"A person who rise to lead in your absence also rise to lead at your death." Niccolo heaved to a seat next to Sonja, speaking more like the captain he had claimed to be. "Is wise to live."

"It hurts them to leave." The prince stared at his hands.

"Hurts who?" Thonra asked.

"The staff. They scream."

She pursed her lips, and Sonja braced. Thonra held the prince's eye, but her expression was soft. Not quite compassionate, but close.

"Everything got worse when you people showed up." Leif sank to hug his knees. "If you leave, it'll go back to the way it was."

Sonja took a breath, letting her mind wander to the way her knee rested against Niccolo's. Warm and steady. "Could I interest you in another story?" she asked.

"Is it a happy story?"

"It's worth it, I think."

Leif scowled. "Maybe that's why you don't tell the stories."

"Not all are happy," Niccolo said. "We try. Sad does not mean bad."

"The best stories are both," Sonja said. "A survivor is incredible because of the circumstances. It's sad that bad people steal and hurt, but that's how you get stories of sacrifices that save lives. Love that is stronger than death."

"Enough," Leif croaked.

"Stories of loneliness are sad, but imagine how inspirational it would be to find that survivor."

"I said enough."

"Sometimes, we tell our own stories to stay safe."

Leif cast out a hand and clambered back into his chambers. "Remove her."

Sonja stood to follow, but a gentle hand pulled her back.

"Is best idea?"

"If he has the other half, he's not safe here."

Niccolo let his eyes fall first, then his hand. She stepped after the prince, ignoring the feeling of Thonra's stare.

The last space was darker than the others. A four-post bed leaned against the far wall, almost a room of its own, with decorative head- and footboards. Winter bed curtains draped across bowing posts, static as if stone carved in place. Something smelled vaguely sour, but the overwhelming aroma was stale. Piles of sheets littered plush carpet. Over the bed, a row of windows seemed covered from the outside with creeping plants or grime. The prince hunched over his hands, thin legs poking out from the drapes.

"How many have stayed with you, Leif?"

"I don't want to talk to you."

Sonja looked down. "I know." She had to keep pushing. "I wish I could tell you something different. This is important."

"I'll have you executed."

"I'll risk it. You have to know what happened."

Everything exploded in an instant of light and color, blinding and harsh. Sonja flinched away, stumbling back into a solid mass. She adjusted slowly to a glow like hearth light, peering at a soldier's impassive face. Dozens of figures filled the room, floating a few inches from the ground, all tall and malformed, with abnormal limbs and rictus grins. Their eyes followed Sonja with a horrible intensity.

The prince screamed. His immediate fear melted into rage, then cut off abruptly with a sob. "I know what happened!"

The room seemed frozen in time. Intricate candelabras illuminated each corner, but the firelight didn't flicker. Dull daylight faded to a shimmering sunset. The ballroom below droned with one ancient chord. Thonra and Niccolo dashed inside for a better look. It was a potent spell; even Niccolo looked between the waxen faces of guards and servants. Thonra lingered near a trio of cooks, the largest wearing an embroidered eyepatch.

Elvy stood closest to the bed, slack-jawed. Her head bobbed lightly, dangerously reminiscent of the bodies that floated below. The eyes, though…her eyes still tracked Sonja with a groggy mistrust. Stern and focused, with a reprimand seemingly posed on her slack tongue.

There were so many. Sonja wondered if they were all staff, including the many children scattered throughout the room. What was this relic truly capable of? She cleared her throat. "You know?"

"The castle is broken," Leif said softly. "I can see it sometimes." His eyes lingered on a corner of the fading manifestation, his voice weak. "They're never coming home."

Sonja didn't reply. He lay back on the mattress, his chest heaving, and the manifestations disintegrated. Morning light returned, filtered through snowy clouds. Her thundering heart drowned out the idea of the next words. A familiar weight settled in her lungs, as if bad news poisoned the air inside her. It had been the same the first dinner after Ulrik. Thonra had disappeared, leaving Sonja alone to recount his last moments. Her fingers tightened instinctively.

Sonja forced her hands together, rotating her rings to keep from digging nails into her skin. She hated pushing him. Hated confirming his pain and crushing his hope.

Niccolo ambled forward, careful of the ashen remains blowing in a wind that didn't truly exist, moving past her to join Leif. He leaned on a knee and twisted to a seated position, back pressed to the side of the mattress. Their eyes met, brief but telling, and he gestured toward the door. He'd handle it from here.

Sonja returned a small nod, the pressure melting away. She left, gently guiding Thonra behind her. Expecting resistance or maybe needing the support herself, Sonja held her sister's arm until they stood on the far side of the toy room.

"He's not what I expected," Thonra said, wearing a mix of unusual emotions. Solemnity, consideration, compassion — all tucked under her usual stony glare. "Maybe it should have been obvious, but he looks as bad as the first."

"It's not that extreme." Sonja's shoulders hunched, and she rubbed at her eyes. "But, yes, he was quite a surprise."

"Half of the relic, then?"

"I think so."

"Why not bring me here first?"

"This is where we were headed."

"I don't believe you."

Sonja slumped onto a nearby bench, picking up a bridger from the abandoned logic game. "You wanted to see the castle." She spun the tiny wooden token between two fingers. "I didn't know what you'd say about him," she mumbled.

Thonra crossed her arms. "I'd want him better guarded. We can't let him wander off, much less get captured."

"Part of me worried you'd find the relic and snatch it right off his body without asking a single question."

A moment passed in which Thonra did not deny the accusations. "He's not what I expected," she repeated. "Things are always more complicated than we can plan for."

"So how do you want to uncomplicate them?"

"Get the boy some food."

Sonja paused, jaw slack. "Okay?"

"He'll need his strength. Even with the magic keeping him alive, that body is falling apart. He's going to have a long recovery afterward."

"Afterward" was the key. It implied that Thonra was only interested in taking the relic. True, it also implied that she hoped Leif would survive the removal, but that felt like the barest minimum of decency. "So, we get him out of here as quickly as we can, then? Nurse him back to health on the way home?"

"Tell me about this boyfriend of yours."

The game pice fumbled out of Sonja's hands and plinked to the floor. She took a moment to recover. "Be more specific."

"You trust him?"

Sonja tightened her lips.

"I see." Thonra nodded. "Can I get any details?"

"What do you want?" Sonja hissed.

"I'm gauging my chances." The eldest leaned on her stool's back legs, crossing her arms and squinting toward the dark room. "Seems trained. Was he really a soldier? Or has he always been a mercenary?"

"Thonra…"

"It's fine if he's not military. Attiettans make good sell-swords. It just changes how I talk to him."

"I don't like what this sounds like." Sonja moved to break her line of sight and waved away another roundabout comment. A churning, sinking feeling roiled in her gut. There was something distant and calculating in her sister's tone. Sweat coated Sonja's palms. It was never a good idea to let Thonra decide on her own. Once she locked on to something, she was immovable. "Explain."

Thonra reached down and retrieved the bridger, placing it decisively in an offensive position on the board. "It's simple. You and the skinny boy get a head start. Travel out for a few days and update your location on the map." She continued to build out a formation. "Learn what you can about the relic and see if he'll show it to you. Your stallion and I will catch up shortly." Piece by piece, a pattern came into view. Not an exact replica of the Larslen Gambit, but it was damn close. A maneuver better known as the "Blind Cliff."

"No." Sonja knocked the board, toppling the pieces before Thonra could finish the arrangement. "No, I'm not splitting up again. Not for anything. You promised—"

"This is important. You said it yourself. The mage is looking for the Kepstan boy. It's our job to make that as hard as possible."

"Not the way you're saying it. It sounds like you're framing this as another goodbye."

"For now, it is." The stool legs dropped with a resonant thud. Thonra leaned forearms heavily onto her knees, several pieces still in hand. "You're being dramatic. If you care, you'll listen to reason."

"I'm not doing this again." Sonja lurched into the dressing area, sure she'd struggle to keep her voice low. "I barely got you back, and I'm not leaving you now."

"Stay with the relic." Thonra strolled in behind her. "As long as you have the fjarfest, you can bring him back."

Sonja swallowed forcibly, feeling tears and frustration pushing against her chest. "There's another way. Let's talk through this."

"I've got it worked out. I'll catch up. We're going to take a pass at the other half first."

"Absolutely not."

Thonra huffed. "It would be foolish to leave without trying to get the entire thing. We need as much of the original runic structure as we can get. If half only sustains starving corpses, the whole thing could—"

"I'm not leaving you." Sonja enunciated each syllable, turning to tower nearly a full head's height over her sister. "If you're staying to fight for the rest of the relic, that's fine. But I will be part of it. I saw what he can do…"

"You are the lifeline," Thonra said. "Energy magic is the key. As long as you and the relic make it back, you'll figure out the rest."

"This isn't some kind of sacrifice," Sonja snapped. She pushed her sister back, knocking a game token away. "It's not an option. I'm going home with you, or not at all."

"We're not arguing this. You're being shortsighted."

"Listen to yourself."

"I could say the same." Thonra's face darkened, and she closed the distance again, voice dangerously soft. "You have the solution to all our problems sitting three rooms away. I'm offering to give us the best chances. If I can add to our win, that's a bonus. If we can't, we'll be quick. Who better to bring to the illusionist honor battle than a null? Valtyr won't know what hit him."

"Valtyr knows," Sonja spat. "He knew Niccolo needed a powerful illusion. This is asinine. He'll kill you both and add your bodies to his collection. We don't leave anyone behind."

"This is about *him*, then? About getting left behind? You're wound up over nothing. I won't lose his pretty little face. I'm sure the mercenary will be more reliable than your last one."

Sonja knew the exact moment her sister regretted the jab. Thonra, reluctantly, appeared speechless. She'd taken it too far. Yet Sonja couldn't feel the hurt. Not fully. It was a small, damp feeling. The memory of a feeling. One she hated and ignored and smothered and cursed. The memory of a promise. A promise to stay, broken at the first inconvenience. The emptiness that followed. Emptiness like the solitary days in the monastery. Emptiness echoing again when Thonra had split off all those years ago.

"I didn't mean that, Sonni…"

"I was worried for my sister," Sonja growled. "Are you listening at all? I'm tired."

"It's one last step to make it all worth it," Thonra whispered. At least she had the decency to show regret. "You can't trust me one more time?" She reached out, holding a game token like a peace offering. It stung the slow-healing burns, but Sonja took it. Another bridger.

Shadows passed by the distant bedchamber door. The boys shuffled closer, still trading quiet words. Niccolo smiled at her from across the room, hollow but sturdy.

Thonra seemed to gain a second wind and gave an exasperated sigh. "Then don't go far. Find somewhere nearby and wait for me. But realize I'm doing this for you."

20

THE TIDES

"It'll be simple."

Sonja didn't look at her sister during the explanation. She aimed for a neutral expression, but that was a losing battle. It wasn't easy to ignore Niccolo as he tried for her attention, but she leaned her stool back and provided nothing more than small, supportive nods when applicable. Because Thonra was right, and fighting was pointless. They would bring Ulrik back, and this was the way to do it.

The prince listened with hunched shoulders and shifting eyes. His temper was subdued, but it didn't make him calm.

"We'll start small," Thonra continued. "The first and most important thing is to put distance between you and the illusionist. Get out of the city and hide. Sonja will contact me once you're safe. Nichol, you and I will stay and eliminate the threats at Kepstadur, then be along a few days behind."

"The army of bodies?" Niccolo asked. "We alone?"

"When Valtyr dies, the revenants will no longer be an issue. It won't be as difficult as you think. You'll see through illusions; I'll solve any magical conundrums. We simply hunt him down and pick off all his fjarfest until we find the one."

"Sonja?" Niccolo asked.

She frowned into the space between them. "It's the logical plan," Sonja said. "Thonra's illusions will do you more good here. You have the advantage of high magical tolerance, and Leif needs an alternator's skill set to stay safe and healthy."

"You are not a healer, yes?"

"I can stabilize if anything goes awry — and it's easier for me to track general well-being." She channeled Thonra's confidence. This plan made sense. Leif was a liability. Just repeat the words.

Niccolo frowned. "But we do not all flee?"

"And leave someone like this to run wild?" Thonra said casually. "The army he's building will only grow. Collecting souls and bodies alike. If you'd seen the research I had, you'd understand. This isn't about money anymore. This is a moral obligation to our fellow man."

Sonja didn't fully believe those words, but no one spoke out. With a satisfied nod, Thonra left to scope the escape route, allowing for some preparation time. Leif packed and repacked a knapsack before scattering the contents. Clothes that wouldn't fit an adult. Sonja promised it'd be their first purchase. The prince scanned her once before skulking into the depths of his chambers.

Niccolo caught her wrist gently, pulling her aside with two fingers. For a moment, he only studied her face. Part of her wondered what he saw. "This is not about armies, yes?"

Sonja considered lying but shrugged. "What Leif has probably isn't enough for full revivals. This is our best chance for your friends and for Ulrik."

"And for his parents?"

Sonja's shoulders fell. She hadn't considered the lives lost here.

Niccolo waved away her response. "Is only a thought. Let Leif believe we will retake the keep. Is something he cares about." She nodded, but he didn't let go. His brows knit together, and he dropped his eyes to their hands. "You will be safe?"

"We'll meet up soon," she said.

Niccolo blinked slowly, then sighed. "I will do as I can to keep her well, though I fear she does not harbor the same feelings."

"She will watch your back. Thonra's a bitch, but she's not heartless."

"As you say." He shifted away. "She thinks I am here for money and treats me as such. Another greedy mercenary of Attietto. Second to her goal."

"That's not true," Sonja lied, growing warm with the shame of her own assumptions. "You'll both make it to Tharvik. You'll have the other portion of the relic, then we'll start reviving your friends."

He smiled, but it didn't reach his eyes.

"That's a promise," she hissed as Leif meandered back. The trio stepped into the dark corridor. Sonja's thumb drew up the bridge of her nose.

Thonra met them in the low light, her gaze focused. "They're moving." Thonra jerked her head toward a horde of revenants shambling up the grand stairs to the balcony. "I say you use the hidden ladder by the entry. I'll cover you until the big door, but Stal and I will need to move quickly. I don't like this pressure so close to us."

"Do you think Valtyr knows?" Sonja asked as they approached the back of the hall.

"If we found this place, so can he. You're in charge of cloaking once you get to the last landing. Yourself, the boy, the door, all of it." Thonra handed over one of her oversized bloshuls, unlatched a half-dozen locks, then pulled Sonja into a hug. "It's good to see you again, Sonni. I'm ready to be home too."

Sonja tightened her grip as her sister tried to pull away. "You keep *Niccolo* safe," Sonja breathed. "I swear to every god who will hear me. Protect him, or don't find me." Deep down, Sonja didn't mean it. Thonra was a constant. She couldn't imagine a future without her sister. Of course Thonra would survive, but Niccolo… "He deserves to live," she added, voice weaker.

When they pulled away, Thonra's face was unreadable, but she nodded. "We'll see you soon." She touched Leif's shoulder, locking him into her illusion.

Niccolo forced the secret door open, weapons poised into its dim green light. Several ever-burning lanterns, the same from the war room, illuminated the drop. He barely met Sonja's eye as she passed. At the bottom, Leif pushed into the foyer, moving a panel so well hidden that Sonja couldn't find it again after it closed.

Gentle crying caught her attention as they turned to leave. The Kepstan Regent knelt in the center of the foyer. Illusion. The Kepstan Regent was dead. She'd died a decade ago. Sonja stepped to block the figment with her body, but Leif didn't seem to notice anything. The regent sobbed Leif's name, but he didn't flinch. Could his hallucinations protect him from this? Would he still use them even now? That seemed wasteful, but maybe. Or this was Thonra's doing. She knew what was there and could control Leif's experience individually.

Either way, they needed to go before he noticed. Sonja led him quickly, dodging a few revenants patrolling the entry stair. In the archery corridor, Niccolo had confirmed all revenants along the route were visible and real, though that could change at any time. At the bottom landing, Sonja reached one hand out to Leif, opening a drip on Thonra's loaned bloshul. "Let's go see Tharvik, okay? And if you hear anyone but me, just squeeze."

He tentatively took hold and squeezed once. Sonja centered and brought him into a new cloaking spell. She couldn't help him how

Thonra had, dampening the whimpering sobs. Sonja pressed her free hand onto the door to lighten it. Something soft stopped the swing from the other side, sparking every instinct in unison as a grey hand slashed into the opening. She yanked Leif out of its closing grip.

"Highness?" a man's voice called from atop the stairs, speckled with fear. "Highness, please. Please, help us."

Sonja pulled desperately against the enormous door, but more limbs piled through. Leif went rigid beside her. "Arvid?"

"Highness?" Desperation peaked the illusion's tone. "Prince Leif, please, we need—"

The pleas cut off abruptly.

"Leif, this isn't real," Sonja said quickly. "This is a trick to make you stay."

"They're hurting him."

She manipulated the weight of the doors — double, no triple. The revenants outside clawed uselessly as those stationed on the stairs ambled down. "This is what we told you. A bad man who wants to find you—"

"He has my friends."

The assertion was true, but not in the way the prince meant. "Leif, this is an attack. We need to keep these bad guys out. Do you know how?" She took his hand again when he didn't answer, guiding them away from the approaching dead. "Come on, now. Look at me. We need to help."

He stared up to the foyer in a trance. Had Arvid's voice faded to only his ears. Had Valtyr found him?

"At the top," Leif finally said. "The blockade gate…"

Sonja towed him back to the foyer, momentarily stunned by the madness. Bodies piled around each other. Men, women, and children with a dozen nationalities. Some soldiers, some common. Some black-eyed, some appearing almost alive. Not a single step sounded in

Sonja's ear. Thonra's silence. One of her favorite tricks.

She turned back to the blockade doors, as Leif had called them. Solid wood, with wavelike designs. She cast illusions of the open doors before jamming them shut. Corpses stumbled toward them, but an invisible force cleaved through their ranks. Niccolo. Covering their escape. She could almost track him in the carnage. Any that passed him proved to be illusions as they stepped through the solid wood.

She gestured at Leif, one hand cupping the other to represent locking. Sonja pointed to the doors, but he was mesmerized by the chaos. She gently took hold of each shoulder, praying that he didn't recognize anyone in the mix — his mother, Arvid, or otherwise.

Leif focused on her slowly, seeming to come to himself, and pried open a small panel to reveal a system of gears. Sonja traced the static assembly with her eyes. Between chains and ratchets, she narrowed in on a pin with a loop approximately sized for a finger, latched on, and pulled. It held stiff, rusted and settled by forgotten years. She poured a manipulation into it, heat that stung against her skin. The pin broke free, throwing Sonja to the ground, but the gears whirred to life. It was an eerie sight in the silence, even more so when the assembly ran out of slack and the chains warbled uselessly by.

She didn't fully understand what had happened, but when she checked, the door to the entry stair wouldn't move. Sonja released every spell but their invisibility, clambering to pull Leif toward the kitchens and away from the worst of the violence. They dodged around writhing bodies and stayed close along the dining hall windows. From this vantage, Sonja noticed what she hadn't in the entry: hundreds of sopping corpses lining the bottommost pavilion, clustered in rows, with those inky eyes. Infinitely more than should be possible to control. Shit.

Leif pointed along the choppy surface of the flooded water, back toward the docks, where more bodies dragged themselves out of the bay, creating a human net along the second level. There was a mix of uniform styles, ages, skin tones. Even the decay varied. These bodies were from past raids on Kepstadur or from the fall itself. And when the dungeons were full, Valtyr had hidden the rest just outside of the port. Shit, shit, shit. If the corpses took the castle, Thonra and Niccolo wouldn't have anywhere to hide.

Was there any escape? The gardens, maybe? They could jump along each tier, then she'd lighten them as they fell. But they'd have to move quickly before every layer flooded with the dead. How many more were waiting beneath the waves?

Her mind pulled in a dozen directions. Save Leif. Warn Thonra. Protect Niccolo. Find Valtyr. Where could he possibly be? How could he orchestrate all of this? How much magic could one man direct? They were out of their depths in this matchup.

Sonja guided Leif to hide among the grand columns, noting his breathing. They were outside Thonra's noise cancellation. "Stay with me, Leif." She scanned the room, willing her mind toward a solution. Her eyes fixed on a single figure in a familiar cloak. It loomed in the window, tucked behind the dividing curtain, staring out over the docks as the dead sloshed into the city. "He'd need to be watching…" she whispered. Before Leif could question, Sonja took him by the wrists. "Stay here. Stay hidden. Assume nothing is real." She gave him her smaller bloshul. "If you're in danger, use this to hide." Faced with his terrified expression, Sonja couldn't fight back the urge to hug him. "If you need me, Niccolo and I have a passcode, okay? Yell *'hurry, can't pray.'* It has to be in that order. I'll come right back."

"*Hurry, can't pray,*" he repeated. "Please don't…"

"Trust me. This will be over soon." With that, Sonja ran. She leapt onto the table and skirted along its length. He was there. Valtyr surveyed his handiwork, arms extended, palms up. Calmly, silently. As if he knew Niccolo was distracted. Knew exactly where the null was.

Sonja widened her bloshul drip to a stream and grabbed her dagger, slinking off the table. She ran in, manipulating the curtain to be sticky as she pushed it against his body.

Valtyr thrashed and tangled further into the material. He reached for her, but Sonja dodged out of the way. He collapsed. She pounced, slashing at the material in search of the little crystal from Felix's vision. Sonja changed the manipulation, weighting it like boulders to pin the mage beneath. Little metal rods in the ceiling groaned and snapped under the magic, falling in a cacophony. She clutched at his robes and arms, searching for the relic necklace, bringing back only dust.

It took several heartbeats to realize she stood over a pile of ash. The sand of a manifestation, fading quickly from her fingers. He wasn't here. It was a trap.

Before she could run, the revenants were upon her. They surged from the foyer and kitchens, closing without hesitation. Scattering their energies only gave her a moment before the fallen bodies reoriented and piled closer. There were too many, all grasping at her limbs, pulling back and down. Panic rang through her ears, too loud to let her think. Sonja swiped with her dagger. She tumbled off balance. Sharp nails and bones scraped her armor, roiling to pin her. Revenant skin wasn't warm like a person's; neither was it fully dead. It was patchy. A haunch of meat cooked only on one side. Each one with a distinct pattern and texture. The salty brine was still thick in the air. The skin churned like a half-full wineskin.

Think. Find a solution.

With a pulse of power, each body she touched lightened. She kicked and thrashed, dislodging many, but couldn't break out. A wave of nausea washed over Sonja as her penultimate bloshul ran dry. She yelled, offering another. Keep going. More and more piled around, latching to her clothes and hair and limbs. Dragging her along the stone. Dragging her to Valtyr.

Heat surged overhead. A bright, lavender sun blinked into existence, dropping toward the writhing mass. Corpses shrieked in half-human tones, skittering away from the light or cowering like injured animals. Sonja fought back a pang of sorrow. It wasn't their fault.

An invisible hand bumped Sonja's armor once, then a second time to pry her into Thonra's spell. Cold eyes glowered down, then pulled Sonja roughly to her feet. The dining hall overflowed with figures. Many wore shifting faces — another of Thonra's favorite tricks — making it impossible to track the number of illusions. Neither sister acknowledged the other.

Thonra climbed onto the table, directing the flow of battle in an almost dance-like kata, while Sonja scampered to the place she'd left Leif. She raked her fingers against the energy of any nearby figment. Some fell, while most were only illusions. It was cheaper to guess than it would be to keep an identification going. She might need that payment when she found the prince.

And there he was. Cowering by the same pillar, eyes and ears covered tight. But the dead were closing. As soon as one bumped against him, the revenants swarmed. A lump formed in Sonja's throat. She was slick with cold sweat. What could she do without hurting him? Sonja dove in, clawing as Leif's panic was lost in the unforgiving silence. Gods. She couldn't let him die. He was a kid. He'd survived for so long.

Uskieru, save him from the fields. Sonja prayed. *Vaernda, hold his heart. Ilsky, keep his breath.*

With a silent shout, Sonja cast a surge of energy. The nearest revenants stuttered and seized, dropping to their knees, eyes and mouths gaping black. She thrashed through their dropping forms, wrapping arms around his chest. She wanted to tell him he was safe, that she wouldn't let anything happen to him. But even without the magical suppression, she wouldn't.

A hand fell on her shoulder, and Sonja flinched. It pulled back, but she curled in tighter. Gods, she couldn't watch another one die. Again, the hand pulled. Urgent, but not hurting her. She looked back to find Niccolo over her shoulder, speaking unheard. Spatters of black ichor marred his face. His soft curls flew every disheveled way. His eyes were intense without being panicked. Sonja pushed to her feet, pulling Leif along with her. She followed in Niccolo's steps as he dodged around revenants and passed through illusions. He didn't fight. His eyes studied the balcony for something Sonja couldn't see. They ducked behind the stairs, sprinting for the closed study door. He barreled through the solid image, slamming it shut in a rush of wind behind them. Finally, Sonja stood in the warmth again. Niccolo's voice rolled around her in waves. Maybe he was speaking in Attiettan, but she couldn't tell. The second door shut. Sonja centered into the peace of the moment.

That is, of course, until a fist slammed into her stomach.

A week's worth of dried fruit and bread threatened a reappearance as Sonja dropped to her knees. Overhead, another thud shuddered books from their shelves. Her mind clawed for meaning around the black blotches floating in her vision. She flopped back, searching for the threat, but what she found was worse.

Niccolo pressed Thonra hard onto the desktop, an arm under her chin. He had both wrists held in his off hand and a knee on one thigh. But Thonra wasn't even looking at him. Clarity dripped back to Sonja slowly. As she stood, she held her sister's hateful gaze. It had been years since they had physically fought, but it was familiar. Thonra would rather end a skirmish decisively before it began. Some things never changed.

"One simple instruction," Thonra growled. "Take the boy away. That's all I needed you to do. And yet, here he is." She tilted her head, and Niccolo tightened his grip.

"Just like old times," Sonja said. The words tasted of blood in her mouth. "Those were the good ole days, weren't they, Thon?"

"I do not believe this," Niccolo muttered with an unfamiliar intensity. Thonra's composure was infuriating.

"Let her up." Sonja put a gentle hand on his shoulder. He waited another moment before pushing off and skulking to the prince. "The entire city is overrun by corpses. There were more hiding in the docks. We couldn't have gotten out without physically climbing over them."

Thonra straightened her clothes, sitting purposefully on the desk. Her eyes were sharp, adding new information to her plan. "So you abandoned your job to add to the chaos I was already juggling?"

"We were looking for a back door and realized where he would be watching. Where it seemed like he'd watch. If I could find the dickhead and give us a chance—"

"You wanted to look for the mage? What a novel thought," Thonra spat. "If only we'd considered doing that."

"She did not know," Niccolo said.

"She shouldn't have to know. That was the point."

"Know what?" Sonja hissed.

"Know we found him already." Thonra rolled her eyes back to stare at the ceiling. "And now he'll have found a better hiding place. Do you know how hard—"

"Enough," Niccolo said. "We make work as is."

"As long as you get out." Thonra narrowed icy eyes. "Let's try this again, the way we agreed."

Sonja unhooked her final bloshul, the big one Thonra had loaned her, and slapped it onto the desk. It sloshed, not even half full, in rolling waves. "I won't make it out. Not without bleeding myself dry."

"Then you're useless." Thonra slid off the desk and padded toward the exit. "We can't give him any more time to regroup. Sit here and stay quiet until we come back."

Sonja met Niccolo's eye in a moment of defeated obstinance. "Or we leave town together. You cloak all four, Niccolo and I make the path, then everyone lives and no one becomes a fighty sack of meat."

Thonra stopped in place, sending a withering glance over her shoulder. "We're leaving with the entire piece. We didn't get this close to choke."

"We didn't get this close to die." Sonja stepped up and placed a hand on the door.

"If you'd listened, no one would have to die." Thonra seemed tired above all else. Not angry or dismissive. Simply tired. A rare state that rattled Sonja's resolve. "So, sit here, and watch the kid. I'll be back, and we'll walk out unharmed." She stormed down the hidden hall and out of sight but didn't fully leave. "Come on, Stallion. One more fight, okay? You can't quit on me now."

He lingered a moment, glancing between Sonja and the silent Leif. Niccolo let out a long breath, dropping his eyes.

"And if there's another way?" Sonja pleaded, as much to Niccolo as to her sister.

"There's not." The door opened and shut with finality.

"Then go die, asshole," Sonja said, stifling the urge to slam her fists into the desk. "I'll revive both your sorry asses. But Ulrik first." She rummaged through travel items she'd once considered left behind, throwing another ration at Leif before flashing Niccolo a sharp look. "If you're smart, you'll help us figure out how to escape. If we move fast, we can—"

"Sonja…"

"I know!" she snarled, leaned onto her forearms, and nested her head in the fabric of her pack. "I'm being unreasonable and should sit here until she gets back."

"The one who is unreasonable is standing alone." Niccolo placed a soft hand on her back.

A deep, comforting chord thrummed along her spine. "Stay here." Tears burned her eyes.

"I promised to protect."

"And if I can't revive you all?" A desperate fear coiled around her arms and neck. "I don't want your promises. So many people…the magic might run out. I don't know how this works."

"You will learn. We will be careful. She will not wait for me." He was gone with the next breath.

She stared at her hands. A scream boiled in her chest, but any illusion over this room had likely faded. Silence melted in the study's warmth. When she looked up, Leif stood in a corner, his eyes fixed on an empty space nearby. His brow furrowed, and his fists tapped repeatedly against his temples.

"Is everything okay?"

"What's wrong with me?" he whispered.

Sonja puffed out a bit of her tension, stepping over beside him. "Nothing is wrong with you. This isn't your fault. You're caught in…"

An image materialized before she could still his arms. It was a rugged, familiar man, but taller, with the bold, unnatural proportions Elvy had. His dark eyes fixed, lightly unfocused, on Leif even as the bearded jaw hung slack. The Kepstan Warlord. Leif's father. Sonja could see the resemblance clearly now. Not identical, but enough.

"What is this?" Leif whispered. More visions molded into place. Faces that hadn't been with Leif before. Sonja recognized Niall among them, Felix's bunkmate. These were new spirits. Not those that Leif had carried most of his life.

Sonja studied each one, looking for the best words to explain. "Your relic. It draws them in, I think. Spirits that passed on nearby to you. These are some that had been attached to your mother's portion…"

"They're dead."

Silence suffocated her reply.

"They're dead, and they have been dead. They're here, and they're dead, and they're trapped, and they're dead. Gods, I see it now." Leif dropped his eyes, clutching his stomach and rocking unsteadily. "I'm dead too."

"You're not dead," she snapped, surprised at the way the words felt raw in her throat.

He lifted his shirt, where a long sash wrapped several times around his waist. He moved the ratty fabric to expose a leather length in the middle, barely long enough to loop around him. It clung to his hip bones like seaweed on jagged rocks. Leif grimaced. "It's holding on to my spirit and their spirits. They can't die because of this. They stay here with me. I've trapped them." He pulled the belt off, holding it by a small, crystalline stem in the middle. His eyes filled with tears as he looked to his father. "I trapped them here."

"You didn't," she said, then reconsidered. "You didn't know. It's an unfortunate byproduct, but what you have is a miracle. Think of all the ways this could help people. Think of..." Sonja couldn't keep pressing, not with the agony written across his face. "Leif..."

The images faded all at once as a smaller firebug flitted off the shelf to land on Leif's hand. Slowly, silently, he turned the fjarfest over, watching the beetle crawl around his wrist. A moment later, Elvy formed. She stood upright, hands crossed at her front.

"You're not real," he whispered.

"I'm here, Highness," the figment responded.

"I've been alone."

Elvy didn't respond, but her eyes were vibrant. Pleading. Hurting. This being was more than a simple illusion.

"She was with you the whole time," Sonja assured him as the spirit's eyes focused in her direction. "This is Elvy."

"But she only says the things that I want her to. Nothing new. Only the kinds of things I remember her saying. The same interactions over again. Even when we disagree, it's my memory of a disagreement." The image dissipated before Sonja could form an argument. "Elvy is dead," Leif said as he stepped into the center of the room and pried at the trapdoor handle. "I'm finished being here."

Things were happening so quickly, Sonja couldn't complete her own thoughts. Escape. Save Leif. Help Thonra. Protect Niccolo. "Is there another way out of the castle?"

Leif shrugged. "There's a way to release them. To release us all."

21

SOLDIER

Thonra was being unreasonable, and she recognized that. It was the principle of the thing. She had plenty of blood to spare, but as soon as she gave Sonni another bloshul or two, she'd be chasing them down the hall. With such little supply, Sonni'd be smart enough to stay put.

Thonra shuffled until the Attiettan caught up, then prowled past dozens of corpses lumbering upstairs. Through the double doors, the royal bedchambers appeared empty. She approached the wall where the Mage of Voices had been imprisoned. A prismatic array of thorns burrowed through wood and stone in some sort of terrible briar patch. It spanned up and along the ceiling, hanging in tendrils with flowering buds. The place where Valtyr had been was the darkest, like a root feeding the system.

It was hard to imagine that kind of torture. Thonra wondered how many escape attempts he'd made. How infuriating the prince's proximity would have been. Had Leif never once come to his parents' room? Why not? What could've kept Valtyr from dawing him in? Had he been too weak to act or hadn't held enough substance to pay for the right magic. Something was missing.

Niccolo stared at his mistake; each clean cut spoke to his ignorance. For Sonni's sake, Thonra didn't comment. In the inner sanctum, a plush bed had collapsed in on itself, the posts at the corners stuck at all odd angles. Multicolored sunlight filtered through the stained glass windows. She wiped away a layer of dust and peered out to find a constant stream of revenants shambling from the depths. Valtyr had quite the collection, not including his illusions. One command, and the revenants would swarm the castle. She had to think.

"He is not here. Let us go." Niccolo's voice startled her back into the moment. He hadn't said much before, nothing outside of verifying invisible bodies. "Cannot leave them for long."

"You're telling me," Thonra scoffed, leaving the bedchambers. "Give her any leeway, and she'll bolt off to get herself killed."

"If any die," the Attiettan lowered his voice, "know this is your own doing."

Thonra stopped abruptly and met his eye. He didn't look angry, but the softness of his expression had melted fully away, leaving only his sharp bone structure and impassive frown. "I see."

"I see this before. The generals take charge and tell cápitans to follow orders, yes? Many times, general knows good plan, and this experience saves lives. Sometimes cápitan is, eh, refined to this position. Will not change bad plan because the general claims to have only this solution. Some soldiers cannot see problems, because how can the general be wrong? Sonja adapts to new problems, and you punish her for insubordination. You do not see this as unfair?"

"Point taken," Thonra snapped. In the hall, she gestured to the next doorway, expanding her spell to encompass it.

He pushed through obediently, but the door thudded into something beyond. Niccolo peered in, then lurched back. "Three!" He rammed a shoulder hard against the wood, then slashed that invested sickle through empty air. A corpse dropped in a heap, the invisibility no longer worth the cost. Thonra widened her cloaking spell and spun, watching as the nearby undead turned and shambled toward them. As she blinked, the number multiplied. With her null busy, she couldn't differentiate real from fake. She opened the bloshul at her chest and set her hand focus. With a single kick, a violet flame manifested across the carpet, moving out from her epicenter. She tempered its heat so that the manifestation wouldn't catch. A real fire would not help them right now. All the same, flames crawled down the hallway, and the corpses stumbled away. Niccolo stepped beside her defensively. He scanned the corridor, blade posed at shoulder level.

With another breath, Thonra broke the flames, then counted to three. Niccolo had told her about the secret door at the end of the hall. She manifested a series of tiny hands to shift the tapestry, all the while pulling the Attiettan in the opposite direction. They hunkered in a corner as the corpses regained their composure. As planned, several noted the swaying curtain and stumbled to investigate. A few more stepped into the room with the downed corpses, their souls drawn into Niccolo's fjarfest.

But the Mage of Voices wasn't a fool. More revenant's shambled through the hall, hands out like a net, closing on Thonra's hiding place. Niccolo grabbed her wrist and stood, leading carefully around the prying hands and through illusions he could not see. The searching line was tight, yet not impenetrable. The mass of revenants had moved from the archery corridor, where Valtyr had previously been. It was unlikely he'd return. Thonra followed Niccolo down the stairs and through the foyer, directing him silently to the ballroom. She caught him staring at the study door, but it still looked secure.

"You jammed it tight, didn't you?" she asked.

"Of course. They struggle to leave, even if needed."

"I'm more concerned about someone getting in."

"Ah, then this will not help," he said, a bite in the words. "When Valtyr realizes this is the only place to search, we simply hope the dead do not burst through. Their numbers are more strong than one old soldier."

"Point taken." She emphasized both words. He probably overruled Sonja at every turn. "I know you'd rather run—"

"I did not say this." Niccolo turned the corner and held up eight fingers, though Thonra only saw three revenants. His boots thudded across the stone, but the sound dissipated without an echo. "This army is dangerous. We cannot let it continue. This will destroy the nearby homes like a flood."

"I could've used that support with my sister. She would have listened to her little stallion."

"Why listen to someone who uses punches to express a thought that needs words?"

She scoffed. "Oh, don't act so holy. You don't think you've hurt people before? In a career like yours?"

"In my career, I hurt hundreds," he hissed. "But they haunt me."

Thonra flinched away from his unexpected remorse. It was sour. Acrid. Far worse than defensiveness.

"And what of you, mage? You are so better? You hurt the same ones again and again, but at least you hurt less numbers than a soldier. This is your pride?" He skulked onto the garden patio, nearly slamming the door behind her. "His name is Bragi, yes? Your married one."

In a fury, she spun to face him. "Keep his name away from your bootlicking mouth. Act like you know us, but whatever she's told you in the stupor of a morning after is as good as meaningless. You weren't there through the hardships. Hurt her, and you'll find I'm not afraid to kill a killer."

"Is strange." Niccolo's tone was even. "I do not need this 'morning after stupor,' yet she tells me of how you leave her to travel and mourn alone. Meaning you are also not there, no? I know you for one hour and see you are too stubborn to admit wrongs. Too centered on self to see what is in the mirror. Can we agree to make opinions of facts, or must you see me as scummy foreigner whore stealing from your sister's pocket?"

Thonra's mouth went dry. Turns out that chain mail was hanging on a spine after all. She didn't know whether to be impressed or infuriated.

"You are going to stand here and gape," he continued, "or is time to revive Ulrik?"

She started to snap back, but the words flattened against her tongue. Thonra purged the emotion from her face. He stepped past, but she caught his arm. Her reply shook with an unexpected emotion. "What did she promise you?"

Niccolo blinked down at her with impassive eyes. "Nothing that will stand in your way. I am not so selfish."

"And will you take her with you?"

"What does this mean? I put her in the bag and drag her to Attietto? This is what you think?" Anger spiked through his voice, a fire she hadn't seen from him. So sharp, she drew back. "I cannot go here. Do you listen? Traitor. Deserter. This is what my home call me. I am damned to your land and damned to your language. Forever. There is not a where I can go that is back." He inhaled like he might say more before storming deeper into the step-stone paths.

Thonra, finally recovered, scoffed, and jogged after him. "That's not what I meant, and you know it. Don't twist my words. She just hasn't seen her family in years now."

He barked a bitter laugh and responded in Attiettan, rapping his bracer against a trellis of dead weeds and sickly blue buds. "To think bad of me is one problem. You think so lowly of her? She is so simple as do as I wish? No thoughts of her own?" Niccolo spun to face Thonra, his first and last finger pointed at her chest. "You know something? Sonja changed as you are here. Is on the edge and angry in a way I do not recognize. I see her nearly drown in the water of ice and still become in a better mood than the — eh. What's the damn word? *No importé*. You drag her down and give no apology. Do not even notice. She wishes to pay for your love, and you make this so she cannot afford." He ran frustrated fingers through his hair and spat something more in Attiettan. "Find another thing for complaining, or leave. My promise is to keep you alive. Wherever this is, I do not care. I rather find this mage myself. Just go."

He spun away before she could respond. Not that Thonra had a reply. Regret gored her. She remembered the day they split up. The morning Bragi left for home.

Just go! Go south.

Thonra had yelled the words. Words that would haunt her dreams for the next two years. Bragi thought they'd follow him. It almost worked on Sonni, but Thonra had stepped in.

I'll go north, and we'll find it. We'll meet up again, and it'll be fine. No, not in the middle. Go the whole way. I'll see you at the Bari Mountains unless we find something first. Stop crying. Do you care about Ulrik or not? My nephew won't grow up fatherless.

Sonja had relented that day, suggesting Kepstadur Keep before they'd split ways. Sympathetic map in hand, Thonra hadn't looked back. It would have broken her.

Niccolo weaved in and around the planters, stopping to stare at the growing army of dead flooding the city. That army poised to kill Sonja and give Valtyr the other half of the relic. And Thonra had punched her in the gut. Shame burned her cheeks and closed her throat. He glanced over her without comment. Was she so easy to read?

"Where to hide if you choose to trap your pursuers?" he asked.

"Somewhere easy to escape," she said with a shrug. "If he's even still here. I'd be halfway across the city to avoid that blade."

"Without Leif's magic, you think?"

"No. I suppose that's the only thing keeping him here. The relic. He's probably looking for us just as fervently." Thonra thought back to the corpses piling into Leif's room.

"And if he waits?"

"What do you mean?"

Niccolo took a deep breath, squinting to stare through the windows into the throne room. "What if he waits? He believes we now have Leif. He does not allow us running. So, he instead predict where we go to keep Leif safe."

"And you know a place like that?" An anxious pit formed in Thonra's gut.

"Is the first place your sister and I camp." Niccolo led the way inside the throne room, shoulders fixed toward the door Sonni had warned her against earlier. "He knows of this place. Watched it even before he is released."

"So it would follow that he may wait there now," Thonra said, understanding rising like the dawn. "He went to Leif's room, assuming the boy was alone. Now that we've confirmed we have him, he waits in the place that you and Sonni once considered safe." Something about that changed the interaction. Valtyr was no frightened field mouse. This was the Mage of Voices. He was the horned monkey, using its snakelike tail to draw in its own meal. Thonra didn't like to be the hawk, so sure she was the only hunter.

Niccolo nodded, mouthing silent numbers as he scanned the room. "Seven. Some at the entry, some at the thrones, some in the centers."

She glanced between the four she could see. That wasn't an unreasonable number compared to other rooms this size. He guided her through the maze, pausing outside the double doors.

She traced the carvings with one finger. "What's inside?"

"Room for war plans," he said. "Big table with a map and such."

"Any other ways in or out?"

"I do not believe."

Only one entry. That spoke to a confidence Thonra grew wary of. "I'm ready when you are." As he pressed gently through, Thonra felt that he'd been right. This was the perfect den: dimly lit, cluttered, largely overrun by cumbersome furniture.

Niccolo sighed. "Or no. There are no watchers here."

She caught his arm, breathing slowly to settle her heart. "He can still be here."

"I do not see any person."

"He knows to account for you. Sonni said so." Thonra closed the door gently behind him, taking in the detailed shelving, the pedestals, and the gleaming chestplate in the center of the table. "Big soldier like yourself would benefit from something like that, yes?"

"You may say this, as this armor is mine."

"He's absolutely here." Thonra stepped lightly forward, drawing her dagger in one hand. "Just because a spell is cheap doesn't mean you can't overpay. If I know I can disappear for three mils, why would I pay twelve? I wouldn't, right?"

He nodded, following behind her, both weapons in hand.

"I wouldn't unless I knew I had to. But the magic will take anything you're willing to give it."

"You tell your magic numbers of blood?"

"It's an example, Stal. You don't *speak* to magic, per say. It's more about guiding intention. The clearer the intent, the better odds it will cooperate." The war room offered plenty of places to hide, but Thonra focused mostly along the exterior. Dense cabinets held the rows of bookshelves, wide enough for a starving mage to stand on. That's where she would hide if roles had reversed. But the armor still called to her. So perfectly placed. So tempting. After a lap around the room, slashing into the open air above the cabinetry, Thonra approached the table, heavy and inlaid with a giant map.

"Bait," Niccolo said, forcibly ignoring the metal. "Sonja believed his previous watcher waited for us to take this. Then it will know to attack. This is why we leave it and all these supplies."

"I can see that reasoning," Thonra said, "but we could use that to our advantage. If we trigger his attack, it could expose where he is. Expose what he hopes to gain." Using a stack-stone chimney for support, Thonra clambered onto the hip-high cabinetry. "You stand opposite me, Stal. That will also let you guard the door. I'll move the plate, and we'll see what happens."

Niccolo grunted in ascent. "If you can, I will like to have this back. Is a useful piece." Before walking away, however, he handed her that wicked sickle. "Is good to use on the dead. They fall and cannot resurface."

"You need this more than I do."

He frowned at her dagger. "I do not agree. Also, I search for the mage who cannot die to this. Is more of use to you." The Attiettan didn't blink until she wrapped tentative fingers around it. Through the handle, she could almost feel it vibrating. The magic inside this relic was hungry. Very hungry. Thonra didn't know how to feel about that.

After Niccolo tucked into the corner nearest the door, Thonra widened her drip. Keeping their other spells in place, she sent waves out along the table, manifesting little hands below the chest plate. Manifestations couldn't be altered by any further illusion magic, so she could only hope nothing was watching too closely underneath. She rocked the plate — it was denser than she'd assumed — waiting a tense breath in case anything changed. When the silence remained, Thonra pulled again, drawing the armor to the narrow side of the table, neither toward herself nor toward Niccolo.

Maybe they had been wrong. Maybe she had projected her own preferences onto the Mage of Voices. It would be a lucky break to make this space her own den, in the process also retrieving Niccolo's belongings. She shot the stallion a gleaming smile. This was far better than she could have expected.

Until five bolts cracked into existence, thundering against the cabinetry bases and exploding into violent color.

22

WITHIN HALLOWED HALLS

Thonra nearly tumbled off-balance, fighting like hell to maintain her concentration. She clutched to stones and shelves to keep from plummeting into the writhing mass of vines snaking up and boring through the woodwork. It took an extra moment for her mind to register what she had seen. Five crossbow bolts, arrayed out and fired toward the base of the shelving. There to catch anyone, even those not standing directly by the table. Tendrils now spread unfettered along the ground and walls. Nowhere was safe.

She gaped back at Niccolo, a question on her lips, but terror ate her words. He hacked at a bundle of vines clawing up his legs and waist. Gods, she should have made him climb the furniture like she had. His sword lacked the efficiency of the sickle he'd given away. The bolt hadn't hit him directly, but he'd been far too close to escape in time. His teeth gritted together, desperate to stay quiet. No one would hear. But anyone could see loops encasing an invisible man.

Whatever shot the bolts would be closing on him.

Thonra prepared to jump, only for something rough to wrap around her ankle. She choked out a scream as thorns like wolves' fangs dug into soft flesh. With a single slash, she cleaved through the vines, marring antiques behind her. The coil stilled but didn't fall away. Pain remained, a burning poison. Gods, she hoped it wasn't poison.

With an unsure leap, Thonra tumbled to the table, scattering little tokens in all directions. Sloppy. Valtyr would find them. She needed time. Thonra enveloped the room in abyssal darkness, filling the void with the sound of rain and thunder. She groped at her ankle, flinching back as a thorn jabbed into her palm. It was certainly poisonous. Shit.

She cast the plant away and crawled to the table's upturned lip, the little war tokens digging into her knees and palms. Carefully, Thonra stood and moved across the map's surface, fingers straining around the fjarfest. She blinked the darkness away, only long enough to confirm that Niccolo was still affixed to the wall, then she started swinging. The first few lopped through nothing, until, without warning, the Reaper blade sunk into something soft. Revenant, likely. The blow was effortless, morbidly comforting in its familiar motion. It reminded her of days playing in the vineyard, shirking work. But the fruit back west had put up more of a fight. The fjarfest completed its arc unresisted. A thunk and clatter sounded, like the tumbling body had knocked over a chair. On the backswing, she dropped another and clipped a third that squelched limply against her, pushing her back. Definitely the dead.

Thonra banished the darkness again, almost surprised to find Niccolo fully freed. Damn, it was useful to have a null around. Sonni really knew how to pick them. He was pale, somewhat off-kilter. Rips in his clothing were soaked with a clear liquid rather than the deep red of blood. She'd need to tend to that quickly.

Tumbling off the table toward him, Thonra examined the downed revenants and their reloaded crossbows. Before she could reach him, plumes of sand grew and solidified. Thonra smacked into several in her path — versions of Sonja and Niccolo, all terrified and scampering around the soft green light. So many manifestations. The null would have no advantage here, except he hadn't expected Thonra. Ash erupted where Niccolo had been, desperation in the movement. He'd be easy to find. She needed to decentralize the destruction.

She fished in her pocket of pebbles — Sonni's trick, but Thonra never let a spell beat her. She reared back and launched the pebbles, heavier, across the room, far from Niccolo's carnage. Clustered together, the manifestations crumbled to dust, giving her an idea. Thonra opened the next bloshul drip and focused on the falling sands. This had been tricky magic to learn. She coaxed the remnants up, calling for the ash to create, but stopping short. It felt like half of a command. The particles surged through the air, buffeting against all the visages of her allies. Amid it all, however, a single, unseen form created an outline. Tall and thin, she could almost see his robe billowing in her maelstrom. Valtyr's silhouette stood in one of the many chairs, invisible arms held to shield his face. Thonra surged forward, slicing through manifestations, adding their essence to her spell. She had a limited time to act. The sand grew obstinate against her mind, seemingly aware it was being misused.

Moments before she reached the table, the dust drew away from her control, collating into hard steel. A cloud of knives hung overhead as if suspended from the tips. The handles pivoted up, many pointing at Thonra, others directing to what she had to assume was Niccolo. There was barely time to think. Thonra dropped to one knee, her momentum carrying her under the table. The chair where Valtyr stood toppled over, likely abandoned.

Knives pattered down, loud and angry as hail. Niccolo cried out. Thonra's breath caught at the sound. She hadn't kept him safe.

Sonja didn't quite hear Leif's words until he had disappeared into the tunnels again. *Release us all.*

She hated the sound of that. "Now, hold on," she said. "Let's talk about this for a second."

"No, this is right." The boy was starkly calm. His voice was listless while his breathing stuttered unnaturally. "If we're released, we'll be together again."

"And how do you plan on accomplishing that?" She didn't fully need his reply. Firebugs reoriented as he passed with the little blue crystal held high. They flocked to him as readily as they had to the Reaper blade. If Niccolo was to be believed, that made this blue rock a dreki object. A tiny part of her mind wondered what kind. "What about all your travel? There's a whole world out there, and you want to see it, don't you? When I tell you that Jrendavar is far more than anything you've seen before…"

He turned over one shoulder wearing a face twisted by fear and sorrow. But his eyes held a harsh determination. Gods, she'd seen that look before. "They aren't supposed to be here. It's torture, isn't it? I'm torturing them. I can't carry them with me like this, live a normal life."

"You can," Sonja shot back. "Do you really believe Elvy and your father and all your friends *want* you to die young? Let's sit and talk this through."

He continued toward the heat. It was the first time she'd seen any piece of this fjarfest up close — broken between the glyphs, then braided into a lattice of leather and wool. "I was supposed to die. We should have all died together. This place is the third hell, and we're too stubborn to escape the cycle."

"You're being rash."

"We should all be together."

An image of that old barn cat flashed through Sonja's memory. Young Ulrik trembling to keep it alive. It only lived another few years after he'd saved it, but that sense of responsibility had been its own anchor. Maybe Leif couldn't see a path forward, so he looked for a chivalric end. He wasn't the cause of the entrapped spirits, yet he buckled under self-assigned responsibility. She couldn't watch Ulrik die again. "Another thing," she pleaded. "I don't think this will work the way you want it to."

"What do you mean?"

"You haven't solved the problem, have you? Sure, *this* relic stops drawing in spirits, but what would happen next? There's a second one upstairs. You destroy that relic, and I'd bet my barn that every spirit drawn to you would suddenly bind to the thief."

This gave him pause, his feet shuffling until he faced her.

"And think of all the other people all over the nation who he'll be able to snatch up if we let him live. Everyone in Tharvik and Batinavik, on and on until someone else stops him. We need that second half, Leif. We can be the ones to save everyone. Like in Niccolo's stories."

"To destroy the second half too?"

Sonja's mouth went dry. "What if we could use the halves together for good? What if we can bring people back? People like Niccolo's friends or your parents."

"And keep them here longer?" he spat.

"You don't want them back?"

Figments flashed around him, malformed and unnaturally upright. Elvy, the warlord, the cook wearing the eyepatch, on and on down the sweltering hall. Their dull eyes were so close to sentient, but not quite. "Like this? No, I don't! You can look at them and say you do?"

She couldn't.

"All I want," Leif lowered his voice, still strained and somewhat petulant, "is to let them go. You say I would go too. Fine," his voice quaked, "I'll go with them. Travel is for the living, and I've always been dead. These are stupid, stupid dreams, and I don't want them." He squeezed the fjarfest as if it might crumble in his grasp. When it held firm, his head and shoulders caved over his fists

"It's a shame," Sonja whispered, her throat too tight for sound. "You just seem like a survivor to me."

The illusions dissipated. Leif turned away, but he kept the crystal tucked in his hand. They walked together in silence, the tension in the air having dulled somewhat. He didn't push deeper into the halls, seemingly satisfied to walk the perimeter where the firebugs were no taller than her knees.

"The world needs more people like you," Sonja said.

He didn't reply, shuffling on with one hand tracing the rough stone.

A thought stuck out in her mind: what if they didn't need to *hold* the second half? These two pieces had originally been one, linking them very strongly. If they destroyed Leif's relic, especially burning it, Sonja could probably transfer that destruction. In a way, it was like her shared map. Sending that heat along threads… No. This was stupid. She smothered the thought. Even if she had the blood for that kind of magic, she wouldn't let Ulrik die — not Ulrik. Leif. Leif couldn't die. He was too young. He'd been through too much.

The prince stalled, looking back down the hall. In the quiet, a faint sound drifted toward them. A thudding. Again and again. Something crashed in the distance. Clattering footsteps cascaded closer — many, many footsteps. More than Thonra and Niccolo would make together. More ravenous than a triumphant return. Firebugs scattered into burrows. The stampede of bootfalls thinned in several directions. Fanning out? Surrounding them?

A flash at the end of the hallway showed the briefest image of a person, their black scleras searching. Searching for Leif.

"Stal?" Thonra struggled to form the word, echoing in the confinement beneath the table. Eerie silence followed, broken abruptly as his knee hit the ground and his hand slammed the table. The heavy breastplate rolled away from him, manifestation sand pouring off its smooth curves. Did Valtyr know the strikes fell true? Thonra scrambled out, catching Niccolo before he could fully drop. Gods, he was an ox. She used her limited momentum to carry him several paces away, dragging him into the only somewhat safe corner.

His eyes wrenched shut, and he muttered through gritted teeth, "*Medicina. Por tossica. Enna bolsan. Enna bolsan...*"

"Just rest. You're going to be okay." But she couldn't move him. Not quickly. Maybe the best thing to do was run. To distract Valtyr with her own bait. Opening yet another bloshul to drip in tandem, Thonra cast the room into darkness again. She pressed a comforting hand on his chest. He was trembling, covered in a thin layer of sweat, but what could she reasonably do for him? "You'll be safe here."

"*Por tossi— por tossica...*" he repeated.

Under cover of her fabricated night, Thonra stumbled toward the door, searching until she found the handle's smooth metal. She forced it open, drinking in chilled, salty air. Thonra took a single step and bounced off something terrible. Solid, yet textured like sour milk. Revenants. Shit. A flurry of arms closed in, searching blindly. Thonra drew up a mix of manifestations to confuse them. Fast and messy. Hide. She had to hide. She fell to her knees and dragged past the slew of limbs, clinging to every spell until she could stand again.

Thonra knew not to go too far. Niccolo had to stay in her radius. That's how he'd survive. Unseen. Out of the way. Gods, Sonni would be furious. Her words echoed in the darkness. *He deserves to live.* Thonra silently promised he would.

She created two final manifestations and let all others fade. After three breaths, she dissipated the darkness, staring at a version of herself that dragged Niccolo away. They were pretty good. She was proud to mimic even his unhealthy pallor, that mild green undertone. Thonra tried not to look at her own double. Leaner than she'd been. White lines of stress already streaking her dark hair. The illusion was crying again. Why did it always cry? Damned magic.

Regardless, it put on a good show, nearly fumbling the soldier to check its other bloshuls, then panicking as if confirming them all empty. Thonra's double pulled more desperately, but fake-Stal was as heavy as the original.

Corpses encircled the manifestations, and fake-Thonra leveled her dagger. They were beautiful little things, hers and Sonni's, but they'd very clearly been designed as ornamentation. Ulrik had liked the history behind them. Some legend about foreign gods who swapped domains, leading both to ruin. It looked so childish in the manifestation's hand.

Thonra craned for a hint of Niccolo, flinching at the sudden tenderness in her leg. He needed to hold on a bit longer.

A gaunt figure faded into existence. Not the bubbling of a manifestation, but an invisibility spell wisping away. This was the real Valtyr. In his many depictions, there were few consistencies. Some showed him as a giant with strong, laborer's shoulders, towering over his victims. Some drew in red eyes or off-color flames that lapped along his beard. But the truth was unremarkable — maybe a little tall, with hair like ink spilling to his knees. Years of captivity had not been kind to him. The Mage of Voices wasn't quite skeletal. He bore weeping puncture wounds just as fresh as Niccolo's, but the veins… The veins were dark purple and red and blue to mirror the roots that grew from those horrible relic bolts. He walked slowly, purposefully, possibly neutralizing a limp, his hands clasped behind his back. Rich clothing hung filthy and torn, and jewelry showed ages of neglect.

Valtyr blinked at fake-Thonra's pathetic dagger, his eyes flicking between the manifestations. This might be her best chance. If she couldn't find the Kepstan relic — apparently a crystal — she could at least look for the fjarfest controlling the dead. Valtyr furrowed his brow, arms crossed at his chest. She swore she saw a significant glimmer on one hand. Gods, if the Myhrs were right about that wristlet…

"You can come out now." Valtyr's voice startled her into stillness. Quiet, yet firm with a mild northern flare. "Let us handle this as adults. As it stands, I have something you want, and you have something that belongs to me. I request a trade."

Thonra ignored him, calling for her illusion to spit at his feet. "Rot in the grave, bastard," fake-Thonra said with impressive vitriol.

Valtyr ignored the manifestation. "Come now, I can be fair. Let us negotiate, yes?" Through the antechamber, movement stilled Thonra's careful approach. She peered around a few bodies, Niccolo's sickle held poised.

A group of revenants dragged Sonni, unconscious and bloody, from the open study door.

-|-

Turn after turn, Sonja dragged Leif behind her, his panting too loud. "Rest a bit." She batted away at a brave cluster of smaller bugs as they flocked to the relic. They weren't in the deepest part of the maze, yet sweat trickled down her temple and the air felt thick in her throat. "We can make it back to the door."

"I have to destroy it." He looked so tired, so old — well into his twenties or thirties. "They're going to kill us and take both pieces."

"There's got to be another way out." Sonja pulled him up, keeping them moving. Shuffling steps sounded from all angles. Not quite surrounded, but close.

"Arvid?" The horror and pain in Leif's voice sent a stabbing heat through Sonja's throat. His whole body shook, but he reached out and squeezed her hand. A figure stood, distinguished but faded in his finery, a crossbow leveled. Arvid's black eyes haunted his bloated face.

It took aim, and she shoved Lief down, instinctively lurching in front of him and manipulating her pack. Cloth hardened to stone, grinding into her shoulder blades and accelerating her fall. Sonja had the clarity of mind to shield her head before impact.

A crunching, rending squeal echoed off the close quarters. Sharp pain jolted through Sonja's shoulders and wrapped her arm. She grunted and released the manipulation, aware of a coldness in her fingers. She froze for a moment, both settling the blood rush and mentally evaluating the wound.

"Stay down." Leif's voice was quiet, taut. Her loaned bloshul hung at his side, sealed but still deflating. Another mechanical twang resonated, followed by a distant, rebounding clatter. She flinched, renewing the pain in the arm, but he kept her down. Footsteps thundered away, leaving only the sounds of their breathing. "They're gone." Leif's second hand twisted into a bizarre three-point focus, held stiffly in front of him.

When Leif shifted away, she twisted out of the pack straps and forced herself upright. Only the tip of the arrow, maybe the length of her smallest nail, jabbed through. Her fingers still worked.

"Is your bag magic?" The prince ran a cautious thumb over the exposed point.

"It's a little trick." Her breaths came slowly, deliberately. "When we make it out of here, I'll show you." She took his arm before he could argue, pulling in the opposite direction. Sonja could feel the revenants nearby. She could hide in an illusion, but for how long? What would that leave if she had to fight? Then again, would they have any chance at all in a direct confrontation?

Leif was only getting slower. Tears streamed along his face as he muttered words too quiet to make out. Determination compiled slowly. "I don't want to," he said, finally loud enough to hear.

They rounded another corner, and the air grew cooler. Were they near the study? Could they lock their pursuers inside? This didn't look familiar, but the stone walls were all a little too similar. It smelled of salt, but she followed it again and again and again until a breeze brushed her sweat-stained face. Sonja sped up. It was darker here. Maybe there *was* a second exit. Maybe there was a way out.

"Sonja, I don't…"

She barely saw the bars in time to stop. A gate, rough texture reflecting in the uncanny lighting, blocked them from a pitch-dark path. The air beyond it was cool and refreshing. A tart ocean breeze compared to the hell of the hallway. Sonja fumbled with the padlock, casting a surge of energetic magic that only sent sparks in all directions. No. Not iron. Not here. They were going to get out. She clawed at the hinges and hung off the bars, but it was sturdy.

Revenants scrambled toward them, a slew of weapons in hand, wearing everything from faded uniforms to tattered nightwear. She corralled Leif behind her and searched for outs. One round of pebbles dropped several, but many rose again after only a few heartbeats. Arvid stood among the front line, that crossbow trained on her chest. Sonja cast a wall of fire, both protecting and obscuring them, but it was ravenous against her resources. The crossbow fired, narrowly missing and clanging into the locked corridor.

Sonja cast another spell against the padlock, only to have it backfire, burning a hole through her cloak. Leif was singing. It was a broken tune, maybe a lullaby, but she couldn't quite make out the words through his sobs. Footsteps echoed against her skull.

She would die here. The least Sonja could do was help the others.

It was a trick. Thonra knew it was a trick. It had to be a trick. The revenants dragging Sonni — no. It wasn't Sonni. It could not be Sonni. The revenants dragging that *thing* ambled into the circle, dropping *it* next to fake-Thonra and fake-Niccolo.

It couldn't be real, yet Thonra's magic spiraled out of control. Young Sonjas and Ulriks flickered in and out of existence. Bragi's sorrowful expression appeared on thirty forms all around her. Her manifestations wavered, sand falling from the elbows and chin. Gods, Thonra was losing it. She was slipping. This was a trap, and it was working. He was an illusionist, the emperor of unreality. This was not Sonni. But gods…

Thonra stumbled toward the mage, dodging revenants and hoping nothing invisible hid in her path. Closer and closer, Thonra saw more detail of a familiar wristlet, one she'd studied since leaving Seglaborg. She searched his other jewelry, still several paces out of arm's reach, but nothing looked like Sonni's description of the Kepstan relic…

Sonni… Sonni was…

Thronra choked down a sob. Older images of her siblings formed around her. Ulrik, sick, but holding his son on one hip. Sonja in the wedding drapes she'd never used. Ma and Dada.

Valtyr could see it all, her pain and weakness. He drank it in with an unreadable expression. Thonra couldn't stop it, so she barreled forward. With her limited control, she called for her double to lunge at Valtyr, which indeed sent him back a few steps. That was certainly the wristlet, and all she had to do was take it.

Thonra slashed down with the Reaper sickle. Sure, the Kepstadur relic, wherever he held it, would protect him from dying, but being maimed? Maybe not. The invested blade cracked, stopping halfway through the arm, as it had for Niccolo. Valtyr bellowed, and the revenants closed on the thing that looked like Sonni. Thonra ripped it away and tried again, hacking even lower on the forearm, but the magic refused to part for the blade. In desperation, she flung the frail mage to the ground, pinning his arm and clutching at the fjarfest chains. They were stronger than she'd expected for how dainty they looked, and, unfortunately, so was Valtyr. He rolled, slamming her back, searching her invisible body, tearing away bloshuls and supplies. His rage continued to echo off the walls, growing manic as long fingers closed around her neck. Slimy, half-living revenant hands fumbled to pin down her limbs. Thonra slashed again, but not for his arm. She missed twice more before the sickle snapped through the chains.

The revenants stalled, going limp before collapsing all around her. Valtyr only shouted louder. He struggled to his knees, shoving her back so that she hit the floor again and again. He seemed to meet her eyes. Was she not cloaked anymore? Thonra couldn't focus long enough to check. Dazed on the terrazzo, her head rolled over, meeting Sonja's unblinking eyes. A rusted spear protruded from her back, held firm by the only two revenants still standing.

"You think this is pain?" Valtyr growled, kicking her closer to her sister. Why wasn't it fading? It wasn't real. It should fade. Please fade. "You wouldn't last a day as I've been. And we can test that."

Thonra blinked up to see Valtyr raising a relic bolt overhead. She was the calf at the altar.

Metallic resonance rang through the throne room, almost louder than Valtyr's choked cry of surprise. Niccolo stood behind the mage, wearing his breastplate and long lines of exhaustion. He wasn't even looking at Sonja as she bled and died. How could he not care?

Thonra rolled to hands and knees, trying not to pass out or throw up or both. A man's scream echoed in her ears as the room flashed a blinding white light.

Another pang, and a crossbow bolt drove deep into the floor, wedged perfectly in the space between two stones. Sonja gawked at it, gleaming in the firelight.

"Do you—" Leif's words cut off in a yelp as one of the forms dropped through the flames. A second fell through, along with a clatter from the far side, then the silence returned. Sonja waited only another moment before dropping her manifestation to find the horde of bodies collapsed on top of each other as far as she could see. Leif pressed past her and fell to his knees. He cradled Arvid's corpse, even as the ichor seeped over his hands. The prince didn't cry, but his gaze was farther away than the sun was from the moon.

"We can't stay," Sonja said after several long breaths. He could mourn here forever, but the revenants might rise again. She threw several of the weapons out of reach into the locked hall, then almost carried Leif away, crunching over the dead. There wasn't enough salt in the world to bless these bodies. What was salt to these? Years in the brine had done little to give them rest.

It didn't take long to leave them behind, but Leif was inconsolable, hitting his chest and scratching up his arms. "I want it gone. All of it, gone. I never want to see this again." He threw the fjarfest against a dead-end wall, falling from her grip. "Kill it," he wheezed through fits of coughing. "Let them die. Promise you'll let them die"

Sonja kept him from collapsing then scrambled to retrieve the relic. Immediately upon touching it, a shock of energy repressed her sleeplessness and amplified her emotions. It was heavier than she had expected, dense but pliant. The anchor felt more akin to soft wood than stone. She rubbed gentle fingers over some common glyphs. *BOND. PULL. LIFE.* There were several she didn't recognize. Older combinations in older tongues.

"Niccolo would be heartbroken," she said, cradling Leif's head and cupping the relic to his chest. "For what it's worth, so would I."

Leif huffed but didn't fight.

Could she do both? Destroy Valtyr's relic with sympathy while keeping Leif alive? Was it worth the risk? She would have tried for Ulrik. But Ulrik was gone. This was not the same boy, not in three hundred ways, so why did it feel like losing him again? "Let's talk about this back in the…"

Around the next blind corner stood a man. His tattered robes and long black hair flared in the heat. He dragged a dark-haired woman, unconscious, across the stone behind him. Sonja stumbled back on instinct. Her insides twisted in horror and alarm. Her eyes burned. She pulled Leif carefully away, one shaky finger held to her lips. She didn't think he'd seen them, but Sonja barely breathed. Valtyr was here. He was here, and he had her sister. He had Thonra. Where did that leave Niccolo? Sonja could barely see through her tears. What had gone wrong? When? Had he always known? Been waiting?

"What is…" Leif whispered.

Sonja's throat was too tight to speak. To even breathe. Was Thonra still alive? Sonja paid for an identification, but there was so much metal. She couldn't find anything but sparks and mist. Gods, she was blind. There was no telling where he'd gone. And if he was invisible… No. No, he wouldn't be. It was better to be seen. Valtyr would use Thonra to get to Leif. Sonja wouldn't let him.

The prince pulled on her arm, pointing to a marker carved into the wall. One that Niccolo had left. The ones that led to the fiery core. Sonja nodded encouragingly. If Thonra was alive, this would save her. If she wasn't, it would save Carita and Helmi, Red and Pierce. All those people living blissfully unaware, a mere half-day's travel from a nightmare. "We'll destroy it," Sonja said. "His too. Keep holding it for now, but let's find that furnace room." With the crystal exposed so deep in the cavern, they were attracting a lot of attention from larger beetles. The firebugs were wary though.

"If you wish her to live, you will cease your running." The voice resonated through the tunnels, loud enough to disguise the direction. "I will not plead. Not the way he did, your foreigner."

Leif looked up in fear, but Sonja had no comfort to give. She was hollow. Filled only with dread and death and loss.

"The soldier was stronger than I gave him credit for," Valtyr continued. "He may even still live. Find him before he bleeds away. These two in exchange for the rest of the relic. This is all I request."

Thonra's voice groaned something incomprehensible.

"Yes, yes," Valtyr hummed. "She is here. She is very near. I'm sure she will come for you."

Leif was growing too heavy, or maybe Sonja was growing too weak. She hated this quest. She hated herself for agreeing. It was a useless venture. What had it cost? Two years, and they were no closer to her brother than the first day. And if they were, would she dare do this to him? Was it living?

I'm sorry, Ulrik. You deserved more than your years. I wish we could have found you a few more. I'm so, so sorry.

She was on the ground now. Sonja dragged across the stone while Leif crawled beside her. She wasn't going to make it. But the firebugs, they seemed bolder. A large beast with a broken leg stalked them from the ceiling nearby. It wasn't as scary, knowing what they wanted. Niccolo's sickle. Leif's relic. It really was simple.

Sonja took his hand and felt that surge of life again. She scratched the crystal across the stone. It left a nice, clear line. Not quite chalky, but any bit would help. She was out of plans, but not out of magic. Guiding the prince's hand, Sonja drew out three intersecting circles, then connected the points in a triangle. Leif didn't seem to be fully cognizant, but he slid closer and allowed her to lead. More firebugs waited, perched in the shadows of the corridor. All sizes congregated together, from little orange matches to huge red forges. She pulled open her last drip all the way and sought out the Kepstan relic's energy threads. Sympathy streaked up and around in far more directions than she'd expected. Maybe the nearby iron was still playing tricks on her. Sonja latched on to the strongest one in her mind, paying out her costs. She pressed her lips against the smooth edge before centering it in her drawing.

No sooner had she let it go than the swarm closed in. Sonja caught Leif as he dropped, seizing against the stone. She scooped him up, back leaned against the wall, almost feeling the waves of pain roll over him. His energy weakened, but the thread was still stubbornly in place for now, so Sonja reached for it. It grew brittle and rough against that part of her mind. How long could she hold on to him? The magic could have anything it needed, as long as the Mage of Voices died. Leif cried out, curling further into her chest. Like holding Ulrik after the nightmares. Sonja knew she was crying but couldn't feel the tears.

She almost didn't notice Valtyr down a nearby hall, his free hand clutched at his chest. Good. If Leif survived, Thonra would be close by. She could help him, even if it took everything Sonja had left. The mage looked terrified, maybe unable to believe what he witnessed. The writhing bugs made short work of the relic, and it burned like Sonja had hoped. That heat needed to transfer sympathetically. She could do this. It was nothing new. Just hold on. Don't let go.

Sand pooled around Valtyr's extremities and fell from Thonra's hair. Manifestations. They'd never been real to begin with. Sonja almost laughed, but the pain was too great. Hopefully that meant he'd lied about Niccolo. Her soldier deserved to live. Maybe, for his sake, he shouldn't find her body. Maybe that would be too much. Thonra would take care of him. She'd promised to keep him safe.

When the thread between the two relic pieces broke, Sonja rocked with the jarring release. Had she not been on the ground already, she'd have crashed into the walls. Ash and dust faded completely, leaving no remnant of the mage's last grand lie. The bugs scurried around, checking for more food, but they left once certain Sonja and Leif had nothing to give.

"We did it," Sonja whispered, clutching Leif's energy.

"They're proud?" His voice wouldn't pass through a flower petal.

"They are." She didn't know exactly which "they" he meant, but she didn't have to. "Go to sleep now. You've done such a good job."

-|-

Thonra hunched on the stone, unable to move or think or process anything that was happening. But Bragi was there with her. She felt his presence. She could almost reach out and touch him. This figment or illusion or psychosis, whatever it might be, caressed her cheek. He had the darkest brown eyes that sparkled in a crowd, eyes that glowed when they met hers.

Niccolo was somewhere behind her, the sounds of his struggle dim in her ears. She'd failed. Thonra couldn't save either of them from this terrible endeavor. She should have let Sonja leave. Sonja wasn't meant for this kind of work. It was better for Thonra alone to bring her findings home, where Sonja would be safe and taken care of. For only Thonra to die if she failed.

That magical brightness faded, until finally, she pushed herself upright and found the gaggle of revenants crumpled on the ground. They stared past her with blackened eyes, leaking a putrid liquid from their mouths and noses. Sonni was gone. So was her growing puddle of blood. Of course the null didn't react. There had been nothing to see. Yet, the emptiness continued to ache. Shuffling grunts echoed overhead, as if a great distance away. She looked back to see Niccolo struggling against the Mage of Voices. One arm rammed a sword through Valtyr's gut as the other fist held them together. Niccolo seemed careful with his footing, maintaining a wall to shield her, no matter how Valtyr thrashed. He had powerful legs, Niccolo. His trousers had been cuffed up to his knees. Powdery blue ointment smeared over puncture wounds on his exposed calves. That was probably good. Yes, better than the poisonous dribble.

Against her own will, Thonra stood. She could hear Bragi's soft encouragement. Without the revenants, the odds were far more fair. Manifestations pulled Niccolo back, but Thonra slashed steadily through each one. They could do this. They could take it. Step by step.

Until more hands latched to Thonra's arms. Until the manifestation of a half-naked warrior slammed his forehead into Niccolo's temple. The Attiettan clattered to the ground, his sword discarded. A blade pressed into her throat. She said goodbye to Bragi, raising her shoulder one last time to brush against the wooden earrings. What message would he get from that?

In the seconds before steel split skin, ash cascaded around her. Thonra searched for Niccolo, who surely had banished the spells, but no. He lay on the ground, covered in that fading dust. Valtyr clutched at his chest, cupping a violent orange glow, so bright as to sear through his skin. In a sickening crack, Valtyr was blown back, slamming into a nearby wall. He slumped to the stone, hands falling away from wretched burns, the smell of which stung her eyes. His head lolled to one side before he toppled over, unmoving.

Thonra's mind was too clogged to make sense of all the things she saw, but her body knew to stumble forward. She rolled the Mage of Voices to his back, finding a seared hole through his shirt. His chest beneath had burned black and still radiated like dying coals. A leather band lay across his chest, as if part of a broken necklace. Maybe it had once held a trinket, but no more.

Thonra felt nauseous. Or exhausted. Or both. They had been so close to Ulrik. He should've been back by now. Her two-month expedition had expanded into years of hopelessness, shoved down again and again and again. But she did it for the family.

Thonra cried. Hot tears that took shuddering gasps to fully release. This had been her chance to go home. How had she come so close, only to fail at the very last moment? She coughed and closed her eyes, shaking with a physical pain that radiated from deep in her stomach. Thonra doubled over and grew still, as it hurt more and more to simply breathe. She would check on the Stallion soon, but first, she needed to rest. At least until the room stopped spinning.

23

FINAL COST

Sonja counted the seconds. Her vision would fade first. It'd be like passing out. She wondered if she'd die like Felix had: aware that she was dead before being called to the Sapphire Orchards. Or had the anchor affected his passing? She hoped Ulrik would be waiting. A guide who could show her around. He'd had years to meet other spirits. Meet the gods, even. He'd have befriended hundreds of poets and historic figures by now…

Her count crossed ninety, and Sonja opened her eyes. She felt fine. Very hot and a little lightheaded, maybe, but far from dead. Sure, the caster's own blood was a rich payment, but that link had been expensive. It didn't matter how good of an alternator Sonja was, she'd never felt so much power. She should have dried up. Unless the magic had taken something else.

Shit. What had she offered?

Sonja surged upright, woozier than she'd believed. There were tales, terrible tales, of magic affecting relatives. A mage would use too much, and it would take something more valuable than blood — an only child, a close relative, a new spouse. Thonra couldn't die, but Niccolo… She couldn't banish the thought fast enough.

Abandoning her pack, she hauled Leif's arms over her shoulders, leaning into the walls and stumbling toward the stairs. She climbed, sorry that his feet thudded against each riser. He groaned weakly, energy still tied to his body, if only because she would not let go. The study warped past her, but she focused on her goal. The secret hallway stretched long and round. Her stomach rioted. Don't stop moving. Sonja dragged him into the light of the foyer, collapsing once she ran out of supporting walls. Black-eyed bodies littered her vision, unmoving. She could almost make out the sound of rain.

She tried calling for help, but it was so cold. The marble floors rocked under her hands, and she couldn't see Leif's thread clearly in her mind. Sonja imagined more and more hands holding him, but it was dull. She didn't know how long she lay there. Maybe long enough to die. Leif's eyes fluttered open and closed, open and closed. He wouldn't make it. Who would go first? Would his eyes turn to those terrible black scleras? What if the sympathy hadn't worked? Valtyr could still be here.

Sonja didn't register Niccolo's arrival until he was over her, cupping her face, talking again, softly and slowly. He was always talking, and she yearned to sit and listen. But he was dead. She'd killed him with her magic, and Leif was fading.

"Whatever you're doing, stop." Thonra's voice rang so clearly. An oversized bloshul dropped nearby as Niccolo pressed a canteen into Sonja's unresponsive fingers. Thonra knelt, propping up Leif, brushing over Sonja's tight knuckles and frowning. She wore a veil of heaviness. Thonra pulled the bloshul cap so that a trickle of blood dripped down the side.

Offering boar's blood didn't take Sonja's dizziness away, but it gave her the clarity of mind to use her words. "He's fading. Don't let him. Don't let him."

"Let go," Thonra snapped. "I've got him. Niccolo, get in my pack. Bottom left pocket — go on, she's fine. The boy isn't. Move. Now."

Niccolo laid Sonja gently on her side and dug through Thonra's belongings.

"Other left, Stal. Come on. There's a wooden box. Find it for me, please." Her tone was serious but not sharp. She almost sounded lighter or kinder…

"Thonra?" Was any of this real?

"Rest, Sonni. We've got him. I can't keep you both. Only so many hands." A gentle thumb brushed across Sonja's forearm.

"Is this?" Niccolo asked.

"Yep, that's it. There's a book with it. Leather. Pages ripped out. Yes, that. Grab those pages."

Sonja faded for a moment, coming to with a roiling nausea, choking on that metallic smell. She couldn't sit there. She had payment now. With so much blood pooling across the floor, Sonja blinked, inverting the colors with an identification spell. At a sweeping glance, this was the emptiest the castle had been. The wall of spirits had dissipated, leaving Thonra's raging energy to contrast Niccolo's gentle glow. The aura of green mist around the Reaper blade twitched and thrashed but slowly leaked out. Very little in the spell's darkness felt distinct. It took a breath to notice Leif's spirit hanging off her sister's. The end was loose and frayed, with a cold cast. She was his anchor. He was alone, and he seemed aware of it.

"… Bunch of stones…" Thonra's voice was muffled. "... All the little carvings. Yes, yes. Grab those…all of them on his chest…"

Sonja pulled lightly on the prince's energy. "We can show you the west." Sonja's voice echoed into the void.

Leif's face shifted in and out of focus, radiating that familiar yellow light. His expression — when she could see it — was distant. He watched her, unblinking, with no reply.

"We'll stop at every food stand we see. You'll fatten up in no time," she said.

"Of where you get this?" Niccolo's voice was far clearer.

Leif turned toward the sound, studying his soft aura.

She reached for Leif again. "You don't have to stay, but it would mean a lot if you did. He doesn't want to say goodbye."

Niccolo's voice rose, just shy of a shout. "Lief drink; make Leif drink. Please, this, I know this. Trust me."

A surge of indigo thrashed around the prince's face, his energy flaring with color, but the threads slipped from Thonra's grip. His face stabilized, eyes wide and watery on Sonja. "I'm scared."

Before she could reply, her physical body lost connection with the blood source, plunging her back into the colors of reality.

"...her away from him," Thonra was saying. "She'll hurt herself."

Blackness snapped back into place as Sonja's body jerked into the air. The movement chilled her weak bones, almost too dazed to keep breathing. Was any of this real? Or simply the thoughts of the dying. She slipped out of consciousness.

No visions. No memories. Simple nothingness.

Sonja fluttered awake to find herself in the regent's study again, the warmth of the tunnels failing to counteract her trembling jaw. She curled into a soft bench, dreamlike and unmoored, until a loud clatter brought her back. The suddenness bounced behind her eyes. With a tired grunt, Niccolo lowered and latched the trapdoor.

"Aye, aye." Niccolo's familiar, admonishing chitter soothed her. He eased to his knees, a firm hand holding her shoulder. "Stay here. Please, drink."

After grumbling something that she didn't even find coherent,

Sonja took the proffered canteen. Half the water sloshed down her face, and he coaxed her to eat some dried meat, watching like she was a lizard that might skitter away.

"What happened?" she whispered, trembling fingers reaching for him. "You look terrible." And he did. Cuts and puncture wounds covered his face and body. Blood had dried, smeared away from his eyes and crusted in the fibers of his clothes. Greenish-blue spots dotted across his skin. His leathers lay discarded by the door, battered beyond recognition, leaned against his breastplate. It was all so damaged, she wasn't sure any piece was salvageable beyond scrap.

A tired smirk warmed his cheeks. "And you are all red." He brushed a thumb across a tender spot near her temple. "Help check pupils."

The tightness in her chest contracted further, refusing to take in full breaths. What if the illusionist… What if he was tricking her? Was this all a lie? She let her fingers catch against the folds of Niccolo's shirt. It was the one he'd loaned her, now covered in rips and grime. One finger hooked gently into a tear and gave the fabric the smallest tug. "Are you real?"

His lips worked around a reply, brow furrowed, before he spoke. "I hold closer perils. Yes. Nothing grey about us."

Tears dropped to her nose as she forced the next words. "Did Thonra survive?"

Niccolo flinched. "She did, she did. You did not see her?" His reply came with an earnest haste, and he took her floating hand gently in his. "Yes, yes, yes, yes. She is in the hall. Is no reason to cry."

"I thought I'd killed you both." The words hung between them as she dropped her arm. "Magic I couldn't afford, but it didn't take me. It didn't, and I don't know why."

Niccolo's jaw flexed, and he sat back on his heels. "The fire is yours, yes?"

"Fire?"

He gave his head a subtle shake, loosening a few waves. "The mage smelled of fire as he died. I do not know why."

Sonja's eyes floated to the little orange beetles climbing on the walls. "My fault. Sympathy magic. Both pieces are gone."

Niccolo nodded, his eyes distant.

"I'm sorry," she whispered. "I broke our promise."

"Promise?"

"To bring them back."

His lips drew into a thin line. Niccolo proffered the canteen again, helping her sit up, but taking his time with the words. "I believed we died. And when we did not, it was a gift. But we still run here. You lie among the dead." He swallowed hard. "The door is open, and there are bodies that lead to the place we left you. I would trade seven hundred relics for you to be alive. Your sister, she…she stops. But you are still fighting when we come close. The armies are still, but you fight on." He smothered his rising voice and whispered. "My dead need rest. I cannot bring them back to become like this."

Sonja looked away. What would it be like in that rotting body? Would they be aware at all? She fought down a shiver, centering back into her surroundings. "What now?"

Niccolo's mouth twitched down. "Your sister may have plans. I do not ask. Maybe to Batinavik? There are many healers."

"That's a long trip. Will Leif make it? Is he still…"

"I do not know."

She pushed upright, accepting Niccolo's steadying arm, waving for Thonra's bloshul. Niccolo hesitated but passed it over, tentatively sitting next to her. Sonja started a drip and slipped into an identification. She hesitated a moment before holding her hand to Niccolo. He took it, and she linked between them. His colors swirled into place.

They gazed through the wall, finding Thonra hunched over, working on a weak light.

"Your sister, she carry Healing Waters from Attietto," Niccolo said. "Helped to make his body strong."

"And that worked?"

Niccolo shrugged. "We wrap Mietitore in many cloths and bind it to him. Is not the same as other anchor, and your sister agrees this is damaged, but she says it has similar properties to maybe help. Her box of relics are added to pockets and bound at his body, but you will know better than I if this works."

Sonja leaned in to point out Leif's spirit. "He's still here. But if his body can't hold on..."

"He will not survive travel to Batinavik," Niccolo whispered. "He will struggle to live to Tharvik."

"I don't know," she said, fading them back into the antique vibrance of the study, "but it seems like our better option. Can you carry him if I watch his spirit?"

He nodded. "There will be healers in both cities."

"I'll stay with him as long as it takes." A moment's hesitation passed between them. "You could stay as well. I know he'd love to see you again. Technically, I promised we'd show him the west."

He met her eye. "You and I show the west?"

She shrugged. "If you wanted to, of course. And at the end, my parents would love to hear wine opinions from Attietto."

His fingers twitched, but neither let go. That expression was back. The inscrutable pain or longing. "Opinions from a soldier?"

The gentle question broke her. "From a soldier, from a mercenary, from a traveler, a storyteller... You're more than what you were."

"A stallion?" he smiled weakly. "Does she think I do not know?"

"I think she prefers it. All the better if it embarrasses us both."

"I am not embarrassed."

Sonja's heart thundered in her ears. He was so close. She could see the yellow around his irises, feel their breaths synchronize. Gently, she leaned in, resting her head against his shoulder. A moment of hesitation passed before he relaxed, disentangling his hand to wrap it around her waist. Without thinking, her fingers returned to the punctures in his shirt, scrunching the material to keep her arm from shaking.

They didn't speak. Not for a long time. As if a word would wake the armies. As if this peace was early spring ice, and the smallest shift could plunge them back into the frozen water. Someone's breathing stuttered on the inhales. Sonja couldn't tell if it was his or hers or both. But slowly, the tightness in her chest resolved into a steady rhythm. She was heady, shutting her eyes as the room spun, clutching the torn fabric tighter. Maybe it was the blood loss, maybe the adrenaline, but the study felt dreamlike. Awash with a sense of safety long lost to Kepstadur's walls. Or maybe her mind simply couldn't process it any other way.

They needed a plan forward. They couldn't hide here forever. After a few more precious seconds, it was time to talk to Thonra.

With a guiding hand, she made it to the door and out into the stormy foyer. Corpses littered the floor, the most concentrated in and around the throne room. Each one was nothing without Valtyr's command. Without the hoard of souls he'd collected. Black sludge pooled over the beautiful flooring. Thonra sat very still, a meditative position, with a thin twine stretched between her rings. All as if she didn't sit in the middle of a soilless graveyard. How much salt would it take to bless them all? Far more than was worth carrying.

"Stable," Thonra confirmed without opening her eyes.

Sonja mirrored the posture across his body, studying the desperately attached fjarfest — most notably that deadly sickle. "Traditional medicine will probably help him more than we can. There's a living town nearby."

Thonra grunted in affirmation. "And then what?"

A palpable pressure built as Sonja sorted out her words. She noticed the same blue smears along one of Thonra's legs. A medicine? Not one she knew. "It's time to go home." Rain poured overhead, some leaking through the broken and untended skylights. The admission hurt, but the state of the dead hurt more.

"I understand."

Sonja's jaw fell slack. She'd been ready for a fight. Screaming vitriol. Every pandering argument she'd prepared faded. "Really?"

"Yes."

"Well, that's perfect!" Sonja's heart soared. "If you don't mind, I'd love to wait with Leif. Give him an opportunity to recover, you know? But Tharvik isn't too bad. We could even relocate to a bigger city after he stabilizes. I don't know how the people would respond to a Kepstan, or if anyone would even believe us. It'll be an expensive trip back, but we can work odd jobs; can you imagine us as mercenaries? Ma and Dada would never believe…" Something in Thonra's expression felt off. "Right?"

Her eyes opened for the first time, but she only looked at Leif's slow-rising chest. "You should go. Be a mercenary. Hug the family for me. I'll follow later."

Sonja recoiled. "This is it. We did it. We searched for years, and now, you're allowed to go home."

"You are, Sonni. You deserve it. I'm going to look a bit longer."

Tears welled in Sonja's eyes, spilling down her face and into her lap. "Not like this. This wasn't the plan. We're going home together. You swore it."

"Things change." Thonra hardened. "The magic exists. We saw it here, and I am not giving up on him."

"Implying I am."

"I didn't say that. Will you listen to me?"

"No, I won't. Where else could you possibly go? This is the edge of Jrendavar. There is nothing else to look for."

"There are always more rumors. I'll leave Jrendavar for a time. Other countries have their own legends we've never heard of. The First Pilgrim had the answers. I'll visit other sites and—"

"This one wouldn't have worked," Sonja pleaded. "When I looked for Leif's energy, I could only see us. The people who were still here. Before, it was only people who died near the relic. Castle staff and townspeople. The souls attached to the Reaper blade. I didn't see a way to find a different soul."

Another flash of irritation marred Thonra's face. "Yet, this castle alone held three different spiritual fjarfest."

"None of which worked how we needed." Sonja rose in a flurry, gesturing wildly at the dead. "Say we could bring Ulrik back. These revenants were little more than puppets. They could follow simple commands, but what would that be like? Would he want that? What would Vann think to meet a dead-eyed man claiming to be his father?"

"Shut up."

"What kind of body could we give him? He's been decaying in the ground for years now."

"With the right fjarfest, it'd be a matter of perfecting the magic. Let me keep looking."

"Why should I?" Sonja raised her voice. "Read the signs, Thonra. We nearly died here three hundred times over."

"I can't give up yet."

"So you'll give up on Bragi instead?" Hurt flashed across Thonra's face, but Sonja pressed against that nerve. "He's living and breathing and missing you immensely."

"This isn't about him."

"Stop hiding from him." Sonja rallied with a desperation she hadn't realized she'd carried. "Can you imagine all the help Ma would have to pay for had they lost all four of us at the same time? And with Tuyet still raising a baby? He was right to leave."

"Just go." Thonra's voice was barely audible. "I'm done arguing with you. Pack your things and get Niccolo ready. We leave once the rain stops."

Arguments piled into Sonja's mind, but the conversation was over. If she kept arguing, Thonra would never let herself reconsider. Sonja might have pushed too far already. She could have ruined it all. The reason her sister wouldn't come home.

24

MORNINGS AFTER

The rain didn't relent. It was a warm, summer downpour that threatened to flood Kepstadur further. It washed away the bile outside, but the corpses remained in their horrifying piles. Sonja and Niccolo were the first to survey the full extent of death, going out and planning their route. He went pale at the sight of it all. "This looks as war," he told her weakly. "Many soldiers, but more civilians. We all hated it in the start. Myself, Castillo, Adelma. But he grew, eh, dull to it all. He stop seeing Danqong as people. We deserve to fight them, like the generals told…" he trailed off as Thonra approached, Leif lightened in her arms but still too awkward for her to carry.

No one spoke as they left the city, nor much more as they trudged through mud on the way back to Tharvik. Upon arrival, they found excited locals dancing in the soaking streets. It was the warmest day they'd known in ten years, and while the rain was still chilly, dozens basked in its long-awaited return.

Citizens watched with unabashed mistrust for the people carrying a half-dead boy into town so late in the evening. Niccolo and Sonja weren't immediately recognized, but when Helmi's guards arrived to handle the situation, familiar mercenaries calmed the unsettled masses and helped deliver Leif to the medic's care. The boy looked a little better, washed by the rain and wearing Sonja's spare clothes, but the medic took note. He was a familiar man, with nigh incomprehensible speech patterns. Sonja was thankful when he didn't ask many questions, but she felt obligated to give him a few details.

"He's all but starved. No telling how long he was out there," she said vaguely, while exposing her mage's rings. "Everything on him is a fjarfest. He needs them nearby until he's stable. We can leave some behind as payment."

By the time she'd wrapped things up with the medic, Thonra was gone, Niccolo having pointed her toward the inn. As things settled, he and Sonja scarfed down a quiet meal, then they shambled toward their designated cots. She hesitated before turning away, but only long enough for Niccolo to catch her hand with a quick, comforting squeeze. Sonja didn't remember even making it to the pillow before, in a blink, it was sunrise.

She was the last to the table, too cold and shaky to rush her morning, too filthy not to wash off. In the dining hall, Thonra sat with more familiar faces — the man with the piercings, and the redheaded woman. Thonra leaned forward, focused in on the man. Niccolo, nearby, was already looking healthier; if nothing else, he was no longer wearing holey, blood-crusted clothing.

"We can track it. That's not a question," Pierce said.

"If you find it, I know how to handle these kinds of creatures." Thonra used her most bored tone. "It won't take but three of us."

Red flicked her eyes over Sonja. "You said thems were related." She raised a faint eyebrow at Niccolo. "You promised two mages."

He shook his head. "Related, yes. Promise mages, no. But I assure you, is worth the effort. Keep her safe, and you will have the monster."

The mercenaries shared a silent exchange. "I'm willing a given old try." Red's face split into a feral smile. "Let's kill a demon."

Sonja noted her sister's eyebrow quirk, but Thonra accepted the woman's handshake, regardless. "I'll be ready in an hour."

The mercenaries, with barely a genial goodbye, skulked off to break the news to Helmi.

"Chasing that bear, then?" Sonja shoveled the last few bites of porridge, hunched over the bowl. "What do you hope to gain?"

"An immortal bear could probably teach me a thing or two. Plus, it'd help the people here."

Sonja pursed her lips. "And after the bear?"

"That trading town."

"Batinavik?"

Thonra nodded. "I'll go there to see what connections they have. Attietto was the first goal, but it's a limited place to search — no offense, Stal."

Niccolo bowed graciously, feigning a regal expression.

"Danqong has a lot of unique beliefs," Thonra said.

"Be safe, both Danqong and Attietto," Niccolo said. "Ask of the fighting before any place. You do not wish to be trapped and hiding in the middle of fights."

"Noted." Thonra neutralized her tone. "I need to get ready."

Sonja softened. "You don't have to."

"I do."

Why did it hurt to hear? Sonja knew that Thonra would go. It wasn't her nature to change her mind. But it still hurt. "Market's expensive here, but you can get most essentials. No dispensaries. There's one in Batinavik you should go see. He runs a textiles shop, out-facing. A good local to know, but he'll push you around. If you want to travel through the Baris, he might help you there too."

A silence followed. "I'll remember that."

"Remember that we'll miss you," Sonja whispered. "Remember, you can always come home. That this wasn't your fault."

"Okay, Sonja," she snapped. That guilt was written like the sun on her expression. "I didn't ask for you to coddle me." Thonra let out a sigh, settling some. "Do you still have your map?"

Sonja frowned. "Not going to do us a lot of good when you leave the country."

"I'll still send updates. You'll figure it out." Thonra fidgeted with the straps on her travel sack. The inn felt public for such an emotional conversation. Her eyes even flashed to Niccolo once; he kept his head down, enthralled in runny eggs. "You'll hug Ma and Dada for me, yeah? Tell everyone I miss them."

"They'd all rather hear it from you, but I will."

Thonra gave only a nod and left. Sonja and Niccolo went to check on Leif before meeting her and the two guards at the gate.

Sonja stepped in for a hug. "Come home as soon as you can. Promise?"

"I promise," Thonra whispered, stretching up to lean her chin on her sister's shoulder. They stayed for an extra breath, and Thonra tightened her grip. "Enjoy it for me, okay?"

Sonja only closed her eyes in response. "I love you, Thonra."

"And I love you." She looked at Niccolo over Sonja's shoulder. "Take care of her, Stal." As suddenly as she'd appeared, Thonra left.

The separation was a fire poker, sharp and hot between Sonja's ribs. The eyes of the locals followed her and Niccolo with a scrutiny that scraped across her skin. "I'm going to hunt."

His steps behind her were hesitant. "This is meant as a dismissing, or is an invitation?"

"It's whatever you want it to be."

She made it to the gate facing Kepstadur before Niccolo caught up. She expected him to say something. To crack a joke or talk her down, but he didn't. They hiked for a long time in that silence. He was thinking. Sonja tried not to think. About her siblings and the vineyard and the long journey ahead. The weather was so nice, and she had pigs to find. But her own thoughts bombarded her. By the time they made it to a decent place, sharing a broad rock for seating, it was too warm and bright. The boars wouldn't be out again until evening. She sat anyway. "What a disaster," she said, tossing acorns into a bramble patch.

"I am sorry for your sister."

"She's doing what she thinks is right." Sonja rolled tense shoulders back. "Well, maybe not right, but necessary."

"She will change her mind?"

"Hopefully one day, but for now, I have to pray she keeps surviving. Thank you for setting her up with guards."

Niccolo gave a small smile. "Is, unfortunately, only way I know to stop her from leaving town at dawn. These are good people, I think. And this deal benefits both."

A second handful of acorns scattered small, unseen creatures into dead underbrush. It would be months before the dormant plant life would recover — if ever. The discolored bushes and black-tipped branches seemed healthy and whole, possibly feeding off a magic potent enough to infect the soil. Would these plants adapt? Would the original foliage be strong enough to retake the forest?

"You are well rested today?"

The question caught Sonja off guard. She turned to study his profile, as he pointedly refused to look at her. "I am. Why?"

"At the keep. You were unwell before, and…" He puffed out a breath. "I fear overstepping. Misunderstanding, yes?"

Sonja's heartbeat quickened. Cautiously, she slipped one hand around his arm. When he didn't flinch away, she moved closer and laced her fingers together. Almost instantly, his tension evaporated and they settled against each other. "You were the perfect gentleman during my near-death experience."

"My memory looking back believes you fall against me rather than choose. I did not mean… If I…"

"Me? Fall?" she said over his stammering. "That's quite unlikely."

Niccolo almost smiled, stacking his hand over hers. "Of course. My words were very sillly." Each breath relaxed their postures together. The summer breeze held no hint of Kepstadur's lost chill. "And the west?" His voice was still hesitant.

"Leif's recovery gives us time to plot the best route." Part of Sonja held on to the hope that her sister might double back. A slow healing could give Thonra the time to change her mind, though waiting could raise different risks, especially for the prince. Something struck Sonja about his question. It wasn't obligation, was it? "You know you don't have to go, right? You don't owe me anything from a deathbed promise to a prince's spirit. He wants to travel; I want to go home. If neither of those things benefits you…"

"There is no better place to go," he said dryly. "Do not take this wording as an insult, but before plans for the west, I believed I wander until something interesting happened."

"That can't be true."

Niccolo shrugged. "Not completely, but is not untrue."

"What can we do to make the journey worth your time?"

"Being with you and being with Leif is enough. If I can help, this is enough."

Sonja did not like that answer. The wording had a distance about it. Something dour and fatalistic. She tried and failed to meet his eye. "There has to be something you want."

He opened his mouth, then seemed to think better. Unsettled fingers traced circles across her bare arm. "What I want, I cannot have."

"So it's a secret dream, then? I'm a very good guesser." She coaxed out a lackluster laugh. "Okay, let's start with nine thousand ronad. A little money never hurt anyone. Then, with your new fortune, you'll build a theatre and start hiring talented performers to tell your most outlandish stories."

The second laugh felt genuine. "I like this plan."

"But it's not what you had in mind."

His breaths stilled. "I had friends and a shop to work in. My parents grow old. I have no siblings to care for them. To know how they think of me. To tell them what happened… I fear my abandoning tainted their memory. Castillo would know to watch them, maybe threaten them. If he can take Adelma's life, who was as a sister to us, what is the worth of my family? What is the worth of my reputation? I know in my heart he watches my home." Niccolo shook his head. "Letters may be captured and may be a danger for them. I know better than to hope to return unless I live longer than the army. There is no goal. I hold the goals of everyone I watched die. I stand here with a gods-cursed sword, and I hold the dreams of the dead." Once the words started, the next had rolled over each other. He wrung his fingers with an absent stare that seemed to see far beyond the forest canopy.

Sonja didn't rush to reply. She watched his chest heave under the weight of the admission and imagined being named a public enemy. What would the vineyard think? Surely some would consider her innocent, but she reconsidered for him. People who knew Niccolo might have always seen a soft-natured boy who had never belonged in the army. Maybe they'd always known he'd desert. "What are your parents like?"

He squeezed her arm, firm but light. Niccolo gazed into the midmorning sun. "Woodworkers, both. They are strong from storms and sand. My father trained by making boats, and my mother of tables. They move to Sierodella and make a business for ships and repairs.

My father, he brings home — er — wandering cats and dogs. My mother tells him we cannot tend to another animal, but she sings when fixing the shed for them. Her aunt lived with us at the time and did much healing for animals. Sometimes people."

Sonja wasn't sure if he wanted solutions, but she might have a few he hadn't known possible. "Was she sensitive to magic?"

"*Mi evietta?* No. No, she works as a medic in the first war when a young girl."

"And in Sierodella? How many people do you think were magically sensitive? Even just a little."

He considered his answer, turning finally to look at her. "Why?"

If a trustworthy messenger could make the trip, it would only take one sympathetic page… Perhaps Helmi might know someone. But to defend against spies… How could she send instructions? "I don't want to over-promise, but there might be a way to contact them magically. Keeping them safe would be a matter of creativity. But with a little research, I could probably… I want to do this for you." The last words slipped out before she'd considered them.

Niccolo's shoulders fell, uncoiling the tight lines that raced up his neck and knotted in his jawline. "I would like that," he whispered.

Mouth suddenly dry, Sonja couldn't quite remember what words were. Instead of the echoing silence of stone walls, the small sounds of the woodlands spun in that space between them. Their first encounter in the study flashed in her mind."Niccolo, about that night, it—"

His eyes widened. "I am sorry if—"

"No, it's not that…" Sonja tightened her grip, face suddenly hot.

For a frozen instant, he only watched tracing her features with his eyes. Down and around her lips. Damn Attiettans, always so close. Niccolo met her gaze again. "Could I…"

Sonja leaned in. The kiss was softer than she had imagined. All his sharp features and rugged appearance meant nothing. He traced tentatively up her arm, holding lightly against the nape of her neck. One hand pressed against his chest, Sonja basked in his warmth and steady heartbeat. For a time, she could forget what she'd seen. She could enjoy the supple oak smell and his hands at her back.

Somewhere in that kiss or the one that followed, Sonja found comfort in her simple goal and the idea that Niccolo would be there for the journey. The ghosts should rest here with the castle. With a bit of time and patience, maybe she and Niccolo could rejoin the living.

-|-

The next days blurred by, mostly spent sleeping, tending to Leif, or preparing to leave. Niccolo had pocketed more valuables than Sonja had realized. A few collections of coins in tithe pouches, but he'd carried out mostly display jewelry or old books. So close to the castle, Niccolo kept those more unique items hidden.

As Leif's condition improved, they discussed different paths, per local recommendations. The prince seemed thrilled to be included in the planning. Leif had yet to comment on their dark conversation shared in the tunnels, and Sonja was not inclined to revisit what had been said. A coward's choice, maybe, but they had plans to focus on. She could hide behind that reasoning a bit longer. For the first stop, Sonja stayed firm. Their priority should be to visit a port or an inland trade epicenter like Govardern. That journey would take several weeks, but the roads were said to be well maintained.

Life got easier after Thonra left again, and, unfortunately, Sonja couldn't deny that. Her own edgy defensiveness had melted away with the winter weather. It even seemed to help Leif, who was up and walking — against doctor's recommendations — within the week. He made friends around town on his strolls, functioning under the name "Ulrik" while so close to the castle. Thonra might have broken Sonja's nose for loaning him that name. Sonja, however, thought it was fitting in a way.

Freshly bathed, newly groomed, and wearing clothes made for a man in his twenties, Leif's biggest improvements were near-instantaneous. Doctor Anders said it would take time for him to fill out to a healthy weight, but keeping him active would be important.

On the day they were to leave, Leif made a special point to visit with all the people of Tharvik he'd met in his brief stay.

Sonja finalized a deal with Helmi, leaving four invitations to Jrendavar. As it turned out, the old innkeeper, Carita, was a decent alternator who agreed to work the other side of a sympathetic sheet. If the letters could draw Niccolo's parents across the border, more options opened up. Even if they were followed, Carita seemed strangely excited to help. Helmi's crew had nine letters. Surely one could make it across the sea.

Niccolo waited at the western gate, checking their supplies for the journey and brushing out their newly acquired donkey, Chamberlain. If Leif was really going to travel across the country, he'd need the option not to walk. There was no way to tell what the prince would do when arriving at the homestead — if he would continue on or settle down. In truth, Niccolo might not stay either, though she didn't spend much time considering those odds.

With all the talk of his parents, Niccolo had picked up whittling, be it to feel close to them or to keep his hands busy. It had been awkward at first, and Sonja wasn't sure how to tell him, but he needed to know.

"Can I give you a warning?" she asked, her tone playful.

He cut his eyes suspiciously to her.

"People back home have certain…associations with whittling. It's an old nuptial tradition."

"Ah yes, I know this word." He smirked at her.

"They'll think you're planning to propose to someone."

Niccolo's hands stalled, knife biting into the grain. He processed that for a moment, wearing a face that was difficult not to laugh at. "Your people… Swords and spoons? Is that not the correct tradition?"

"Not where I'm from. Maybe here in the southeast, but if someone, say, in my family were to notice, you would get quite a few questions."

Before Niccolo clambered together a response, Leif bounded over, ready to leave.

Thonra did not arrive before the party left Tharvik.

The first leg was a trial run, as Leif would need to camp two nights before their destination. Their concern was unwarranted, as the prince was eager to learn new and useful skills. Spirits were high as the first stop's gates faded into view. A medium-sized city by the name of Velsmarkent. At Helmi's urging, they arrived in time for the summer solstice. The streets lined with vendors and swelled with patrons in colorful robes bound with bright white sashes. The mix of smells pulled Sonja in every direction at once. It was not quite the same as the stubborn grapes that grew at the vineyard, but she slept easier on that journey home.

25

PROMISING

It took nearly three weeks to hunt and kill the terrible bear. Big brute was dying already — Thonra suspected it had stumbled on a piece of the Kepstan relic, though she couldn't imagine how. When she, Asta, and Gunnar made it to Batinavik, the town lauded them as heroes. Thonra barely paid it mind. This was penance.

After a day of recovery, she wandered through the back alleys in search of the smooth wooden door and the removable plaque bearing interlocking circles. She pushed inside, triggering a small chime. Despite bloshuls full of the blood she'd harvested in the wild, she shifted a stool near to the large casks and sat heavily on it.

"Good afternoon, and welcome." The shopkeeper beamed, stepping down into the back room. "How is it that I may help you today?"

Thonra didn't spare him a smile. "My sister recommended your services. Says you can find me passage through the mountains."

"Right to business." The merchant reset his posture. "I can respect that. And you want the Bari Mountains. Anywhere in particular?"

"The most magical place you know." Rows of shelves behind the man looked suspiciously set up for displays, despite being empty. Thonra imagined the cubbies filled with relics, but saved for what he might consider a "serious customer." She subtly rested a hand on Valtyr's broken wristlet, hidden attached to her belt. Maybe this salesman truly was valuable.

As she memorized the room, this merchant appraised Thonra's features. "A sister you said? I might know the young woman you're referring to. You favor."

She flinched as if flicked in the face. "We don't favor much at all these days."

He held his breath for an extra beat, then swiped a finger superstitiously along the bridge of his nose. "So the castle took her too, then?"

"It did," Thonra whispered. In a way, Kepstadur *had* killed Sonja. The part of her determined to save Ulrik. The part vying for her sister's approval. Thonra had watched it die.

"I am sorry for your loss."

"The guide," she said to reorient the conversation. "Tell me about them. How many times have they taken the journey? What have they learned?"

Nearly three hours passed before Thonra left the shop, her coin pouch lighter than she had anticipated. Information wasn't cheap here, and unfortunately, this vendor was tight-lipped about any potential fjarfest in his storerooms. But he had provided value. She returned to her half-priced room — a gift for the bear's severed head — and considered how much money she'd need to convince either of her traveling companions to continue along this path. There was no telling what the Stallion had paid them. She didn't like thinking about Niccolo. He'd said things she couldn't refute. Terrible things. And so much of the horror came from the truth his words held. Thonra didn't deserve to go home. To bring that spite. To drag Sonni down. Sonni had never been callous enough to save Ulrik, and Thonra had wasted years of her sister's life.

But this search was far from over.

Somewhere in the days that followed the keep, Thonra developed a new habit: fidgeting with her earring. It was a bad time to go soft. She couldn't dwell on Bragi. Yet she couldn't bring herself to pack the earring away.

He had visited her when she didn't think she could stand again. That image was clear in her mind. Bragi had been beautiful, standing with her in Kepstadur's halls.

Thonra smothered the sentiment, draining a bottle that burned as it went down. Instead of sleeping, she prepared the runes and focuses for her sympathetic map. Sonni had it so easy. She could just make it happen. Energy magic was so expensive. Hard to track threads, hard to hold on. Before casting the spell, Thonra drew a line of mountains along the edge of the page. Sonja wouldn't see that, but it would help keep track on this end.

Thonra connected to the sympathetic link and pulled, searing slashes in the shape of an arrow toward the hastily drawn peak, then again with a mark that this path seemed "promising."

ACKNOWLEDGEMENTS

Hello, it's time to acknowledge.

A very important thank-you to my editing team: Kourtney Spak, Jaime Dill, and Sam Willow. You made this first expedition into publication far easier than I expected. Additionally, this story would have never gotten to the editors without my wonderful early readers, specifically Jackson and Soraya. I'd also like to thank Zoie for feedback on sensitive topics. I am so grateful for everyone's thoughts and input and energy; it was invaluable.

A huge shout-out to my ARC team who came in and provided that first boost of reviews to help gain visibility and traction, and lastly, thank YOU, dear reader. Whether you found this story through my website or online retailer, in a brick-and-mortar store, in your local library, or floating in a mysterious beam of light: thank you for giving this debut author the chance to tell her story. More soon, and I can't wait to see where this road takes me. Latest info at my website.

rgsartain.com

Until we meet again!

A tidbit for making it this far:
The chapter one glyph reads SEARCH.

www.ingramcontent.com/pod-product-compliance
Lightning Source LLC
Chambersburg PA
CBHW020400110726
47899CB00006B/1799